Carol Marinelli recently filled in a form asking for her job title. Thrilled to be able to put down her answer, she put 'writer'. Then it asked what Carol did for relaxation, and she put down the truth—'writing'. The third question asked for her hobbies. Well, not wanting to look obsessed, she crossed her fingers and answered 'swimming'—but, given that the chlorine in the pool does terrible things to her highlights, I'm sure you can guess the real answer!

Melanie Milburne read her first Mills & Boon novel at the age of seventeen, in between studying for her final exams. After completing a master's degree in education she decided to write a novel, and thus her career as a romance author was born. Melanie is an ambassador for the Australian Childhood Foundation and a keen dog-lover and trainer. She enjoys long walks in the Tasmanian bush. In 2015 Melanie won the HOLT Medallion, a prestigious award honouring outstanding literary talent.

THE SICILIAN'S DEFIANT MAID

CAROL MARINELLI

CINDERELLA'S INVITATION TO GREECE

MELANIE MILBURNE

MILLS & BOON

First Published in Great Britain 2022
by Mills & Boon, an imprint of HarperCollins*Publishers* Ltd,
1 London Bridge Street, London, SE1 9GF

www.harpercollins.co.uk

HarperCollins*Publishers*
1st Floor, Watermarque Building,
Ringsend Road, Dublin 4, Ireland

The Sicilian's Defiant Maid © 2022 Carol Marinelli

Cinderella's Invitation to Greece © 2022 Melanie Milburne

ISBN: 978-0-263-30077-2

04/22

MIX
Paper from
responsible sources
FSC® C007454

This book is produced from independently certified FSC™ paper
to ensure responsible forest management.
For more information visit www.harpercollins.co.uk/green.

Printed and Bound in Spain using 100% Renewable Electricity
at CPI Black Print, Barcelona

THE SICILIAN'S
DEFIANT MAID

CAROL MARINELLI

MILLS & BOON

PROLOGUE

'ALICIA, HAVE YOU been telling fibs again?'

'I don't think so...'

Alicia frowned as she and Beatrice made their way along the private path that led from their tiny school and their residence towards the convent. Even half running it was a good ten minutes along the rugged coastal headlands of Trebordi in Sicily's south.

'Maybe a few white lies...' Alicia admitted, deciding that it might be safer just to apologise in advance. 'I'm sorry if I've got us into trouble.'

'Again,' Beatrice scolded. 'It is hard work being your twin sometimes.'

And, although she was being told off just a little, Beatrice's words made Alicia's heart soar because—well, it made them family.

Even if technically they weren't.

They had arrived at the baby door of the convent within a few weeks of each other and had been fondly referred to as twins at first. Though others had long since stopped, between them the term had remained.

In days gone by the baby door had been used regularly. Its use was rare now, but a benefactor ensured that it remained open. Baby girls dropped off at the convent, if not adopted, lived in the private house and were given a free education at the school in the convent grounds. Baby boys were cared for in the same residence up until the age of one, unless adopted.

'It's lucky we're girls,' Beatrice would say. 'It's such a good school. At least...' Beatrice would wrinkle her nose, '...compared to the one in town.'

'Well, I wish I'd been born a boy,' Alicia would say, and sigh, because she hated school and ached for a family with something akin to hunger. A desperate, insatiable hunger. 'But then, if I were a boy,' she would say with a smile to Beatrice, 'I wouldn't have you.'

Though they were not actually twins, nor even biological sisters, Alicia preferred to think of them that way, and would introduce them as such to any doubtful tourists who might make the trek along the headlands to the nunnery and stop to make a purchase from the produce shop.

'Twins?' They would frown dubiously, for Alicia and Beatrice could not be more different in either appearance or nature.

'Yes,' Alicia would say as she wrapped their parcels. 'Though not identical, of course. Our parents died in a house fire. Mamma passed us out of the window to the firefighters. It was the last thing she did,' she would add with a wistful sigh.

'Alicia Domenica!' Sister Angelique rarely spoke, but when she did it was to tell off Alicia, or report her to Reverend Mother, who would scold her for her fanciful tales. 'Why on earth would you say such a thing?'

Alicia's answer was always simple. 'Because it sounds so much nicer than saying we were abandoned.'

It sounded as if they had once been loved.

Alicia had arrived at the convent first, early one September. A feisty and very Sicilian baby with curly black hair and blue eyes which would quickly darken to a deep brown.

The nuns had guessed she was a week or so old, for her cord had been a shrivelled stub, which meant that—for a little while—she had been cared for and loved. She had been bathed and dressed before being left, and there had been a pair of Italian gold hoops pinned to the little baby suit she wore. Despite appearing well nourished she had seemingly arrived hungry—grabbing at the bottle and sucking greedily, then grabbing a finger and clutching on—although the nuns had soon found out that was just her nature. She was frantic not just for milk but for attention. Wanting more, ever more, of any brief taste of love…

They had named her Alicia after the nun who had found her. And she had been given the surname Domenica for she had arrived on a Sunday.

Then, three weeks later, deep in the night, the bell had rung again, alerting the nuns that the baby door had been used. This time around there had been barely a cry, and the babe had been fragile and skinny. She'd still been covered in vernix and the cord had been crudely tied off, meaning the infant was likely just a matter of hours old.

This baby had been as blonde as Alicia was dark, and so silent in comparison that the nuns had been worried. So worried that, despite it being late summer, they had lit the old wood stove in the kitchen and, after feeding and wrapping her, had put her in the same crib as Alicia for extra warmth.

A mistake, perhaps, for after that Alicia had sobbed loudly whenever they were parted.

She had been named Beatrice Festa. Beatrice after the nun who had found her, and Festa for the festival that had been taking place in town when she'd arrived, and they were rather sure she had come from there. Still, it had soon been decided that she was misnamed, for Beatrice meant bringer of happiness, and *festas* were fun, yet she was an unsmiling, serious little thing.

Alicia loved her so very much, though—even when she was prim and cross and attempting to communicate to her the trouble they were in.

'Have you been swimming with Dante Schininà in the river again?' Beatrice asked.

'No!' Alicia was telling the truth. 'Ragno wouldn't come—he says he's too old for all that. Anyway, the water is getting too low.' She called him *ragno*, meaning spider, because he was tall and skinny and all arms and legs.

'Thank goodness.' Beatrice tutted. 'Or we really would be in trouble.'

'For swimming?'

'It's not just swimming. I know when the river is dry you two go into the cemetery.'

'What's wrong with that?' Alicia shrugged. 'We look at the names.'

'It's morbid,' Beatrice said.

'No.'

'And you're lying again—you can't read.'

'Ragno doesn't know that.' Alicia smiled, for she hid it so well that even Beatrice had only recently found out.

'He's trouble, Alicia.' Beatrice turned to her as if to warn her.

'Not to me.'

'You were seen holding hands.'

'I like holding his hand,' Alicia said.

'The nuns think you get up to…' Beatrice's voice trailed off.

'To what?' Alicia let out a scoffing laugh and then made a gagging noise, for she could think of nothing worse than kissing. 'Oh, please—we are friends and that is that. I don't understand why everyone is so mean about him.'

'I wasn't being mean.'

'Yes, you were,' Alicia said. Though she loved Beatrice, she still stood up for her friend Ragno. 'You were being mean. I can hear it in your voice that you are cross. Everyone always is when they speak about him.'

'Because he roams wild. He sleeps in sheds most nights, and he steals—'

'Eggs,' Alicia said. 'For breakfast.'

Beatrice paused then, and nodded. 'His mother is a disgrace.'

'She's been kind to us, though.'

Alicia did not understand Ragno's mother. She barely housed or fed her own son, yet he had given her a bag a few weeks ago, from his mother, and in it had been sanitary pads and tampons—a far cry from the awful strips of cloth the nuns allocated them. Alicia and Beatrice had spent a few nights reading the tampon insertion instructions, agog! As well as that there had been a glossy magazine, and Alicia had pored over the pictures of gorgeous dresses within, running her finger over the pages as if she could feel the fabric. It hadn't swayed Beatrice's opinion, though.

'She's unmarried,' Beatrice whispered as they entered the convent and then climbed the staircase and took their seats outside Reverend Mother's office.

'So?' Alicia shrugged. 'We're probably bastards, too, yet the nuns take care of us.'

'Don't say that word,' Beatrice warned. 'Anyway, it's not just because she isn't married. You know what they call her?'

'Yes,' Alicia said. 'And it's because she's a beekeeper.'

'She isn't though.' Beatrice shook her head. 'That's just what the locals call her.'

'Why?' Alicia frowned.

'Because she gives away honey.'

'I don't understand,' Alicia admitted.

Beatrice rolled her eyes. 'For someone who's getting bosoms, you don't know very much.'

That was another way they were different, Beatrice was still like a stick, and Alicia was starting to fill out. It horrified her—she had thought she was dying when she got her first period, and she hated the little buds of her breasts. She wanted her old body back—the one that had let her swim in her knickers and run...

'Men go to her home,' Beatrice explained.

'Ragno already told me that.' Alicia shrugged again. 'They go there to play cards.'

But then she recalled the slightly sarcastic edge to his voice when he had said that, and the accompanying roll of his navy eyes.

Alicia turned to Beatrice. 'What does it mean to give away honey?'

'I don't actually know,' Beatrice admitted.

'Ah, so there *are* some things that the genius doesn't know!'

'Shh…' Beatrice warned, for Sister Angelique seemed to be beckoning them to come into the office.

But as they duly stood and stepped forward, the nun put a hand up to stop Alicia. The signal was clear—Alicia was to remain outside.

She sat on the bench, trying to rack her brains as to what she might have done now! It had been weeks ago that Dante had handed her that bag from his mother, and she hadn't been down by the river, nor lied to any tourists of late.

Whatever it was must be terrible, though, for the door opened and Beatrice came out, her face pale, her eyes wide. Gosh, it must have been a terribly big lie she'd told, as all Beatrice did was shake her head and mouth the word *no*.

And now Sister Angelique was pointing for Alicia to come in and see Reverend Mother…

Not a minute later Alicia shouted the very word that Beatrice had mouthed.

'No!'

She was urgent as she raved on.

'Reverend Mother, you can't split us up. No, no, *no*. Beatrice would never agree.'

Reverend Mother sighed at the perpetual drama of Alicia.

'You can't separate twins,' Alicia pleaded. 'It's not right, it's cru—'

She was halted.

'Alicia, you are to stop this nonsense,' Reverend Mother warned. 'You don't even share the same birthday. This is an incredible opportunity for Beatrice—a full scholarship in Milan!'

'It's so far away that it's almost Switzerland.'

'Alicia, you stand here weeping, saying that you love Beatrice,' Reverend Mother said reasonably.

'I *do*.'

'So surely you want what's best for her?'

Of course she did. But the absolute truth was that Alicia

thought *she* was what was best for Beatrice. Everybody considered Beatrice cold. She had heard the nuns say that her emotions had been cut with the umbilical cord, and even that she—Alicia—must have got Beatrice's share. Yet Alicia knew otherwise. Each year in September, when the festival came to town, poor Beatrice would climb out of the window at night and go looking for her mother. And in the weeks afterwards, when the festival had long gone, she would cry herself to sleep and then wake screaming after the most dreadful nightmares.

Alicia's answer came from the heart. 'She needs me.'

'Are you sure it's not the other way around?' Reverend Mother checked, planting a little seed of doubt. 'Alicia, Beatrice is very gifted...'

It was true. Another thing that set them apart was the fact that Alicia struggled to read, let alone write, whereas Beatrice always had her head in books. She excelled in French and was intently studying Latin.

'There is a reason I have told you separately,' Reverend Mother explained gravely. 'Your reaction to this outstanding offer for Beatrice matters very much. If you carry on like this—crying and sobbing—then she won't go. Is that really what you want?'

Alicia was the silent one now, as Reverend Mother watered that little seed and watched it sprout.

'Beatrice has a real opportunity to further herself. Would you prefer her future to be working in the shop on the grounds, selling our produce? Or in the nursery when we have a baby arrive? Perhaps she could get a job one of the village cafés...'

'She could get a job in town!' Alicia shivered. 'In the library. She loves it there!'

'What a selfish young lady you are turning into,' Reverend Mother said. 'Quite the rebel too, I hear.'

Sister Angelique happily broke her silence then. 'Alicia has been seen holding hands with that ruffian—'

'I'm aware, thank you,' Reverend Mother cut in, glancing

down at Alicia's emerging figure and then back to her eyes. 'Sister Angelique will take you to the donation cupboard and find you something suitable to wear underneath your school dress. Then it will be time for evening prayers—use them wisely. I do believe you care for Beatrice, and I trust you will do the right thing.' As Alicia turned to go, Reverend Mother added one more thing. 'And, Alicia, choose the company you keep more carefully.'

Her heart felt shorn by the news that she was losing Beatrice, but Alicia's fire remained. 'I do choose carefully, Reverend Mother. I only have two friends...'

'You have many more.'

'There are people I play with and speak to and like, but true friends are something precious.'

'You are maybe a little young for this lesson, Alicia, but I feel it necessary to tell you now—there are certain young men a young lady would be well advised to stay away from.'

'But I thought we were supposed to be kind to the homeless and the hungry?'

Alicia frowned as if she had misunderstood something and watched as Reverend Mother swallowed.

'Most nights Dante Schininà is both.'

The donation cupboard smelt musty and of mothballs. Alicia's eyes drifted to a beautiful sequined dress, but then sagged in disappointment as Sister Angelique handed her a bra, already long faded from pink to grey.

It was a very long walk back from the convent to the school chapel, where she sat for evening prayers, feeling just a little relieved that Beatrice wasn't there so that she could properly think.

After prayers she made her way to the small residence for boarders, where she and Beatrice shared a simple bedroom. Outside the room she stopped at the wooden door and wished mirrors were allowed, just so she could check her face. She didn't want Beatrice to know she'd been crying, as Alicia really was not one to cry.

She was confused, though—deeply so. After being punished for all the little fibs she had told, now Reverend Mother was *telling* her to lie. And it would be the biggest lie she'd ever told, for she did not want Beatrice to leave.

Beatrice jumped up from her bed as Alicia walked in. 'I'm not going,' she stated immediately. 'I've told them I'll only take it if you can come too…'

'They're not going to give me a scholarship to a posh school in Milan.' Alicia laughed at the very notion. 'I can't write or do sums, but you're so clever, Beatrice. I think you should go.'

'You're just saying that.' Beatrice shook her head wildly. 'You've been crying.'

'Yes.'

'You never cry.'

'I was told off about Ragno,' Alicia said. 'You were right; we were seen holding hands. I am to choose my company more wisely.'

'We swore we'd never be separated, though—that we're as good as twins…'

'But we're not twins,' Alicia said. 'We're not even sisters.'

'We're sisters of the heart.'

'Yes,' Alicia agreed, 'and that means you had better study hard, so that when I'm old enough I can come to Milan and see what you've made of yourself.' She pushed out a smile and squeezed Beatrice's hands. 'Then we can be together again…'

CHAPTER ONE

Milan

ALICIA WOKE BEFORE her alarm, as she often did. And she lay there, as she often did.

But today was not a usual day.

It was not the dark of night she hated but the silence.

The absence.

Falling asleep with no one to wish *buona notte*.

And no one to offer a *buongiorno* to in the morning. Of course, as she constantly reminded herself, even if she and Beatrice had kept in touch they would hardly be sharing a room at the age of twenty-eight.

But even if they would have been past sharing a room, in Alicia's fantasy world they might have shared an apartment. Or even caught up for lunch once a week.

Hell, she'd have been happy with even just a phone call now and then, to catch up on Beatrice's no doubt glittering career. Or they would drink cocktails and sigh in exasperation over Alicia's disastrous attempts at dating.

And then she would not feel so alone with her secrets and her shame for all that had happened since Beatrice had left Trebordi—the forbidden touching in the river, the making love in the hut nearby. There had been no shame at the time, but the heartbreak and heartache and scandal that had followed had nearly broken her.

A heartache so deep she had left the island she loved, left her life.

'Alicia...' Reverend's Mother expression had been bewildered when she'd told her of her decision. *'I thought this was everything you ever wanted?'*

She hadn't understood it herself.

'So did I. Can I say goodbye to him, please?'

Alicia screwed her eyes closed. Even now she dared not be alone when she examined that time.

And she *was* alone. For despite tears, and promises to write every week, and the hope of being together someday, Alicia had received just two cards from Beatrice since she'd left Trebordi.

Trebordi.

Three jagged cliff-edges that disappeared into the Mediterranean Sea. She felt as if she stood there alone now, on the sheer drop.

No more.

Today was the day that things might finally start happening, after so many futile attempts to find Beatrice. This morning, if God and fate were on her side, Alicia would come face to face with Dante again.

She had long ago stopped thinking of him with the childhood nickname of Ragno.

She had never allowed her mind to linger for too long on the memory of Dante, or the forbidden fruit she had tasted but once.

So forbidden.

And so far from sweet!

The once beautiful memory of them had been so besmirched and tainted that Alicia refused to think of that time.

Or at least she did all she could not to.

Today might be the day she faced him.

Alicia showered quickly, pulled on underwear and a pretty loose dress and sandals. Her clothes were still second-hand, but at least she chose them herself, and she loved going to the markets and vintage stores.

She left her tiny, very dingy studio apartment, and quietly made her way down the many stairs to the street.

It was a fifteen-minute walk to work, and still a good hour until sunrise when the Duomo came into view. After almost a decade here, the sight of Milan's cathedral still brought a pause to her stride. It was so magnificent and imposing, yet so delicate, too. As if the most amazing pastry chef had piped intricate details onto the vast structure.

'Help me,' Alicia whispered into the silence as she paused. 'Please.'

She needed all the help she could get. This seemingly 'chance encounter' had actually been two years in the making and had already been thwarted a couple of times.

Alicia looked over to the luxurious hotel where she worked and up to the top floor, where presumably he slept.

Alicia had no idea how a poor boy from Trebordi had made it to the penthouse. Nor how the lone wolf that Dante had been could have changed so much. For he partied hard and moved with the rich set now.

What she *did* know was that Dante Schininà was now a man of great means.

And that she loathed him.

But if there was to be a hope of finding Beatrice then she needed this rich man on-side and would swallow her pride.

Alicia entered the hotel through the less than glamorous staff entrance and made her way to the changing room, where she chose a locker and put in her code. Stripping off her dress, Alicia took a fresh mint-green uniform from the laundered pile and did up the poppers one by one, then tied on her apron. She took her compact mirror from her bag and placed it in her apron pocket, and from her locker she took out flat, soft-soled shoes. She tied back her thick, black, wavy hair and twisted it into a neat bun with a little more care than usual, because she wanted the best of the room allocations—certainly she was not grooming herself for Dante.

'*Buongiorno.*' Alicia smiled at the head of housekeeping, and then to each of the morning crew as they arrived, but her greeting went pretty much unreturned by the bleary-eyed crowd.

She stood trying to feign nonchalance as the room allocations were given, although her heart was racing.

'Grand Presidential Suite…'

The woman had started at the top, and Alicia knew that this suite was the best, and the one reserved for Dante when he was in residence. This was her chance.

'Rosa.'

Damn!

Alicia exhaled heavily, reminding herself that there was still time. Dante Schininà was in Milan for three nights on this visit, and only one of them was already gone.

'Rosa?'

Alicia looked up and saw that her superior was frowning.

'Where is she?'

'I haven't seen her,' someone said.

'I'm here!' Rosa had arrived—*almost* on time for her five-thirty start, but a moment too late for the best and rather more prominent role.

There was a reason Alicia was never late.

'Alicia?'

'Sì?'

'You can take the Grand Presidential Suite—the guest is Signor Schininà…'

Alicia was second choice but she didn't care—she had the job. The head of housekeeping took a moment to read out the relevant requests on his booking. Alicia's reading, despite her best efforts, was still poor, and as guest preferences were sometimes hard to decipher she was glad the woman was reading them aloud. Dante's didn't really veer from the standard, even though he stayed in the best suite.

'You are to leave the breakfast trolley at the butler's kitchen but deliver his coffee. Knock on both the main entrance and the door to the bedroom suite. Even if there is no response you are to take in his coffee, open the drapes on the Duomo view and then offer to pour.'

'*Si.*'

'Pour even if he remains asleep—which is likely, since he only just got back.'

Alicia felt her nostrils pinch as the head of housekeeping explained that Dante and his international guests had taken a helicopter to Switzerland for a night at a casino.

'Signor Schininà likes still iced water, no lemon. Black coffee, with two raw brown sugars. Although ensure cream is on the coffee tray in case he should have company.' As Alicia nodded and moved to walk off and get started, the head of housekeeping offered an added insight into this esteemed guest. 'Alicia, may I suggest that, even if you get no response to your knocking, you pause and listen before going into the bedroom suite? Knowing Signor Schininà there is every chance he will be *active* at this hour, if—'

'Of course,' Alicia interrupted, her throat suddenly tight. 'If that is the case I'll return the coffee to the trolley and leave it for the butler to pour.'

'Excellent.'

Alicia smiled, but her smile soon faded as she headed to the kitchen to check the trolley contents with the head chef. He kindly checked and ticked off the list for her, informing her that the pastries included Signor Schininà's preferred anchovy, spinach and ricotta—*yuk!*

Although she nodded, her mind was largely elsewhere. *Active* at this hour, Alicia thought angrily. How disgusting! What sort of animal…?

Alicia stopped herself then, refusing to stoke her own ire. It would serve no purpose for her to arrive at his suite flushed and resentful when it was imperative that she smiled. Many guests were…well, *active* in the morning, and it was part of her job not to interrupt.

But as the chef covered the 'just in case' breakfast for two with heavy silver cloches, Alicia pondered what her reaction might be if she found Dante lying beside someone.

She should expect it!

After all, she had seen him with his models and his actresses a couple of times as he strolled through Reception.

As the service elevator slowly trundled its way up to the penthouse floor, Alicia took out her compact mirror from her apron pocket. It was her most treasured possession and had actually been an eighteenth birthday present from Dante's mother. The picture on it of the lady was fading, the gold plate long since gone, and she couldn't read the engraving. But she would never part with it.

Alicia stared at her brown eyes and saw the contempt she held for him there, as well as in the tight press of her lips, but then she reminded herself why she was doing this.

Beatrice.

Reminding herself also what a brilliant liar she was—it was her super-power, in fact—Alicia pushed out a smile. She had to be nice when she saw him. Act surprised...

If he was asleep, she would gently wake him. And if he didn't recognise her she planned to blink and say, *Oh, my God. Dante, is it really you?*

She must appear friendly—though not too much, of course. Especially if he had company.

He was Sicilian, though, and from Trebordi, no less. There were certain ways that were simply adhered to. Alicia expected him to at least extend an invitation for her to join him for a drink at some point. Just to be polite, of course.

We should catch up, he would say.

Dante would expect her to nod and say, *For sure*. Which was the Trebordi way to politely decline.

But, oh, no. She would not be declining. Alicia *would* get her audience!

The elevator doors parted and she wheeled the large silver trolley quietly along the carpeted corridor, then left it outside the butler's pantry. Thankfully Enzo, the butler, was doing what he did best and dozing in his seat, waiting for his guest to press the bell before he jumped to attention.

Finally her long-awaited moment was here, and to her own

surprise Alicia found that she was calm. Resolute. Possibly because she had been rehearsing this for a very long time.

Be nice, Alicia, she reminded herself as she added ice but no lemon to two still iced waters and then picked up the tray set with coffee for two. *Do not let Dante see that you hate him with a passion.*

And, given she was Sicilian, she had passion aplenty. So much so that she allowed herself just one truculent gesture and deliberately removed the cream from the tray. His lady-friend, if present, would just have to go without!

She knocked on the main door gently. 'Coffee, Signor Schininà.'

No response.

Quietly she let herself into the entrance hall of the Grand Presidential Suite and turned on the permitted dim lights. She walked through the lavish lounge, noting that there was the faint scent of cologne in the air—but of course she had never known the Dante who wore cologne.

She came to the master suite and listened for a moment. Silence.

Only…not quite.

Well, there was silence emanating from his suite. It was the sounds in her own mind that had made something akin to panic arise unbidden within her. For, like a radio signal, it was as if she had tuned in to the noises *they* had once made. And not just the sounds of their lovemaking, but of the illicit hours before. Her first kiss as they lay by the river, feeling the furnace of the first blasts of hot *scirocco* wind. Deeper kisses as they played in the water…

The cups were rattling in their saucers on the tray she held as, in her mind, Alicia heard again the ragged sound of his breathing in her ear. It was a noise she had long since attempted to block out, even though it crept into her dreams some nights…

She stood desperately trying not to tip the tray and block out the babble of sound that beckoned her to replay that time again. Her own gasps as his kiss brought her close to a place she had never been. The sound of his hollow shout followed by taste of their shared air in her mouth as they savoured what had just occurred. Despite her absolute inexperience, she had known Dante had just come, as she had.

Oh, God...

Now the moment was here Alicia wanted to turn and run, for there was one thing her scheming had not allowed for—the fact that she might enter his suite replaying the one memory she had never dared to.

No!

Whatever internal switch her memory had flipped, Alicia turned it to 'off' and took a deep cleansing breath. She saw that the cups and saucers had stopped rattling, and with calm restored she knocked for a second time. Then, as per his request, she quietly announced her arrival. 'Coffee, Signor Schininà...' When still there was no response, Alicia pushed down the silent door handle and let herself in.

A bedside light had been left on, and when she saw that he was alone she let out an involuntary sigh of relief.

He was sprawled on his stomach, one long leg straight, the other bent at the knee, and his arms were spread as if he were swimming, perhaps doing the front crawl, with his face turned to the side to breathe...

She blinked, for it really was better not to remember their time in the river.

Oh, but even in dim lamplight Alicia could see that, as if to taunt her further, Dante had changed.

Each time she saw him he grew finer.

The boy she had called Ragno had been scruffy. Feral, some had called him. Trouble. Yet not to Alicia. When Beatrice had chosen to study or read she would take the secret path he had shown her to the river and sometimes find him there.

Together they would swim and jump logs, or swim underwater, seeing who could hold their breath the longest. Or they might play in the empty stone hut. He would eat the food she had brought, while Alicia would pretend it was their home.

He'd made summers fun…

Then Dante had turned into a youth, and the boy who'd had no friends except her had become the boy all the girls wanted. Alicia had not been able to see what all the fuss was about.

Until she suddenly had.

But by then they no longer held hands.

She had been fourteen when he'd left for Rome to find his father, though their lazy days by the river had started to peter out well before then, and jealousy had invaded her as he'd slept his way through the village girls but would never so much as kiss her.

He had returned a man—and a very beautiful one at that. Dark, brooding and completely forbidden, he had taken her within hours of his arrival.

Well, not taken, exactly… Alicia had been willing.

More than willing…

She had asked him to be her first.

Yes, she might have seen him in the hotel foyer a couple of times since then, but he'd always had company and walked straight past her. Now he lay dark and unshaven, his back muscled, his buttocks barely covered by a silk bedsheet and the soles of his long feet incredibly clean. Alicia knew his every toe—and that was why she hated him so.

Yet there was also an unforeseen urge to touch that naked shoulder and gently stir him awake. To feel his skin beneath her fingers again as she gently called his name—*Dante*…

Instead, she kept to the script she had so carefully crafted. 'Signor Schininà…?'

He didn't stir.

Alicia put down the tray and then turned and took in the rich disarray of his room. His jacket lay discarded on the floor, there was uncorked champagne in the ice bucket and plates with the remnants of cheeses, figs, grapes… But Alicia ignored them and moved towards the many windows, opening the first of the drapes on the Duomo view.

The vista from here was stunning, and she focused on the

cathedral. It looked like a fairy tale, lit up against a bright blue sky with sunrise mere moments away.

Perhaps he had timed his request so that he could watch the fingers of light...?

No. He definitely had not.

'*Chiuse*—' Dante groaned, and told the maid to close the drapes.

He knew full well that the sunrise would be too much for his fractured mind. She perhaps did not hear him, given his throat was dry, but as he peeled open his eyes he forgot where he was.

Standing looking out of the window was a woman—though it was not the feminine curves that had him taking another look, more the way her hands were resting on her hips.

It was the way Alicia would stand and gaze out at the view from the clifftop, or look up in awe at the trees that sheltered their stretch of river.

God... Dante closed his eyes in case a herd of pink elephants started marching past, for he was clearly hungover indeed if he was conjuring up Alicia.

Another night spent wining and dining international clients at a casino... Soon, Dante told himself, he would never have to set foot in such a place again. Soon, Dante thought, he could give this life a Sicilian kiss goodbye and turn his back on the lot of them.

Then came a voice, somehow familiar, even all these years on. 'Would you like me to pour?'

What the actual hell...?

He frowned at her...at the shadow she cast as she approached and turned off the bedside lamp. Slender olive-skinned fingers poured coffee into a cup, and he recalled slender olive-skinned fingers exploring him elsewhere. May God forgive him, he chose not to look up, lest he spoil the fantasy he intended to return to the moment the maid had gone.

Or rather the memory.

Of taking Alicia.

But then her voice came again. 'Dante?' She sounded bewildered. 'It really *is* you!'

He felt seedy, hungover, and he had a morning erection that was less than comfortable when he was lying on his front with a maid smiling down on him. But, good God, it really was…

'Alicia?' he croaked.

'Yes!' Her reply was too enthusiastic for this hour—but then that was Alicia. 'I saw the name on the tray, but I told myself it couldn't be. I mean…'

Of course she didn't add *given how poor you were*, but even in his cognitively challenged state he felt the implication.

'What are you doing here, Alicia?' Mistrusting by nature, and even more so now compared to the Dante she'd known, he asked the question point-blank.

'Earning a living,' she responded, as if it was obvious. 'Would you like me to pour?'

No, I mean what are you doing by my bed…in my suite?

He didn't say that, of course. But he nearly did. He was so rarely caught off-guard like this.

Holding the sheet, he turned and sat up a little and pulled up a knee, then reached for one of the glasses of water and downed it in one before leaning back on the pillows. Dante was jaded and bitter enough with the world to be suspicious. He'd been shunned like a leper growing up, but in more recent years suddenly people wanted to know him.

Yet, because it was Alicia, he gave her the very rare benefit of the doubt.

'Two sugars?' she checked.

'*Si.*' He nodded and ran a hand over his very heavy morning shadow, trying to work things out. *Milan, Milan…* But of course. Her so-called twin had moved here.

Dante was *not* a morning person. And neither did he tend to think out loud. But the shock of seeing her almost moved him to speak before coffee, to enquire after her and her sister, or whatever Beatrice actually was…

His brief silence was her undoing, though.

'It's *such* a surprise to see you again.'

Her voice was forced and it had Dante looking up to her oh-so-innocent smile, and the blink of her gorgeous velvet-brown eyes, and the benefit of the doubt he had so briefly given her faded. This was no chance meeting.

He had always known that Alicia Domenica was a liar. It had made him smile once. But it didn't today. Instead it disappointed him. It was an emotion he was not used to feeling, for he anticipated the worst and was usually right—as was the case on this breaking day.

'Such a coincidence,' Alicia said, her smile too bright, her eyes too wide.

And he knew he would by far have preferred to keep his last memory of her, instead of replacing it with this very beautiful fake.

It was no coincidence.

And so, instead of responding, Dante yawned. And as he did so he watched her gorgeous full lips pinch in slight frustration at his refusal to engage in conversation.

Yes, he was being played.

Go for it, Alicia, he thought.

No one ever beat Dante.

CHAPTER TWO

ALICIA HAD WATCHED him position his knee in the same way he'd used to. She clearly recalled it now, as she poured him his coffee. He had been hiding his erection as they lay together, pulling down his clothes, lifting a knee...

She hadn't known then what he was doing—not really.

Until he'd told her.

Taken her hand and shown her.

'How long are you in Milan for?' she asked, but he responded with a question of his own.

His voice was husky, dark and deep, as if he had been shouting, or smoking, or both. 'How long have *you* been here?'

'Years.' Alicia glanced up and smiled. 'Nearly a decade now.'

'I meant how long have you been working at this hotel?'

'Oh...' She remembered to be casual. 'It must be eighteen months—no, maybe two years now.'

'I always stay here—well, when I'm in Milan.'

'Really?' Alicia pretended to check her memory. 'Actually, now you mention it, I thought I saw you departing from the hotel once...' She maintained her smile but could no longer summon it up to her eyes. 'I was polishing the revolving brass doors, though you didn't notice me as you passed...'

Alicia could hear the little note of bitterness in her voice as she recalled how it had felt to have the one man she had ever kissed, ever slept with, just walk on by with another woman on his arm, but she fought to check it.

'Anyway, it's so good to see you again!'

He did not return the compliment.

She stood unsure and a little perplexed, because this wasn't in any of her carefully planned scripts—Dante recognising her and then basically ignoring her. Or rather, ignoring them and what they had once been. But then, mid-sip of his coffee, he glanced up. She smiled brightly at him.

'Oh, *scusi...*' Alicia watched as he put down his coffee, reached for his wallet and took out a couple of notes. *'Grazie.'*

Alicia's heart, which had been tumbling since her alarm had gone off that morning, suddenly landed.

It was an awkward landing, though.

A not particularly medal-worthy landing.

'You're tipping me?' Her voice was incredulous.

'Why else would you still be waiting there?'

He dropped the money onto the bed in a take-it-or-leave-it motion, and it was then that all of Alicia's carefully rehearsed scripts went out of the window.

'Is that really all you can think to do? All you have to say after all this time?'

'What do you expect me to say?' He frowned. 'Okay—it's great to see you, Alicia. You look incredible.'

'In my chambermaid uniform?' she flared. 'You knew me in rags, and now you see me in a maid's uniform and tell me that I look incredible—?'

'Hey, if I'd wanted acrimony for breakfast I'd have ordered it,' he cut in, and Alicia fought to check herself.

'I was just...' She offered her palms skyward. 'Well, it's just *such* a shock to see you.'

'So you already said.'

Dante's intention had been to shrug, to dismiss her—yet for once he was curious as to what this claimant might want.

Now he was rich so many people petitioned him.

But Dante had never thought Alicia would do so.

She was the one person who had appeared on the stage of his life without resentment or agenda. The one person whose trust he hadn't had to pay handsomely for.

Until now.

But it wasn't just curiosity as to what she wanted that was winning.

How could it still be good to see her, even when he knew it was a ruse?

And he might have been being a little facetious, but she really *did* look incredible. The pale green was perfect with her olive skin, and he'd instantly noted her bare, toned calves. She still wore no make-up—none. Her shape was *more*... More breasts, more hips, even more appealing, and incredible was still the correct word.

'Actually,' Dante said, 'while you're here, could you open all the drapes? I might as well see the sunrise now that I'm up.'

He watched as she set to work and he could feel her silent fury even as she tried to quash it and attempt a recovery from her little outburst. 'It's so early...' she said.

'It's the time I specified.'

'No...' She let out a little false laugh. 'I mean six a.m. is not the best time for conversation.'

It was the only time he'd misread her.

An easy mistake—for how could he have guessed that she was merely angling for a coffee invitation when it was as if he could see images of them together flickering on the walls and ceilings? When with each turn of the kaleidoscope he was shown another intimate moment they'd shared.

With such potent energy coursing between them, unseen and yet so tangible, Dante assumed her plan was first to seduce and then to ask for whatever it was she wanted.

His response was world-weary. 'Am I supposed to ask at this point what six a.m. *is* the best time for?'

'I just meant that there are better times in the day to converse.'

'Did you, now?'

'Yes,' Alicia said, evidently waiting for him to remember his Sicilian manners. And as she tied the final sash she made one last attempt to engineer the conversation. 'It really has been ages…'

'Since when?' Dante asked.

'Since we last saw each other. It was at your mother's funeral, I believe.'

Not the best seduction line, Dante thought, and was about to give a slight scoffing laugh and call her out when he forgot his own rules. And it was Dante now who veered from the script.

'That wasn't the last time we saw each other, Alicia.'

Alicia straightened, and then fiddled unnecessarily with the privacy curtains as he spoke on.

'Are you forgetting what happened *after* the funeral?' he asked. 'When we took shelter from the blood rain?'

'No…' Alicia croaked.

'Before that we swam, though,' Dante mused, and though his voice was low and soft it was not meant to soothe her, but to inflame her as he added, 'If I remember correctly.'

'I'm not sure…'

'I am,' Dante said. 'Though of course we didn't actually swim…and we politely didn't mention what occurred beneath the water.'

She stood with her back to him. 'The *scirocco* makes people crazy.'

Alicia felt dizzy, and was suddenly desperate to flee. She'd been playing with fire, she realised, a long-smouldering fire that was now starting to flame.

She dared not turn. In fact, she went to swish open the thin curtains under the drapes.

'Leave them,' Dante said. 'I don't want anyone seeing in.'

'Fine,' Alicia croaked, and dropped her hand to her side. Even with her back to him she could feel his eyes upon her. She tensed, as if an ice cube had been dropped down the back of her uniform and melted on contact.

'Just what *are* you doing here, Alicia?'

Was it Dante or a VIP guest asking her this very direct question? Because if it was the latter then he had every right to be furious at her scheming ways. And if it was the former…

She should go now—give him a polite smile, leave that damn tip he had tossed on the bed and walk out. Yet it felt as if it were Dante asking the question…

Her legs would not move and she dared not turn, because that switch had been tripped again—only Alicia was struggling to locate the 'off' button now! *Help*, she silently begged the Duomo again. Only it was a rather different request now—*Please don't let me fall back under his spell.*

'Alicia…'

Dante's low drawling of her name felt like a feather brushing from the nape of her neck right down to the very base of her spine. And further down. Alicia could actually feel a pulse throbbing between her legs.

'What?' she asked, still staring out at the view, because it was so much easier than turning around. For she knew that voice—it called to her in a place that only he knew.

'Any minute now I'll wake up and it will be that doddery old butler in here and this strange coincidence won't have occurred.'

Dante's voice filled the strange silence that hovered between them.

'Perhaps.' She attempted to shrug, saw the cathedral blurring before her eyes.

And then the *scirocco* might well have just arrived in this suite, for it felt as if she were breathing those hot African winds that swept across Sicily at times…the same hot air that had wrapped around them a decade ago.

'It is strange…' Alicia attempted vainly, still clinging on to her lie, for it was the only thing she had to hold on to as the pull of Dante lured her.

'Tell me what you're doing,' he said.

She did not know how to. And when hate should surely be dominating, desire overrode it. The woman he had made her—

the woman only Dante knew—was frantic to see again the navy of his eyes, her senses flooded with the master's return.

The realisation should make her want to weep—finding out, a decade on, that her buried feelings had not diminished one iota, had merely been hibernating, and now they'd awoken, blinking at the sun after the bleakest of winters.

Alicia stood frozen, not knowing quite what to do with the surge in sensation. She looked out at the new morning as she relived a day of old, caught in a time warp between past and present. The future rendered irrelevant.

It was the oddest moment in her life as a decade of anger was displaced by the hot rise of passion. Every thought, every practised moment evaporated, and all that remained was the blissful recall of naked, heated, slippery bodies entwined, taking shelter from the storm and creating their own…

'You still haven't told me what you're doing,' Dante prompted, but she gave him no response.

She could feel his eyes roaming her body, as if he was aware of the tumult within her despite her still stance.

Walk away, Alicia, she told herself. *Get out now.*

He wasn't going to enquire further about her, nor was he going to ask about Beatrice. Certainly he wasn't going to invite her for a drink…

This was the very end of them.

Only this time it would be on her terms, Alicia decided. She would be the one to walk away, as he had so easily done, without so much as a backward glance.

'I think about that day sometimes,' Dante said.

And even with her back to him she heard the edge of surprise in his voice and knew that he was frowning, as if the information he'd just imparted had surprised him.

Indeed, it probably had, for Dante was not one for sharing his thoughts. Nor was he one to be lied to…nor swayed by feminine wiles.

'So do I,' Alicia responded, her voice the husky one only he had ever heard.

'I'm thinking about it now,' Dante said, and each word tautened her within.

Alicia half turned her head, but not enough so that she could see him. He was taking her straight back to the woman he'd met a long time ago. One who *could* deal with the sulky darkness of Dante.

She knew, too, that her back would be a reminder of long ago, and that her voice, her words, were pure seduction. Yet this was unrehearsed, for her talent was untrained and exclusive to Dante…

'I, too, am thinking of that day…' Her voice was tuned to his, low and husky, yet breathless and carnal.

'Turn around, Alicia.'

They would lead each other to danger. The path she stepped on would be as familiar as unlatching the little gate behind the church and disappearing into the rushes that led down to the river and the place only they knew.

Oh, she'd missed him, Alicia acknowledged as she turned and saw him, lying on his side, those navy eyes on her.

Yes, one final kiss, she decided as she walked towards him. Time for a new memory to whisper into her dreams at night. God knew she needed one after ten years.

And, because it was Dante, not for a second did he question her approach to the bed.

He knew she was not walking over to claim the tip that lay discarded.

He would kiss the truth out of her, Dante decided. He would hold her wrists and have her look him in the eyes as she revealed her reasons. He would get her to admit what she was up to, albeit with gentle tactics.

And so he held out an arm, and as she neared he reached for her hip and pulled her closer. 'I knew it was you,' Dante told her, 'before I had even opened my eyes.'

'Liar…' she said on a breath as she closed her eyes.

And because it was Dante, his kiss to welcome her back

was not on the lips. Instead, his unpredictable mouth met the fabric that covered her stomach, pressing his face against it as his hand stroked first her bottom and then moved up to the ribbons of the apron she wore. He located the ties easily, as if he had been planning on doing just that.

Alicia guessed that he had, for she had felt the heat of his stare.

'*Did* you know it was me?' he asked, flicking the lower poppers. And now his tongue met the soft skin of her stomach in a long velvet kiss.

'No,' she said, and felt a little giddy as he stopped kissing her stomach and then took not her hand, but her fingers.

'You're sure about that?' he checked.

'Not till I saw your name…'

She breathed out a shaky breath as he kissed her palm, slowly at first, and then wet and deep. Until now Alicia had not known that there was a line that ran directly from her palm to between her thighs, but with each lick of his tongue, each decadent kiss, she felt the ache of arousal.

'Alicia,' he demanded, and his large hand was around her wrist now, holding her as he looked up.

But whatever he'd been about to say no longer mattered, it would seem, because his head went back down and he kissed her forearm, then the inside of her upper arm, pushing up her short sleeves and breathing in her scent. Then his mouth moved to her breast. But perhaps he considered the wet trail his mouth might leave, for he removed it.

'Please…' she implored, looking at his mouth as she hurtled back a decade to a place where she was wanting and willing.

Dante accepted her plea and moved so that he was sitting up, and then pulled her onto the bed, into his lap.

Alicia went easily. She was so pliant—as if all thought had left her, just as it had that day long ago. Her legs clamped his thighs, but Dante hitched up her dress in a practical manoeuvre so she could more widely straddle him. And she was so terribly willing. For it was she who lowered her head towards him. And the feel of his lips against hers was so sublime that she closed her eyes and drank from him.

Yet his kiss was different now. Even as he gave her his mouth she felt it was a more refined kiss. He was no doubt more skilled now, but that was not the kiss she wanted.

'Dante…' She was demanding as they kissed, arguing with his tongue, wanting to feel again the intemperate thrill of his deepest kiss. Rising onto her knees and asking for *that* kiss with her tongue.

For a moment she found it, and his new practised kiss was lost as he briefly returned to the kind of kiss to which Alicia owned exclusive rights. His hand came to the back of her head and he pressed her face into his, their mouths melding, panting, knowing the other again.

Alicia took over the pressure then, holding his head, kissing him hard, freeing his hands to do as they chose. And they chose to bring her back down to his lap, only closer this time.

Their tongues were wet, his jaw was rough, and now his hands were stroking her bare thighs—and not gently. They were rubbing her skin as if making fire, and then they came up to her buttocks, and *this* kiss, the return of *his* kiss, was an unexpected relief.

Unexpected because walls she had not known existed were collapsing, and the tiny bites and licks to each other's mouth were mutual. She was at his neck, licking the salty skin, as he pulled her dress higher up, and now his erection was lodged against her knickers, damp and swollen on her stomach. She lifted herself up and Dante rubbed the head of his erection against cheap red satin.

'Tear them…' she pleaded, for he would be so worth the waste.

'Hold on…'

Dante was panting, as if from the sheer exertion it was taking for him not to take her now, and for Alicia it was the same—she was desperate for him as he peeled apart the rest of the poppers of her dress.

'I want to see you.'

Though he didn't really get to look, because she was smothering him with her full breasts.

'Oh, God…' Alicia gasped, desperate for his mouth to claim her breast through the lace. It did, in a deep, sensual suck, and then another. But when satin and lace were too much of a barrier he pulled his head back—to expose her breasts, she guessed. But instead he held her still. He made no move, just held her by the arms.

Her eyes flew to his in question. Alicia saw anger blazing in his navy glare, and his words were pure venom.

'This is a set-up.'

CHAPTER THREE

'DANTE!' ALICIA WOULD DIE, she would lie, she would give anything not to be left like this. She was on the edge, desperate to answer the call to breach the void. 'It's not a set-up. This is *us*...'

She was trying to get back to his mouth, but he turned his face so she only got his cheek.

'Come now, Alicia,' he said, and he pushed her away, pulling the sheet back over himself.

He looked down at the red panties and so did she. She saw the little diamante heart, the silky black hair of her triangle, and even his erection peeked out for another look.

Angrily, he covered it. 'Nice underwear for work.'

'My underwear is not your business.'

'It is when you bury my face in your breasts.' Dante tipped her off his lap. 'I knew you were lying all along.'

'I wasn't,' Alicia attempted—except she had been...right up to the last second.

'Jesus, what is it you want?'

'Dante—'

'Whatever it is, just say it.'

She stood dishevelled, doing up her poppers, retrieving her discarded apron. She was mortified.

'I don't want anything,' she told him.

'Oh, please,' he sneered. 'I can't even sleep without someone coming after me for something.'

He reached to the floor for a jacket and pulled out a packet of cigarettes. And that confused her further. Because not only did he not smoke, but also… 'Dante…*è contro il regolamento*. It's a non-smoking hotel…'

'Don't you dare try and talk to me about hotel policies,' he warned, lighting one. But then he pulled a face and angrily stubbed it out on the saucer. 'I don't even smoke.'

'Why do you have them, then?'

He didn't respond, but the look he gave told her she had no right to question him. None. It was Dante who was firing the questions. 'Is it money you want?'

'No.' Alicia shook her head. 'I told you—I don't want anything.'

'Oh, I'm quite sure there's something.' He watched as she tied the apron. 'I'm assuming there are no condoms in there?'

'Meaning?'

'You'd have let me take you bare. You didn't want me to wear one last time either.'

She refused to examine that memory now, but she understood his implication. 'Damn you!' she swore. 'The very last thing I want is your baby.'

'I know a set-up when I see one,' Dante told her.

Alicia was too embarrassed to admit he was right, and as she did up the final poppers on her uniform she lied again, to her own detriment. 'Well, you're wrong.'

He was angry.

Very.

And that feeling of sick disappointment was back.

Alicia—or at least the Alicia he had grown up with—had been the only person who had smiled when she saw him. The only person who had never made him feel filthy or an unpleasant burden the way his teachers or the locals had.

As his own mother had.

She had taught him that it was possible to trust—perhaps a little too well. Because when his father had reappeared in his life—well, Alicia had made him believe in the power of family.

What a let-down *that* had been.

Though it had hurt less than this.

He thought of their games. How she would demand to know how he would react in certain extreme scenarios. And, how if a gun were to be held to his head, if he were forced to come up with one person in this world he trusted, Alicia Domenica would have been the name he'd have given.

Not now.

He was angry. Not just with Alicia, but at how far it had gone. His intention had been to confront her by the bed, catch her wrist in his hand and look right into her lying eyes.

Instead, he had sought the skin of her stomach, her hand, her arm…

'Dante,' she said, 'you and I go way back—'

By way of interruption he made a scoffing noise. 'You wouldn't believe how many exes message me. The richer I get, the more they seem to recall the good times we had.' He looked right at her then. 'The trouble is they weren't all that good.'

It was a cheap shot, but he was more hurt than he cared to admit.

'We *were* that good Dante…'

Her voice was thick with unshed tears, and her certainty when many might crumble gave him such a blinding flash of days of old that for a second he closed his eyes, the glare of memories too bright.

'You accuse me of a set-up,' Alicia added as she pointed to the window where she'd stood, 'but just who was seducing whom back there, Dante?'

He said nothing.

Alicia said it for him. 'It felt very mutual to me.'

It had been—although he refused to concede that point. So what if the attraction was still there between them? Alicia Domenica was here with an agenda. Of that he was certain.

'Is it money you want?' he asked again.

'I told you—no.'

'Revenge?'

Her jaw tightened for a moment, but then she visibly steeled herself. 'Nothing like that.'

'So you just happen to be working in the same hotel I frequent?' He glared at her. 'Just happened to be *bitterly* polishing your brass door as I walked past one day?'

'I'm not bitter.'

'Oh, Alicia, the hell you aren't.' She flashed him a dark, angry look that told him he was right. 'And if you ever pull a stunt like this again I'll have you escorted from the building before your feet can touch the floor.'

'Dante, please...' She was embarrassed, dying inside, appalled at how wrong it had all gone, but he clearly didn't want to hear any of it.

'Alicia, go and tidy yourself up in the bathroom.'

'What?'

'I'm summoning my breakfast in precisely two minutes,' he told her. 'So go and tidy yourself before you head out—because right now you look as if you've just left my bed...'

He gestured to the bell that would summon the butler and, bastard that he was, then proceeded to set a timer on his phone.

'Two minutes.'

'Dante...'

'I would take my advice if I were you,' he warned. 'Isn't screwing the guests frowned upon in that policy manual you just quoted from? One minute forty-five seconds now...'

Alicia headed into the sumptuous bathroom and saw that unfortunately Dante was completely correct. Her hair was wild, her mouth swollen, her neck and chest dappled like some old pony, but in red...

She splashed her face with water, and then buried it in a hand towel for a moment, appalled at the turn of events. She lifted her face, did her best to tame her complexion, and then retied her hair and hastily straightened her clothes.

'Better,' he said as she walked out.

He was about to press the bell, effectively shutting any

further communication down. At least if she valued her job. And now that sense had returned, suddenly Alicia did.

'*Mi scusi, signor...*'

He told her, in rather rude Italian, exactly what she could do with her apology, as well as the sudden use of the word *signor*. 'Just get the hell out.'

'Dante, I never…'

Perhaps it was self-preservation that halted her. For how could she admit that, ten years on, all it had taken was the low purr of his voice to have her walking towards him. In some ways it would be easier to let him think this morning's events actually *had* been intended rather than let him know the power he still held.

Yet for her own dignity Alicia decided she *would* correct him on one thing. 'Can I say one thing before you summon the butler?'

He rolled his eyes.

'The most embarrassing moment of my life was when you saw me in my *nonna* knickers and my donation cupboard bra…'

She watched his jaw clamp, and rather than look at her turned to the view, but she saw that he'd closed his eyes. It would seem that he, too, would like to block out the memory of that time—or, knowing Dante, callously disregard it.

Alicia forced herself to push on. 'With my first pay cheque I bought some nice underwear. It is my one indulgence.' He said nothing. 'What I am wearing beneath my uniform is for me, not you.'

Still he refused to look at her. 'Just go.'

'Bastard.'

Now he looked at her. 'You have no idea how right you are. Don't attempt games with a black heart, Alicia. It never ends nicely.'

It ended now, Alicia decided and flashed him a smile. 'Here is the butler now, *signor*. Enjoy the rest of your day.'

CHAPTER FOUR

ALICIA DID NOT enjoy the rest of her own day.

'Where on earth...?' The head of housekeeping was waving her hands when she reappeared.

'A guest asked me—'

'Fine. The third-floor breakfasts are late.'

That was it.

No one would guess that Alicia, who just did her job, day after day after day, and was too shy with men to get to a second date, had just been almost taken by Signor Schininà.

She felt ill as she worked—too ill to eat. And so when she was given a late lunch she hid in one of the linen cupboards on the sixth floor and sat on a bench there, trying to breathe, her elbows on her knees and her fists clenched at her temples.

For all her planning there were things that she hadn't considered. That her feelings might remain. That she might jeopardise her job. Might cross the room and move directly into his arms, as easily and as readily as that.

How was it possible that he could lure her so easily? His betrayal had once almost broken her.

She buried her face in a towel and tried to dilute that, to tell herself that it hadn't been that bad—except it really had been.

Dante had returned to Trebordi for his mother's funeral. The briefest of visits—one night, maybe two. Conversation, kisses, solace, grief...all building to something precious. Or at least she'd thought it had been precious.

Until nine months later.

Alicia felt as if Sister Angelique was standing over her in the linen cupboard now, as she had in the early hours of that morning. She'd been summoned out of bed and had stood there bemused when accused of using the baby door.

And then she'd been ushered into the nursery, where she sometimes worked when there was a baby left.

It was his baby. Right down to his toes. She'd been able to see that—and so, too, had Sister Angelique.

'He must have been busy in the short while he was back.'

Alicia's thoughts had been too jumbled for her to get the implication at first as she'd looked at the babe.

'It would seem you're not so special after all.'

Clearly not.

She'd been left holding Dante's baby.

Just not hers.

For close to two years now she had sought an audience with Dante.

No more.

Whatever game she had started, all Alicia wanted was for it to end, and she was grateful when her long shift finally finished.

Physically weary and emotionally drained, Alicia pulled on her dress and sandals and removed the tie from her thick black hair, but had no energy even to comb it.

Walking out of the staff entrance, she made her way along the road she had come that morning, when there had still been hope, but there were new troubles she was dealing with now.

'Alicia!'

The low sound of his voice, while not a complete surprise, still made her jump. Alicia briefly closed her eyes and took a breath to gather herself before turning around.

'Dante.' She could barely look at him. She couldn't bear to take in the beauty of him in a suit, for it was a cruel reminder of the day he had taken a whole lot more than her heart.

'We need to talk,' he told her.

'We really don't.' She went to walk off, but he reached for her arm and pulled her back, turning her around to face him.

'You've clearly been trying to speak with me, yet now you're running off.'

'I'm hardly running—my shift is over.'

'Let's go for dinner.'

'Why?'

'What do you want me to say, Alicia?'

'How about, *It would be nice to catch up*?'

'That would be a lie,' Dante said. 'I don't enjoy rehashing the past. And I don't appreciate that I am suddenly popular now.'

'Meaning?'

'You wouldn't believe how many people try to get hold of me—people from the village. *"Oh, Dante, remember the village dance." "I was just thinking of you, Dante..." "Dante, Dante, Dante..."'* He looked at her. 'It is not just women who rewrite the past, I get offers of business from the same men who once would not even let me clean their chicken coops.'

Alicia took in a breath, recalling how cruel those times had been.

'The head of the school I attended writes annually, asking me to give a donation and return to give a speech. I remind him that from the age of ten I barely attended. I'm very used to being looked up—although I have to say your methods are a little more ingenious.'

'So I am in the same basket as old acquaintances or your headmaster. We were *lovers*.'

'Alicia, we were hardly lovers...' He leant in, and her throat tightened as he told her in less than romantic terms that they had had sex only once.

Her eyes flashed, yet still she refused to meet his. 'No wonder the nuns warned me about you.'

'They were right to.' Dante shrugged. 'I, too, warned you not to get involved with me.'

He had.

'Yet here you are,' Dante said.

'No.' She corrected. 'Here *you* are, Dante. I was actually on my way home.'

'True,' he conceded. 'And although I don't usually take old *lovers* out for dinner…' he paused and gave her a black smile '… I'll make an exception for you.'

'Why?'

'Because I owe you an apology.' He looked mildly pained to admit it.

Alicia was about tell him he most certainly did, but she stopped herself—because even if she wasn't very responsible with her own heart, when it came to a child's she was. And to unleash her hurt might cause dreadful pain to Roberto and his adoptive family.

'I can't be seen with a guest at the hotel…'

'We'll go elsewhere.' He shrugged. 'Up to you,' he said, in that same take-it-or-leave-it tone he'd used before, and then he walked off.

Was it for Beatrice that she considered following him? Or was it to gauge whether she should tell him he was a father? Maybe just to end things on a better note than they had this morning?

It took her a moment to collect herself, and another moment to catch up, because he did not slow his stride.

And, although it felt strange to walk again with Dante by her side, there was a certain familiarity to it that she dared not examine.

He was stunning.

Or rather, he stunned *her*.

Of course she had seen it this morning, his raw beauty. Dante before he faced the world had been so perfect that she had wanted to lick him, to kiss his face off, to be lost in him. Not much had changed now, except he was dressed in all his finery—a tailored suit, hand-stitched shoes and a tie that had certainly cost more than her entire wardrobe combined.

And his scent…

Dante even *smelt* rich now.

But there was also the familiar scent of him beneath.

Be careful, she warned herself. For while once she might have been able to handle the knife-edge of Dante with ease, that dark edge had clearly sharpened.

'Not here.' She made known her protest as he halted outside one of Milan's smartest restaurants. 'Dante, I'm hardly dressed for fine dining…'

Her words died as he took her elbow and the mere touch of his hand shot a million volts through her.

'The food is good here, and…' He paused. 'You look fine.'

He spoke to the greeter and asked for their most private table. Perhaps he didn't want to be seen with a rather scruffy end-of-shift chambermaid in public. He walked so confidently as Alicia followed behind him—looking at his broad shoulders—into a room so dark it didn't feel like just after six on a summer's night…

They were led to a booth, and now that her eyes had acclimatised she could make out more easily the exquisite dark walnut and the engraved partitions.

'It's like a confessional,' Dante said.

'We might be here for a while, then,' Alicia retorted smartly.

'Really?' he asked, rather tongue in cheek. 'What have you been up to, Alicia?'

He turned and confidently ordered wine to be brought before the menus, then resumed his teasing.

'Do you make a habit of sneaking into guests' rooms?'

She knew he saw her discomfort, and he would know that it was rare from Alicia, because she was usually fiery and confident.

'Look, before we get into whatever you want to speak to me about, I do want to apologise,' he told her.

Alicia swallowed, wondering if he even knew of the chaos he had left behind—though it would seem the span of Dante's conscience ran to a far tighter timeline…

'As much as I don't approve of your methods this morning, I should not have commented on your underwear and accused you of dressing to seduce me. You are correct. What you wear beneath your uniform is none of my business.'

She gave a small nod, feeling awkward about what she'd told him. She was relieved to accept a menu from the waiter as he reappeared, and as the wine was poured she tried to gather herself.

There were little lights clipped to the menus, and she pretended to read before saying, 'I'm really not hungry.'

'Then you can watch me eat.' Dante shrugged. 'Grow up, Alicia, and order. The veal *scallopini* is very—'

'I'm not a big meat-eater,' Alicia interrupted.

'Since when?' He frowned.

'For ever.' Alicia shrugged. 'Although there was not much choice when I was growing up, there is now.' But, given she could not read the vegetarian options, Alicia did what she always did when dining out. 'I'll have *spaghetti al sugo*.'

It was the safest option, as she had long since found out. Just a plain tomato sauce and pasta. Even if it wasn't on the menu the kitchen staff could make it easily, perhaps with basil or cheese, and of course it was always delicious—except she would love to try more.

Dante also ordered a pasta dish, though it sounded so much nicer than hers and she pressed her lips together.

He would read her envy, her jealousy. He always had and he always would—the same way he would have noticed the missing cream from the coffee tray this morning and known it was no accident.

'You can change your mind…' he said.

'No, I'm happy with my order.'

They sat in silence, and then Alicia offered not so much an apology of her own, but an acknowledgement. 'Thank you for not reporting me.'

'Did you think I would, Alicia?'

And as she looked over at him the cruel deserter and the lavish playboy seemed to fade, leaving just Dante, the man who had once been her friend.

She'd missed him so.

'No,' she admitted. 'At least not the Dante I knew. But, as you said, perhaps things weren't as good as I recall…'

'I was very cross this morning.'

'Yes.'

'If you wanted something you could have called, or written, or…' He watched as she closed her eyes. 'You could have called out when I passed you in the foyer.'

'You were with someone, Dante. I don't think she would have appreciated it.'

'Fair enough.'

And still he could surprise her, for he was suddenly kind.

'How have you been?' he asked. 'I really would like to know.'

'Busy,' she said. 'Working, mainly.'

'No husband?'

'I would hope not, after this morning.'

He smiled at her response. 'How many broken hearts have you left behind, Alicia?'

'Fewer than you, I'm sure,' she retorted.

'You know, for someone so beautiful there is so much venom in you.'

Her throat caught. He had called her beautiful as if he meant it, and maybe he did. He had always made her feel so. 'There's no venom.' She shook her head.

'Yes, there is,' he refuted. 'Why?'

She ran her tongue over her lips, unsure how to answer this very direct question. Truly unsure if she should.

Dante hazarded a guess, wasting no time in getting to the point. 'I told you I was leaving that night. I told you it was a one-off.'

'You did.'

'I didn't leave you pregnant?' He frowned. 'I know I took care, but if…'

'Dante…' her top lip curled just a little in a sneer '…it wouldn't have taken me ten years to find you if you had. I would not have allowed my baby to starve while you played fast and loose with your tarts…'

'Tut-tut,' he said. 'That's not a nice way to speak, Alicia.'

No. It wasn't.

'I take that back.'

'Good,' he said, and took up his wine. 'Let's try and keep this civil.'

The waiter draped a white serviette over her lap but did not approach Dante. Alicia had never eaten in such a place, and wondered if the serviette treatment was just for women, or the aura that surrounded Dante silently warned that he wanted no contact.

He'd always been like that.

They sat in silence until their meals were served. Dante was waiting her out, and Alicia was overwhelmed, unsure now whether to ask for his help.

The spaghetti was generously covered in grated cheese, black pepper too, and finally they ate. There were few days that Alicia could recall when she had *not* eaten pasta, but she was so awkward now that it felt as if she held chopsticks.

'So,' he asked, 'how is Milan treating you?'

'Well.'

'How often do you go back?'

'Back?'

'To Sicily.' He gave her a thin smile. 'I could have saved you the trouble. I have a hotel on the east…'

'I'm not in Milan for *you*, Dante.'

'That was actually a joke,' he said. 'So, how often—?'

'Here is home.'

'Seriously?'

'Milan's beautiful.'

'Indeed. So you don't go back?'

'Why would I?'

They were fumbling—or she was—through the catching up. And she skipped over Beatrice because she didn't know what to say now.

He asked about friends, and if she was seeing anyone—all of it like squeezing blood from a stone, really.

'No.' Alicia went a little pink at the last question, for she found this topic exquisitely uncomfortable.

She had had first dates—many, *many* first dates—but even the good ones had led to the inevitable... After all, a good date should end in a kiss, and ultimately Alicia had found that she could not go through with it.

'I've actually just broken up with someone...' She gave a tight shrug, thinking of the most recent disaster. 'You know how it is... We wanted different things...'

Alicia stared at the orange flame of the candle between them rather than at him. It was dawning on her—or rather, she was finally admitting—that her issue with other men was that she'd prefer they be him.

'You would certainly be...' Dante hesitated, for they were heading into dangerous territory indeed.

Oh, she sat demure now, twisting her pasta, yet holding Alicia was like being handed a bolt of lightning. She came full pelt out of the gate. Always, and not just with sex. She just lunged into passion, headed straight to devotion, with no moment to catch your breath in between.

Still, he was not here to give Alicia Domenica dating advice.

She persisted, though. 'I would certainly be what, Dante?'

'A challenge.'

She gave a mirthless laugh. 'I'm sure women would say the same about you.'

'I meant you would certainly not be looking for a...shall we say a *temporary* arrangement.'

'You don't know that.' Alicia lifted her eyes to his. 'Are you forgetting this morning?'

'So you would have simply dressed and left?'

'I would have wanted dinner tonight,' Alicia answered smartly, and gestured to her plate. 'But I got that without sleeping with you.'

He said nothing to correct her, but the slight raising of his brows stated that it was only his control that had stopped them.

'Are you?' she asked.

'What?'

'Involved with anyone.'

'No.'

'The woman I saw you with in the foyer...?'

'Is this a trick question?'

'You don't know who I'm talking about, do you?' Her voice was derisive as she looked around the restaurant. 'This is early for you. You're more after-parties and casinos...'

'Actually, no.' He shook his head. 'The truth is I only gamble when I'm working. I'm a good host, though. Got to keep the investors happy...'

'I never thought you'd be one to succumb to peer pressure, Dante.'

He moved the candle from between them very deliberately and leant forward. Cross now, he looked right into her eyes and jabbed a finger towards her.

'We all do what we have to to survive, *bella*.'

She wanted to snatch his finger.

Hold it, press his hand to her face or her breast.

He was *that* potent.

She felt as if his hands were almost on hers under the table. When he'd leant forward she'd almost reached towards his fierce kiss, but Dante wasn't here to make out.

'My father can't keep up with the lifestyle, so...'

She startled at the news. 'You found your father?'

'He found me,' Dante said.

'Tell me!'

'What?'

'Do you have brothers, sisters...?'

'A brother—well, half...'

'Older or younger?'

'Two years older, apparently, but really he's a spoilt teenager.' He rolled his eyes and leant back against the velvet of the booth. 'Believe me, be careful what you wish for, Alicia.

Family is not so easy. You must have seen some of this when you were doing your "research" on me?'

'No.' She shook her head.

'Right…' His disbelief was evident.

'Dante, please… Tell me how it was to finally meet—?'

'I don't want to get into it.'

'Dante?' she urged. 'Please don't do that.'

'What?'

'Whatever you think of me *now*, can you please for a moment remember *then*? We used to speak about this…dream of this.'

'No, *you* did.'

'Dante, we would sit in the cemetery or lie by the river…' Her breath hitched as she recalled their innocence and lying by the river like two fat starfish, holding hands and deciding who their family might be. 'I was there at the beginning. Please let me know how it ended.'

He never discussed such things, but it was her dream, he knew. Hours and days they had spent together as she anticipated the moment she'd find her parents, or he'd meet his father.

Well, it had been Alicia's game that they'd played, and so he would tell her a little more.

'Very well, it was…' He searched for the right words. 'Conditional, I guess.'

She shook her head, not understanding.

'I didn't really trust him.'

'You don't trust anyone.'

'I'm aware of that, and so I tried. But I'm not very good at being grateful.'

'I can imagine.'

'There had to be compromises made from the start—some I wasn't comfortable with…' He took a drink of his wine and watched as so, too, did Alicia. In fact she even pushed her half-eaten food away.

'What sort of compromises?' she asked.

'What if I told you that my father asked me to take his name?'

'So?' Alicia shrugged. 'I'd take my parents' name in a heartbeat. I'd be so happy…'

'Well…' he gave a grim smile '…for what it's worth I would be sorry to hear you were no longer Alicia Domenica.' He said it with a sincerity that elicited his own surprise, given it came from someone so cold. 'And you would now be sitting opposite Dante Ricci.'

'No…' Alicia frowned, for that was not the man who sneaked into her wildest dreams. 'You're Dante Schininà.'

'I told my father the same,' Dante said. 'For all her faults, my mother at least made some sloppy effort to take care of me the first few years and gave me her name.'

'She did,' Alicia agreed. 'What other compromises?'

'I have an older half-brother, Matteo, and my father has a wife Giustina…'

'Your stepmother?'

'There are no steps to her ever being my mother. However, she is his wife. My mother *was* the local *poutana*, Alicia.'

'Oh, yes.' She guessed that would take some explaining! 'Remember when I thought she was a beekeeper?'

For the first time he actually smiled.

It felt like a victory.

Growing up, Alicia had thought Dante smiled easily. It had only been when she'd seen him with others that she had realised what a rarity that smile actually was. So beautiful, though, to see that full sulky mouth spread and the reward of his white teeth, and sometimes…just sometimes…there was the greater reward of his laugh.

'So, how did he explain you to his wife?'

'Death can be kind to those left behind.' Dante shrugged. 'It allowed my mother to go down in his history as a long-time lover.'

'And Giustina was okay with that?'

He should leave it there, Dante knew. Certainly, he usually would. But Alicia was the one person he'd been able to talk to, and even after ten years that hadn't changed.

'I think she's always been happy for him to take a lover if it means she can sleep alone.'

'Really?'

They were leaning towards each other a little now.

'However, she was not happy that her golden goose had laid another egg—me. Do you know what the name Giustina means?'

Alicia shook her head.

'Justice,' he said. 'Impartial.' He gave a sardonic roll of his eyes. 'If ever there was a woman who was wrongly named—' He broke off as Alicia started to laugh. 'What's so funny?'

'The nuns used to say the same thing about Beatrice—how Beatrice Festa was an inappropriate name when she was such a cold little thing.'

'How is she doing?' he asked.

It was like the wood stove in the convent kitchen slowly staring to heat up, because that was what Alicia and Dante had been like. Cold, warm, warmer, and then so, so hot.

She must remember the inevitable freeze of the plunge pool post-Dante, but Alicia felt warm now, and she did not want to pull away. She knew how difficult it was to get Dante to reveal anything, and as he was starting to do so now she didn't want to lose the moment.

'Beatrice?' he prompted.

'I want to hear more about your family first.'

'They're rich, with boutique hotels in Florence and Rome. I was given an apartment, a bank account…suddenly I had a life I was told I'd always wanted…' He swirled his wine. 'Basically, for almost a decade, I've worked for my father.'

'But?' Alicia pushed.

'I've also been my own entity. The Sicilian side of things are mine.'

'That's good. Isn't it?'

'For me it is.' He nodded, then gave a black smile. 'My contract's up soon.'

'You're walking away?'

He shrugged.

'Now you've got what you wanted?'

'No, no,' he said. 'He got what he wanted, too. I don't think he contacted me without an agenda.'

Colour flooded her cheeks and she stood. 'Excuse me a moment.'

The restrooms were more like a boudoir, and it was really more than a moment's escape—ten moments, maybe.

Her brain was spinning after a whole day of Dante, Dante, Dante, and she was startled when she saw her reflection in the mirror. Her hair was tousled, the red of her bra strap was exposed, her cheeks were flushed and, although it had been more than twelve hours ago, she still looked exactly as if she had just left his bed or wrenched her lips from his.

Could he see what she did? Alicia thought with a dart of anxiety.

He'd tipped her upside down so much so that she startled the woman next to her by suddenly asking the time. *'Che ore sono?'*

'Sò ottu ore.'

Only eight?

Time had always moved differently when she was with Dante.

Her mind kept flicking back to their time together, to blood rain kisses and words uttered, lingering in that afternoon for a dangerous second.

She dared not let it venture there for long.

It would kill her to recall it completely, and yet she could feel the need to fully examine their time building—a mounting pressure within.

Forbidden hours that she had buried for more than a decade.

Yet her body was reliving it now and she felt inflamed.

Oh, she really did want Beatrice now. For her to be at home

to talk to or call. She needed someone who would understand how lonely times had been back then.

For him, too.

More so than she.

So much more so.

She was appalled now at the spite in her thoughts as she'd walked to work today, how she'd decided she needed Dante the rich man on-side...

She had been planning to use him, or at least try to.

But not in *that* way.

Because the very last thing she needed was to desire him.

Her napkin had been folded and returned to the table and the waiter came with dessert menus as she took her seat.

'No, thank you,' Dante declined on behalf of them both.

'Coffee?' the waiter offered.

'No,' he said.

She was both hurt and relieved that he was wrapping things up, but she made a vague joke as she sat down. 'I don't get any dessert?'

'You can have what you like, but I need to get on. So just say what you want to say.'

'I'm sorry.' She knew she couldn't even look at him, but she tried to. 'I do want something.'

'I know.'

And again he was being kind at the oddest of times.

'Alicia, I get it. Just tell me what you need.'

She had her audience, but she loathed her methods so much.

'Come on.'

'I've lost contact with Beatrice.'

'Did you have a row?'

'No, nothing like that. I lied to you that afternoon...'

That afternoon...

'I'm not with you,' he said.

'When you returned for the funeral I told you we were

in touch, but the truth is I haven't seen her since she left the convent.'

'But you said you wrote to each other all the time. That she was studying law.'

'I exaggerated a little,' Alicia said. 'Quite a lot, actually.'

'So how often did you write?'

'Not as much as I would have liked to. Not as much as I told you we did…'

'How much are we talking?'

'She sent me two cards.'

'Since when?' he prompted. 'Since I went to Rome? Since the funeral?'

'Since the day she left.'

'Only two cards?' He was blunt.

'We promised that we'd stay in touch and be friends…'

'You were just children then.'

'No.' She shook her head.

'People move on, Alicia…'

'No, we were so close. I've searched for her. That's why I came to Milan. On the weekends I go to the library, and I've visited schools, universities… I've even taken the train to Florence and Rome and done the same there…'

'You're stalking her as well as me?' He saw her flinch and abandoned the joke. 'Have you tried a private investigator? They do that sort of stuff all the time—'

'Listen to you!' She stared, wide-eyed. 'We don't all have your endless resources.'

He gave a black smile. 'I've been working my ass off since I was ten—not cosy in my convent school and warm bed. I've earned what I have.' He looked right at her. 'Don't go for the sympathy vote, Alicia…'

'I'm not.' Her cheeks were on fire. 'I just want to find out what happened to Beatrice.'

'Okay, tell me what you know.'

'You'll help me?'

'I'll ask one of my team to put someone on it.' He took out his phone. 'Festa?'

She nodded.

'Middle name?'

'No.'

She told him the little she knew and he typed it into his phone. Clearly it wasn't enough.

'You must know the address of the school she was sent to?'

'The nuns always wrote the address on my envelopes. It would have been a big church school, I assume…'

'Her date of birth?'

She told him—or tried to. 'I am not sure what the official certificate would say. They might have put it as the day before she arrived as she was a few hours old when she was found…' Alicia gave a helpless shrug. 'We're both Virgos…'

'What does your star sign have to do with anything?' He stopped typing into his phone, clearly irritated at the scant details. 'What else?'

'Beatrice always thought she had been left after the festival. She used to have the most terrible dreams…'

'I mean practical stuff.'

'She was good at languages.'

'Did she ever find out about her family?'

'Dante.' She was reproachful now. 'I had to wait till I was eighteen to be told anything. You know that.'

He did…

But they were heading back to that afternoon again, and neither was willing to go there.

'It's not a lot to go on, but I'll get someone on it.'

'Thank you.'

'I have to go now. A happy hour meeting.' He pulled a face. 'I hate cocktails.'

'I've always wanted to try one.' She shook her head. 'I'm not angling to come along.'

'Believe me, you'd hate tonight.'

He stood, and they walked out of the restaurant and onto the busy street. It was bizarre to Alicia that it was still light.

That she'd seen him and he was going to help her.

It felt both safe and unsafe to be back in contact with Dante…to know there would be time for her to more sensibly ponder if she should tell him about Roberto…

'You'll need my number,' she said.

'No, no.'

'In case you find out anything.'

'Gino, my head of legal, will contact you and keep you informed.'

'Well, *he'll* need my number.'

'I don't want your number, Alicia,' he said bluntly. 'I will help you because we were once friends.'

He'd slotted her right back into the past.

'I hope you gave your family more chances than you give old friends.'

But he was not up to taking advice. 'Gino will be in touch,' Dante said, and it was clear he was about to go.

Given who she was dealing with, Alicia knew it was the end of them—that she would probably never see him again.

'Dante?' She called after him. 'Before you go, can I ask you something?'

He considered it for a moment, and then nodded.

There were so many things vying for the top spot on Alicia's list of things she would like to ask. All the questions she had suppressed over the years seemed to have been unleashed by this morning's events. But there was one that was essential.

'If you had a child,' she ventured tentatively, 'would you want to know?'

'Alicia, please don't play your cryptic games. I've already asked you—'

'And I've answered.'

'So what is the point of your question?'

Alicia took a breath. 'What would you do if you found out, years later, that your child had been left at the convent's baby door?'

Dante frowned.

'I'm really not talking about me,' Alicia cut in.

Yes, you are, Dante thought, for her face was on fire and he was certain he knew why.

'Have you found out more about your parents?' he asked.

'No.'

'You have, haven't you?'

'No, I'm just asking you. If, years on, you found out you had a child, would you want to be a part of its life?'

He could still read her expressions, see the turmoil in her eyes, and given her search for Beatrice it would seem that Alicia was on a mission to gather up the people she had decided should love her.

And from the little he knew about her parents, this would likely not end well.

So he cut it off at the neck.

'No.'

'You don't mean that.'

'What? Because you don't like my response it has to be wrong?'

'I think you *would* want to be a part of your child's life.' She was insistent. 'Blood is thicker than water. There would be a pull—'

'Not for me.'

'Not even if you saw your own flesh and blood, face to face?'

'I did,' he reminded her. 'Alicia, people use the baby door for a reason.' His phone was buzzing, obligation calling, and he did not have time for Alicia's hypotheticals. 'Let it go, Alicia. Seriously.'

And then, to prove how easy it was to walk away, he

left—just as he had a decade ago, with but a single word 'Ciao,' and not so much as a backward glance.

Just as the endless men he had seen leave his mother's house had.

It had never entered his head that someone might watch them go.

His mother certainly never had.

'Happy cocktail hour, Dante,' she called to him.

He lifted his arm in a dismissive wave she knew only too well.

She would never understand him.

But she wanted to.

CHAPTER FIVE

GINO DID MAKE CONTACT, leaving a message for her at the hotel, and she sent him every piece of information she had. And then there was nothing.

Every day Alicia checked at Reception to see if there was a message, or a call, or some news about Beatrice.

Any word from him.

Dante Schininà.

An official-looking envelope came a week or so later and she took it to the head chef, who helped her with stuff like that.

'You have to display your parking permit prominently,' he said, explaining the contents of the letter.

'I don't drive.'

'We all got one,' he said with a shrug, and handed it back.

'Thank you.'

She continued to check each and every day, but quickly became tired of waiting.

It was five a.m. on a Friday, and as she dressed in the dark she realised how tired she was. But it wasn't the hour that exhausted her, nor the thought of the long shifts ahead this coming weekend. She was simply weary of clinging on to people who so clearly didn't want her in their lives.

No more, she decided, fastening the clasp on her bra. On her next day off she was getting back on the dating site. She would meet someone at a cocktail bar, Alicia decided, and she would find something fabulous to wear for the occasion. She was going to kiss another man. Make love, even…

Well, perhaps not quite yet, but at least she would dance. Yes.

But of course just when she'd got brave, and had decided it was time to move on, Dante pulled her back as if there was elastic between them, tightening, snapping her round to face him as she approached the hotel.

He walked towards her, looking depraved before dawn, a wolf slinking back to his lair, for Alicia knew Dante hunted at night.

He wore a suit and his morning shadow, and she did not want to get close lest she smell a scent that wasn't his.

Of course she was wearing exactly the same dress as she had been a fortnight ago. Part of her wanted to point out that she *did* have other clothes, but it would reveal that she cared what he thought.

And although she broke her stride, it wasn't because she was shocked to see him. It was more that her body was trying to prevent her from breaking into a run.

Towards him.

Years from now they might be allocated chairs next to each other in a nursing home and her heart would still soar, Alicia knew.

Her own passion angered her.

Frustration at his lack of it bubbled like lava beneath.

And so she was at her scathing best when he stopped in front of her.

'How is your new hotel?' She knew he had changed his location in Milan.

'A bit boring.' He shrugged. 'The maids aren't quite as entertaining.'

'And how was your night?' she asked, with just a dash of derision. 'I assume you were in Lugano?' It was a very deliberate assumption, for that was where the largest casino was.

'Lake Lugano and a full moon is a sight to behold.' Dante smirked.

Oh, he had *not* been walking by the lake and gazing at the moon, Alicia knew. 'The moon is not actually full until Sunday.'

'Then I might have to go back.' He paused, and very deliberately put a stop to their verbal sparring. 'Alicia, I'm not here by accident.'

She swallowed, for she had already guessed he didn't generally slink around outside hotels in the early hours of the morning.

'Can we sit?' He gestured to a bench in the square.

'No, I can't be late.'

'I'm sure you're ridiculously early.'

True.

'Come on,' he said, and gestured with his head as he took her elbow lightly.

Something in the way he said it told her he was here to talk about Beatrice. She perched on the edge of the bench rather than sit. She'd been waiting for this moment for ever, but was terrified now it was here.

'It's not good news,' Dante said, but then he immediately moved to put her mind at rest. 'She's not dead or anything,' he added. 'At least, there's no evidence to suggest that.'

Her breathing was shallow, and she wanted to get up and run, but then Dante took her hand.

He'd used to do that.

Dante knew how to hold her hand like no one else.

His hands were the kindest she knew.

She looked down at their fingers, laced together, and discovered how right they looked clasped together here on the edge of dawn. Though his nails were now manicured and neat, his hands were so familiar, and she clung on for just a moment.

Gathering herself, she lifted her eyes to his. 'I remember the day you stopped holding my hand.' She looked down again. 'We were walking through the rushes.'

He said nothing.

'Well, I think it was the last time, apart from our wild afternoon.'

Still he didn't respond.

She doubted he even remembered.

'Do you want me to tell you what Gino has discovered?'

She took a breath. 'Yes.'

'Gino has good contacts, and he sourced a top private investigator. He's seriously good, but he's been on the case for two weeks and turned up nothing.'

'Nothing?'

'Nothing.'

'There must be *something*.'

'The trail goes cold at the village. He chased up all the name hits, but none were her. And all the schools—not just in Milan, but all of Italy. It's just a complete dead end.'

Alicia closed her eyes for a moment. Of course it was not his fault that the news was bad. If anything, it helped a little to know it wasn't just her poor reading skills that had led her down blind alleys to nowhere.

'Maybe she's married now,' Alicia said.

'I think he would have found a record of that.'

'She might be in witness protection.'

'Perhaps… But have you considered that she might not want to be found?'

His voice was kind, though the question was brutal. But Dante really did know how to hold her hand, for he took it into his lap as he asked it, and held it gently even as it clenched.

'Yes,' Alicia finally admitted. 'I've thought of that a lot of late.'

'People move on,' Dante said, his grip tightening as she went to pull back her clawed hand. 'I haven't kept in touch with anyone from my past…'

'You're stone-cold, though,' Alicia said.

'So was Beatrice,' Dante reminded her, probing the parts of her that hurt with a tenderness that didn't actually surprise Alicia—for just as he'd accepted her fiery nature, he'd respected, too, the quiet intermissions. The lulls where she gathered herself. Faced facts and regrouped. 'Was it you keeping the friendship alive?' he asked.

'Maybe.'

'Is it time to let go?' he asked, and then one by one he unfurled her fingers as they sat there, as if unknotting a necklace, her hand the sole focus of his attention as Alicia thought things through and drew her conclusions.

'I can't,' she finally admitted. 'I mean, in many ways I have. I've got good friends here, and I'm doing well at work. Most of the time I can put it aside. But then I see a blonde woman who looks like her... Beatrice once said we're sisters of the heart, and for me, at least, it's still true. We shared a crib, Dante...'

'*Bambino oca...*' He sighed. 'Like little goslings... They love the first person they lay eyes on and follow them around.'

'Maybe.' Alicia nodded. 'But I'll never stop looking.'

'You mean that?' he checked.

'Yes.'

She could smell a woman's perfume now, and she noticed for the first time that there was lipstick on his cheek. Combined with the news he'd brought, it made her feel a little ill.

'Well, thank you for trying.'

'I haven't really tried,' Dante said as she stood.

'You just said—'

'Alicia, sit down. I want to put something to you.'

'What?'

'Just sit for a moment.'

'I don't have time. I'll be late.'

'Be late for once, then. Look, Beatrice has to be somewhere. The detective has suggested he goes back with you to—'

'No.' She shook her head. 'I don't want to go back.'

'Even if it means you find Beatrice? You need to sit down with the nuns—or whoever's still there at the convent. With someone who knows what to ask.'

'I've already done that. I asked them so many times.'

'Yes—as a teenager. You're a woman now. You're working and independent—they won't be able to intimidate you as much and you'd have the investigator with you.'

'I don't want to go back to the convent. I don't want to go back to Sicily at all.'

Dante's eyes narrowed. She knew he had always known when she was flustered, but he chose to let it go—for which she was grateful. No doubt he'd file it away, though, as he often did pieces of information.

'Anyway, you just told me you had Gino put the best person on to it.'

'Yes, and I did—as a favour for a friend. I don't owe you anything now.' He said it quite coldly. 'However, I can have the investigator build a team, bring in some fresh eyes—not just in Sicily and Milan, but beyond.'

'Then do it.'

For a brief second Alicia really thought it was a simple as that—that Dante was offering to help her because of their shared past.

'Oh, no.' He shook his head. 'If there's one thing that my mother taught me it's that you don't give the honey away for free. If you want my help, then you have to come back to Sicily with me. Today.'

She laughed—not an amused one, just a tired one—and hitched up her bag and walked towards the hotel.

He easily caught her up. 'I mean it. Just listen.'

'No,' Alicia said. 'Don't try bribing me with Beatrice. You should *want* to help…' Her voice faded a little. Dante already *had* helped. What he was suggesting now was a whole new level. 'Why would you want me in Sicily?'

'I've messed up.' He moved her into a doorway. 'I suggested to my family that they come with me to Sicily for the weekend and meet someone.'

'Why?'

'Seemed like a good idea at the time. Not so much now. Look, I've had a think, and maybe I don't have to sever things with them so absolutely. You could be my excuse to pull back. I could say that I'm basing myself in Sicily more because of you...' He smiled. 'I'll tell them that you're hot-headed and needy.'

'Get one of your actresses.'

'Alicia, I think the best chance I have of pulling this off is you. Anyway, I am *not* giving some stranger details on my dealings.'

'You've already told them I'll be there, haven't you?' she accused.

'Yep. I told you. I've messed up.' He almost laughed. 'Your lies are catching.'

She leant against the wall.

'Come on—it would just mean a family dinner with them on Saturday. In return you'll have a fleet of investigators doing all they can to find Beatrice.'

'I don't want to go back to Sicily.'

'I'm in Syracuse...'

Alicia gave a tight shrug. Geography wasn't exactly her favourite subject, given she couldn't read a map.

'Ortigia is practically its own island.'

'I know that.' She snapped out the lie.

'I'm just pointing out that you won't run into any of your past there.' His hand came up to her arm as he said it, as if he was anticipating her walking off, and then his face came a little closer. 'Or whatever it is you're running from...'

Her eyes narrowed and met his. 'It doesn't mean I'm running just because I don't want to go back.'

'You're as Sicilian as I am, Alicia. You miss it like hell.'

He knew her far too well.

'Seriously...one dinner with my family.'

'No.'

'Maybe a couple of wanders around holding hands—we're good at that bit.'

He tempted her with that alone.

'Sex?' she asked.

'If you want,' he said. 'And I think it was established the other morning that you do.'

Alicia was suddenly incredibly grateful that she hadn't

admitted that her ruse had never included bedding him. That he didn't know it had been sheer lust that had pulled her across that room.

'I was playing you, Dante.'

'So you *don't* want me?'

'I want a lot of things—not all of them are good for me.'

It was the best she could come up with. He was like cake in the baker's window—tempting, delicious, but it went straight to her hips.

Or in Dante's case between them.

'No sex, then.' He shrugged.

His hand was by the side of her head now, and his face was so close she almost dared not breathe.

'Come to think of it,' Dante said. 'I prefer to remember you sweet and willing, and those little gasps that came from here…'

His finger moved to her throat. Her heart felt like a bird trapped in a net as he taunted her with his words.

'I prefer to remember you pleading for me not to go slow while I thought I would die trying to come.'

Alicia no longer knew how to breathe as he took her back to that sultry afternoon. 'I'm not sharing your bed,' she said.

'Fine with me. I don't like sharing a bed, anyway. It's a palazzo, Alicia. There are his and hers chambers…' He smiled. 'Nice, huh?'

She stared at the lapel of his jacket.

'The flight leaves at midday. That gives you a few hours to get ready.'

'It will take more than a few hours to turn myself into one of your lionised—' She halted herself, hating the evidence of her jealousy.

'A few clothes…' He watched her blink, as if remembering how much she liked the pretty things. 'A designer wardrobe shouldn't pose a problem. After all, we *are* in Milan…'

'I have to work.'

'Call in sick.'

'And tell them what?'

'Have you been living under a rock, Alicia?' he mocked. 'Say that you kissed a Sicilian…' he said. 'That you just got pinged…'

She stared.

'Or you could fake some gastro issue? No hotel would want you working…' He put a hand on her stomach. 'Not very sexy, though.'

His hand was warm through the cotton of her dress, and there was a certain security to be had in her loathing. The bliss of their afternoon together had been so tainted by the evidence of her lack of exclusive rights, Alicia doubted she'd ever get over that fact.

'We're not sexy any more, Dante.' She was lying through her teeth, but convincingly maybe, because he dropped all contact.

'Fine with me.' He pulled back, and as he spoke she could feel where his hand had been on her stomach. 'One weekend, Alicia. I get to bow out of the entertainment circuit my father has me on. Even playboys need sick days.'

It was tempting.

Perhaps, after a weekend together, she would be able to gauge better whether to tell him about his son… She thought of his baby, whom she had cared for, and how her heart had broken at removing herself from Roberto's life.

Ultimately she would never have access to this much help with her search for Beatrice again, Alicia knew. A trained team searching for her would get her so much closer to her goal.

Yet it was not her twin nor even his son that had her on the edge of saying yes.

It was him.

Dante was the temptation.

And not just because she wanted him. It was more that she wanted to know again that moment in the sun.

Yes, she was bitter, and jealous of the women pictured on his arm these days, and pitted with self-loathing that he had seen her that long-ago day in her appalling underwear. And although she was proud of her job, of the life she had forged, she didn't want to be remembered as his maid.

Alicia wanted the sun.

And she wanted one full moon with Dante.

From the doorway where they were huddled, Alicia called in sick. 'I have an inner ear infection,' she told her manager as Dante stood listening. 'It's terrible. I'm on antibiotics and I thought I might be okay to work, but I was so dizzy when I stood... Yes, probably vertigo. I've almost fainted walking to work...the Duomo is all blurry...' Dante rolled his eyes at the drama of her. 'No, don't send a driver. I'm nearly home...' She ended the call. 'Did I sound convincing?'

'Alicia, I nearly took out my phone and called an ambulance.'

They had breakfast with the investigator in a private room at the rear of a patisserie. Well, Dante had coffee and sat a little apart from them as the guy had Alicia raking through her memory for any more clues.

Dante had heard the details so many times these past few weeks, because he'd seriously had people looking, and so many pointless, fruitless updates.

And so Dante sat bored on his phone as she went through Beatrice's likely date of birth and the Virgo thing again.

'I gave Gino copies of all my photos,' Alicia told the investigator.

'Any correspondence at all?' he asked.

'Just these.'

Dante looked over as she took from her bag the two cards Beatrice had sent her. 'You have them with you?'

'Of course I do,' she snapped. 'I carry them everywhere.'

'Are these the original envelopes?' the investigator was asking.

'Yes.'

'You didn't think to say before?' Dante snapped. 'Jesus, Alicia, are they postmarked?'

'Illegible,' the investigator answered. 'I'll get them looked at properly, though.'

Alicia looked as if she was about to cry, and he regretted snapping. He knew she was overwhelmed, and tried to make light of things to ease the sting of his reprimand.

'Told you,' Dante said to the investigator. 'She's a goose.'

Yet watching her hand over those letters he felt a little sick, because it was like watching her hand over a piece of her heart.

Things moved quickly in Dante's world.

For two hours she sat with the investigator, and then she was told she was to head to Quadrilatero d'Oro, the golden rectangle, the fashion centre.

'I won't know where to start.'

'My assistant has booked you in to a store and told them what's needed. They'll help…'

'Good. Will you come?' she said. 'While I get to look "suitable" to be Dante's partner?'

'I hate that word.'

'Am I your girlfriend, then?'

'How about we stick with Alicia?'

'So are you going to come?'

'God, no. I'm going back to the hotel to have a shower and get changed.' He nodded towards the driver. 'He'll be back for you at eleven.'

Shopping turned out actually to be fun—though the assistant did try to steer her into capri pants.

'No, not with my bottom,' Alicia said.

'Well, how about some shorts, in case you go on the water?'

'I would feel like a sailor,' Alicia said. 'I like things loose… I like dresses…' Her eyes lit on one. 'I love this.' She held up a silver dress which came to just above the knee. However, this was to be a *family* dinner. 'I think it might be more appropriate for a nightclub, though…'

'Try it.'

The dress was beautiful. It slid like liquid mercury and it shimmered and it clung. And there was not a bra in the universe that could be worn under it.

'Better not…' Alicia sighed, but soon she was the owner of a gorgeous wardrobe suitable for a family weekend. It cost more than… Well, she didn't dare add it up.

The assistant looked over her selection. 'Oh, you'll need flat shoes for walking, some wedges for the evening…'

'No, I like heels.'

'The streets are likely to be cobbled, with lots of steps.'

She didn't care.

Alicia looked over the selection too. Shoes, so pretty, and some dresses, and sarongs rather than shorts, in case they went out on the water, and bikinis too. Then there were sets of underwear so divine she knew she would wash them by hand and love them for ever.

And the most gorgeous nightwear.

The assistant had smiled when she saw Alicia's evident surprise as she'd held up a gold slip nightdress with a silk wrap to match.

Alicia was sipping iced tea when Dante called, watching as her outfits were wrapped in tissue paper and placed inside designer luggage.

'Are you ready?' he barked.

'I think so…'

'The car has been outside for fifteen minutes. I told you the plane departs at midday, Alicia.'

'What happened to the flirting Dante?' Alicia asked. 'Or is that how you speak to your hired staff?'

She turned off her phone and placed it in her brand-new leather handbag. She would never jump to his command.

'Actually,' she said to the assistant, 'I'll take the silver dress after all.'

And sell it online.

Bastard.

'Finally!'

Dante was sprawled on a seat when she boarded late, wearing a pale lemon shift dress, her black hair in a high ponytail tied with a strip of yellow velvet.

Then he pulled out his manners. 'You look very nice.'

'I'll take that with a pinch of salt,' Alicia said.

She was uncomfortable in such luxurious surroundings, and feeling defensive, and so underwhelmed by his reaction to her.

'Given that I looked "fine" in a white dress, "incredible" in my maid's outfit, and now, dressed in designer clothes, I pass as "very nice".'

'Alicia, I don't do all that flattery stuff. If we were actually dating you'd know that. You're the one pretending to be *my* partner—not the other way around. Try and remember that.' He reached into the pocket of his jacket. 'Here...'

'I am *not* pretending to wear your ring.'

'God, no—no one would believe it for a moment.'

She opened the box he'd handed her and found it was a pair of silver drop earrings, each with a glittering red stone at the end.

'I saw you didn't have any earrings.'

'I lost one of my hoops,' Alicia said, holding her new earrings up to the light. 'The red glass is like the centre window at the church. The one above—' She stopped herself from reminiscing about the windows of her old church. Now she was returning, she was filled with nostalgia for home. 'Well, they're very pretty. I'll wear them tomorrow night.'

He nodded. 'You always loved your earrings.'

It was hard to believe that just this morning she'd been on her way to work and now she was heading home to Sicily with Dante. But she had to force herself to remember that Dante didn't actually *want* her in his life.

It was either that thought or the sound of the jets powering up that had her breath hitching.

'It's fine...' He must have heard her, because he glanced over. 'Private jets are smaller so it brings a more rapid ascent.'

She nodded, embarrassed to admit to this suave version of Dante that she had never flown before.

'And descent,' he added.

Like you, she wanted to say. For he took her straight to the highs, then dumped her in the lows.

And yet she was the one who had stepped onto the ride, Alicia thought as the tyres sped across the runway.

CHAPTER SIX

AND THEN THEY were up.

The sky was blue and clear, and they were a mere two hours away from…not quite home, but Dante was right.

She missed Sicily so.

It almost hurt to admit how much.

'The drink of home,' Dante said as two shots of Limoncello were placed on the table between them. *'Salute.'*

It was then that Alicia started to get excited—to believe that she might even find out about her sister. And even if she didn't, she would have given it her best.

'He was very thorough.' She could feel him watching her. 'The investigator.'

'Don't get your hopes up.'

'Why not?'

'What if it's bad news about Beatrice?'

'Then I'll know.'

'Do you *want* to know?'

'Yes, I do,' she said.

'Do you know what *I'd* like to know?' Dante asked as she went to take a sip of her drink.

'What?'

'The reason for your hate.'

'There's no hate.'

'There is.'

She said nothing.

'Seriously,' Dante pushed. 'We were friends…we had sex

once when we were young. Now, years later, I'm doing all I can to help you find your twin—and, yes, you're helping me out in return—but there's so much anger in you, Alicia.'

'No.'

'Yes,' Dante said. 'There is. So before we attempt to play lovers, let's have it out now, Alicia. Why the animosity?'

He really had waited for his moment. They were face to face and she had nowhere to go.

'The restrooms are there.' He gestured his head. 'If you want go in there and hide for the flight, go. Or we talk.'

For the first time in her life Alicia found she'd rather be in Reverend Mother's office—because this really was a question too big for her to handle.

Aside from her upset and pain, it actually wasn't about her.

'Alicia?

His calling of her name was a demand for a response, so she gave him the part that was her own. 'I heard some talk in the village.'

'Such as…?'

'The usual.'

'Are we really having this conversation again?'

'There was a lot of talk.'

'So what's new? I told you not to listen.'

'I tried not to.'

'Clearly not that hard.'

'It felt personal.' She was being as honest as she dared to be.

'Was it about us?' He frowned. 'Were we seen?'

'No.'

'Was it because you were late back?'

'It wasn't about us!'

'Then who?'

'I don't know!' Alicia said. 'I don't know who she was.'

'So, a vague rumour?' He gave her a tight smile. 'Thanks, Alicia.'

He ignored her then. But even though she was tired she was too nervous to try to sleep with Dante sitting opposite, his scent light in the air. Nervous that his foot would tap hers when he stretched out. Nervous that if she fell asleep she would go back in her mind to their intimate time, recall it in detail when she had spent years trying to deny it.

Alicia forced her eyes not to close.

'Get some rest,' he suggested.

'I'm fine.'

She had spent a decade fighting memories of them, and she did not want to relive them with Dante nearby.

It was a fruitless task.

Their time together was no doubt a mere passing thought to him—a pleasant memory that occasionally drifted past like one of the thin clouds the jet was now searing through.

But for Alicia that one day, their short existence as one entity, felt more like a season, with the seeds planted then bearing fruit even now.

Now, as she found herself headed back to Sicily with Dante, Alicia was fighting not to remember every last moment they had shared...

CHAPTER SEVEN

Sicily, a decade ago...

THE *SCIROCCO* WAS SAID to send people crazy.

And with a funeral to attend too...

No wonder Alicia was on edge.

As hot desert sands were lifted in Africa and made their approach across the Mediterranean, Alicia wrestled with her black tights. They were far too heavy for the heat that even by Sicilian standards was fierce.

And they were dreadful.

At least they covered the vast awful knickers—only not quite, as the elasticated waist of the flesh-coloured cotton stuck out above the black of the tights.

Alicia looked down at the odd bra. It was an off-white satin, with padding and wires and seams that squashed her breasts into two strange points. Hating it already, Alicia pulled on the dress Sister Angelique had chosen for her. It was black nylon with a built-in slip, long sleeves, and a lot of pleats as well as buttons and zips. Her shoes were Cuban-heeled dance shoes, again from the donation cupboard, and a size too large so they kept slipping.

There were no mirrors allowed in the residence, and although Alicia had that morning received a small compact mirror, she chose not open it up. She did not need the contraband to confirm that she looked a fright.

Tears were trickling down the back of her throat and she swallowed them down and scolded herself.

This was no time for vanity.

Yet she was in an odd silent frenzy.

It was the approaching winds that were driving her crazy—everyone said they sent you mad.

And then there was the absence of a birthday card from Beatrice.

Her eighteenth birthday had come and gone unacknowledged.

Well, there had been a difficult conversation with Reverend Mother—and, yes, there had been cake that evening, and the parcel with the compact yesterday. But there had been *nothing* from Beatrice and that hurt.

Dreadfully.

Despite frantic promises that she would write each week the correspondence had soon faded. Now, a full week after her birthday, Alicia's hope that Beatrice would make contact was fast fading.

Certainly she had reason to be upset, Alicia told herself. There was the absence of Beatrice, and now, of course, the shock of Signora Schininà's death.

It had nothing to do with the beastly black dress!

The nuns had seemed both surprised and displeased that Alicia was attending the funeral. In truth, apart from the occasional nod if they saw each other in the village, she and Signora Schininà had never really spoken. Ragno had left four years ago, to find his father, but even if Alicia didn't approve of how the woman had treated her son, she held a certain fondness for Signora Schininà.

A fascination, almost.

She had been so beautiful.

Seriously beautiful.

Her eyes had been a different blue form her son's, almost violet, and her lips had always pressed into a slight smile whenever Alicia saw her in the village. And, although the locals had so visibly disapproved of her, somehow Signora Schininà had looked down her nose at them.

And then there were the parcels...

Even after Ragno had left the parcels had kept coming each month, with no explanation nor any note. The final one had arrived yesterday. It had spooked Alicia a little, to know it must have been sent just before she died. And Signora Schininà had remembered her birthday, for apart from other provisions there had been a little gold compact mirror inside.

It was beautiful. On it, a drawing of a woman with long curls who was looking down. There was an engraving that Alicia couldn't read, but it was a true gift and she knew she would treasure it—especially now.

Stepping out of the relative cool of the building, she felt the vicious heat slam into her. The sky had a coral hue, and out towards the ocean there was a still, heavy mass of dirty red cloud making its slow approach.

As she took the path towards the village two nuns approached her, their habits billowing. 'Sisters,' Alicia greeted them respectfully.

'Alicia...' Sister Catherine returned the greeting. 'You are going to the funeral, then?'

'Yes,' Alicia said, and held up the basket she carried in an oddly defiant gesture. 'I baked.'

No one else had.

'I have prayed for her soul and I shall go now and light a candle,' Sister Catherine said. 'Hopefully the storm will hold off.'

Sister Angelique stood still, and Alicia knew she would not waste either a candle or idle words on Signora Schininà. Her disapproval was evident.

She wasn't the only one.

The funeral would be a very quiet affair.

None of the local women were friends with Signora Schininà, and certainly neither their husbands nor their sons knew her!

Nor the men who sat at the bar this midday, as Alicia walked by in the oppressive heat.

The village was quiet, and so too the little square outside the church. Usually for a funeral there would be cars lining the streets either side. People would come from outside towns and villages to pay their respects. But today there were just a couple of expensive cars.

One Alicia knew to belong to the doctor who had found her... The other...

Alicia was nervous to see her old friend again. He had left a few years back, and in truth things had become a little awkward between them before he had gone.

No more swims in the river...

They would lie beside it talking sometimes, but it had simply caused trouble if Alicia was off the convent's grounds for any length of time, and aside from that the ease of their conversations had gone.

Today must be hard for him.

Alicia received just a small stipend for her work at the convent, but she had spent as much as she could afford on some peonies. Not just to thank Signora Schininà for the parcels, but also because she couldn't stand the thought of an empty grave...

'Alicia.' The priest greeted her.

'Father.'

Alicia looked around and saw just how small the gathering was—herself, the good doctor, and a couple of attractive ladies Alicia presumed to be from the House of No Bees, as she and Beatrice had called it in the weeks before she'd left.

'Should I go in...?' She gestured to the church.

'It's a graveside service,' the priest divulged, looking less than pleased. 'Signora Schininà was very specific in her wishes regarding today. I have chosen to honour them.'

'Oh.' Alicia had never known just a graveside service before.

'If you want to go in and pray before we start her son is in there,' the priest offered.

'I've already prayed,' Alicia said, for she had been to the chapel attached to the school that morning. 'Where should I put this?' She held up the basket.

'Leave it there.' He pointed to a bench under a tree, but then as the hot wind caught both his robes and his words he suggested otherwise. 'Perhaps the vestibule.'

'Dov'è la veglia funebre?' Alicia asked where they were gathering afterwards, but the priest shook his head.

'Signora Schininà specifically asked for things to be kept simple.'

'I see…'

Alicia, a little bemused, took the steps up to the gorgeous baroque church. It brought tourists to the village, for the nave had survived the great earthquake and the rest of the church had been faithfully and beautifully rebuilt.

Grateful for the cool of the vestibule, Alicia placed the basket down and heard footsteps. She stood, straightened up and turned, about to step out of the shadows and greet Ragno. Except the mosaic tiles, the dome, and the delicate windows with their gorgeous stained-glass, all seemed to blur as he walked towards her.

He didn't walk *to* her, though, for his eyes were fixed upwards. Perhaps it was because the coral sky through the stained-glass windows was casting a dull red glow. Or perhaps he simply didn't notice her, standing in the dark vestibule dressed dourly in black. Maybe he didn't recognise her, nor particularly remember her, even?

After all, he had been *extremely* popular with the girls…

Whatever the reason, he walked straight past her, and Alicia was actually relieved that she hadn't been seen. For it was at that very second that, to Alicia, he became Dante.

Ragno had been a boy, a bit of a rebel, then later a youth who'd run wild. A lone wolf, the locals had called him…

Yet on many occasions, and fearlessly, Alicia had played with the wolf. Nothing sexual—unfortunately for Alicia. They had been just friends.

And then he'd no longer wanted even that.

He was taller than she recalled…broader too. More poised. His thick black hair that had been scruffy and long was now beautifully cut, accentuating high cheekbones and a strong jaw. He was clean-shaven and wore a very smart suit and polished black shoes, all of which Alicia took in as he walked past her.

She let out a breath as he took the stone steps and now just his scent remained. Crisp and fresh, it cut through the slightly musty air.

Dante Schininà had turned into a man.

Well, of course he had.

With a mind that was flummoxed, Alicia attempted to reason. She was eighteen now, so he must be twenty.

She hadn't been expecting such beauty, though…

Alicia Domenica was lying.

Even to herself.

His beauty had become evident to her before he had left, and now she stood in the silent vestibule and acknowledged that her upset and tears over her appearance today were purely selfish and in regard to him.

She stared down at her pointed breasts and the endless pleats of the dress. Oh, why did they have to meet again with her looking like this?

But then she reminded herself that Dante would have far more on his mind than what she was wearing.

Alicia walked towards the small gathering, where he stood tense and a little apart, making not a single attempt at small talk.

She left it to the priest to announce her arrival. 'Ah, here she is.'

'Alicia.' Dante nodded without really looking at her. 'Thank you for coming.'

'Of course,' she said. *Le mie condoglianze…*'

She offered her condolences and then they kissed in polite greeting, but their cheeks did not even touch. Their faces just moved forward and to each side in the familiar practised moves.

Except they no longer felt familiar.

His hand, despite the scorching heat of the day, felt like ice in hers, and when she looked up and saw his grey complexion and gritted jaw she wanted to wrap her other hand around his, or reach up and touch his face.

Of course she would not.

Could not?

'Well, shall we…?' the priest said, gesturing towards the cemetery as if he was inviting them to move through to the lounge.

It was just a short walk up the hill, but in truly vicious heat, and as they started to head off Alicia was pleased to see that the florist must have had a change of heart and closed up her shop and come over.

Her son Guido was with her too.

The grocer came then.

Followed by the postmaster.

There were ten or so in the end.

The priest went first, holding his thurible and trailing smoke, with Dante walking behind him.

Dante was very composed; his stride did not falter and nor did he look behind him.

He simply walked alone.

As he always had.

Signora Schininà had all but banished Dante from the house when he had turned ten—that was common knowledge. He had had supper with her after school and then slept in the shed or wherever he could find.

Dante had explained to Alicia why once. 'I'm bad for business,' he'd said.

The gates to the cemetery were open, and the small procession made its way in. But to Alicia's mind they turned in the wrong direction. The Schininà family were over on the other side, she thought frantically.

She and Dante had used to come here to look at the names and wonder if her real surname was here amongst the plaques and stones. Well, Dante would read them. She had memorised them, based on what he'd read out.

But they were turning towards the lone graves on the edge and it dawned on her—Carmella Anna Schininà, the family shame, would be buried apart from her ancestors. Alone.

Dante briefly halted then, his shoulders lifting and his breath catching, before resuming his stride.

Alicia soon found out the reason for his brief hesitation— her own breath caught and her eyes widened in surprise when she first saw the grave site, for it was clear that despite the meagre attendance there were many mourning today. She had never seen more flowers at a funeral—her small offering was almost smothered with deep red roses that clashed with *girasoli*—sunflowers—and glorious cascades of lemon mimosa too. Orchids, lilies… The blooms were a blaze of colour and unexpected beauty in a regretful day.

Despite the poor turnout, there were clearly many people thinking of her with sadness and fondness today, even if they might not say.

On top of the coffin there was a delicate spray of white chrysanthemums—they meant joy the world over except for in Italy, where they meant sorrow.

Alicia was certain they were from Dante. And as she took her place the sorrowful simplicity of the chrysanthemums brought tears to her eyes.

Oh, he must be in agony this day, Alicia was sure, for he and his mother's had been a complex relationship—or rather, almost no relationship.

Years ago, Dante had told her something he'd never told another.

'She wanted to leave me at the baby door.'

'But she didn't.'

'She wishes she had.'

'No.' Alicia had been insistent.

'She's told me herself,' Dante had replied. *'Many times.'*

Now the son she'd never wanted stood as the priest offered prayers and sprinkled holy water. As he cleansed the coffin Alicia found her gaze drifting away, for it was here and with such indifference that Dante had said goodbye to Alicia.

They had come here, to a lone grave in the corner, the quietest part of the cemetery where there were seldom visitors. It was overhung by trees, and she had tried not to cry because her friend was leaving.

Their mood had been odd, Dante brooding and sulky, clearly wishing he wasn't there. Alicia had insisted they meet before he left, and told him that it was right they say goodbye. She'd worn an awful checked pinafore and a top that smelt of mothballs and wished she could look nice, as the girls at the dance hall surely did.

'We're friends,' she'd reminded him.

They'd sat beneath the wisteria on the bench with little left to say, and the journey ahead of him had seemed so daunting to Alicia. 'You don't know anyone in Rome…'

'No.'

'You don't even know where your father is…'

'Alicia, there's no work for me here. *Her* family don't want me around,' he said, referring to his mother.

'Even so…' She'd been doing her best not to cry.

He'd taken her hand then, and it had been so long since he had, and it had felt so nice, that her fingers had coiled into his.

His skin had been hot, and she'd felt as if the sun was beating down on them, and she'd felt awkward suddenly… nervous, perhaps.

She had tried to fill the silence. 'I wish we'd found out.'

'Found out what?'

'Who my parents are.' She had turned and smiled. 'I won't know anything till I'm eighteen…' That was four years away, though. 'You'll have to come back if you want to find out.'

'I'm not coming back.'

'Your mother is here…' she'd attempted, when really she'd wanted to say *Me—I'm here, Dante, please don't leave me too*.

But they had sat there silent. He had turned and looked at

her, and more than his gaze she had felt the strain that had been ever-present between them in those days.

'Hey, maybe I'll find out that we're related.' She'd turned to him and smiled. 'You might be my brother. Then we'd be family and you could stay…'

Dante had not returned her smile. Instead he had stood. 'I'm going.'

'Now?' Alicia checked. 'But we've only just got here.'

'Yes, now,' he'd snapped. *'Ciao.'*

No embrace, no kiss, no promise to keep in touch.

Gone.

The service was soon over.

No gathering afterwards, just a handshake, another air kiss and another offer of condolences and then life went on.

Of course not.

'Come to the bar, Dante…' one of the ladies called. 'We can all have a drink…'

He just waved a dismissive hand, his back already turned as he walked out through the cemetery gates.

'Dante,' the florist called out. 'Would you like to come over? Stay for supper…?' But then she shook her head, for he had already gone. 'Like a black ghost,' she muttered.

'You tried,' the grocer said, and shrugged. 'What can you do?'

Not much, Alicia thought. Really, none of them had ever done much for him. All of them blaming him for hanging around, or daring to be hungry, or too smart with his mouth when he was told to move on…

'Come and have a drink, Alicia,' the florist said. 'Cool down a little before you walk back.'

She gave a polite smile. 'Thank you for asking, but I'm expected back…'

She wasn't, particularly, but it was not an hour with the florist and her doe-eyed son that Alicia craved!

She retrieved her basket from the church vestibule and drank some water from the tap. A little hungry, she selected some fruit, but instead of heading back through the village she walked behind the church and opened the little latched gate.

It really was a gate to nowhere.

Well, it led to a meander in the river, but there wasn't even a path behind it—that was how unused this route was. Dante was here, Alicia knew, for the rushes were freshly parted and trampled.

She was hot. It was by far too hot. And she was by far too heavily dressed to be walking through the rushes. She passed the empty stone hut where they had sometimes played, and then continued further on. The too-big shoes were designed for dancers rather than goats, she decided as she lost her footing a couple of times on the steep slope down the bank that led to their old place by the river.

And there she found him, sitting with his elbows on his knees and drinking wine. He didn't even look over his shoulder as she approached.

'Go back,' he said. 'You don't want to be seen alone with her son.'

'I don't care for all that.' Alicia sighed deeply and joined him. 'Anyway, your mother deserves a wake. I baked…'

'No need.'

'Please…' She pulled back the lid to reveal the food she had made but he shook his head and snubbed it.

Alicia rolled her eyes as she was reminded first-hand of just how difficult Dante could be at times. He was like the old wood stove in the kitchen at the convent, which was rarely lit and so slow to warm you almost didn't notice it at first, but then…

'I can hear you rolling your eyes,' Dante said.

It was something Reverend Mother said, and they shared a little laugh sometimes when Alicia was inevitably told off.

'I hoped you'd be here,' Alicia said.

'I thought the river would be dry,' he said.

'There was a big storm in the mountains last Friday…' Her

voice trailed off, for that was the day his mother had died. 'How long have you been back?' she asked.

'A couple of days.' He stared ahead.

'When did you find out?'

He just shrugged, clearly in no mood to divulge specifics, so Alicia attempted to be practical. 'Do you need help sorting out the house?'

'No,' he said. 'All done. She just rented a room there, so she didn't have much, and the other girls helped pack it. It's all there.' His head gestured towards the hut.

He was shivering, as if they sat there in the middle of winter, and yet he was sweating a little too.

'I'm so sorry…' Alicia said again, although it came straight from the heart this time. 'I don't know what to say.'

'There's nothing to say.'

'It was a nice service.'

'No,' he refuted.

'I thought it was,' Alicia said. 'Straightforward.'

'Well, she was far from that.'

'And how about all the flowers?' Alicia said, and saw his slight smile.

'How about them?' he agreed. 'No wonder the florist offered me supper. She would have made a fortune today. All cash, I'll bet…' he said. 'In blank envelopes…'

'Really?'

'For sure.' He nodded. 'There'll be no names on any of the cards.'

'Well, I put mine.'

'Did you see the mimosa?' he asked, and Alicia nodded. 'It means secret love. There were a lot of bunches…'

'I bought peonies,' she said.

'You didn't have to do that…'

'I wanted to. They mean discretion. You know, after you left she would send me a parcel every month.'

'Did she?'

'There was always a religious statue.' Alicia smiled. 'I think she knew it would appease the nuns if they asked me what was in them… The packaging never said who they were from, but I knew. It was the stuff she used to get you to give me. Sometimes there would be deodorant, or some skin lotion or nice scented soap…' Alicia swallowed, unsure whether or not to tell him what had occurred. 'A parcel came yesterday.'

He stared ahead.

'She must have sent it before she…' Her voice trailed off. 'There was a present for my eighteenth. My only one… Well, there was cake but…'

'She liked you.'

'We never even spoke.'

'I think she knew what it was like to be a girl growing up there…'

'She was at the convent?' Alicia checked, for that was something she hadn't known.

'Yes, she lived there like you. Her parents couldn't handle her…' He gave a thin smile. 'Anyway, I doubt they have a plaque up for her—she was not exactly valedictorian of her class…' He thought for a moment. 'She could have been, though…she was incredibly clever. Unwise, but so clever.'

'And beautiful,' Alicia said, and she wasn't being shallow— his mother really had had a rare old-fashioned beauty. Quite simply she'd been the most beautiful person Alicia had ever seen. Or had been until this day. For that title now went to her son.

She saw now that she had never fully seen the perfection in him. How had she once lain her head against him and laughed and chatted so easily? How had they sat holding hands? Because now she no longer knew how to look into his eyes.

'She had it all,' Dante said. 'Or she could have. She just didn't want it, though…'

'A woman of mystery.'

'Well, I don't have to worry about her now.'

'Did you worry a lot?'

'Every day of my life.'

Dante closed his eyes, for he did not want to tell Alicia that he slept on cardboard, or couch-surfed. Sometimes in winter his friend Gino, a law student who did shifts at the bar where he worked, loaned him the back of his car.

Nor did he want her to know that the suit and shoes he wore today were Gino's too. Or that every envelope he had sent his mother, every scrap of cash he had scraped together, he had found yesterday in a box. Some of his letters had been sliced open, some were still closed and unread. All the money he had sent was unspent…

Right now, Dante felt as if his head would explode, for he did not understand how or why his mother would rather do *that* work than use what he'd sent.

And the fact that some of his letters had gone unread…

'I will never understand her,' Dante said, and as Alicia's hand came down on his shoulder he shrugged it off, perhaps a little too harshly. Dante loathed touch. 'Sorry,' he said, as she pulled back her hand. 'It is not you I am cross with.' He was silent for a very long time and then he looked over to her. 'No more.'

'She's at peace…'

'No.' He shook his head. 'I'm not talking about her.'

Dante was speaking about himself.

Or rather he was not talking, just thinking of the chaos and the responsibility of loving another person.

No more.

Dante shook himself, as if from a dream, and then peered into the basket she'd brought and selected some cake. But instead of eating it he pulled it apart and fed it to the birds.

'Did you ever find your father?' Alicia asked.

'Nope.' He shook his head. 'Did you find out about your parents?'

'Sort of.' She gave him a tight smile. 'Well, not their names… But last week I was told by Reverend Mother that my mother got in touch when I was a year old. She and my father were from an hour or so away, a young couple. Scared, I suppose.'

'Will you meet them?'

'No.' She shook her head. 'Reverend Mother made an

approach just before I turned eighteen.' Alicia swallowed. 'Well, an approach to the woman she believes is my mother. She married my father a year after they had me and have a family...' She took a breath. 'She told Reverend Mother to never call again.'

'Surely you can know their names?'

'Reverend Mother says she was never given them. That really it is just her guesswork.' Alicia gave a tight shrug. *'Non destare il cane che dorme...'*

She had been told not to awaken the sleeping dog. Dante agreed. 'You're better off without family.'

'No.'

'I mean it.' Dante really did. 'Hey, how is...?' He paused, not because the name was forgotten, more in quiet surprise as he suddenly acknowledged to himself how relieved he was that Alicia was here. 'Thank you,' he said, 'for being here today. For the cake...'

'The birds are enjoying it.' Alicia smiled, because he hadn't eaten any, and he returned her smile.

It was his first genuine smile in God knew how long.

'Beatrice,' he said suddenly.

'Ah, yes.' She blinked as if she had lost track too.

'She must be finishing school soon?' Dante prompted. 'Or is she at university now?'

Alicia Domenica lied.

She often did, and always had, but not quite so much with Ragno.

Only she did not know how to bare her soul to this man— to Dante. Perhaps it was simply that she was too embarrassed to admit that not a soul seemed to want her in their lives.

Not her parents, nor Beatrice...

Even Reverend Mother, as kindly as she could, had told her that the convent's duty to her was done, but had offered her a year's grace before she would be forced to make her own way in the world or marry. And Reverend Mother had just the young man in mind!

No, she did not want to tell Dante that, and so she lied.

'She's applying to go to university,' Alicia said.

'To study what?'

'Law!' Alicia responded, because he'd said his friend was doing the same, or maybe because it was the cleverest thing she could think of. 'She writes to me all the time...'

'That's good.'

'We're thinking of getting a flat together.'

'So you'll see your twin soon.'

He had always called them that, and played along with Alicia's games. 'I hope so.' At least that part was true. 'So you're still in Rome?'

'Yep.' He did not elaborate, just squinted at the blowing sand. 'I'd forgotten how hot it was here.'

'Get used to it,' Alicia said. 'It will last for days. We'll all be crazy by the time it's done.'

'I told you—I'm going tonight.'

'Will you ever come back?' Alicia asked, trying to dim the needy note of hope in her voice.

'No.' He was blunt. 'I hate the place. I have no good memories of here.'

That hurt, and Alicia could not hide the fact that it did. 'Thanks a lot.'

'What?' He was obviously too cross with the world to navigate her emotions. Today, if anything, he seemed determined to deliberately trip them. 'We just used to swim and play stupid games...'

She flinched.

'Go,' he said. 'Seriously, Alicia, just go. You didn't deserve that.'

'So you do have some good memories of our time here?' she nudged. 'Tell me.'

'You're so damned *needy*.' He gave a half-laugh. 'Yes,' he conceded, 'there are some good memories.'

Dante kicked off his shoes and peeled off his socks, just as Alicia ached to do with her tights. He stood up and she looked at his long feet and toes, and was jealous of their freedom. It was so hot that the leaves seemed to be drying above them as the heat intensified.

He took his jacket off, speaking as he did so. 'I had no sleep last night,' he admitted, 'or the nights before...' He paused as a box of condoms fell from his pocket and her eyes followed his to them.

'I can see why!' she retorted smartly.

'Alicia—' he started as she reached out and picked them up. The condoms must be Gino's. 'Leave them.'

'I want to look.' She took out the foil-wrapped packages and he watched her count all four of them, then look at the number twelve on the box. 'You have a far more interesting life than me...'

Dante didn't. Well, he did and he didn't.

Dante's reputation in the village had all been lies, and it would seem his name was misused frequently. And, although he could easily have pulled any girl, the simple truth was that he loathed kissing and detested physical contact. Being raised in a whorehouse had turned him off even the thought of it.

He had grown up knowing way too much, and yet had been taught nothing at all. Aside from holding Alicia's hand, he'd never really known touch. Together they'd explored the world—or at least the rocks and the river and the logs. And then at some point people had questioned that, the nicest part of his life.

No, he had said, they were just friends.

Alicia too had vehemently defended their friendship—to Beatrice, to her teachers, to the nuns. There was nothing like that between them.

Then his own body had proved him a liar.

So he'd seen her less, pulled back, but he'd known he must go.

He recalled with detail the moment he had dropped Alicia's hand. They had been walking through the rushes on their trampled path as they so often did.

'Slow down...' she had moaned, and he'd turned.

She'd been bent forward, grabbing at her long hair. Then she'd straightened, holding it in one hand as she tied it with the band she wore on her wrist, as she so often did. Only this time as her arms had lifted he'd seen not just a glimpse of brown stomach but the shape of her breasts, and so he'd turned and kept walking.

'Wait!'

She had caught him up and her hand had slipped into his, but he'd dropped it. 'Too narrow,' he'd snapped.

'What's wrong?' she'd asked later, as they lay in their shady spot in silence.

He simply hadn't responded.

'Dante?'

She had poked him, and he had caught her hand to stop her.

'Let's go back.'

'We've just got here.'

'Well, I'm bored.'

That was the very last time they had been by the river. Until now.

'Here.'

She handed him the packet of condoms and he took them silently, then replaced the box in the pocket of his jacket, which he then dropped to the ground.

'You know...' She looked up at him as he rolled up the sleeves of his shirt and untucked it. 'The nuns all think we used to come to the river and kiss and make out.'

'So?'

'They thought that was why we went to the cemetery too.'

'I don't care what they think,' Dante said, and lay on his back, his hands behind his head.

'Nor do I,' she admitted. 'But I care that you never once tried.'

'I can't win, can I?' Dante said, squinting as he looked up at her.

'Meaning?'

'Alicia…' He closed his eyes. 'Just leave it.'

'I don't want to leave it. You slept with half the village and never even tried to kiss *me*.'

'I told you—you shouldn't listen to gossip,' Dante said.

'It's hard not to,' she snarled, and then lay down beside him. 'I am going to die in this heat…'

'Then go home,' he told her.

'I don't want to.' She felt a tear squeeze out of her eye and fall into her hair.

He rolled onto his side. 'Are you crying?'

'No,' she said, screwing her eyes closed. 'It's just the sand…' But then she told him the truth. 'I don't want to leave you alone today.'

'Maybe I want to be alone.'

'Do you really, Dante?'

He didn't answer.

'If you want to be alone, just say so and I'll go,' Alicia said.

'I think you should go.'

'No.' She would not let him off easily. 'Tell me you want me to leave and then I shall.'

'Stay,' he said, for on this day he did not have the energy to lie. 'Please.'

His hand found hers then, and the feel of his fingers interlaced with hers was so incredible, so beautiful. So beautiful that she felt the sting of tears in her eyes again and she closed them.

'Stop crying,' he said. 'You never cry.'

She could blame it on the funeral, or the *scirocco*, or the heat—even on Beatrice—but she told a rare truth. 'Maybe you just never noticed.'

He dropped her hand and Alicia regretted her words, her admission, but then she felt him turn beside her.

'I noticed,' he said, and her heart seemed to stop, for his voice was close and his breath was on her cheek.

He kissed her where her tear had fallen and it felt so nice—not hot, like the sun, but soft and warm, like velvet brushing her temple. So nice that more tears fell.

'Please don't,' Dante said. 'I can't bear to see you cry.'

CHAPTER EIGHT

TEARS HAD NEVER BEEN her weapon of choice and Dante knew it.

'Alicia, don't cry,' he said again.

'You just left,' she accused. *'Ciao...'* She threw back his final word to her. 'You left cross.'

'No...' he said. 'Alicia, I didn't want to get you into trouble. I didn't want things to change between us,' he said. 'But they already had.'

'How?'

'Because of this.'

His mouth was on hers, and when her lips parted so did his, and she felt the slip of his tongue, and forgot how to breathe, and then he lifted his head.

'You taste of apples,' Dante told her.

'I ate one as I was coming here,' she said. 'You taste of wine...'

He smiled down at her. 'I wanted to do that so badly the day I left...' She stared back at him. 'Then you spoiled it...'

'How?' she asked—and then she recalled that she'd declared they might be related and went very red. 'I was joking.'

'Well, it didn't help matters,' he reproached.

'I wish you *had* kissed me,' Alicia said.

'You don't,' he refuted. 'Alicia, you'd have jumped out of your skin.'

'You don't know that.'

'Oh, I do. Because we used to lie here together like this and you had no clue...'

'Of what?'

He took her hand and guided it beneath his untucked shirt.

She felt him under the fabric as she looked into his eyes. 'I would probably have screamed.'

She smiled, shocked even now, but loving the feel of him, but then he removed her hand.

Alicia touched his cheek as she had wanted to earlier today, and pushed back his raven hair. She ran her finger around the shell of his ear, just so relieved to touch him, to finally touch his face.

She cast her mind back. 'I wanted you to kiss me.'

'Then why didn't you stop talking?'

'Nervous.' She smiled. 'I think.'

'Are you nervous now?'

'No,' she said, and tried to think of the right word. 'Impatient.'

He gave her the kiss she had thought then she wanted. Dante was correct. She had not been ready for his intensity back then.

His head blocked out the sun and he moved his body so he was half over her. Alicia loved the weight of him, and the way, if she put her hand to the back of his head, he kissed her harder and their tongues duelled. And then he pulled back, and she licked her lips and looked at his wet ones, and she met his eyes and they were black with passion.

'Kiss me again,' she asked him.

He obliged with a deeper kiss, his weight coming over her and Alicia decided she could be held like this for ever. His tongue was probing, his jaw rough, and when he moaned into her mouth she arched in response and tried to squeeze her body under him further, just for more of this bliss.

'Hey...' He was moving away, a little breathless.

'Please don't stop.'

Dante ignored her.

They were boiling, and sweaty, and so overdressed—not just for the blistering heat, but for the edge they were both on.

Alicia sat up and removed her shoes and glanced over. 'I wish I was wearing socks.'

'Take your tights off.'

'Look away, then,' she said, not wanting to flash her awful knickers.

'Why?'

'Just look away.'

He lay on his back, looking up at the sky, as she lifted her bottom and manoeuvred the thick heavy nylon. It was a relief to peel them off and to join him in lying down.

'Better?' he asked, turning and positioning himself on an elbow.

'No,' she admitted, for she was warm in new ways now.

Dante gave a low laugh and lightly kissed her, his hand coming to rest low on her stomach. Close, so close, to where he had lit the fire that was now starting to burn.

'Please…' she gasped, not knowing for what she asked, just that his fingers were hotter than black nylon in the Sicilian sun and it was more of this heat that she craved.

He kissed her again, deep and slow, and this time when he stopped she cursed.

'Alicia!' he warned, in response to her filthy mouth.

She turned to protest at the halt in proceedings but, as she rolled onto her side, she could see the strain of his erection. It felt as if she had one herself, so aching was she.

'Dante…'

She went for his belt, but his hand caught hers.

'Alicia!'

'What?'

'I'm taking the train back to Rome tonight,' he pointed out.

'So? We're just kissing.' She smiled, undoing his shirt. 'Nothing more than that.'

'Yeah,' he said, 'right.'

He caught her hand to halt her, but he wasn't *that* much of a gentleman. Dante was far too aware that if her hand moved lower it would be over.

Her fingers persisted though, grazing his chest and suddenly he wanted what he'd never had.

Skin and touch.

He took a strand of her black hair and liked the way they sometimes smiled, saying so little at times, but also so very much.

They were both olive-skinned, but the heat was beyond them. Her face was red, her hair wet with sweat...this was not the weather to lie out in.

'Remember how we used to swim?' he said. 'We could cool down.'

'I thought you were too old for all that?' she teased.

'Maybe I was waiting for you to grow up,' Dante said.

'If we keep our underwear on then we're doing nothing wrong,' she said, but she was negotiating with herself rather than him.

'Agreed.'

She felt brave as they lay together, so confident in herself, and yet as they stood she held her breath, not quite so confident as he undid the rest of his shirt and she saw the dark hair on his chest, his strong arms. Her cheeks were on fire as she looked at his flat stomach, and as he stripped off his trousers she saw his long, muscled legs were hairy too, and she was, for the first time, shy.

Not scared—just a little daunted by his magnificence.

And also ashamed.

Alicia knew what she wore beneath her clothes.

She was ashamed to undo the final buttons and zip of the beastly dress.

Dante helped her out of the awful contraption, and thankfully she did not see his reaction to her underwear, for her face was wrapped in pleats of polyester when he first saw the pointed bra and vast knickers.

Alicia wanted to hide. She was silently crying in shame

and she wanted to draw up her knees and cover herself from his eyes. But he held out his hand.

'Come on,' he said, now just in his boxers, with his erection jutting out. 'Let's go and do some more kissing.'

She was so flushed, so red and sweaty from the heat, and so loaded with desire. This time he did not notice her tears, for they ran silent and mixed with the rivers of sweat that poured from both of them.

The water was warm, not quite refreshing but still a relief, and the river was so low it only came to Dante's waist. They waded further then swam to the logs where they had once played dangerous, childish, hold-your-breath games, but this time they did not climb out onto them.

Her face stung as she dipped it under the water, so wind-burned was she, but when she surfaced Dante had one arm on the logs and with the other scooped her into him. It was then that the pointed bra with awful wires that was by far too big and the vast knickers faded into the recesses of her mind.

'*You* are my nice memories of here,' he said, and Alicia knew this was the closest to romance not just she but *anyone* would ever get from him.

It wasn't love he gave, but neither was it lust. It was the most precious moment of her life.

'I'll treasure this kiss,' she told him.

'And me.'

It was a kiss that would not be halted, yet so delicious and patient. The water slowing Dante just enough to relish rather than unload. His hands glided over her waist, his fingers spanning her ribs. All Alicia had to do was hold his head, or rest her arms on his shoulders, and be so deeply kissed.

His hand came to her breast but, aware of the wretched padding, she removed it and guided it back to her waist. Her consent made itself known elsewhere, for beneath the water her legs coiled tightly around him and they kissed harder, deeper, as the hunger that seemed to have existed since she was born was satisfied.

'Oh, Dante...' She was in bliss, and somehow knew what to do next.

Latched together, they moved up the bank so that he could stand but now with both his hands free. He held her hips beneath the water, and on the surface they kissed in ways that were gentle, tender and subtle, denying the power beneath.

The wind stung but his mouth did not. Her arms were locked behind his neck and they were looking right at each other and his erection was wedged between them.

'We're just kissing,' she said, as he moved her slowly up and down the length of his shaft.

Dante didn't answer. They were position-perfect and his heat was on her.

'Dante...' Alicia gasped, just a bit bemused—because how could she not have known that such bliss existed? His hand left her waist and she welcomed the shared indulgence as he held himself and pressed *there*, right into her knickers. 'We could...' she breathed, almost weightless and yet still pressing down. 'Just a little way.'

They were looking right at each other, and his eyes were as blue as a summer night as he denied her.

'No.'

He moved her back against his length, then he kissed her shoulder and her neck and she started to tremble—to climb up him, almost. Except he was gripping her hips, holding her tight.

She started to moan, for it was as if the tide had suddenly turned, as if they were being dragged down, and yet she was being held so very safe and still, as a power she did not know was unleashed.

It must be the same for Dante, too, because his sudden shout was hollow, the sound of a secret shared, and she smothered it with her mouth. They came with lips locked and clung to each other, sharing each other's breath as the frantic moment passed, his hands becoming looser on her hips and her legs relaxing.

Their bodies were sticky from the heat above the surface but sated beneath…almost.

He looked at down at her spiky eyelashes and swollen mouth and wild wet hair, which he lifted. 'I've marked you,' he said. 'Wear it down…'

She nodded, and rested her head on his shoulder, her legs still loose on his hips, looking at the swirling silty river, glad the water was not clear today.

'I meant what I said,' Alicia admitted. 'I want to feel you in me.'

'I'm ignoring that,' Dante told her.

'Please don't ignore me.' She kissed his shoulder with deep care, just kissed that one salty spot and tasted his skin, wondering how what had felt like too much just moments ago felt like not enough now. 'I want it to be you, Dante.'

'Alicia, you know you'll regret it.'

'No.'

'You're old-fashioned, and you want an old-fashioned family, and you'll never get that from me.'

'I know that.'

'Go and be with Guido!'

'Guido?'

'Don't play games, Alicia. Why do you think he was at my mother's funeral? Certainly it wasn't for a glimpse of *me*.'

She pressed her lips together, because part of her knew he was right. That her year of grace would, if the nuns had their way, end in a 'suitable' marriage.

'I think I'm too impatient to work in a florist.'

'Don't joke about this.' He was very serious now. 'I *am* leaving tonight.'

'I still want it to be you, Dante.'

She felt a sting on her back but ignored it, still resting her head on his shoulder, and then there was another sting. The first heavy drops of rain.

'You should get back,' Dante said, unwrapping her from him, 'before it really hits.'

'No.'

'Come on,' he said, almost pushing her away from the logs and further into the water. But then he stopped, and as they stood in the waist-high water she watched the frown on his face and looked down at herself.

'I'm bleeding…'

'No,' he said, and they both looked around them, taking a moment to register the phenomena.

She had heard of blood rain before—distant sands hitting cooler air and staining the rain red—but never seen it.

'Let's get out the water.' The sky had turned to fire, like a red and black sunset, and they were being pelted with heavy, stinging drops of red-sand-laced rain. 'Come on…'

They grabbed their clothes and ran beneath the trees.

'Alicia.' He caught her. 'You need to get back…it's blood rain…'

'I've told you already,' she said. 'It has to be you.'

CHAPTER NINE

THEY RAN. NOT JUST for shelter, but out of need.

Grabbing their clothes and the basket and running through red puddles, their bodies sandblasted as they dashed for the stone hut, they tried to breathe in air so hot it burnt to take it in.

'I am leaving tonight.'

He was stripping the awful bra from her, warning her, telling her, and she cared not a jot. Alicia was truly the happiest she'd been.

They might have been paintballing, so red was the sand that smeared them, but who cared? He was massaging her taut round breasts and the relative cool of the hut was fading. Her only shame had been in what she wore—bared, she felt brave.

Even more so as she peeled off her knickers and felt as if she had just burst from some cocoon. She shook damp hair rather than wings, and climbed into the deep, ancient sink that was more like a trough and prayed for water.

'Don't waste it,' he warned, for if there was any water there would not be much.

As they stood together he pulled the release and hot water drenched them.

'Like a luxury hotel,' Alicia said, for she was used to cold showers, and started to rinse her hair. He was rinsing himself, and she watched how carefully he washed the silky black hair surrounding purple flesh.

'Wash your breasts,' he told her, and she looked down at her puckered nipples and saw sand.

But as she washed she noticed his hungry eyes, and saw that he grew, and realised he was not merely being thoughtful.

'Wash down there too,' he said, still cursing about the sand, and she stood, feeling awkward about touching herself.

He took over, catching at the water, so gentle and thorough, and then a finger slid inside her and seemed to hook her.

'Ouch!' she exclaimed.

'Better now than with gritty fingers,' he said. 'Turn around,' he told her while they still had water. 'Bend.'

He washed the last of the sand away. As he did so the water reduced to a trickle, and she felt the stab of another finger and closed her eyes as he stretched her.

'Ow… Ow…!' she said, holding the wall with one hand. And then she turned and smiled. 'Don't stop.'

'Out!' he told her.

'Not yet…' She was panting, still bent over, holding on to the wall as he did delicious things with his fingers as the last of the water dripped on the base of her spine.

'Alicia…' he warned.

She knew he could take her there, but he removed the pleasure of his hand.

She did not move. 'Go on.' His hand had moved to his length and she was tense with anticipation. 'Please…'

'We need something.'

She was sulking as she straightened and turned around, but then they kissed hard, and before climbing out she looked at him closely, and it was wonderful to be able to search his face.

'Stop.' He turned his cheek, her scrutiny clearly too much.

They were still so hot, and he went to a backpack she hadn't noticed before and they both gulped the water he found there. Then he took out a sleeping bag and spread it down. It was all so matter-of-fact, the most natural she'd ever felt.

'You're sure?' he asked. 'Because guilt—'

'Is better than regret,' she cut in. 'I want it be you, Dante.'

'It's so hot…'

Even now there was a sheen of sweat on both of them. It was just so humid, yet so sexy to be naked and slippery with him.

'Your skin…' he said, as if he had never seen skin before.

He was stroking her waist with the side of his finger in a light kittling that made her shiver inside, and then he kissed her lightly, but it was just taunting her, so she kept lifting her head to chase his mouth as he pinched her nipples and made her gasp. And then he tasted them so nicely that her mouth was lonely, wanting the same bliss. He flicked her nipple and then gave her breast a deep, slow suck.

Her mouth was even more lonely. But then she was biting his shoulder as his hand slid down to her triangle and he played with her curls there, and then slid to where he had been, but so gently now.

'Sorry I was rough.'

'I never said you were.'

'You don't want sand *here*,' he said, and with one finger he held her in balmy bliss.

'Oh…' she breathed, and closed her eyes as his fingers found a place forbidden to her own touch and stroked her there, so exquisitely that her thighs clamped on his hand. But then they parted as his middle finger circled her entrance, his incessant thumb almost a distraction.

And then her hand found him, and Alicia looked at him, so swollen and hard, and wondered how on earth he would ever fit in. Only he was slippery in her hand, and she was so turned on that she lifted her thigh and stroked him, drawing him close to where his fingers were.

'Hey,' he warned, and began to release her, she presumed to get protection.

She briefly let go of his erection and caught his wrist to stop him from leaving. 'Just a moment more,' she breathed. 'I want to feel you there.'

'You're dangerous, Alicia,' he told her, and he would not be swayed.

'Don't go,' she moaned as he arched his back and reached over for his jacket and the box.

He kissed her sulking mouth as he ignored her command. 'I'm not leaving you in trouble.'

She knew he would not.

She pouted as he rolled the condom on. 'Why did you choose blue?'

'Don't you want me now?' He smiled at her protest.

'You know I do.'

They got back to kissing, and the large flash of blue mattered not when he came atop her and kissed her hard in the reddish light as the wind still screeched around them.

His weight over her was what she had been waiting for and never realised, and Alicia was crying as their teeth clashed and their frantic want combined.

He moved up on his elbows and she lifted her leg. He nudged in, and it hurt so much that she tensed and cried out.

He pulled back.

'Please…' she said.

He tried again but she was still too tense. They kissed some more and then, as if it had to be, he seared in, so hard she arched, his hand in the hollow of her back, and they were one.

'Oh!' She was trying to breathe and waiting for the hurt to recede, yet already desperate for more of the pleasure he gave. He moved inside her and Alicia saw black, and then his mouth kissed her eyes, and it was an exquisite moment of tenderness that they both knew was unsustainable. He moved slowly and their hot skin slid. Her legs gripped his loins and she felt the restrained energy of Dante within her.

Alicia had been so lonely and now she wasn't. It was as simple as that. The hunger she had been born with was gone.

They were kissing, hard, hot kisses, and in between she was finding her rhythm. There were deep, dirty kisses, like a mini refuel, and then he'd thrust some more and she was wild.

And then there were no more little refuels. There was nothing that could have hauled them apart. And when he pulled up higher on his forearms he was watching her, and she was nodding.

It was as if he was taking her to the very edge she was trying to get to, and then he pushed her so hard, and she felt as if all the tension he shot into her spread through her and clenched her, and she found out why they should not have been alone at the river, because had she known this bliss then she would have been there every hour of every day, and she was telling him so as they came down.

'We both would.'

He was thrusting his last, and then he collapsed on her. It was too hot to lie like that, with him on top, but it was as if they were the same person. She tried to draw air into her lungs and he lifted off her.

'You can't go back yet.'

He was looking at her and she felt a thrill of joy, because clearly there was more to come. But she'd misunderstood.

'They'd know.'

'No.'

'Believe me...'

They faced each other side by side in the hot, humid air and he tried to comb her hair with his fingers.

'You're burnt...' He ran his hand over her sore shoulder.

'I think from the wind.'

'And your back...' He turned her over. 'You've been bitten too.'

He was touching the tiny bites she'd got, courtesy of a hot summer day in slow water. The elements and the insects had not been gentle, but his fingers were as he soothed the bites and then rolled her back.

The wind was still screeching but the rain seemed to have slowed, and she listened for a moment and then looked at him. 'Maybe I should get back.'

Please say no, her eyes begged.

'Yes...' Dante said. 'I'll see you back to the church.'

Wrong response, Dante!

'I could come…' She moved to touch his cheek. They had been playing with each other's faces for hours, as if they had only just discovered touch and sight.

'Where?'

'To Rome.' She tried to keep the wobble from her voice. 'There's nothing to keep me here and…'

Her voice faded as he removed her hand from his cheek.

'There's nothing for you there.'

Alicia had bowed out gently once before—with Beatrice she had lied to make her leaving easier. She didn't want to repeat that mistake.

'You're there.'

'Alicia…' He closed his eyes. 'I knew you'd regret it.'

'I don't regret it. I just don't like…' Alicia knew that she was being by far too needy and she tried to reel herself in. 'I don't like this part, Dante. I don't want to say goodbye to you with no prospect of seeing you again.'

'I have no prospects,' he said.

'I don't care.'

'Well, you should,' he said. 'Alicia, I don't want anyone in my life. I mean that.'

'You don't.'

'I do. I'm like my mother…'

'No!' She did not accept that for a moment.

'Yes.'

'So you want to be without a family? Banished to a lonely grave?'

'Alicia, she wasn't banished…' He pulled on his clothes, his shirt pink from the rain and muddied. 'My mother chose to be buried alone.'

As she dressed her reluctant body in damp clothes she did not want to put on, Alicia recalled the priest saying how specific her instructions had been.

'Put on your tights,' Dante told her.

'It's too hot.'

'Alicia…' he warned, for she knew he could guess at the

trouble she might find herself in if she returned bare-legged after spending time with him.

Reluctantly she sat down, pulling them on, and then stood, angrily hitching them up.

'What are you going to tell them, Alicia?'

'That I took shelter from the storm,' Alicia said. 'I just won't mention with whom.'

'God, no. And remember to wear your hair down for the next few days.'

They did hold hands through the rushes, but near the edge he dropped all contact. It was so hot and sticky, with steam rising from the street, and it was such a sad ending—but still she did not regret what had happened.

'I'll leave you here,' Dante said.

'Where are you going?'

'To the cemetery. And then I'll see if I can hitch a ride to the station.' He looked at her burnt face. 'I hope you don't get in too much trouble.'

'I'll be okay.'

He nodded. 'You'd better go or we might be seen.'

'Yes.'

'Ciao.'

He walked off and she kept waiting for him to look back, to change his mind, to do something… But he did nothing. Not once did he turn.

His standoffish farewell actually helped. The complete lack of romance at the end, the absolute removal of hope, drew a line so firmly that it proved a basis for her to stand upon and actually strengthened her.

She made her weary way to the convent, through the village that looked as if the apocalypse had hit. An occasional car passed with lights on and wipers going…red rivers were still running along the sides of the streets and forming puddles. There were trees down and the sound of sirens in the distance. And yet Alicia felt oddly calm—even when she found Sister Angelique waiting in the residence.

'Where on earth…?' She was almost shaking with suppressed fury. 'I have been waiting for hours.'

'I took shelter,' Alicia said. 'I honestly thought the world was ending.'

She lied so well—except both of them knew the storm had blown in long after the funeral.

'I've never seen blood rain before.'

'You've lost an earring, child,' she said, and Alicia's hands flew to her ears. Sure enough there was an empty space. 'They were a gift from your parents, weren't they?'

Had she lost an earring yesterday it would have hurt—unbearably so. Yet there had been a greater loss today.

But she had found something too.

Courage.

'I'm going to change,' Alicia said, and offered neither her feelings on the matter nor an explanation. 'Thank you for your concern, Sister.'

Dante had infused her heart in a way that could not be easily explained, and their forbidden afternoon made her feel a little loved and a whole lot brave.

She had been told she could stay there in the residence for an extra year, but now she considered going to Milan to track down Beatrice. That night, though, she dreamt of heading to Rome. There was nothing to keep her here, apart from the fact that she loved Sicily so. At least her little slice of it.

But without her two friends it was lonely.

Nothing happened.

She worked in the produce shop and Guido started to drop by and the nuns would smile.

Alicia not so much.

She tried for jobs in the village, but to no avail, for there were locals who could read and do maths.

In winter it rained high in the mountains, which meant the river was full, and she would sit remembering when the water had briefly run red.

And then spring arrived, and time started to gallop. Alicia started to ask more frequently to use the phone, calling hotels and agencies in Milan, but the jobs were all casual.

Turn up and see.

'How is your young man?' Sister Angelique asked one day.

'Who?' Alicia frowned, but she knew she meant Guido.

Yes, she could see the writing on the wall—but, no, Alicia was determined to make her own way. And whenever her conviction as to how she might survive started to waver she reminded herself that Dante had left with no money or qualifications.

But then the bell rang on the baby door at the convent.

Of course Alicia did not know that it had, for it was an hour before dawn and she was still asleep in her bed. But there was an angry rap at the door of her bedroom.

Alicia startled awake and opened the door.

'Is he yours?'

Sister Angelique stood there, her eyes bulging and with spittle at the edge of her lips.

'Tell me now. Is the baby yours?'

'Baby…?'

'Have you been hiding it?' She glowered.

'Hiding a baby?'

She was so bewildered Alicia thought the nun was going to check the wardrobe or under her bed, but her mind had not fully woken up.

'I saw you unkempt and with your earring missing that day. You were missing for hours with that Schininà boy. And nine months later there's a baby at the door.'

'Sister, I don't know what you're saying…'

It was late spring, and the night sky was already bright as she was marched to the convent and taken down to the small infirmary, where the cries of a newborn grew louder as they neared the nursery.

'He's not mine,' Alicia insisted, and then stilled when she saw the tiny infant. His head was to one side, he was angry and red, and…

'That baby is pure Schininà,' Sister Angelique sneered as she stated the obvious. 'He must have been busy in the short time he was back.'

'What do you mean?' Alicia asked, but she answered her own question.

Dante had barely been here.

One, maybe two nights.

It didn't even matter if she'd been before or after, because in that very second all the bliss Alicia had found fell away.

Sister Angelique's spiteful words merely twisted the knife. 'It would seem you're not so special after all.'

Alicia just stood there, the sound of her own pulse in her ears blocking the infant's cries. She had thought that day mattered. That, however fleeting their time had been, something precious had occurred.

Clearly not for Dante.

'Don't just stand there,' Sister Angelique scolded. 'He needs feeding.'

'I can't.'

'Come, now,' Sister Angelique said. 'It's hardly the child's fault. I shall get a bottle ready and then I must prepare for morning worship.'

'I can't,' Alicia insisted.

But it fell on deaf ears, for Sister Angelique was making up a bottle. She placed it in a steel jug to cool, and then left her with the new arrival in the nursery.

Alicia lifted him, and as she fed him she tried so hard not to notice the perfect arch of his eyebrows, nor the shape of his jaw, tried to deny the clear evidence.

Then his little feet kicked out of the blanket...

Who would have thought toes could be so revealing? They were long, as were his limbs. *'Poco ragno,'* Alicia whispered as she tucked him in—little spider.

Of course she could not be sure, and it would probably never be confirmed, but her heart knew that Sister Angelique was right—he was pure Schininà.

Dante had gone and left her literally holding the baby.

Alicia truly hated that blue condom.

Absolutely she did.

For in all honesty it would be so much easier if the tiny infant she was charged with taking care of was her own...

CHAPTER TEN

Sicily, now...

DANTE HAD NEVER seen Alicia asleep.

For all the past they had shared, for all they had done, there was the odd realisation that he had never seen her sleep.

Or really even at rest.

Always busy, or talking, or imagining, or lying, or testing him. What he would do if...how... When there was silence, she filled it.

He knew her smile, her pout, her frown, knew when she lied, when she was upset, but he had never seen her asleep.

She was tough—he knew that. But not always.

Were they on for the weekend or off?

He knew the woman who'd been in his bed the other week...but not the one who'd walked into his suite with a feigned smile of surprise. And it was the oddest feeling to have Alicia back by his side.

For all the surprises she'd brought into his suite that morning, the biggest for Dante was that she'd never been back home.

It troubled him perhaps more than it should.

He wasn't expecting an easy weekend, but he had no issue with slaying a few of her demons.

So long as she left his alone.

'Alicia.' He tapped her foot with his. 'Look.'

She startled awake and looked at him for a moment with resentment, and then she too found her mask and smiled.

'I dozed.'

'So did I,' he said. 'I asked the pilot to take the scenic route.'

As he would have done for a client, but that was not so pleasant as her smile now, as she gazed out of the window.

'To your left you can see Syracuse and Ortigia Island.'

They were over the Ionian Sea and now circling back towards Catania, the pilot informed them.

Though her village was in the south, still it felt as if she was coming home, for there was no other place on earth that sang to her soul the way Sicily did. It reached into the forgotten corners of her heart too, for she could recall Beatrice trying to drum into her the maritime borders of the Ionian Sea before it gave way to the Mediterranean.

Alicia, embarrassed that she could not read the names, had pushed the map away and shrugged. 'Why would I need to know that?'

For moments like this—because after glimpsing their destination she found herself craning her neck and scanning towards the south, wondering if Trebordi was visible on this clear blue day, but too embarrassed to ask Dante. She was unable to meet his eyes, the recall of them so intense she could almost feel the windburn.

But then the plane suddenly dropped and she held her stomach. 'Told you,' he said. 'The descent in a private jet is more rapid. Well, in comparison...'

'I have nothing to compare it with, Dante. I've never flown before.'

'You should have said it was your first time.'

'Would it have changed things?'

He shrugged. 'Maybe.'

Alicia inhaled deeply as they disembarked. She stood, hands on hips, blocking the exit for a moment and just taking it all in. The sky was a different blue here, and more familiar, the needle of her inner compass almost settled in relief as she stepped back onto Sicilian ground.

'Alicia!' Dante prompted, impatient. 'Can we please move?'

The drive to Ortigia was for the most part accomplished in silence. Alicia gazed out of the window as heaven unfolded before her eyes. It really was an island—a separate entity, almost.

'It's just linked by bridges...'

'Three,' Dante said, glancing over, back in entertaining client mode as he started to tell her all the myths. 'Asteria turned into a quail.'

'And threw herself to the sea.' She could remember Beatrice reading the story to her. 'It's beautiful,' she said as they took one of the bridges, and she felt as if she was crossing into another time zone, for it really was an ancient world they were entering.

'We are going there...' He pointed to an elegant palazzo within the citadel as they exited the bridge and the vehicle slowed. 'The roads here are not really made for cars.'

'Can we walk, then?' Alicia said. 'Show me...'

'This afternoon we can—'

'I meant now.'

Dante was surprised—he was more used to women who liked their views from a penthouse suite.

'I slept on the plane,' Alicia pointed out.

Her energy was refreshing—but then he reminded himself that this was exactly what he and Alicia had loved to do. They'd used to spend their days wandering. It was how they had found the little meander in the river—a place to this day where neither of them had seen another soul.

He was surprised, too, at the pleasure he found in showing her the tiny island that burst with the history and rich beauty of this ancient place.

'It's a maze!'

'No, it's just small,' he said as they walked under an archway. 'If you get lost, you always end up back here.'

They stepped out into a central square with a beautiful fountain in the middle, but Dante's attention was elsewhere.

'Tomorrow we dine there...' He pointed to a very sophis-ticated-looking restaurant and she took in a nervous breath.

'It's quite relaxed,' Dante said.

He thought she was intimidated by the surroundings, Alicia knew, but it wasn't that. It was the thought of a family dinner that made her both excited and anxious.

Another first.

'I'm so nervous about tomorrow,' she said.

'Why?'

'I want them to like me.'

She made him laugh, and that was unusual, and both of them sort of knew that it was.

'I don't even think they like *me*.'

He wanted to say they would love her, tell her to relax, but he knew it was a snake-pit he was bringing her into.

'We'll have cocktails to take the edge off.'

'Being drunk is not a good first impression.' She turned. 'This fountain is beautiful.'

'Fontana Diana...' he said. 'The goddess of hunting. See? She carries a bow...'

'The goddess of childbirth too,' Alicia said, because she loved all the myths and knew them well.

'Then let's not get too close.'

But they were like iron filings to magnets as they stood there side by side.

If only it were just about attraction...

There was all this history clinging to them and all these secrets dragging at them, fighting each other silently.

She looked up at the stunning structure of mermaids and babies and though it was heavenly, she was choking down sudden tears.

He stopped playing tour guide then, because something had obviously upset her and there was nothing about that day to regret.

'She's the goddess of virginity too,' Dante said and turned

her to face him. 'Arethusa took off her clothes and bathed in the waters, and when Alpheus saw her beauty the river was full of desire. Like us...'

'She was clearly not wearing awful knickers, then.'

God, he hated what he had said about her underwear the other day. How what she had been wearing a decade ago still upset her.

'Alicia,' he said, 'I don't even remember them.'

'How nice of you to say that you don't recall.'

'Hey!' He was sharp. 'I meant I wasn't really concerned with your underwear that afternoon. Why do you do that to yourself?' He sighed. 'You don't know how to let things go, do you?'

She breathed out and thought that perhaps he was right. She had sullied that memory too much with the bits she hated when there was so many nicer parts to it.

'You really don't remember it?' she asked.

His eyes narrowed as they gazed deep into hers, inciting a dangerous, deep recall between them, and she felt her heart hammer, as he drew the memories to mind. 'I remember that if you hadn't been wearing it in the water... I wanted to remove your bra...you wouldn't let me...'

'It was pointed, like an old lady's...'

'You have a mole just above your left breast.' He held her hips. 'I remember that very well.'

'And?' She swallowed.

'This isn't boding well for a sex-free weekend.'

'I say things I regret sometimes.'

'I know.'

'In haste.'

'You can repent at leisure,' Dante said. 'But I shall tell you what I recall is that your knickers were see-through when they got wet—I do remember that—and then pink from the rain...'

Alicia wanted to pull away, except her body held its ground as he kissed her. It was not the frantic kind of kiss that had unfolded in the hotel, and neither the younger kiss of discovery. This was slow, and far, far more dangerous, because it gave her a glimpse of another Dante.

She was kissing him back, and when she grew too urgent he slowed her with his mouth, taught her the kiss of lovers who had waited all day with the certainty of night—at least until she heard someone call his name.

'Dante!'

He pulled back and then turned. 'Hey...' He smiled. 'Matteo.' Dante appeared to remember his manners then, but she knew he had lost them long ago, and was certain that kiss had been for an audience. 'This is Alicia. Alicia, this is my brother Matteo and his wife, Rosa...'

She was blushing through the introductions, as if embarrassed that they had been caught kissing, except in reality it was a blush of anger.

'We were just about to get a coffee,' Matteo said. 'Join us?'

'We'd love to,' Dante responded. 'But Alicia is tired, and we haven't even been home since we touched down.'

'For sure.'

'We'll see you tomorrow,' Dante said.

'You knew, didn't you...?' she said once they were a suitable distance away. 'That's why you kissed me then.'

'No,' he said. 'Had I known my brother was here I would really not have been making out with you for some kick.' He looked at her. 'Don't act as though I'm some sleaze. You didn't mind the prospect of a morning shag when you wanted something from me.'

It was as simple as sex to him.

And she'd let him think it was the same for her.

'Come on.'

They walked through the cobbled streets and ancient archways towards his residence. Then there were some narrow, rather steep steps that seemed to stretch for ever and she actually paused midway.

'Do you have to carry your supermodels up these?' Alicia asked.

'No, we stay at the hotel, where I have a private elevator to the penthouse,' Dante informed her. 'Keep going,' he said, 'we're almost there.'

And then he put her out of her misery.

'There is an easier way in, but if we'd taken it then you would have missed out on this view.'

'Oh!' The whole of Sicily was stretched out before them, so glorious it brought a fresh batch of tears to her eyes. 'I've never seen it…' She was breathless. 'I mean…'

'I know what you mean.' Dante said. 'The best views are from a distance.'

She looked at the little fishing boats bobbing alongside yachts in the harbour, and beyond to the ships in their channels, and then back to the sight of the island she loved so. 'I lived there for eighteen years and I've never really seen it—well, not like this…'

It was like a portrait, or something from a picture book, except there was wind on her face and salt in the air and the images were real. It was home, and Alicia knew then how very much she had missed it.

'Can you see…?' She hesitated. 'Can you see it from here?'

'No,' he said. 'It's too far to the south, tucked away around there.' He pointed. 'It's just a couple of hours drive away, though.' They both drank in the majesty. 'Wait till tonight, when it's all lit up,' he added. 'I hope the sky behaves while you're here.'

Being back was even more emotional than she'd anticipated, and as they walked on to his residence for the first time Alicia was actually pondering that drive.

'I'll take you into town later,' he said, 'so you can see the hotel.'

'Is it yours or still with your family?'

'Always mine. They've never seen it.' He took a breath and softened his stance. 'There is a little north-south divide with my dear stepmother. One both she and my father are perhaps coming to regret.'

'In what way?'

'Just leave it.' He gave her no more than that. 'We always knew God was in his heaven here.'

There was not enough room in her mind to dwell on it. There was the thrill of being back, the absolute beauty of Ortigia, the splendour of his home and simply being here with him.

'It's incredible.' Alicia looked up. 'Was it really a palace?'

'For minor royals, maybe. In truth, it's a lot of work,' Dante said. 'The initial plan when I bought it was that it would be a boutique hotel someday, but there's a lot that needs to happen. Half of it is closed off...'

'For renovations?'

'Hazardous,' he said. 'Then there are the permissions needed for everything...'

He pulled a face, but as he showed her through, Alicia could tell he loved it down to the last hazardous brick.

'I brought you in this way to see the view, but usually I take the front entrance. You can actually drive up to it.'

She was grateful now for the endless stairs and the glittering surprise at the top.

'My residence is on the second floor—it's not in such disrepair.'

There wasn't a hint of disrepair.

Gorgeous rugs softened the stone floor and the furniture looked rather more inviting than the imposing edifice. French doors opened on to a large terrace, and she knew she would love to stand there and take in the view of the harbour.

'We'll eat out there tonight.' He opened a little door. 'More stairs,' he said, and then added, 'Your luggage might be a while.'

'No problem.'

'I mean it probably won't get here until dinner.'

'I'm not in a rush.'

'Good.'

Another climb and they came out into a long stone corridor with just little slits in the walls high up and barely any light. 'Left or right?' Dante said.

'Right.'

They walked along to a door, and as he opened it she stepped from darkness into a pretty chamber in pink. It really should have been gaudy, with so much pink, but it was pretty, and sensual, and it had an ocean view too. It was the prettiest room she had ever been in, Alicia realised, with a rosewood bed.

She pushed open a door to an equally pink bathroom. 'Wow.'

Alicia was looking forward to soaking in that gorgeous tub—she would not be telling him she had only ever had a shower—and when she walked back into the bedroom she found she wanted to bounce the bed just to feel it. But she would do that alone.

'Is this your room, Dante?' she teased. She knew she should not even be edging towards flirting, but it was just a joke.

'Yes,' he said.

'What's this for?' she asked, pointing to a velvet rope above the bed.

'Come on.' He pointed down the long corridor. 'Your room is down there,' he said, though she knew he meant his.

'Can I see it?'

And that was not flirting—it was honest curiosity.

'Oh, gosh!' she said as they entered Dante's room. It was very male, dressed predominantly in jade, and the bed was made of a dark carved wood that was imposing rather than inviting. More like a torture rack. 'That doesn't look very comfortable.'

'It's a medieval bed with a very modern mattress.'

'Oh!'

'It's also built into the building's structure and it can't be taken out.'

Here the rope hanging from the ceiling was of thick jade velvet. She went to pull it, but stopped short when he said, 'Better not.'

'Sorry.'

She wandered into the bathroom, which was more like a temple with its mosaic tiles.

'It's designed like a compass,' he said, looking up. 'It's a bit spooky.'

'Please don't tell me it's haunted.'

'Okay, I won't. But we can swap for tonight and you can have the pink room.'

'*Is* it haunted?'

'I have been known to switch rooms some nights, but I promise I'll go to the couch if the ghost comes out.'

'I don't know when you're joking.'

The skies did behave for Alicia.

Dante made them lovely drinks on the terrace as stars started to dot the night sky and the lights of Sicily went on across the water.

Then their luggage arrived, along with a butler who made the one at the hotel look sprightly. 'I'll take it up,' Dante called out, but the man was already doing it.

The most beautiful dinner came up through a service hatch. Under a big silver cloche there were slabs of ravioli in a buttery sage sauce.

'So, your family are at the hotel?'

'They are.' He looked over at her. 'Don't lecture me and say that they should be here. The cook and the butler are a married couple,' Dante explained as he served up. 'They make your hotel butler look young, and dinner for six would kill them. Of course, they're complaining that they're not eating here too.'

'Your family are complaining?'

'No, the staff. We're back in Sicily now. They rule the place. I can't tell them, though.'

'Is that why I couldn't pull the rope in your room?'

'No, that summons a lover. There's a cord between the rooms, so don't pull it if you only want coffee.'

God!

'Gino messaged. He suggests you meet him on Sunday. He feels that if you're with him when he visits the convent…'

'I don't know.' She was slicing into her delicate ravioli as if it were steak.

'Alicia, did something happen?' he asked. 'You hear all these things…'

'Nothing like that.' She took a drink. 'They were good to me—well, for the most part—and I had a nice childhood.' She was struggling now, but for the first time she was really debating going back, asking for advice.

And not about Beatrice.

'I'll come if it helps,' Dante offered. 'I have no issues having some straight words with Reverend Mother.'

'Really, no.' Absolutely she would *not* be going back with Dante. 'Let me think about it.'

'Sure. Now probably some *osso bucco*,' he said, 'made with love by my wheezing cook.'

But it was *caponata*. It was a very Sicilian dish, rich, sweet and sour, with aubergine and capers, olives and roasted peppers, and there was fresh crostini. It was so nice when scooped on the crisp bread.

'Thank you,' she said.

'For what?'

'For remembering I'm not big on meat.' Gosh it was good to relax and eat her favourite dish from home. 'I'll eat whatever comes tomorrow, of course…'

'It's a restaurant.'

'Yes.' She nodded. 'Just dinner.'

'I'm having breakfast with my father on Sunday, but he knows what's coming—that I'm going to walk away. I've given him ten years, Alicia. And they're hardly lambs to the slaughter. My father, if you can call him that, played me.'

'How?' She shook her head, because from where she sat, from every vantage point of her life, no one had ever played Dante.

'He caught me off guard.'

'You are *never* off guard.'

'Well, I was.' He looked at her. 'And he exploited it. The proverbial long-lost son whom he'd share his wealth with, bringing me on board with his business…'

'That sounds like a father to me.'

'You know what charisma is?'

'Of course,' Alicia said. She was sitting opposite it.

'My father has it in spades. He can close a deal, charm the birds… My mother had it too. When she smiled every man thought she was his—at least for his allotted time.'

'You got a double dose?'

'Maybe,' he said, 'but it's not just an inherited skill, Alicia, you have to hone it. Matteo, who you just met, has none. He has been pampered and spoiled all his life. Nice guy—just no drive because he's never needed it. However, my father is not a miracle-worker, and if he knew if he wanted to keep his empire going he needed…'

'You?'

Dante nodded. 'I don't like how he goes about his business. Shady, sleazy… But I don't scratch anyone's back—' Dante halted, perhaps recalling the time he had scratched hers. 'He has a lot of international backers, and when they're in Europe they want to be entertained. He was starting to struggle. He couldn't be everywhere. Matteo would happily sit with his mineral water on his phone and then leave early, because he had a marathon or a cycling event he was training for. He was into racing cars for a while, but useless at that…'

'Whereas you're a showman?'

'I'm sick of casinos and my father's way of doing deals. All of this—' he gestured to his home and the beauty beyond '—was correctly done. All my dealings are clean. And now I'm just stepping back. Devoting more time to you, my love…' he mocked, and blew her a kiss. 'Believe me, I'm being far nicer than I intended to be.' He looked at the view. 'They're not getting their hands on this.'

'Do they want it?'

'They want the boutique hotel it could be. Still, the bed-room arrangements at present would suit my father and Giustina. I've never been able to figure out why she stays if she knows he cheated so regularly...'

'Perhaps she has a lovers of her own.'

'Giustina?' He snorted. 'Good luck to her, then.' But he considered it for a moment. 'You think?'

'I've no idea.' She shrugged. 'But people always have their own reasons for staying, even if they're not all on display...'

She was here after all. Sitting opposite him and pretending it was easy, that her heart could handle being exposed again to the ice of Dante.

'I wonder who summoned who in the old days?' Dante said.

'The man would summon,' Alicia said. 'Women probably weren't allowed to.'

'Please...' he refuted. 'They were at it all the time in days of old...'

'Really?'

'They had none of our hang-ups and promises of one person for ever—perhaps I should have lived then.'

'Perhaps,' she said, gazing at the huge moon over the water.

'But why the rope above the female's bed, then, if she couldn't use it?' Dante's mind was clearly lingering in its usual space. 'I guess it depends on who ruled at the time. So if I were King, I'd summon you. If you were Queen...'

'You'd have to wait for my command.'

He pulled a face. 'I don't think I'd be a very good Queen's consort... No. Mind you, the truth is I do prefer to sleep alone.'

'Really?' She frowned in disbelief. 'That's not what I gleaned...'

'I'm not talking about sex.' He gave her a smile, his lazy evening conversation unfolding. 'Of course it would be rude to say so after the event, but if I could, then, yes, I would have sex and then return to my suite or she to hers. I hate the noise of another person and the feel of them by my side...'

'Truly?'

He nodded. 'I can't sleep—not properly.'

'Well, I love it,' Alicia admitted, and then coloured a little. 'I mean…' Gosh, she didn't want him knowing that their one afternoon had been her only time. 'Even when I was little it made me feel safe, hearing Beatrice and knowing she was there. I love the sound of someone breathing…'

'I can leave my door open and snore if you'd like.'

'Yes, please.'

'I was joking.'

'Well, I wasn't,' Alicia admitted. 'I hate silence at night. It reminds me too much of the room after Beatrice had gone, and how—'

She stopped, not able to tell him how she had cried when he'd left at fourteen and there had been no one to hear. Not at eighteen, though. For a little while she had been so glad to hug that secret to her and close her eyes to the memory of them. All that had stopped abruptly when the baby had been born.

'I hate sleeping alone.'

'Don't tell anyone that.' He looked over. 'Guys, I mean.'

'What's it to you?'

'Just some free advice,' he said.

Their tongues were growing looser now, and more honesty was creeping in as the lights started to darken in the distance. Sicily was retiring as they stayed lingering over the view.

'I can also tell you why things don't work out in your relationships…'

'Oh, you can?'

He nodded assuredly.

'Go ahead.'

'You're sure?'

'Please do.'

'Well, you're beautiful, funny, and the sex is…' He gave a very Italian wave with his hand.

'But?'

'You fall hard.'

'No.'

'Alicia.' He looked right at her. 'Your devotion is instant. Beatrice is a case in point—ten years on you're still searching for her.'

She managed a half-laugh and then just stared at the moon—which then gave in to Dante Schininà too, for it hid behind a cloud for a moment's pause as Dante confirmed his findings.

'We had sex once and you were ready to pick up your life and move to Rome.'

She sat silent. Did he think she was like that with everyone she met? Really? That she tore off her clothes, she bent over on command—that she would actively choose to feel like this? Put her hand up for this kind of hurt?

Yet she had.

And for the chance of one full moon night with Dante, she was sitting here being told how to pull better.

Because that was all he did.

She really had chosen to swim with a shark.

'Just slow down…reel it back a bit…' He was warming to his theory. He smiled. 'Then you will have guys eating out of your hand.'

'Thank you, Dante.' She gave a tart smile. 'It's nice to have a playboy's advice.'

'No problem.'

'Do you want mine?' Alicia offered. 'I mean, while we're sharing our thoughts on this beautiful night.'

'No, thanks.'

'For free?'

'I don't need it,' he said.

'Oh, Dante, you do.'

'Oh, Alicia, I really don't,' he said. 'Because I don't want a relationship that works. I don't want the same things as you.'

He didn't even hide it.

'So how shall we say we met?' Alicia asked. 'I'm sure your family will ask. Do we say—?'

'Say you're from the south too…just be vague.' He named a couple of nearby towns. 'But say we met in Milan.'

'What?' She stared at him. 'I'm not supposed to mention we knew each other as children?'

'I'm hardly going to tell them about our time at the river after my mother's funeral...'

She felt a flash of tears in her eyes and blinked them back, trying to not show how much it hurt that he could so readily erase their rich past, the little stitches in the tapestry of her history reduced to sex by the river.

'I am going get some sleep,' Alicia said, trying to hold on and hide her hurt and silent fury. 'I was up early. I'm sure you want me looking fresh tomorrow.'

'Alicia.' He caught her wrist. 'Don't storm off.'

'I'm not storming off.'

'Oh, *bella*, you are...'

'I'm really not.'

'A silent storm.'

'No,' she said. 'Just tired.'

She was white with fury as she slipped off the lemon dress and for the first time in her life had a bath.

Only so that she could give in to the tears as the taps ran.

How had they first met?

She thought of the grubby boy who had pulled out her first tooth when she hadn't dared. Of how, as Beatrice would silently read, she would kneel on the bed and look through the window at a world that beckoned and know that Dante was out there.

The river, the woods, the hut, the cemetery... He was written on almost every page of her childhood, and he was in her teenage years, too—and now she was late twenties and back to the start...

Oh, gosh... She was playing the most dangerous game with her heart now, pretending to be his lover, a part of his life...

Lying up to her neck in the warm water filled with bubbles, she felt her body aching knowing he was near. Her breasts were loose in the water and it was nice, relaxing, and after a real cry it was nice to just lie there, floating in the scented water.

She stepped out and wrapped herself in a towel when she was done, her hair damp, only to find the bed had been turned back. It really was five-star luxury he lived in each day.

She slipped on the gold nightdress and climbed into the bed. The sheets felt like silk as her head rested on a pillow soft as feathers.

And then the door opened.

'*Buona notte.*'

She lay there silent.

'Alicia,' he prompted, 'don't let's go to sleep on a row.'

'We're not rowing.'

'Then say goodnight.'

'*Buona notte,*' she answered.

And there was a certain relief when he left the door a little ajar—just enough so she could hear him prepare for bed—for tonight she would be able to sink into the comfort of having another close.

And even in the dark, even when she was angry, it appeared Dante could still make her smile. Because the little bell above the bed rang, just once.

Of course she ignored it.

And she ignored, too, the temptation to reach up and pull her own rope, to have him lie next to her, to be held in his arms again…the place she felt safe.

CHAPTER ELEVEN

ALICIA AWOKE TO the sounds of the harbour rather than the city, and lay there not really ready to get out of bed.

She knew her eyes were probably puffy from crying, but she would just blame it on a terrible night's sleep, she decided.

Except, with Dante close she had slept beautifully.

How shall we say we met?

Alicia stoked her own ire by recalling his answer. It was far safer to remain cross.

She had a feeling that today would be more difficult than even she could anticipate, for she would meet his family and watch him walk away from them. And then, when he had finished with them, his destruct button would turn to her.

Dante would walk alone again.

As he always had.

There was a knock on her door, but it would seem that here in Ortigia they did not await a response, for Dante came in holding a cup and saucer and wearing nothing but a towel, his face as unshaven as it had been on the morning when he had lain in the hotel bed and roughly kissed her.

'It would seem I am the maid this morning,' Dante drawled.

Alicia refused to smile.

'M'lady,' he said, and as he put down the cup and saucer on the bedside table she caught the freshly showered scent of him and hated herself for feeling suddenly alive beneath the sheets. 'Can I do anything else for you?'

'Actually, yes.' She threw back his own words. 'While you're here can you open the drapes.'

'Sorry, no.' He sat on the bed instead. 'I've decided I don't like being the maid.'

'Guess what, Dante? Nobody likes been the maid.'

'I would if we were playing for rewards.'

He squeezed her thigh through the sheet, and his hand was warm and her limbs were too fluid for someone who was trying to be taut with anger. She refused to react, and yet it was like being back in the river, for above the sheets she sat poker-faced, and beneath them she was alive. Aware of the warmth of his body and the weight of him on the bed, his gorgeous back... And then, when he turned to speak, she flamed as she tried not to remember kissing his shoulder, her lips on his chest.

'What do you want to do today?' he asked. 'Shop?'

'I did that yesterday.'

'Well, unfortunately we can't spend the day in bed, because you've decided you're allergic to all that.' He gave a sad smile, but then brightened. 'How about we go out on the water?'

'You have a yacht?'

'That I do.'

'No,' she said. 'I didn't bring anything suitable.'

'Liar,' he said. 'I have the itemised bill, and you have bikinis and sarongs. No shorts, though...'

'I feel like a deckhand in them.'

'Yes, you always were a tomboy in a dress.' He smiled. 'Come out on the water.'

'No, you don't want to miss dinner.'

'We won't.'

'Oh, we very much might,' Alicia said, her Sicilian temper gaining ascendancy. 'And tomorrow's headlines might read "Billionaire Missing at Sea".'

'So you're sulking?'

'I'm not sulking,' Alicia said. 'I just don't think a full day in your company is wise, if we're to appear as the happy couple tonight.'

'You're a compulsive liar, Alicia,' Dante pointed out. 'Yes, you are sulking, and have been since you stormed off last night! What did I say that was so terrible? Was it my dating advice?'

She shot him a look and then angrily pushed away the sheets.

Rather more used to sleeping in knickers and a T-shirt than a nightdress, she gave him a quick glimpse of very dark hair as her legs scissored out of bed.

Both politely pretended he hadn't seen.

Both knew he had.

Where the hell was her robe? Alicia thought. Because her nipples felt like studs sticking out. She had to get away, so she walked through to the lounge, deciding she would retrieve her robe in a moment.

She wasn't cut out for this charade, Alicia knew as he came into the lounge behind her.

'Here.' He offered her a pastry. 'Anchovy and…'

She discarded it with a shake of her head. 'I happen to value my arteries.'

'Suit yourself,' Dante said, and put the pastry down, watching as she selected a plump strawberry and then picked up a slice of apple. They perhaps both recalled in that moment that she had tasted of apples the first time they'd kissed.

She went on to the balcony, and of course Sicily's morning sun was fire…or was it her cheeks?

He followed her out.

'Leave me alone.' She tossed the words over her shoulder as she had that first morning and then swept back inside.

'Hey,' he warned as she walked off, and not gently, for she brushed past him angrily. 'This is my home, and in it are my staff,' he reminded her. 'I shall go out today and leave you alone with your mood, but I will tell you now—don't be wearing it tonight.'

She swallowed, trying not to cry. She was just not up to this, and she knew he hated it when she cried.

'For God's sake…' His patience was clearly starting to run out. 'What the hell did I say wrong?'

'How shall we say we met?' she snapped in her hurt.

'What the hell…?'

'Are you ashamed to admit to your family that your "designer girlfriend" was raised by nuns?'

'That's your hang-up, Alicia, not mine.'

'You dismiss our friendship so easily.' She jabbed at his naked chest.

'Do you really want me to tell them?' He did not back down; in fact, his face came closer. 'I was trying to save you any awkwardness. Giustina is like a dog with a bone where my mother is concerned.'

She didn't believe him. 'No, you just don't want to admit how close we once were!'

'Oh, so you want me to tell them we had sex after my mother's funeral?'

'Damn you.'

'No.' He took the hand that was still jabbing at his chest. 'I think you're upset about the real truth, Alicia.'

Her eyes were wide, and she was suddenly terrified that he knew she loved him. Terrified as she admitted to herself that she absolutely did love him. And had for the whole of her life.

It wasn't hate that she'd nursed—it was hurt.

Hurt because he was the nicest, kindest, most brutal, direct, sexiest person, and he would never, ever love her in the way she loved him.

But Dante had less trivial things on *his* mind. 'You're upset that I might tell them how you looked me up and found out the hotel I stayed at.'

'I'm not a stalker.'

'Perhaps you're worried I'll tell them how you walked into my bedroom at dawn… I think *that's* the part you want to erase.'

'No, no, no.' She was shaking her head furiously.

'Yes,' Dante said. 'You tried to play me that morning, and you hate it that I called you on it!'

It was Dante who had trapped her in her own lies.

'No!' she insisted.

'No, what?' he demanded.

'I didn't intend…'

'You just *fell* on my lap, did you?'

'It was never my intention to sleep with you,' she admitted. 'I just wanted us to go for coffee.'

'Alicia.' He held her hips against his and they both knew the towel had gone. 'You had no intention of sleeping with me?' he checked. 'Not even a thought that we might get it on?'

'Not even a thought.' Not a tangible one, anyway, but she could still see those cups rattling before she'd stepped inside.

And she'd woken breathless in the night and denied to herself it was from thinking of him.

Endless hope, maybe.

But what would he know about that?

'Not a thought,' she insisted.

'You're so good at it you don't even know when you lie.'

And suddenly they were kissing. So angrily, so deliciously, so urgently. And between frantic kisses there were angry words.

'Liar…' he said, pulling down the spaghetti straps of her nightgown and claiming her naked breasts with hands that knew them. 'You wanted me…'

'No,' she insisted, because for years and years she had thought she nursed hate, and had sworn to herself that was all it was… At least until she stood at his bedroom door. 'I didn't—'

But she was back at his neck and kissing him hungrily, her short nails digging into his back. And she was such a liar, even to herself, because this man had crept into her dreams. No matter how she'd tried to push him away by day, Dante had always been there when she closed her eyes at night.

'Yes.'

She left his shoulder and rested her burning cheek on his chest, thinking that it might be her own heart she could hear beating in his chest. And it might as well be, for he dictated the very beat of it, the pace, the pulse. He dictated her breath too, for she held it in angrily as she denied the truth...

And then, as if to his command, she finally let it out, exhaling her truth. 'Yes, I did.'

'Wanted or want?' he said, and it was his heart she heard now, two hearts each testing the other.

'Both.'

She did not care if it was just sex, because she loved 'just sex' with Dante.

He lifted her just as easily as if they were back in the river, and she wrapped her legs just as readily around him.

It was reckless—but then they both had been at times.

But she knew Dante had never been as reckless as this, as insistent on another admitting their want. And Alicia loved being reckless—but only with him.

He could feel passion in every limb wrapped around him. All the fakery and restraint they had attempted was receding, and it was a relief to give in to the person who knew him the most.

It was like being swept into a wind tunnel. They were both frantic for each other, not caring for a moment that they both knew, meeting in the urgent, frantic coupling that they had been building towards since she'd stepped back into his life.

She was coming as hard and as fast as he, because both knew if they gave it one second of thought they'd stop.

She was shivering tightly around him even after they'd come, and then they stopped, both silent and breathless, both knowing they were wrong. Knowing they'd regret it, but still okay with what they'd done.

Or just accepting of their punishment? He didn't even know as he let her down.

Alicia tried to pull her straps up, but one was broken and she looked up at him, at a loss, as they stared at each other.

'It's okay.'

Dante didn't even know his own voice. He was stunned.

Not so much that they had had sex—that had been inevitable since the second their lives had crossed paths again—but at the intensity of it.

He never lost his head, and yet the world could have ended, the sea could have pulled back, the sky gone dark, and he wouldn't have cared. And it was still there. For there was need, want and care between them.

He brushed her hair back from her face as he tried to find words.

She dragged air in and nodded, but then a frown flickered across her features. 'Dante, we didn't use anything...'

He closed his eyes, just for a brief second, and tried his best to reassure her. 'Alicia...' He was breathing as if he had been for a morning run. 'I swear I have never done it without one, ever...'

She shook her head. She didn't believe him; she'd nursed the proof of his failings in the contraception department after all.

'You're on the pill?' he checked.

'Of course I'm not!'

He swallowed, saw the anger and panic in her eyes. 'It will be fine.' He wasn't being dismissive, he was trying to be practical, but clearly all the anger he'd been holding in his arms hadn't quite dispersed.

'Don't give me your "it will be fine". You're a liar, Dante. Don't tell me that was a one-off...that you're always careful.'

'Alicia.' Still he remained calm, but curt, sharp. 'I am telling you that is the one thing we don't have to worry about. Christ, you were there when we did it the first time. I was the one who stopped.'

'Well, clearly your methods aren't failsafe. Given that nine months later...'

Oh, her anger had definitely not been dispersed—and now nor had his.

'What?'

His voice was like a whip cracking beside her and she actually jumped, felt the wobble of her exposed breast.

'What did you just say?'

Her voice quavered. 'That it isn't the first time you've gone without.'

'I meant the "nine months later" part.'

'What do you think I mean, Dante? You have a son!' she shouted. 'You have a son named Roberto.'

'You choose to tell me now?' He was white with fury. 'Why not five minutes ago? Or do you want him to have a sibling?'

'Not me…' Oh, she was really angry now. 'Whoever else you were with while you were back in the village had your baby. Clearly I wasn't that special.' She repeated Sister Angelique's spiteful words. 'And clearly,' she added, 'you don't always use protection.'

'God, you outdo yourself, Alicia,' Dante said. 'Your lies know no bounds.'

'I'm not lying, Dante.'

But Alicia was already hating the way she had told him—or rather the way she must now tell him—that he really did have a son. 'I never meant to tell you…at least not this way.'

His eyes were wide.

'There was a baby left at the convent in the same way I was—your son.'

He scoffed.

'Dante, even Sister Angelique knew it was your baby. "Pure Schininà", she said…' Her face was pale and so were her lips, but he'd stopped being sure when Alicia was telling the truth, or even if she believed her own lies. 'She saw I had an earring missing when I came back that day…'

He knew he was hearing the truth now. 'Tell me.' It was Dante who was pale now. 'Stop the games and tell me exactly…'

'That's it,' Alicia said. 'Sister Angelique knew I'd been away too long. I said I'd taken shelter and she took great delight in pointing out I'd lost one of my earrings.' She gave a tight shrug. 'Nine months later there was a baby left in the door. She assumed it was mine but of course it wasn't.'

'So I'm responsible for all the babies who were born nine months after I visited?'

'Please don't.' She could not bear to hear his lies. 'He was yours.'

'Where is he now?'

'He has a family who love him—no thanks to you.'

She turned accusing eyes to him, hating his carelessness. Hating herself, too, for the decision she had taken to walk away from his baby. It was the darkest piece of her, so unexamined that she dared not flip that little piece of the puzzle over. She hated him for the decision his recklessness had ultimately forced her to make.

'How could you, Dante?'

He would really like to ask her the same, but he was trying to be practical with a mind that was working a little too fast now. 'Do you know the mother?'

'It's an anonymous baby door, Dante.'

'Don't be smart, Alicia. These rumours you were talking about on the plane—that's what the hate is all about?'

'Yes.'

He waited.

'There was a lot of talk in the village about you visiting the house when you came home.'

'What house?' He looked at her. 'Do you mean when I cleared out my mother's belongings?'

She nodded.

'I was busy—a night vigil, a funeral, you.'

'Dante, you were there. How *could* you?' she repeated.

He just stared at her for a long time.

'No,' he finally countered. He had again been about to ask the same thing of Alicia, but then he looked right at her and didn't. 'I don't have to explain myself to you.'

'Because you can't.'

'Because I don't need to.'

'Because you *can't*.'

He brushed past her then and she stood there, feeling ill at the way she'd blurted things out, waiting for round two. But then Alicia was suddenly frantic.

She followed him up to his bedroom where he angrily dressed.

'You're not going to the convent, are you?'

He ignored her and she watched him pulling on his jeans.

'You can't go there,' she said. 'Dante, please don't rush in and disrupt his life.'

He didn't answer.

'I shouldn't have told you.'

'Clearly you could no longer contain your resentment.' He looked at her. 'I get that feeling, believe me,' he said, making it clear he was struggling to contain his. 'Could you please stop coming uninvited into my bedroom?'

'You at least owe me an explanation.'

'Actually, I don't.'

He looked up, and it was then that she realised there would be no round two. She wasn't worth a row, and he reminded her why.

'We're not a couple, Alicia. I told you—I don't do all that. And, believe me, neither do I ever want to.'

'Are we friends then?'

'Seriously?'

He was the most haphazard she'd seen him in years. He was in immaculate black jeans and a black top, but the belt he'd threaded through was undone and he was untucked and unshaven and closer to the Dante of old that she hadn't seen in years. Only now, she was in the *Do Not Approach* zone.

'I don't think so.'

'We were friends.'

'Does being friends mean holding on to some decade-old rumour waiting for your moment?' he asked. 'No, thank you, then.'

'I have every right to be upset—'

'Enjoy it, then,' he said, sitting on his medieval bed and pulling on his boots.

The real torture was his indifference. 'Where are you going?'

He didn't answer.

'Please don't disrupt his life.'

'Don't worry.' He was at his sarcastic best. 'I'll pick up some blue balloons and teddies on the drive there—*Daddy's home!*'.

'Please don't go and find him.'

'Go to hell, Alicia.'

She was frantic to stop him—insensibly so. 'We have your family dinner tonight…'

'You're not serious?' Dante didn't even look over, instead he was looking for his car keys, as if an eerie calm had come over him. '*We* don't have anything.' He picked up his phone and turned it off in front of her. 'Believe me, there'll be no family dinner.'

'Don't say that.'

'I am saying exactly that. I don't want one.'

'So where are you going?'

'To find a more sensible conversation.' Even as they looked at her, those navy eyes didn't really meet hers, and they were so unreadable they seemed opaque. 'Do you want me to arrange your flight?'

'You're kicking me out?'

'I don't kick,' he said. 'Ever. Oh, but there were rumours though, weren't there? When I was teenager…when the baker's was broken into. Did you believe that too, Alicia?'

'No!' She was appalled. 'They were lying. I *always* defended you, Dante.'

'You did,' he said. 'But it stopped long, long before the funeral.'

'That's not true.'

'It is. Before you demand honesty from others, take a look at yourself.'

CHAPTER TWELVE

'REVEREND MOTHER IS unavailable, *signor...*'

He had not stood waiting at the gates of the convent for half an hour just to be told this.

'Please tell her that if she fails to make herself available then I will attempt to deal with the situation myself.' Dante was very good at getting his own way, and never had he needed to more than now. 'However, I would appreciate her guidance on a delicate matter that has come to light this morning. Could you tell her that, please?'

Dante waited just ten minutes this time.

'Please, follow me.'

He walked up large staircase which was almost familiar for Alicia had told him about it—how she and Beatrice would chatter on their way up and then sit nervously on the bench he was looking at now.

No doubt his mother had sat there too, waiting to be summoned. Chastised.

'Please,' the nun said. 'Take a seat.'

He didn't get a chance to, though.

'Thank you, Sister Angelique,' said a tiny figure as it appeared at the doorway. 'I shall take it from here.'

Reverend Mother gave a tight smile as they took their seats in her office. 'You want to see me regarding a delicate matter?'

'A baby,' Dante said.

'*Signor...*' she put up her hand '...can I stop you there? I say this with the utmost respect, but before we continue you must know that words once said cannot—'

'I am not here to disrupt anybody's life,' Dante stated. 'But the fact is I believe my brother was left here—'

'Your brother?' Reverend Mother interrupted. 'I thought you were here regarding—' She stopped herself.

'I don't have a son,' Dante said, and met her eyes. 'My father returned for my mother's funeral. He watched from a distance and I am guessing he—' Dante halted. He would not be getting into salacious presumption with Reverend Mother. 'Certainly the baby was not mine.'

'Then I owe you an apology, *signor*.'

'No need,' he said. 'You weren't the only one to jump to the same conclusion.'

It galled him that Alicia had simply assumed the worst. It smeared the sacredness of the time they'd shared—the one decent memory he had of this damned place—but for now he kept his thoughts in check.

'I really can't discuss this further with you. It was different when I thought you might be the father of an infant left here.'

'I accept that you can't discuss Roberto in detail,' Dante said, purposely letting her know that he knew the boy's name. 'Please tell me only what you are comfortable sharing. I do have some questions, though.'

Dante was here about more than a baby.

Their conversation was thwarted, though, when they heard footsteps and then a knock at the door. Sister Angelique appeared with a tray.

'Signor Schininà and I have decided to go for a walk,' said Reverend Mother. She looked to Dante. 'Unless you would like coffee first?'

'A walk sounds good.'

It was windy on the headlands, but nice to walk after his drive, and he was comfortable with the silence, knowing it would be broken only after deep consideration.

'He's happy,' Reverend Mother said. 'That much I can tell you. He's with a loving family and he is thriving.'

'Can I ask how long he was here?' The detail mattered to him; he didn't want his brother to have been here for long, for he knew how much his mother had hated it.

'A few months. Initially there was a young couple we hoped might adopt him, but that didn't work out.'

'So he was moved around?'

'Oh, no.' Reverend Mother shook her head. 'Roberto was taken care of in the nursery here, and he was very loved. Another couple adopted him when he was nine months old. They have since...' She looked over and smiled. 'Well, he has a sibling.'

'Will he be told about his start in life?'

'I can't discuss that. I do keep letters and such in my safe, though, should a situation arise when they are asked for. If you choose to do so, can I suggest you wait?'

'For what?'

'It's harder in the long run if people make promises they cannot keep. It will be better to wait until emotions have settled down.'

'I'm not an emotional person,' Dante said.

Except being back, walking across these grounds...perhaps he was fooling himself.

He wasn't fooling Reverend Mother, though.

'You just found out this morning.'

Her question, or rather statement, was wry. She turned and smiled, and he almost returned it.

'Okay, maybe a bit emotional.'

Yes, maybe a bit emotional—especially now, as they came to the tiny stone school.

'My mother attended school here.'

'Indeed.' Reverend Mother nodded.

'She was a challenging student, I believe.'

'Yes.' Reverend Mother's voice was grave. 'We should have done more. I can see that now.'

'Times were different.' Even the fact that they were having this conversation was evidence of that. 'And you did take her in when her parents didn't.'

'I meant we…we should not have left that challenge to you.'

'You can only have boys here until they are one.'

'Still, we should have stepped in, and I regret that we didn't. I apologise again, *signor*.'

He looked at the school. He had never been on the grounds before, for he had attended the local one in town.

'She could have done well. It was a very esteemed school.'

'It is not so esteemed now.' The Reverend Mother gave a tight smile. 'But we try.'

'It was a great school.'

'I don't think our benefactor anticipated the digital age…'

Here we go, Dante thought.

But perhaps Reverend Mother heard the roll of his eyeballs, as Alicia had once sworn she could, because she glanced up.

'I have just told you that I regret how we handled things, both with your mother and you, her child. I am not so barefaced that I would ask for a handout. Are you so cynical that I must guard my words?'

Was he? 'Please don't do that.'

'It's not just about being an esteemed school. There are children we could have done so much more for—like your old friend…'

'My old friend?' Deliberately Dante frowned, refusing to show his deep interest and yet relieved Reverend Mother was not guarding her words.

'Alicia,' Reverend Mother prompted, unaware that it was needless, because really there had been but one friend for him.

'Ahh, yes,' he said as if he *almost* recalled her.

'She was as bright as a button, but she couldn't read or write. Who knows what she could have been if she'd had access to all the things that are available now? Prime Minister, probably. She was very sharp.'

'She could read, surely?' He frowned, sure the nun was mixing the children up. 'We used to go to the cemetery and look at the graves—or am I confusing her with someone else?' He kept his query light. 'Are you sure you mean Alicia?'

'Oh, she hid it very well,' Reverend Mother told him.

'She had a twin,' Dante said, and turned and looked when the Reverend Mother flushed a little, her head down. 'Beatrice?'

'They weren't actually twins. That was just another story that Alicia made up. Still, as is the case with real twins, one always took up the slack—Beatrice. She didn't even know she was doing it.'

'I don't understand…'

'Beatrice would read to Alicia, who would memorise things.'

'That's clever.'

'Indeed she was—and kind. You know…' She hesitated.

Dante turned to her and smiled deliberately. For when he smiled a certain way he knew that rocks could be moved. Yes, it could be used for bad, but not in this case—for he had to know. And so he smiled his navy-eyed smile and then looked ahead, safe in the knowledge that he had charmed even Reverend Mother.

'Alicia cared for your brother in his first months of life,' she confided to her new friend.

Whoa!

'Did she?' he said, and he hoped she couldn't hear the cursing in his head, because even he could see that must have hurt her.

'Yes, she worked in the nursery. So you can rest assured that he was always well looked after and loved.'

Dante closed his eyes as he walked.

'In fact…' Reverend Mother was the soul of indiscretion now '…the other couple I was telling you about…'

'The couple you hoped would adopt Roberto?'

'Yes. One of them was Alicia. She was engaged to marry and there were plans that she would adopt Roberto.'

He didn't know what to say.

'She always took special care of him when she worked in

the nursery. Still, it was not to be. No. It would seem mother-hood and settling down were not for her. Poor thing.'

God, what a mess.

They had come full circle and were nearing the convent again, and now it was Reverend Mother who had a question.

'Have you made peace with the memory of your mother?'

'I've had enough trouble acknowledging my father,' Dante admitted. 'I think peace is a long way off.'

'It doesn't have to be so. Remember one nice thing.'

'There are some good bits,' he said. 'She cooked good eggs.'

'Come on, Dante, you can do better than that.'

'She actually did.' He was not being facetious. 'We had nice suppers sometimes, and she was good to a friend of mine.' He was not going to be counselled by Reverend Mother. 'I'll get there.'

Next century, perhaps, but for Alicia's sake he asked one more thing.

'Alicia's twin,' he said, as if the memory had just been stirred. 'She got a scholarship, didn't she?'

'Goodness, that was years ago. I can't remember what happened to all the children. There have been so many of them...'

Dante stopped walking and turned to face her.

'You remember my mother,' Dante said, very slowly, 'and you remember Alicia. So you remember the difficult one, and the disadvantaged one, yet not the star of the class?'

She was silent, but she did meet his eyes as he spoke.

'I told you at the beginning, Reverend Mother, I don't want to disrupt anybody's life.'

'Non destare il cane che dorme...'

She repeated what she had said to Alicia all those years ago, but Dante was not scared and he was not eighteen.

'Reverend Mother,' Dante said. 'Sleeping dogs awaken stronger.'

CHAPTER THIRTEEN

IT WAS A dreadful morning.

He would not take her calls, and she was shaking and crying after her handling of things. She didn't know what to do.

'Dante, please call back,' she pleaded when she got his voicemail. 'Even if you're cross, please tell me what is happening.'

Did she go to the airport? Ask for a hotel?

No.

She laid her dress out on the bed—a sophisticated grey, with a high waistband that fell into gentle ruches and was kind to curves, she'd been told.

She added wedged shoes that were pretty, but practical for walking on cobbles.

There was a heavy black pearl clasp for her hair, which matched the earrings he had given her.

But that was more for something to do than anything else.

Alicia didn't need to be able to read to make out the writing on the wall, but she couldn't leave and not know what had happened when he went to the convent. She didn't want to have messed up this part of his life too.

So she lay on her bed and rang him again, and she even pulled the velvet rope and heard it ring in his room, but there would be no more games now.

Finally, late afternoon, he picked up.

'Pronto.'

'Dante, I am so sorry for the way I told you.'

He said nothing.

'You might not believe me, but I was going to ask to go to the village tomorrow. I just wanted your family dinner to be perfect, and then I was going to ask Reverend Mother what to do.'

'No need for that now. I've spoken with her.'

'I'm not allowed to ask, am I?'

Again he said nothing.

'Can I ask that you don't mess up tonight?'

'Do you really believe I'm thinking about some dinner?'

'I've known for ten years and you've known for less than ten hours. I know I've handled this badly, but please, *please* don't let me have messed up your new family, too.'

'Family?' She had no clue, and he didn't even know what to tell her. It was more messed up than she knew.

'Where are you?' he asked.

'At the airport,' she lied, for she couldn't yet bring herself to leave. 'You?'

'Driving.'

'The birds are very loud, then. Are you at the cemetery?'

No, for he knew there was no solace there. He was at the river, which was as dry as he felt, but remembering what Reverend Mother had said about how sharp Alicia was did make him half smile, then it faded.

'You cared for him, didn't you?'

'I did. And I'm sorry I couldn't, well...'

'You're not expected to raise every Schininà.'

'Dante, your baby was the easy part in the end. It was the other part... I wasn't crazy about his father.'

'I gathered that this morning.'

Even now he didn't get she meant Guido rather than him, or perhaps it was time to simply accept he just didn't want her love. 'Dante, I was going to marry someone because I was told to. If I had done it I might have been a bit like Giustina when it came to Guido.'

Now he smiled. 'You did the right thing,' he said. 'Well, that part at least.'

'Dante, you were right. I did stop defending you.'

'Leave it.'

'No, I was upset when we stopped holding hands. I stuffed my bra, I flirted, I tried. And I thought there was something ugly about me because you never once... I was very jealous.'

'I'm going to go,' he said, ending the call.

He would write to her, Dante decided. Nicely, kindly, when he had sorted his head out, and tell her properly that it had all been him and not her.

Then he remembered that she couldn't read.

What wasn't made up or a lie?

Alicia's suspicious mind had got one thing right at least, and maybe possibly two—she had known for ten years, and for him it wasn't even ten hours.

Maybe tonight was not the best time to confront his father.

The thought of seeing his family was wearying, especially with what he now knew, and yet they were tied... contractually, at least.

Not for long.

Dinner, Dante decided, and then breakfast with Daddy Dearest tomorrow and a little talk about Roberto then.

It should be easier to think with her gone—except he kept thinking of them running through the rushes and him dropping her hand. And the wasted guilt because all the time she'd been trying it on.

They would talk, he decided, when his head was clearer.

He called the restaurant to say he was running late and returned home and let himself in—only to be reminded again that Alicia Domenica had lied.

'You are kidding me?'

She sat huddled in her gold robe with heated rollers in her hair, and the clock nudged past seven when he walked through the door.

'I'm leaving tomorrow,' she told him. 'I am.'

'Fine,' he clipped. 'Don't ask,' Dante warned, as he dropped his keys and headed straight for his chambers.

She followed him in but he ignored her—simply stripped off, because he honestly felt as if he'd spent the day digging up dead bodies by hand. He would like ten years to think about today; instead, she stood uninvited in his bedroom again.

'That's not fair,' she said.

'Why have you got rollers in your hair?'

'In case you still want to go to dinner. I know I promised not to mention it, and if you don't want me to come that's fine. Either way, I put out your suit.'

'I can dress myself.'

He stepped into the shower and started soaping up. And he couldn't believe she came and sat on the edge of the bath.

'Are you going to see your son?'

He shot her such a look. 'I don't know. I stopped by the House of No Bees rather than think of it.'

He knew what she and Beatrice had called it.

Should he tell her now that Roberto wasn't his?

Light another fuse before he spoke with his father?

He came out and whipped up a towel, then lathered up his face to shave.

He glanced at her in the mirror as he shaved. 'I spoke with Reverend Mother. I'll tell you more when I'm ready, but I am not in a very good mood right now, and I want ten minutes' peace before I meet the people who call themselves my family.'

And then she surprised him.

'Do you want to have cocktails and casual sex?'

'You don't do that.'

'I think I might like to tonight. Unless you really have been at the House of—'

'Alicia,' he warned. 'I'm not in the mood to joke. And if you are coming, I suggest you take out your rollers.'

'We're going?'

She was so delighted, and in this odd mood he couldn't even begin to read her.

'It's dinner, Alicia.'

'I know!'

'It will be hell.'

'I don't care.'

'I shall not wait one second for you to be ready. Clear?'

Alicia was no longer waiting.

It would be their last night, she knew it for sure, and she was so sick of her own needy self.

She pulled out her giant rollers and shook out her hair, then picked up her 'meet the family' dress.

It was beautiful.

Demure.

Elegant.

She pulled her thick curls together to swirl them into a knot and clip it with black pearls, and then looked out to the harbour and stood watching the near full moon rise above the water—a reminder of the one night she had asked for…a night just for her.

When she recalled it later she wanted her full moon night with Dante to be the night she wore silver. It felt cool, and as she tucked her breasts into the little shelf and turned and looked at her almost bare back she decided it might be more modest to wear her hair down.

She slipped on velvet heels and picked up her tiny little evening purse. Taking out her little compact mirror, she tackled her eye make-up.

She drove him crazy.

The way she'd stood watching him shower, the way she'd hurled questions as he shaved. The way, when she had got things so wrong, she was so blindly determined she was right.

He did not want to care in the way that he did.

About any of them.

Yet, as much as he didn't want her to come to dinner, he knew it would be better to have her there.

He suited up with the same enthusiasm that he would for a funeral, then combed back his hair and splashed cologne.

Tonight was the night he had waited for.

Soon he would be free of the lot of them, and tomorrow he would finally be able to breathe.

The king would be in his castle and very happily alone.

'Alicia!' he called.

'One minute,' she said as she decided against eyeliner, opted for a quick dash of mascara.

'No minutes!' he said.

A slick of lipstick and she popped her compact into her purse and stepped out to the sight of Dante in a suit and a tie—and a scowl.

'Is it too much?' she asked.

'Do you like it?' he asked.

'I love it.'

'That's good, then, because there isn't time for you to change. We need to get going.'

He gave her nothing.

Not a compliment, nor his thoughts.

They strolled through magical lanes so ancient, so beautiful, it felt as if they had entered a portal into another world.

As he guided her across an uneven kerb she acknowledged that heels really were an unwise choice.

But she felt unwise tonight.

She felt his hand on her arm, and the entire problem for Alicia was in that moment—that gesture. His reluctant arm was bliss.

'Grazie, caro mio,' she purred, thanking 'her darling' with a sarcastic edge. 'You haven't said anything about my dress.'

'Why would I?'

'At least pretend to be romantic.'

'We're not pretending yet.'

'Please tell me what was said today,' Alicia said. 'At least tell me if Reverend Mother mentioned Beatrice.'

'Not really.'

'Did she mention me?'

'I was actually there about *me*, Alicia.'

God, she felt shallow. 'I'm nervous,' she admitted.

'About what?'

'I've never been to a family dinner before.'

Stop melting me, Dante thought. *Leave me the hell alone.*

Except he turned her to face him.

'You're better than the lot of them,' he told her. 'Just relax.'

'I'll try.' She gave him a half-smile. 'If we were real partners I'd be terrified, so...' She took a breath. 'We caught up in Milan, and we...'

'Come on,' he said, taking her arm. 'Let's just wing it.'

Her dress was not too much. She would have looked dowdy in the sensible choice, Alicia knew, for the dress was just stunning and people here were dressed more for a ball than for dinner.

There was music, and a dance floor, and the hum of conversation—and Alicia knew, straight away, who was his family.

They were just as beautiful as he was.

'This is Alicia,' he introduced her.

'How lovely to meet you, Alicia,' said Vincenzo Ricci—and, gosh, his father was handsome and, yes, he had the same lethal charm, though he was more open and expressive than Dante.

'So sorry we're late,' she said, appalled, because she had never been late in her life.

'I don't blame Dante in the least,' he said, and he actually gave her waist a little squeeze as he kissed her cheeks.

Yikes.

'We've just ordered cocktails,' Vincenzo said, and raised the slim cocktail menu. 'Join us.'

'No cocktails for me.' Alicia smiled. 'I would just like water for now.'

Dante looked down at the cocktail menu and thought just how hard life must be for her, in so many different ways.

He knew her food order tonight already. Could see how it all had to be planned out. And it pulled at him in ways he did not want, for he did not want to care about her.

'Why don't we just have the house cocktail?' he said. 'They're a bit lethal, with Limoncello, vodka… God knows what else…'

'Okay. Yes, please.'

'So we finally get to meet you,' said Vincenzo Ricci. 'I can see why he's kept you hidden away.'

Was his father *flirting*?

'Sicilian?' Vincenzo checked with Alicia as their cocktails arrived, his head to one side.

'Yes,' she said.

'Dante said you met in Milan?'

'Yes,' Alicia agreed. 'I've been there for almost ten years now.'

'I'm trying to lure her back,' Dante said, clearly reminding her that this wasn't a real getting-to-know-you session.

'Yes, I'm more here than there these days.' She turned and smiled at him fondly, but he was already pushing his chair back.

'Excuse me a moment.'

She gripped his arm in a silent plea for him not to leave her with his family, but Dante ignored her and was gone.

Alicia took a breath and remembered to smile. Matteo was on his phone, to his father's clear annoyance, and Rosa sat looking beautiful, but very vacant.

Giustina was just staring at her, the new arrival, and Alicia dared not glance in the direction of his father.

She picked up the menu and pretended to read through it. She was still doing it when Dante returned. 'I think something plain,' she said, closing it. 'Just *spaghetti al sugo* for me,' she said.

The waiter came to give his recommendations and Giustina moved to wave him away, but Dante put a hand up. 'I want to hear.'

He nodded at the mention of swordfish, and Alicia perked up when the man recited a couple of vegetarian options.

'Oh...' She turned when the waiter mentioned that the *pasta con ricotta e pistacchi* was famous here, and it would seem that she didn't want the *sugo* after all, but the ricotta and pistachio pasta.

'That sounds nice,' she said, as if she'd been swayed. 'I think I will try that.'

And for the first time when she was out Alicia also ordered a starter because it was bliss to have the food described to her.

She had no idea it was on instruction from the man who sat beside her.

It was all very civil on the surface.

Dante asked if they were comfortable at the hotel.

'It's excellent,' Vincenzo said. 'You were right about this location...'

'It's not too late to get on board,' Giustina said. 'You said yourself that your residence would be an ideal location.'

'I don't think so,' Dante said.

'You're not getting attached to it, are you?' Vincenzo asked. 'Emotional investments are not wise ones.'

'Yes, you've told me many times.'

'Matteo,' Giustina said, and actually took the phone from his hand. 'We're talking about family business—pay attention.'

'Actually, we're not,' Dante corrected. 'We're talking about *my* business.'

'Dante's right,' Vincenzo said. 'Let's enjoy the night, and the beautiful company.' He raised a glass to Alicia.

Thankfully the starters were delivered then, and Alicia honestly didn't know if his father and his wife had heard the warning shots Dante had fired. They were eating, conversing, seemingly oblivious to the current beneath them.

Alicia couldn't ignore it, though, because Dante was not appeasing, he was almost confrontational, when this dinner was supposed to be about stepping back quietly.

'So, whereabouts in Sicily are you from?' Vincenzo asked her.

'The south,' Alicia said, trying to be suitably vague.

'Trebordi,' said Dante, clearly regretting telling her to white out the past.

Giustina addressed her for the first time. 'Where Dante was born?'

'Yes.' Alicia nodded, seeing now just how awkward it might make things and regretting their row and her impetuous self even more.

'We grew up in the same village,' Dante said as he took her hand and gave it a squeeze.

'Did you go to the same school?' Rosa actually asked a question.

'No,' Dante answered. 'Alicia went to the convent school.'

'Your family…?' Giustina gestured for her wine glass to be filled again. 'Are they still in the village?' She said it with a slight sniff.

Oh, yes, there was definitely a north-south divide with her; Dante was right. Alicia saw better now why he had suggested they say they'd met in Milan. It was easier to move them a few decades on, because the past was something she'd never been able to face before—though she was surprised to find it was easier now.

'I was raised by nuns…' Alicia said it out loud for the first time. 'I was left at the baby door of a convent.'

'Goodness,' Giustina said. 'Do you know who your parents are? I mean, do you have any idea…?'

Dante again answered. 'Actually, we just found out that we're not a legal couple. We're half-brother and sister—but don't tell anyone.'

'Dante!' Alicia laughed, and was grateful that he'd lightened the mood even with his own dark self. 'He's being ridiculous,' Alicia said. 'Yes, I have an idea who my parents are, but they don't want to meet me. They were young and it was before they were married.'

'So they've since married each other?'

'Giustina,' Dante cut in.

They made it to the main course without further incident, but Alicia was very aware of Giustina's shrewd eyes, and it soon became clear that she had a fascination with her husband's long-ago lover. For when her beautiful main course was almost entirely eaten Giustina again addressed Alicia.

'You must have known Dante's mother?'

The table fell very silent, and she felt Dante tense at the thought that his mother's name might be dragged through the mud again. God knew it had been done enough already in his life.

'A little,' Alicia said. 'She was very beautiful... I've always remembered that. And it was not just her looks—she was kind, too. She used to send me a parcel each month.'

'Did she work?' Giustina asked.

'I really can't remember...' Alicia frowned as if scouring her mind. 'Actually, now I think of it, we used to sell her produce in the convent shop. She kept bees, I think.'

She felt the squeeze of Dante's hand and saw the relief in Vincenzo.

But Giustina did not leave things there.

She really was not a gentle person.

'So how come you met up again after all these years?' Giustina asked. 'Did you get in touch because you read how well Dante was doing?'

It was just a little too close to the bone, for Alicia had done exactly that, and for the first time tonight she was lost for words.

'Thank God she did,' Dante said. 'I'd been looking for her for a very long time... We were friends as children.'

He put an arm around her shoulders and she wanted to lean her head on it. She wanted this to be real. She wanted this Dante to be real—or at least the one she carried now in her dreams.

'I used to call him Ragno,' Alicia said, 'because he was so tall and skinny. And then he broke my heart, because he got off with every girl in the village except for me. Well, in my jealous mind he did.'

She turned and looked at him then, as if she loved him—which, of course, she did. And because she was meant to be acting, she got the chance to speak her truth.

'I saw he was in Milan and I couldn't resist looking him up.' Her hand stroked his cheek. 'Who can blame me?'

And then, because she was Alicia, she took it too far, her lies blurring the truth, her wishes stronger than reality.

'I think his mother knew about us...' she said. 'She gave me a beautiful compact mirror for my eighteenth birthday.' She felt Dante still. 'I treasure it, and I carry it everywhere with me.'

He took her hand from his cheek and for the sake of their audience gave it a squeeze, but she felt his tight warning. And as the desserts were served he spoke into her ear. 'A little less syrup, Alicia.'

Giustina was now more curious about Alicia's parents.

'So you're saying they had you, and then went on to marry and have more children?'

'Giustina.' Dante looked over at her. 'Really?'

He knew Alicia would be upset, and perhaps biting her tongue—a very hard thing when you had Sicilian blood pumping through your veins. And it was he who turned and looked straight at the less than impartial Giustina.

'You never did tell me, Giustina...' Dante gave her a black smile. 'How did you meet my very rich father?'

She shot daggers back at him, and it was tense at the table as the affogato was served.

Before she poured her shot of coffee on her ice-cream, Alicia excused herself. 'So warm in here...'

Dante looked over to Giustina and his eyes fired a warning. 'Don't talk to her like that again.'

He got up and went out for air too—or rather went to join her.

'Sorry about that—she's a cow.'

'It's fine,' Alicia said, staring out at the night. 'And excuse my ramblings. You know me... I just can't help myself when I start.'

'Yes, well...tone it down.' He gave a wry laugh. 'Do you remember how you would say to the tourists that your parents died in a house fire?'

'Yes,' she said with a laugh.

There were some advantages to tonight being a ruse, she thought. Because if they were a real couple, it might be dreadfully awkward to tell him. But, given they weren't, what the hell?

'I can see where you got it from,' she said.

'Got what?'

'Your father has spent half the night flirting with me. He's insatiable. Please make sure I don't have to dance with him!'

'I promise.' Dante smiled. 'Every dance is for me.'

'Giustina really has it in for me.' She glanced back at the table. 'Or for you. I can't work it out.'

'She's cross. I think Giustina is starting to realise that her son might not be able to drag his eyes off his phone long enough to steer the ship away from the iceberg if I pull back from the business.'

'Are they in trouble?'

'No, but I do a lot. I have not been idle.'

'Can I say one thing?'

'Alicia, I don't want a lecture on family tonight, please.'

'No. I want to say I get it.'

'What?'

'You deserve to step away. I can see there are limits.'

'I wasn't expecting that.'

'Nor me,' she admitted. 'I'm going in,' Alicia said, and left him out on the terrace.

She sat with a vast brandy now the drinks were flowing, and saw there were some couples on the dance floor, dancing to the beautiful Italian music.

Matteo actually put down his phone and took Rosa to dance, and Vincenzo dragged a reluctant Giustina to the floor.

I want love, Alicia thought, as Dante walked towards the table. *And for too long I have been knocking on a closed door.*

She could do it no longer.

They would not make it through tomorrow.

So they only had this one night.

Her *almost* full moon night with Dante.

And she would enjoy every minute, and move with his body, and then her life would go on.

'Come on,' Dante said, and held out his hand.

He held her lightly and they danced their first and last dance. She even laid her head on his chest, but Alicia knew it wasn't real. Even as his fingers stroked her bare spine it was her body reacting rather than her heart.

'You're in an odd mood,' he said.

'I've had two cocktails and a brandy.'

'Guess what…' he said to her ear.

'I don't need to guess,' Alicia said, enjoying the turn-on and the thrum of their bodies and allowing herself no more than that.

But she had guessed wrong.

'Reverend Mother apologised,' he whispered, and she pulled her head back.

'She doesn't ever do that.'

'Twice. For not stepping in—not just for my mother, but also for me…'

Please don't make me cry tonight, Alicia thought. *I want to be wild and happy.*

'Did it help?'

'A bit,' he said.

'I am so glad.' She kissed him then. Maybe today hadn't been a complete train-wreck if he had got his apology.

'You don't want to know the reason for the other one?' he asked.

'I thought you said she'd apologised for both of you?'

'That was one apology,' Dante said. 'She also apologised for assuming that Roberto was mine.'

'Assuming…?'

'Like father, like son,' Dante said.

'I don't understand.'

'As I said—a romance of sorts. My father attended my mother's funeral from a distance. And perhaps stopped by the house.'

'Oh, God.' Alicia felt her eyes grow wide. 'There was a car…'

'I have another half-brother.' He gave her a very triumphant smile. 'I accept your apology.'

She was too Sicilian to give it meekly. 'What was I *supposed* to think, Dante?'

Old hurts rose like hot lava, but they were beaten by tears.

'Not here,' he said.

'He doesn't even look like you.' She looked across the dance floor to his father, who gave them a rather cheery wave.

'Sometimes you can see it. We have the same feet…'

'Oh, no…'

'Do you want tell Giustina, or shall I…?'

She was starting to cry.

'Stop it.' He pulled her into him. 'It's fine. I'm not saying anything. I think, though, it is time we said goodnight.'

They tripped home, holding hands.

'I was so jealous.'

'The baby was the image of me, apparently.'

'Are you angry?' she asked.

'Not with you,' he said.

'You are.'

'I'll get over it.'

'Can we go the long way?'

'In those heels?'

She tried, but she ended up with her shoes off and riding on his back, as if she was on a donkey.

This was the best of them, Alicia knew, and she would remember these moments from a distance, with fondness. She was not going to get upset tonight, because it had been such a hard day, and it was such a lovely almost full moon night.

'It's the best view,' she said.

'I don't know… I like the cliffs in Trebordi,' he said.

'Three cliffs,' Alicia said. 'Not now, but…'

She had two—Roberto was safe, Dante would be fine, and Beatrice…

'Thank you,' she said, turning towards him. 'I really mean it. I can't believe I have an investigator and everything…'

She smiled, because she didn't want to spoil tonight, and they kissed instead against the cold stone wall and she thought she might die there and then as his hands slid over silver.

He was really dreadful for her self-control, because he moved her into a dark archway and kissed her hard and deep, pressed against her.

It was better than anything she could imagine.

'Don't stop.' She was breathless. 'No one comes here at night…'

She was at his erection, and she made him laugh.

'There's a night tour,' he said.

'You're bad for me, Dante.' She smiled. 'Maybe we're bad for each other.'

Maybe not.

Soon he was climbing the stairs with her on his back, and she didn't feel heavy, and she was glimpsing little glimmers of possibility, like the stars that battled for attention beside an almost full moon.

Glimmers where there had been none.

'Whose room?' he asked as he put her down, all shining in silver in his lounge.

'Whoever gets naked and rings the bell first,' Alicia said.

She wanted to pull that rope just one time, and she knew she would win because she had on just a dress and no shoes or bra. Except she sat naked and alone on the pink bed for a moment, and felt both as happy and as sad as she knew how to be. So she took out her mirror and reminded herself that she would not be telling him that this was love.

He'd known her long enough.

Then she heard the bell.

'Merda!' It was Alicia who swore.

'Language!' he called from the other room.

And so she was off to the torture bed, and his arms, and she was so glad they'd waited, because he was able to take his time kissing every bit of her skin thoroughly.

She lay on her stomach as he kissed every rib and moved down her spine, where water had dripped that long-ago day, and she tried to fill in the lost years, and all the things she had never done.

'Turn over.'

And he kissed down her thighs to a place only he could be, and she was holding her breath so tight she thought she might faint.

He was impatient, and thorough, and then impatient again, and then he just burrowed in deeper.

Such an odd mood, Dante thought. Because he could feel her on the edge, not giving in to the bliss that was waiting.

He was also holding back—but for different reasons.

They were fighting an odd fight.

But he won, because he felt her let go of his hair, and then the shudder and the pulse on his lips.

'Dante…'

She wanted recovery, to somehow catch her breath, but he'd only given her a glimpse of what this day would be like, and there was none.

He was inside her and he was holding her arms up and they were locked in one another's eyes, and then, when she found herself near, he pulled out and turned her around.

'Dante…'

'Remember in the hut?'

'Yes.'

His hands were on her the small of her back, and then one slid round to her stomach and she felt it glide around her slick entrance. And then he slid in so deep that he hit her cervix with each thrust, and she didn't know how he couldn't want this for ever.

In the end it was Alicia who couldn't last.

She was still moaning as if someone had died when he came, and she heard the hollow shout she'd first heard in the river, and she felt all that power unleashed in her. And then a lovely calm and stillness descended, and she was glad she wasn't facing him because she was crying, and not just at the bliss of him.

He was more complicated than that.

And she was straightforward.

Wasn't she?

God, his bed was lovely, and as they lay together he told her something nice.

'A better finish to the day than the start.' He paused. 'Although I do like you cross.' He smiled at her. 'I like you a lot of ways.'

'Not in the ways I want, though.'

'Alicia, come on…let's just breathe. We're friends again. "Lovers", as you call it.'

There wasn't any time left for breathing, and she was aware of that. But she had made a promise to herself on this long, lonely day, while waiting for him to call.

'We were lovers ten years ago.'

'Can we not have a decade gap between drinks in the future? Be regular lovers?'

'What does that mean?' Alicia asked. 'What does it mean to be your "regular lover"?'

His lack of reply meant she rolled on her side, but it was to a new bliss, because he was playing with her hair and it felt so nice.

'When I'm in Milan, or you're here, or…'

'And when I'm not in Milan or here?' she asked. 'What do you do when you can't sleep then?'

'I'm just saying let's take it slowly, see how we go. You make it so complicated.'

'No!' she told him so. 'I'm straightforward.'

'Straight to something that wakes us up all night and cries and smells. I'm just saying I want slow.'

'The answer is no.'

She stared at the waxing gibbous moon—almost full, and so beautiful—but there was a dark edge to the moon, and a darkness in Dante by her side—a man literally incapable of using the word *partner*. A man who refused even to put a toe in and test the faithful waters.

'I am too demanding to be your lover.'

'Oh, you're demanding,' he agreed, and got back to playing with her hair.

Did she tell him there had only ever been him? That she'd loved him for what felt like all her life? No, that would be by far too devoted for Dante.

It was the hardest thing, though.

To be loved so fiercely and then suddenly not.

To know that at a time not of her choosing she would be handed back her heart and would have to nurse it from broken to functioning.

'I'm going to speak to the investigator tomorrow afternoon,' Dante said. 'Do you want to come?'

'You would think there would be something by now. Some news,' Alicia said.

'Give them a chance. It's not the same…'

She could feel he was half asleep. 'Same as what?'

'Well, there are no trails. She didn't even have a phone.'

'I doubt she'd have answered if she did.'

'I mean phone records and tracking and all that. Bank records and stuff. They are looking.'

'I know. Will you tell your father about his son?'

'Doubt it,' he said. 'And I'm scared to do that DNA thing. I could have relations everywhere. Nightmare.'

They were so, so different.

She put her hand up and stopped him from playing with her hair, but he didn't mind a bit. He rolled over onto his stomach and went straight back to sleep—though she would hardly describe it as the sleep of the innocent.

Was he beautiful? Oh, yes.

Would she be lying here now if she hadn't sneaked in and stripped at his bedside? No.

And it was just her luck to love him.

She slipped out of bed, but there was no sulking, no storming off. He didn't even notice she'd gone.

A good thing—because right now Alicia would prefer to be alone.

CHAPTER FOURTEEN

'How come you went to your own suite?'

'I'm the perfect woman.' Alicia gave a tight smile. 'What time are you meeting your father?'

'Now.'

'How long do you think you'll be?'

'A couple of hours or ten minutes. Think about coming to see the investigator this afternoon, maybe? And we need to speak about that window.'

'What window?'

'We had unprotected sex yesterday.'

'Thank you for the reminder.'

He gave her a kiss as he left but Alicia pulled her head back.

'Ciao.' It was Alicia who said it this time.

'Ciao,' Dante said.

Clearly he did not feel the need to go scavenging for affection or a deeper kiss before he headed down to meet with his father.

It took more than ten minutes but less than two hours, and there would be no need to speak with his legal team.

The sun seemed so vivid, the bay so blue, and as he climbed the stairs all was right in the world.

Or about to be.

'Alicia!'

He called her name and was met with silence.

'Alicia?'

He met absence. The actual *feel* of real absence.

She had gone for a walk, Dante decided, or shopping. Yet he knew he lied to himself, only without the skill of Alicia, because he didn't believe it himself.

'Alicia!' he called a third time, even though he knew it was pointless, for her clothes were gone and the open doors meant not even the linger of her perfume remained.

And then he found out what it was like to have several worried calls go unanswered.

'Do you know where she went?' he asked the staff in a voice that didn't quite sound like his. But they didn't know and, no, Alicia had not used his driver.

She was sulking, Dante told himself. Because he'd suggested that they needed to take some precautions because they hadn't used protection and he wasn't on bended knee twenty-four hours in.

But he could feel an odd panic.

He had shielded himself from loss so fiercely that this frantic feeling was almost alien.

He caught sight of himself in the mirror, grey and sweating—and, yes, he looked as cold as if it were a winter's day.

'She's probably stormed off to a hotel,' he told the butler, but that was quite usual in Dante's life, and this didn't feel like the same.

'Don't worry,' his ancient maid said as she came in. 'She won't be far. She left her bank card—'

'Where?'

He went down the very narrow steps and knew exactly what he would find as he opened the drawer next to where her card lay.

She'd won.

And although he knew this wasn't really a game, Dante knew he'd lost.

'And she forgot her phone.' His maid was wheezing from her trips up and down the stairs.

'We need to go to the airport,' Dante told his driver, but

then wavered, because there were several ways to leave this island—three bridges, the ocean, and a whole lot of sky.

Think, he told himself, before he spun in any one of the directions she might have gone.

He was meant to know her best.

So he knew how much he'd hurt the person he cared about most in the world.

Ever.

She sat at the Fountain of Diana wearing a white muslin smock, with a flash of her red bra on show and her case beside her, and he knew to approach with gentle caution.

'Alicia?'

She looked up at him, eyes brimming with unshed tears. 'How was it with your father?' she asked.

'Let's not worry about that now.'

'But I do,' she said. 'Not about him, but his children. Including the giant one standing in front of me. Although maybe not any more.'

Dante sat beside her and Alicia was glad that he did, for it meant she didn't have to look at him as they said their last goodbyes.

'I hate this fountain,' she told him.

'I might soon,' Dante agreed. 'Please don't leave.'

'Why?' she sniped. 'Because you've got no one left now? Did you tell him about Roberto?'

'No,' he said. 'I told him I was going to be here more often, and that I was done with being his front man, and then we had a bizarre hour in which I gave my father a very stern lesson about contraception and how angry I am, and how he needs to lift his game fast. But we're still talking. Maybe.' He looked over to her. 'I've also been doing some thinking—'

'Dante,' she cut in. 'I've done a lot of thinking too.'

'That sounds ominous.'

'All those years, all those letters… Beatrice knew where to find me, but she chose not to.'

'You don't know that.' He was unsure what to say; he did not want to give false hope. 'I think Reverend Mother is being evasive. I'm sure there's more.'

'Of course there is. But if she's alive then she's a woman now. I've sat like some forlorn dog waiting. I've spent the last decade trying to find her…' She gave a shake of her head. 'I'm glad that you're beginning to sort things out with your family.'

He was silent.

'I'm glad you're not just walking away without a backward glance as you walked away from me,' Alicia said boldly. 'We had a whole childhood of memories and then that day as young adults—that one glorious day—and then you walked away.'

'I was twenty.'

'You're thirty now,' she said.

'And I'm asking you not to walk off.'

'No.' She could no longer hold it in. 'You had every means available and yet you never looked me up. If it wasn't for my actions we'd never have seen each other again… If I hadn't pursued things we'd never have met again. You'd have let me go like Beatrice did, like my parents did…' She shook her head. 'I am sick of chasing people…running after crumbs…' She was crying rivers and didn't even try to wipe them away. 'So, thank you for a wonderful weekend. We're done. I mean that.'

'No, you don't.'

'I do. I'm going to sell these clothes and these earrings and then I'm turning into a swan.'

'Well, they're not glass,' he told her, 'so get them properly valued before you put them online.'

'I shall—and I'm going to give this body to someone who craves it, and give this love to someone who wants it, or…'

'Or what?'

'I'm going to dress up in the silver dress and go to a bar and pick up a man…'

'Are you?'

Alicia nodded. 'I am going to have sex with a stranger.'

'You deserve to,' he said. 'I don't want to love you,' Dante said. 'Because you make me care and worry. I have guilt, and all the things I don't want to know, that I swore I had had a gutful of with my mother. But I do. And it's a different type of worry and caring. You're right. I never wanted to come back for you, but I could never let you go.'

'Oh, you say the nicest things now that I'm leaving…' she sneered. 'Last night you wanted to be nothing more than part-time lovers.'

'You were right—that would never work,' he dismissed. 'Can't blame me for trying, though.'

'Trying what?'

'Not to get hooked!' He was clearly being honest. 'But I am…probably always have been…'

'Oh, save your smooth talk for your international guests,' she said. 'Your *syrup*…' She threw back his word from last night.

'Alicia, I just froze for a moment last night. That compact mirror was from me.'

'No.' She would *not* let him rewrite things. She would *not* let him add to the fantasy of him she had carried for far too long. 'It was your mother's parcel. I know her writing.'

'Gold-plated tin, with a picture of *La Scapigliata*?' Dante said.

'Dishevelled?' Alicia frowned.

'It's the name of the portrait. I bought it for you.'

'No, you must have seen it when I took it out.'

Except mirrors still felt like a guilty pleasure, and she only checked her reflection in private.

'When would I have seen it?'

'Perhaps you went through my bag.'

'Why would I do that?'

He wouldn't, Alicia realised, because he wasn't interested enough in her to snoop, and she must never forget that fact.

'So, you gave me a mirror…' Her voice quavered. 'And

that's supposed to mean something? Make me believe you cared all these years?'

'I bought it in Rome because I wanted you to have something special for your birthday, but I almost didn't send it...'

'Why?'

'Because it might give you hope. I was worried you'd read too much into it,' Dante said. 'Because you might hitchhike to Rome and I didn't know how to take care of myself let alone you. Did you read the engraving?'

He watched her shrug, and it made him ache that she couldn't tell him why.

'You said last night that you carry it with you everywhere.'

'I only kept it because I thought it was from your mother.'

'Show me.'

Reluctantly she opened her bag and took out the little compact she had carried with her for a decade.

'This is a picture by Leonardo da Vinci,' he said. 'It's called...'

'La Scapigliata,' she snapped. 'You said. So you thought I was dishevelled?'

'We both were back then,' he said. 'Apparently the great man carried this portrait with him everywhere. It was never really finished as he would constantly add to it. Did you read the engraving? It's one of his quotes.'

'Dante, it was a gift from your mother ten years ago. I can't remember what it says.'

'Of course not,' he said, and took the mirror.

He swore that one day she would trust him enough to tell him that she could not read, but he would let her keep her secret until she chose to do so.

'It's almost gone,' Dante said, looking at it closely, pretending that he was struggling to make out the words. 'It's really faded but...' He paused before reading the words that felt as if they had been etched on his heart from the moment he had read them. '"L'arte non è mai finite, he ma solo abbandonata." Art is never finished, only abandoned.'

She looked far from impressed.

'So you sent a mirror reminding me that I was abandoned—and not just by my parents!' She let out a tense breath. 'Thanks a lot.'

'It's an unfinished portrait,' Dante said, recalling how he had felt on the day he had purchased it.

Twenty years old and wishing he had the courage to send it, while worrying if he should even spend this much, when surely the cash would be better used by his mother. At the time it had been the biggest purchase he had ever made. Wasted, almost. But then his mother had died and he had returned home, and he had slipped it into the package he had found and mailed it.

'I felt we were unfinished.'

'We slept together once.' She said the same as he had to her.

'I bought this before we slept together, Alicia.'

Now she turned and looked at him.

'I wanted to come back and I wanted to say yes when you suggested coming to Rome.'

'Yet you didn't.'

'I was homeless,' he said.

'Dante, you had an apartment a short time later. You had family and money—'

'Alicia.' He was very serious. 'You don't just wake up and life is better. At least that was what I thought,' he said. 'That morning in Milan was like a dream come true. I'd been trying to sort out my life, and I think I was trying to sort it out for you...'

'I don't want to hear it.'

'So why are you sitting here at the statue?'

'I was thinking of Beatrice.'

'No.'

'I was reminding myself how you used me, kissed me, just because Matteo was nearby.'

'You are such a liar, Alicia Domenica,' he accused with

a smile. 'You were waiting for me. And I am glad that you came to the fountain.'

Alicia nodded. 'Say what you have to, Dante.'

'Can we go back to mine?'

'No. We can talk here.'

'There are a lot of people.'

'Say what you have to here.'

She wasn't so bold when he did.

'Have you slept with anyone other than me?'

'You have no right to ask that!'

'I actually don't want to know the answer,' he admitted. 'Or I didn't. I am messed up,' he said. 'Not as messed up as I was, though, believe me. Alicia, do you know why I dropped your hand that day? Because I was full of raging hormones and I didn't understand that that was normal.'

She frowned.

'I hate it that I made you feel ugly when you were flirting with me. And do you know what else I hated?'

'What?'

'When you listened to all those rumours and I asked you not to. When you insinuated I was paying you or using you. Alicia, I watched men walk away from my mother without a glance; I thought that was normal. I heard what happened in her room and I hated it. I couldn't stand anyone to touch me, but I loved holding your hand. Until things changed—because we changed.'

Alicia swallowed.

'You asked if I would want to know if I had a child…'

'You said no…'

'Because I thought you were asking about your parents. I was so cruel, because I knew that unless it was with you there was no baby.'

'I'm sorry,' she said. 'They said it was a girl from the house…'

'I can't even drive past it, let alone get it up in there! Alicia, when I brought you here the other day I was kissing you, and then I backed out of telling you.'

'Telling me what.'

'You weren't the only virgin that day.' He waved at the lady who was sitting near them and had turned around. 'There was no one before you, and for long while after, and then I went a bit wild… Quite a bit.'

'Dante, I thought you knew everything.'

'God, no. I'm better with my fingers now, I hope.'

'I only know you.'

'I understand that now.' The responsibility of love no longer daunted him, it was losing it that terrified. 'Will you come back with me, please? I have something to show you.'

'I don't know.'

'Come on.'

He took her hand and led her the gentler way to his residence—and yet it felt steeper and more risky than the stairs. He led her back to his chambers and the bed she had left. She stood next to it as he went to a dresser.

'Come here.'

He opened up a small, heavy wooden box, and inside were two things that perhaps mattered to him more than anything else—two dried flowers. One peony, the other a chrysanthemum…his and hers.

'From your mother's grave?' Alicia said.

'I don't often think of that when I look at them,' he said. 'Maybe sometimes. But mostly I think of you…'

She looked in the box and there was a photo of him with his mother.

'It's the only one I have her. I swear I don't have mummy issues, but I did speak to Reverend Mother and she said I need to think of one nice thing to help change my memories of her. I am so glad she sent you those parcels, as odd as that was, because it meant you kept that mirror. I think if you had known it was from me then you might have tossed it away.'

It terrified her to think of it.

'We'll take it slowly,' she said.

'No need now,' he said. 'As I mentioned, I've been sorting myself out, quitting the casinos and stuff, and I think I was working my way back to you. I have my nice thing to think of when I think of my mother and I have peace. But I'd have more peace with you.'

'I would too.'

'Aren't you going to look at the photo?'

'Am I in it?' She smiled, but she was teary as she looked at the image.

'No, just me.'

It was very small and faded, his mother so beautiful and Dante just a child. As she lifted it, more curious than someone who didn't love another should be, her breath caught at what lay beneath.

There, nestled in velvet, was the earring she had lost so many years ago. The sliver of gold she had lost along with her virginity and also her heart.

'You found it.'

'I didn't *find* it,' Dante said. 'It was hooked in the lining of my jacket and clung on all the way back to Rome…'

She was crying and smiling as she picked up the earring and held it.

'You kept the other one?' He answered his own question almost before he'd finished asking it. 'It's in your bag, isn't it?'

'Yes.'

'Go and get it.'

Alicia was shaking as she took out the earring she had carried with her since that day.

It was Dante who unknotted her fingers from around it, and returned it to its other half.

'I will love you for ever,' Dante said as he gently replaced the hoops in her ears. 'You can believe me or not, and we can argue at length in the years to come, but I shall prove it, and I shall help you find Beatrice.' He had given it some thought. 'I know she loved you.'

'How?'

'Because it's impossible to stop.' He looked right at her. 'We'll get married…'

'You have to ask me first,' she reminded him. 'On bended knee.'

'Alicia…we both know your answer.' He wasn't at all romantic, but Dante sighed and got down on bended knee. 'Alicia, will you marry me?'

'On one condition.'

He gave a slightly incredulous smile, because he knew he had this in the bag. For the first time ever Dante was certain in his love. 'What's your one condition, Alicia? Ten babies?'

'That this goes in the box.' She put her hand back in her bag and took out a ferry ticket.

'Salerno?' He went a bit grey. It was thirteen hours away!

'I paid cash, too.'

'I taught you too well. Alicia, I don't need reminders of how close I came to losing you.' He looked at it. 'I would have found you.'

'Maybe.'

He sighed, but as he went to put it in the box Alicia took it from his hand. 'No need.'

'Just letting me know I have to behave?'

He knew her so well. 'I would love nothing more than to marry you, Dante.'

He took her hand and they both looked at their entwined fingers. For Alicia, her hand had always felt empty without his. 'Back together,' she said.

'For ever.' He looked at Alicia and told her a truth. 'The woman of mystery is you, Alicia.'

'Gosh, no… I'm really very simple…'

'No, no,' he said. 'The mystery is how through it all you loved me. Now we make up for lost time.'

A power was unleashed then, and he was kissing her.

'We have a lot to make up for,' Alicia said as he kissed her. 'Ten years…'

'You were my first, and I promise you this—you will be my last.'

He kindly omitted the wild in-between years as he lowered her to the bed.

She looked up at him and told him a truth of her own. 'You are my always.'

EPILOGUE

ALICIA HAD FALLEN in love with Dante as he'd walked down this very aisle.

Not towards *her*, though.

This time things were very different.

She stood in the vestibule with Reverend Mother by her side and a priest who was willing to break a little with tradition.

Cars lined the street, for Alicia and Dante were back and all were curious.

Alicia didn't notice them, though.

She stood in a very simple dress in the palest green and held a bunch of *pomelia*, or frangipini as they were known in other parts of the world. Here, though, the white and lemon fragrant blooms were the flowers of Sicily.

'Are you nervous?' Reverend Mother asked.

'No,' Alicia said, even though the *pomelia* shook as if she was. She was reminded of the time she had stood at the door to his suite. 'I am impatient, I think…'

That was the better word.

Impatient to see him and to be with him.

Now Alicia stepped out of the vestibule and into the light of the church, which was bright and clear through the windows.

Dante stood beside Gino. He trusted him.

His family were there too, smiling as she approached.

There was just one person missing…

The congregation was minus that one blonde head she felt she would search for for ever.

But today she at least was home.

Now she walked towards her future husband.

Her hair was up and she wore the gold hoops in her ears. Not just because they were from her parents, but because Dante had carried one half of the pair all these years.

'You look so beautiful,' he said when she reached his side.

'So do you.'

He wore a suit so immaculate, but it was the scent of him that she breathed in.

'Are you nervous?' she asked.

'No.' He smiled, then leant closer. 'Though I think my father is at being here...'

He made her laugh.

And, while it was a very traditional wedding, for a rather untraditional man, he knew certain things. Just before she handed her bouquet to Reverend Mother Dante stroked a waxy petal.

'Flower of Sicilia.'

'Yes.'

The flowers would be taken to the cemetery later, but first, before they had even started, he removed one perfect bloom and added it to his lapel.

Alicia knew it was going to be added to a certain box he kept.

Then the service was underway, their hands held together as the priest offered a card from which they could recite their vows...

'Io, Dante, ti prendo... Alicia.'

His voice was deep and confident as he told her he took her as his wife and promised to always be faithful, in joy and pain, health and sickness, and Alicia's tears started to fall when he told her he would love and honour her every day for the rest of her life.

'E di amarti e onorarti tutti i giorni della mia vita,' Dante finished.

And now it was Alicia's turn, and she took a very deep breath. *'Io, Alicia...'*

She looked down at their hands as she wavered, but not for the reasons anyone might think.

'Dante,' Alicia whispered. 'I can't read.' She dared not look up.

'The priest will recite the words...'

'No, I just don't want us to go into this with secrets.'

He really did hold hands so nicely, for he held hers so steady, and his mouth was so close to her ear, the congregation all wondered what on earth they were discussing.

'I think that after all the trouble I've given you, you deserve a few secrets,' Dante said. 'Anyway, I think you might already know this part off by heart...'

'Yes,' she admitted with a half-laugh.

'Then go ahead and tell me again that you will love me for the rest of my life.'

Her voice was crystal-clear.

Because it was a relief, in fact, to declare the truth.

Alicia loved Dante.

No secrets now.

* * * * *

CINDERELLA'S INVITATION TO GREECE

MELANIE MILBURNE

MILLS & BOON

To Polly, my gorgeous miniature poodle,
who crossed the rainbow bridge recently.

You were the most amazing dog. Always submissive,
always sweet and loving, a wonderful mother to Lily
and adoring grandmother to the late Gonzo. And an
especially fabulous granny to your human grandkids!

I wrote 90-plus books
with you lying on your bed next to my desk.
You are greatly missed.

CHAPTER ONE

RUBY PENNINGTON DROVE up the long hedgerow-lined driveway of Rothwell Park with a flutter of moth wings in her belly. Coming 'home' to the grand Yorkshire moors estate always triggered a mixture of emotions. Never more so than when she knew Lucas Rothwell was in residence. And, as much as she longed to catch up with her grandmother over the long weekend, it was Lucas she really needed to see.

Thick, bruised-looking clouds scudded across the sky, with the sun appearing weakly between them again and again, as if still deciding whether to call it quits for the day. In the distance, rain was sweeping in from the moors in slanted grey sheets, and the wind was whistling and howling like a siren announcing impending doom.

Ruby brought her car to a stop near the old stables and turned off the engine.

Don't be nervous. Don't be nervous. Don't be nervous.

Her mentally chanted pep talk was falling seriously short. The moth wings in her belly had turned into bats. Hundreds of frantically flapping bats. It was impossible not to be a little jittery around Lucas Rothwell. How long had it been since she'd seen him face to face? Years. She never usually came home unless she knew he wasn't there.

But this time was different.

She *had* to see him.

As soon as Ruby got out of the car the biting wind whipped her hair around her face and needles of ice pricked her skin. Just as well the wild and capricious weather of the Yorkshire moors was exactly what her American celebrity client wanted for her wedding. It would be the highest profile wedding Ruby had done so far, and she owed it to her best friends and business partners, Harper and Aerin, to secure this venue. Their business, Happy Ever After Weddings, was making good progress, but this wedding would lift their profile way more than they could have dreamed possible when they'd first brainstormed a business plan on the back of a napkin in their favourite coffee shop.

Ruby brushed her hair away with her hand and walked towards the imposing front entrance of the castle. The centuries-old estate was a spectacular setting for a fairy tale wedding. The gothic-style castle with its multiple turrets and grandly appointed wings could house numerous guests, and the industrial-sized kitchen was perfect for catering for a crowd.

Pulling off this celebrity wedding gig would be her way of proving she had what it took to rise above her hardscrabble beginnings and being viewed as nothing more than the unwanted kid of a drug addict. Ruby didn't allow herself to think of failing once she set out to do something. Failure had been modelled to her by her mother, and Ruby was determined not to follow her example. Besides, her friends and business partners were relying on her.

And when people relied on her she delivered.

Before Ruby could put her key in the lock, the door opened a crack.

'Ruby, lass, what you are you doing here?' Her grandmother's shocked expression wasn't exactly the welcome Ruby was expecting. It had been months since she'd been to Rothwell Park. And, although her gran wasn't the overly effusive sort, surely she could summon up a teensy bit of enthusiasm?

'I told you weeks ago I'd be here for the Bank Holiday weekend.'

Her grandmother cast a furtive glance over her shoulder and then, keeping the front door only just ajar, whispered, 'Now's not a good time. The master's here and he doesn't want visitors.'

Ruby mentally rolled her eyes at her grandmother's old-fashioned habit of referring to Lucas Rothwell as 'the master'. Clearly her gran had been watching too many period dramas. And as for Lucas being in residence—that was the whole reason for Ruby's visit. Her gran had mentioned a few weeks ago about his planning to be in Yorkshire this weekend, after spending months flitting between Greece and Italy for work. Ruby wouldn't have travelled all this way from London if he wasn't going to be home.

'Why? Has he got one of his supermodel girlfriends here?'

It wouldn't be the first time Ruby had come across Lucas entertaining one of his glamorous partners. She had spent her childhood and adolescence pretending not to notice his brooding good looks and the way his lovers gazed up at him adoringly. She had pretended not to be jealous that he never looked at her the way he looked at those beautiful women. But then, as the homeless ten-year-old waif who had come to live with her housekeeper grandmother after the imprisonment of her mother, Ruby had been practically invisible to him.

Her grandmother pursed her lips, but still kept the door half closed. 'He's alone, but—'

'Great—because he's the one I really need to see.' Ruby smiled and, pushing the door open a little further, bent down to give her gran a smacking kiss on the cheek. 'Not that it isn't always lovely to see you,' she added.

'Get away with you, child.'

Her gran brushed Ruby away as if she was an annoying insect but there was no malice in it. After a rough upbringing herself, her gran had trouble showing and receiving affection, and even while Ruby had longed for more kisses and cuddles growing up, she didn't feel any less loved. Her gran had taken her in and raised her, and for that she would be for ever grateful. Rothwell Park had been the first stable home she had experienced. The castle and its grounds had provided her with security and shelter, which had been the complete opposite of the chaos of moving from one flea-infested bedsit to another while her mother tried to outrun her debts.

Ruby stepped past to enter the castle and her grandmother closed the door behind her with a soft click, her expression still troubled. 'I shouldn't have mentioned he'd be home this weekend.'

Her gran's stage whisper echoed eerily through the large entrance hall and made the fine hairs on the back of Ruby's neck stand up at the roots.

'He expressly told me to keep out all visitors.'

'I'm hardly a visitor.'

Her gran wrung her hands in an agitated manner, her eyes flicking towards the grand staircase as if she was expecting to see Lucas come striding down to fire her on the spot for disobeying his orders.

'You can't stay. He won't allow it.'

Ruby scrunched up her face in scorn. 'Oh, don't be so dramatic, Gran. Of course he'll allow it. This was my home for years. Besides, I have important business to discuss with him. Where is he?'

Her gran's throat moved up and down over a convulsive swallow. 'The library. I was about to take his cup of tea up to him. But—'

'I'll do it for you.'

Why Lucas couldn't fetch his own cup of tea was not worth arguing about with her gran. Beatrice Pennington was an old-school housekeeper. The upstairs and downstairs divide had never been breached in the whole time Ruby had lived with her grandmother.

Lucas's parents, Claudia and Lionel, had occasionally invited her and her gran to join them for Christmas and other gatherings, but Beatrice had been adamant about keeping the distinction of employer and employee in place. Ruby had quietly and covertly rebelled by finding a hideout position, from which to observe the grand and often raucous dinner parties Claudia and Lionel had hosted. The Rothwells had lived in a completely different world from the one she had been born into.

She'd been endlessly fascinated by their glamorous, exciting whirl of wealth and flamboyance and over-the-top decadence.

Ruby couldn't help noticing her gran wincing as she prepared the tea tray. 'Have you hurt your arm?' she asked. 'Here, let me look at you.'

'It's nothing.'

Ruby took the kettle out of her grandmother's hand and set it back on the bench. She turned her gran's wrist over and saw the angry red welt of a recent burn. The skin was raw and weeping, the edges a purply-red that hinted at a possible infection. 'Gran, that needs dress-ing. It looks like it's getting—'

Her grandmother pulled her wrist out of Ruby's hold. 'Stop fussing, lass. I've had worse in my time.'

'Maybe, but you're older now, and wound infections can turn nasty in a blink. You really should see a doc-tor. You might need a skin graft or something. I can take you after I've spoken to—'

'I don't need a doctor,' her gran said with a deter-mined edge to her voice. 'Now, take that tea up to the master before it gets stone-cold.'

Ruby shook her head in frustration, and then glanced at the tea tray. 'Oh, yum, parkin. I haven't had that in months.' She reached for a second cup and plate, and placed them on the tray next to the others.

Her gran looked aghast. 'What are you doing?'

'I'm going to have afternoon tea with Lucas.'

'You'll have me fired, that's what.' Her gran's tone was gruff, but her expression was set in deep trench lines of worry.

Ruby scooped up the tray. 'You know, you really

should think about retiring. This place is too big for you now, and you're not getting any younger.'

'I'll retire when I'm good and ready and not a moment before.'

Ruby knew better than to argue with her gran in one of her mulish moods. But that was another conversation she would have to have with Lucas Rothwell—about her gran's retirement.

'I'll help you with dinner after I've spoken to Lucas.'

The library was on the ground floor, several hundred metres from the kitchen, which only reinforced Ruby's concerns about her gran's increasing age and frailty. The harsh Yorkshire winters would be hard on her gran with her aching joints. How long did Lucas Rothwell expect her grandmother to wait on him hand and foot? Even though he spent less time at Rothwell Park than he had previously, it was ridiculous to expect a woman nudging eighty to remain in domestic service without help.

It was clear the castle was not being cleaned the way it used to be. Dust bunnies were in their dozens along the corridors, and cobwebs hung like lacework from the wall lights, as well as from the chandeliers. It gave the castle a ghostly atmosphere that was a little creepy to say the least. Surely Lucas could afford a team of people to run his damn castle. There were three gardeners, for God's sake. He had made a fortune as a landscape architect, working on massive projects all over Europe. Why not have three housekeepers?

There was a service lift to the upper storeys of the castle, but that was no help with the long corridors and galleries in each commodious wing. The library was in a wing all of its own, overlooking the rolling moors in the distance, divided here and there by dry stone walls and hedgerows. The door was closed, so Ruby placed the tray on a nearby hall table and then gave the door a light knock with her bent knuckles. The *tap-tap-tap* sound echoed hauntingly along the wide corridor.

'Come in.'

The deep burr of Lucas Rothwell's voice sent a light shiver along the flesh of Ruby's arms and set those bats' wings in her belly flapping again. He could be intimidating at times, but she was no longer a timid child. She was a proud and successful businesswoman, and she had an important business proposition to discuss. She would not be bashful around him now. She would be brusque and businesslike.

Game face on, Ruby turned the door handle and then picked up the tray and nudged the door further open in order to enter the library. But something stopped her going any further. The room—dark at the best of times, with all that ancient woodwork and the shelves stacked with valuable old books—was cast in long ghostly shadows.

Lucas was sitting with his back to her in one of the two wing chairs set in front of a quartet of tall narrow windows, situated between sections of the floor-to-ceiling bookshelves. The sky outside had clouded over even more since her arrival—it was now a gunmetal-grey—and specks of rain hit the windows, pecking at the glass like tiny invisible beaks.

'Who is it?' Lucas's voice sharpened and he rose

from the chair and turned to face where Ruby was standing in the doorway.

He was dressed in a black rollneck jumper and black trousers that made him seem even taller than his impressive six foot three. And he was wearing sunglasses, the aviator sort, which were as effective as a *Keep Out* sign. He cocked his head, his nostrils flaring slightly, like a wolf trying to pick up a new scent. *Her* scent.

The thought sent another shiver coursing over her flesh and a warm blush over her cheeks. If only she didn't blush so easily around him. What was it about Lucas Rothwell that made her feel like a gauche teenager instead of a fully grown adult?

The Embarrassing Incident—Ruby always capitalised it in her head—when she was sixteen was partly to blame. More than partly, if she was honest. Whenever she was in his presence—which was rare these days, thank God—she couldn't help but think of the clumsy, tipsy pass she'd made at him at one of the Rothwell parties she had sneaked into. And the stern dressing-down he'd given her that had rung in her ears for hours afterwards.

Eleven years had passed since that cringeworthy night, but it was as fresh in her mind as if it had happened yesterday. But she would *not* let it get in the way of achieving her goal. Harper and Aerin were relying on her to secure Rothwell Park as a wedding venue for Delphine Rainbird, a famous American actor, who was marrying her bodyguard, Miguel Morales. The exposure for their wedding business would be fantastic, let alone the amount of money Delphine was willing to pay

to have her fairy tale wedding in a castle on the wind-
swept moors of Yorkshire.

'If you'd turn a light on or take those sunglasses off,
you'd see it's me.' Ruby carried the tray over to the table
next to the wing chair he had just vacated. 'Why are you
wearing them inside on a day like today? There's not exactly blinding sunshine coming through the windows.'

There was a beat or two of silence before he answered in a hollow tone. 'Headache.'

'Oh, sorry. I'll try not to rattle the cups too loudly.'
She proceeded to pour the tea into the two cups, and
the *glug-glug-glug* sound in the silence was as loud as
a waterfall.

'What are you doing?' His voice contained a note or
two of irritation and his eyebrows were drawn together,
his mouth pulled into a tight line. He remained standing in a stiff and guarded posture that was more than
a little off-putting. But Ruby was not going to waste
the opportunity to spend some time alone with him to
present her proposal.

'I'm having afternoon tea with you. Anyway, you
can't possibly eat all that parkin on your own.'

'Take it away. All of it. And close the door on your
way out.' He turned his back on her and stood staring
out of the rain-spattered windows, his hands thrust deep
into the pockets of his trousers.

Ruby let out a long sigh. 'Look, I know headaches
can make the most even-tempered person a little irri-
table, but I've come a long way and I'd like to talk to
you about something. Something important.'

'Now's not a good time.'

'When would be a good time?'

There was another cavernous silence. The old book-shelves made a creaking sound, and the howling wind outside whipped up a few stray leaves on the ground and sent them past the windows in a whirligig.

Lucas finally released a long, ragged sigh and then lifted one of his hands out of his trouser pocket to rake it through his black hair, the tracks of his fingers leaving deep grooves in the thick strands.

'Is it about your grandmother?'

The quality of his tone had changed, the sharp edges softening slightly. He remained with his back to her, and the broadness of his shoulders and his strong spine tapering down to lean hips stirred a flicker of female awareness in her body. An awareness she didn't want to acknowledge, even to herself. Men like Lucas Roth-well were way out of her league. He only dated super-models—not homely, girl-next-door-types with freckles and acne scars.

'Partly, yes.' Ruby figured discussing her gran would at least give her a good lead-in to her business proposal.

Lucas turned from the window and reached out with one of his hands for the back of the wing chair, lowering himself into it. He stretched his long legs out, crossing his feet at the ankles. His pose was casual, but she sensed a coiled tension in him. Was it because of his headache? She couldn't remember him ever being ill. Was it a tension headache or a full-blown migraine? She had heard migraines made bright light unbearable to the sufferer and often caused vision disturbance. No wonder he was wearing sunglasses inside.

'You can pour.' He nodded in the direction of the tea tray.

If it hadn't been for his headache Ruby would have insisted he say please. While Lucas was taciturn and abrupt at the best of times, he was not normally flat-out rude. Well, not unless she was tipsy and begging him to kiss her. *Argh.* Why couldn't she blot out that wretched moment from her memory for good? On that occasion he had been brutally rude. And from that day her teenage crush had switched to a blistering loathing.

She'd avoided him for months after that, leaving a room as soon as she found him in it, or taking long, arduous detours across the moors if ever she saw him on one of her walks. By the time she was eighteen, she'd left to find work in London, only coming back to see her grandmother two or three times a year. Most of the time when she saw Lucas now he was in a gossip magazine, with yet another stunning woman draped over one of his arms. His success as an award-winning landscape architect saw him travelling the world for his high-end clients. He only visited Rothwell Park intermittently now, which meant she had to make the most of this time with him.

Ruby poured tea into the two cups. 'Do you still take it black, no sugar?'

'Yes.'

She handed him the cup, but his fingers fumbled against the saucer, which made some of the tea slosh over the side of the cup. He let out a curt swear-word, not quite under his breath, and quickly steadied the cup by holding his hand over the top.

'Sorry. Did it burn you?' he asked.

Ruby took her cup of tea and sat on the other wing

chair. 'No, but speaking of burns… Have you seen the scald mark on my gran's wrist?'

Even though he was still wearing his aviator glasses she could see the lines of a frown form on his forehead. 'No. Is it bad?'

'I think she should see a doctor to have it properly assessed. I'm worried it might need a skin graft. But you know what she's like about seeking medical attention.'

'I do know,' Lucas said, his frown deepening into a two-pleat groove visible above the silver frames of his sunglasses.

'You can take a look at it and see for yourself. Maybe she'll listen to you rather than me.'

A flicker of tension flashed across his features. 'I have no experience with burns. But there's a first aid kit in the downstairs bathroom. A medical friend of mine put it together a while back. Feel free to help yourself.'

'Thank you. I'll see what I can do.' Ruby eyed the delicious parkin on the tray between them and her stomach gave an audible growl of hunger. 'Would you like some of Gran's parkin?'

'No, thank you. But you go ahead.'

Ruby took a slice of the rich black treacle, brown sugar and ginger treat and placed it on a plate. But then, suddenly self-conscious about eating in front of him, especially as he wasn't indulging, she put the plate to one side.

He frowned again. 'What's wrong?'

'I'll save it for later.'

He made a soft sound of impatience and placed his cup back on the table. 'Don't be ridiculous. Eat it. Isn't it your favourite?'

'Yes, and that's why I'd better not eat it. I won't be able to stop at one slice.'

One side of his mouth lifted in an indulgent-looking half-smile. It took years off his face and made him seem less brooding and intimidating. 'I thought you'd learned your lesson about overindulging?'

There was a mocking note in his tone that made her squirm in her chair. Ruby could feel a hot blush crawling over her cheeks and buried her face in her teacup, taking a sip or two before changing the subject.

'I have a favour to ask.'

She put the cup and saucer down, and was annoyed she couldn't control the tiny rattle of crockery. It betrayed her nerves, as if she was still that gauche, hero-worshipping, knobbly-kneed schoolgirl.

'I have a celebrity client who wants to get married in Yorkshire and—'

'No.' The flatly delivered negative cut through the air like a gunshot and his expression closed like a shutter slamming.

'But you haven't let me finish—'

Lucas put his cup on the table, rose from his chair and moved back to stand in front of the windows, his back turned towards her again. 'It's out of the question.'

The intractable edge to his tone sent a ripple of anger through her. She *had* to sell the proposal to him. So much depended on her securing Rothwell Park as a wedding venue. Her business partners were depending on her to nail this location for their client. She couldn't let them down. Harper and Aerin were her family now. Failure wasn't an option. Failing was what her mother did, not her. Ruby set goals and achieved them. She made plans and carried them out. She made promises she delivered on without fail.

'But why?'

Lucas gave a grunt of humourless laughter. 'You mean apart from me loathing weddings?'

Ruby let out a gusty sigh. 'Not all weddings are like your parents' ones. I mean, not many couples get married to and divorced from each other three times.'

He turned around to face her, his expression etched in intractable lines. 'You're wasting your time, Ruby. I won't budge on this.'

And there she was thinking her grandmother was stubborn. Lucas took obstinacy to a whole new level. Seriously, he made the most obstinate mule look like a pushover.

'But Rothwell Park is the perfect setting for a wedding. There's so much space and the huge kitchen is a dream to work in. My friend Harper is desperate to photograph the wedding here. The gothic setting really appeals to her. Remember you met her once when she came to visit me here? We met in care. And the wedding planner, Aerin, will organise everything, so there's nothing you'll have to do. She's such a perfectionist—nothing will be left to chance. You wouldn't even have to be here. I'll bring my catering team in a few days early to set up. Please, Lucas, at least think about it before you say—'

'No.'

Ruby sprang from her chair, almost knocking the tea tray off the table. She stood in front of him with her hands balled into tight fists, anger stiffening her spine and frustration heating her cheeks. She couldn't let him stand in the way of her goal. She couldn't let him thwart her carefully, meticulously laid-out plans. She couldn't allow him to make her break her promise to her friends and their celebrity client. The wedding *had* to go ahead. She would find a way to convince him, even if it took longer than the weekend.

She. Could. Not. Fail.

'I can't believe you're being so unfair. This wedding is the biggest we've ever done and it will boost our profile so much. All those rooms are lying vacant upstairs. We could house all the guests—some of them very important people. Do you realise the revenue we could raise from this? It's a dream come true for—'

Lucas turned back to the bleak view of the brooding sky. 'Please leave.'

'No. I will *not* damn well leave.'

Before she could stop herself, Ruby placed one of her hands on his arm to force him to face her. He jolted as if she had touched him with a live wire. A tingling sensation travelled along the length of her own arm and she was acutely conscious of the firm male muscles tensing under her hold.

She couldn't recall touching him since that awful night when she was sixteen. But the electric sensation was exactly the same. A strange fizzing energy that sent tiny buzzing pulses along the network of her nerves. She was standing so close to his imposing height it sent her heart into a crazy hit-and-miss rhythm. The citrus and woodsy notes of his aftershave teased her senses into a stupor. Although he clearly hadn't shaved for a week, possibly more, and the rich dark stubble peppering his strong jaw and growing around his sculpted mouth gave him a rakish look.

Eek! Why had she looked at his mouth?

The top lip was slightly thinner than the bottom, their vermilion borders and the philtrum ridge between his nose and top lip so well defined they could have been carved by Michelangelo. It was a mouth that had inspired many a teenage fantasy. And all these years later Ruby still wondered what those firm lips would feel like against her own. Hard and insistent? Soft and sensually persuasive? Or something irresistibly in between?

Lucas placed his broad-spanned hand over hers and lifted it off his arm as if it was speck of lint. 'Do you really think that tactic is going to work?'

His tone was liberally laced with scorn and another wave of heat flowed to her cheeks.

Ruby glowered up at him, but all she could see was her own furious reflection in his aviator glasses. 'Firstly, I'm not leaving until you agree to hear me out. And secondly, I can't leave my gran struggling all by herself with a burned wrist. Why haven't you engaged another housekeeper? This place is clearly too much for her now.'

'She insists she doesn't want to retire.'

'But can't you see how neglected this place is at the moment? There are cobwebs everywhere.'

His mouth went into a thin tight line. 'No, I *can't* see.'

Something about his bleak-sounding tone made Ruby frown. 'But there's heaps of them. Look at that one at the top of the window, and on the light there. You'd have to blind not to see them.'

The line of his mouth became embittered. 'But that's exactly my point—I am blind.'

CHAPTER TWO

LUCAS HEARD RUBY'S sucked-in breath and the sound of her gripping the back of one of the wing chairs as if his news had shocked her to the core. But then, when he'd been hit with his diagnosis just over a month ago he'd been knocked sideways too.

Even if he did fully regain his sight, post-surgery, how was he supposed to juggle his work commitments in the meantime? How was he going to manage day-to-day life? He was not the type of man to depend on others for anything. He was fiercely, ruthlessly independent and could not imagine any other way of living.

'Blind?' Ruby gasped. 'But how? I mean, what happened?'

'I had a pituitary tumour removed last month.'

'A tumour? Was it…*malignant*?' She whispered the word, as if it terrified her to say it out loud.

'Thankfully, no. But the surgery resulted in considerable swelling against the optic nerve.'

He heard the sound of Ruby swallowing and the creak of a floorboard, as if she was shifting her weight from foot to foot. He could imagine her small white teeth pulling at her plump lower lip and his blood thickened and drummed softly, deep and low in his body. It was a faint pulse that strengthened into a pounding beat as his mind kept running with memories of her understated beauty.

Touching her had been a mistake. An error of judgement that had caught him off guard. *She'd* caught him off guard. The smell of her—the intoxicating peony and tuberose and summer scent he always associated with her—made him want to get closer to her, to breathe her.

Why was he so aware of her all of a sudden? It made no sense. He had done his best to ignore her since she was a kid—especially since that night of the party. Her sixteen-year-old schoolgirl crush might have been flattering to some, but to him it had reinforced his conviction that infatuation masquerading as love was a disaster waiting to happen. His parents had demonstrated that three times with their rollercoaster relationship that consisted of passionately falling in and out of love.

That day he had made it clear to Ruby where the boundaries lay. Those boundaries had been in place for eleven years and he was determined they would stay that way.

'Is it…permanent? I mean, your loss of sight?'

'My specialist is cautiously optimistic. Usually sight does return, but in rare instances it doesn't.' Lucas released a breath he hadn't been aware of holding and added, 'I can see shapes, but there's no definition. And light and dark. But that's about all.'

'I'm so sorry… And here I was, gabbling on about blinding sunshine and why can't you see the cobwebs.

Oh, God, I'm *so* sorry.' The anguish in her voice was palpable.

He pictured her cherry-red cheeks and in spite of everything smiled to himself. He had never met a young woman who blushed so much. Those fiery blushes made her freckles stand out like nutmeg sprinkled on a dessert. 'Please. Stop apologising.'

There was a loaded silence.

Lucas was aware of every breath she took, every movement she made. The rustle of her clothes, the squeak of her shoes, the swish of her fragrant hair. Aware of her in a way he had never been before. Or maybe that was because he'd been alone for weeks without a visitor, apart from the occupational therapist who had taught him how to navigate his surroundings and manage basic tasks such as dressing and eating and drinking.

While the OT had been excellent at her job, he still occasionally bumped into furniture, and the last thing he wanted was anyone witnessing it. He'd given his housekeeper, Beatrice Pennington, strict instructions to keep all visitors away. But he hadn't realised Beatrice had injured herself. But then how could he have? He couldn't see a damn thing, and she was loyal to a fault—the type who wouldn't dream of letting him down at his lowest point.

'Lucas... I meant what I said about Gran. I'll have to stay a few days to help her. And if I can talk her into retiring, then I can help you interview new applicants and—'

'I don't want anyone else here while I'm recuperating,' Lucas said, barely able to keep his tone civil.

The thought of his trustworthy housekeeper retiring was out of the question for now. How could he protect his privacy with strangers traipsing about the castle? He only needed another month or two to see how his sight was progressing.

'The whole point of me being here is to keep my condition out of the press. As far as I'm concerned, the press have had their fair share of Rockwell scandals to report. I will not allow myself to become yet another one of them.'

'But Gran needs—'

'I understand you're worried about your grandmother. Take her to a doctor for treatment, but you'll have to leave after that. I'm not interested in replacing her until my sight returns.'

If my sight returns.

He didn't say the words, but they hovered in the air like some of those cobwebs she'd mentioned.

Ruby gave a heavy sigh and he heard her clothes rustle again, as if her shoulders had slumped. 'You can't stay holed up here for ever. You have a business to run and so do I—which brings me back to Delphine Rainbird's wedding.'

Lucas ground his teeth. 'How I run my business is no concern of yours. And I've already given you my answer about the wedding.'

'But you don't understand how important this is to me.'

The pleading note in her voice was almost his undoing. Almost. But the last thing he wanted was a media circus at his private residence. Paparazzi and drones and helicopters trying to get the money shot. He was a private man at the best of times. What the press would make of his loss of sight was anyone's guess, but he was not going to do anything to risk exposure.

His childhood had been full of media intrusions as journalists had tried to get the latest on his parents—either their recoupling or their uncoupling. Some of the press had even taken to tailing him, asking for a comment on his parents' current relationship status. Not only had it embarrassed him, it had made him determined never to allow his emotions to become so out of control that the press would find any relationship he conducted newsworthy.

As if that had worked. He loathed the way the press was always tagging him, speculating on his love-life, documenting his every move.

'I'm sorry to disappoint you but it's not going to happen. You'll have to find somewhere else.'

'But there's nowhere quite like Rothwell Park. It's got such a wonderfully gothic atmosphere, and I know it'll make Delphine's wedding all the more spectacular—especially with Harper's photography. Delphine came here as a child with her parents, to one of your parents' parties. It left a big impression on her and she's dreamed of being married here ever since. Some of the world's biggest celebrities will be coming—possibly even royalty. It might bring Harper and Aerin and I more high-end clients. In fact, we're counting on it. This is what we need to lift our business to the next level.'

Lucas tried not to imagine Ruby's imploring expression, but it filled his imagination regardless. A beseeching spaniel had nothing on her. He could picture her toffee-brown eyes, fringed with thick long lashes and framed by dark eyebrows. Her full-lipped mouth—no doubt downturned at the corners right now—her ski slope nose, her high cheekbones…

She wasn't classically beautiful, more understated girl-next-door than over-the-top glamourous. She lightened her mid-brown hair to blonde, but her roots nearly always grew through an inch or two before she got around to touching them up. He often wondered if she coloured her hair so she didn't resemble her mother, who had chosen a life of crime over her. Ruby wore the bare minimum of make-up and mostly casual clothes. She was proud and feisty and she had a streak of obstinacy—no doubt inherited from her grandmother.

But Lucas could be stubborn too. And on this issue, he was not going to budge. 'I hate to disappoint you, but there's not going to be another wedding at Rothwell Park while I'm the owner. Do I make myself crystal-clear?'

'I can understand why you want your privacy. I'd be the same. But I need this wedding so badly.'

He heard her proceeding to load their cups and saucers back on the tray, her movements ordered and methodical, but he sensed her frustration all the same.

'What am I supposed to tell my friends?' Her lowered tone made it sound as if the question was addressed to herself rather than him. 'I can't let them down… I promised.'

The teaspoons clinked against the saucers and he heard her let out a long-winded sigh. Lucas knew all about broken promises. His parents had made numerous promises to each other, and to him, and they had all been broken. Some faster than others, but still ultimately broken.

'I'm sorry, Ruby, but you shouldn't have made a promise before you were absolutely certain you could honour it.'

'But all you have to say is yes and I *will* be able to honour it. You're standing in the way of my success. And I know you're only doing it because of—'

He heard her suck in her breath, as if she had decided not to continue with her rant.

'Because of...?'

The things on the tray rattled as she picked it up from the table. 'Because of what happened all those years ago.'

'Nothing happened.'

Lucas had made absolutely sure of that. Yes, he had been a little brutal in telling her how inappropriately she had behaved, but back then the seven years difference in their ages back had been a chasm that couldn't and shouldn't have been bridged.

'I suppose I should thank you for not taking advantage of me.'

'Perhaps I should apologise for being a little curt with you.'

There was a pulsing silence.

Ruby drew in a breath and released it on a stuttering sigh. 'I'm not going to give up, you know.'

The steely thread of determination was back in her voice.

'Neither am I.'

He could sense her eyes on him. He could see the vague outline of her standing stiffly in front of him, with the tray in her hands. He wished he could see her face, see those flashing toffee-brown eyes and the shape of her lips. But wishing was not going to bring his eyesight back. Only time could do that.

Ruby left the library and took the tray back to the kitchen. Thankfully, her gran wasn't there, so she'd have some time to process her thoughts over Lucas's revelation.

It was such a shock to think of him without his sight. To think of a man who had built a global career on constructing beautiful gardens for his clients no longer being able to see anything but vague shapeless outlines.

He was a proud man who had locked himself away from the public eye while he waited to see if his eyesight would return.

What if it didn't?

Her heart squeezed at the thought of him robbed of such a vital sense. How would he run his business? How would he be able to design gardens if he could only see shapes but no definition? He was a man who attended to detail. He was meticulous and thorough in all he did. Now it all hung in the balance while he waited to find out if his sight would return.

She mentally retraced every word of her interaction with him and a wave of shame coursed through her. If she hadn't been so focussed on delivering her proposal she might have picked up on the clues a little earlier. He was wearing sunglasses. He was sitting in the darkened library with no book in his hands or on the table beside his chair. There was not a mobile phone or laptop in sight—things that rarely left his side when he was working on multiple projects.

He had touched her hand whilst reaching for the teacup.

He'd touched her...

Ruby looked down at her hand and flexed her fingers where his hand had so briefly lain. A shiver shimmied down her spine and she closed her hand into a fist, trying to stop the fizzing sensation that lingered in her flesh from the heat of his touch.

She gave herself a stern mental shake and left the kitchen to fetch the first aid kit from the downstairs bathroom. She opened the bathroom door, but then caught a glimpse of herself in the gilt-edged mirror over the basin and suppressed a groan at the sight of her pink cheeks.

She wasn't the blushing sort when it came to interacting with men.

But with Lucas…

Ruby released a shuddering sigh and pulled open the cupboard below the basin to find the kit. She had to get a grip on herself. Because she was not leaving Rothwell Park until she had his agreement on the wedding, and nor was she leaving her gran on her own. Leaving without his agreement would be failing—and she could not fail.

This wedding was her chance—to help expand Happy Ever After Weddings This was her chance to build the sort of financial security that would allow her to put her poverty-stricken past well and truly behind her. The potential was at her fingertips, and she couldn't allow Lucas to snatch it away from her.

Besides, Lucas clearly needed more support than he was currently receiving. She could offer it at the same time as helping her gran…

Ruby found her gran in the sitting room in the servants' quarters. It was only used by Beatrice these days, and was comfortable in a spartan way, which was how her gran preferred it.

'You could've given me the heads-up about Lucas's condition,' Ruby said, and set the first aid kit on the lamp table next to her gran's armchair.

'It's not my place to be revealing the master's private information.'

'I would never tell anyone.'

Her gran narrowed her eyes. 'What about those friends of yours? And all those social media things you're on? One slip of the tongue and the world's press would be on the doorstep.'

'They won't hear it from me.'

Ruby opened the first aid kit and took out antiseptic wash and some cotton wool pads.

If by some miracle Delphine's wedding went ahead, the world's press would indeed be on the doorstep. But there was no point discussing that with her gran—not until she was sure Lucas could be won over.

Her gran winced as Ruby wrapped a crepe bandage around her wrist. 'Not too tight,' she said through pinched lips.

Ruby unwound the bandage a little, a frown tugging at her brow. 'I'm going to take you to the doctor right now. The sooner you have this seen to, the sooner it will get better. You can't risk losing your arm.'

'Don't be daft. I won't be losing my arm…' But her gran's tone had a tremulous note of worry in it that hadn't been there before.

Ruby secured the bandage and met her gran's troubled gaze. 'This has to be seen to today. I've done first aid, Gran, so I know a bad burn when I see it.'

Within a short time Ruby had made an appointment with the local doctor, who advised her to pack a bag for her gran in case she needed to be admitted to hospital. Another hour or so later, once Beatrice had been assessed by a no-nonsense doctor who had advised intravenous antibiotics and a hospital stay of at least a week, Ruby drove back to Rothwell Park, comforted that her gran was finally receiving the medical attention she needed.

Before informing Lucas of her gran's hospital stay, Ruby took her phone upstairs to her room, so she could have a three-way call with her business partners.

'I'm going to have to stay a little longer than I thought. My gran has been admitted to hospital for treatment for a burn.'

Although she wanted to tell the girls about Lucas's situation, and implicitly trusted their discretion, she could not bear to betray his trust.

'Oh, your poor gran. Is she going to be okay?' Aerin asked.

'She'll be fine if she does what she's told. The doctor wants to keep her in for a few days for the antibiotics to do their job. Gran wasn't happy about it, but I managed to talk her round.'

'Did you ask Lucas about Delphine's wedding?'

Harper asked, and the eagerness in her voice made Ruby feel awful for not being transparent about the situation.

'Yes, but I'm still negotiating with him.'

'I'm not sure I like the sound of that,' Harper said. 'We need to lock in the date as soon as possible. Delphine has her heart set on Rothwell Park. It's perfect in every way. She wants the guests to stay on site, and the castle is big enough to accommodate everyone—including her security team. Besides, I want the photos I can take there for the website.'

'I can't plan anything until we know for sure,' Aerin said with a hint of panic in her tone. 'We're on a tight timeline in any case. And it's a remote location, so things will take more time than—'

'I know, but leave it with me. I think I can convince him.'

Ruby wasn't feeling as confident as she sounded to her friends, but her determination more than made up for that. She had to find a way to convince Lucas that holding the wedding at Rothwell Park would be a win-win situation. It was going to be a hard sell to someone who was almost phobic about weddings, but still, it was worth a try.

Lucas was making his way upstairs to his suite of rooms when he heard the sound of the stairs above him creaking. The sound of Ruby's light footsteps as she approached him sent a frisson of awareness through his body. The fragrance of her wafted in front of his nostrils, making him want to press his face to the side of her slim neck and breathe her in.

Rein it in, buddy. He gave himself a stern talking-to. *She's off limits. She's always been off limits.*

'How's your grandmother? Did you take her to see the doctor? I heard your car leave a while back.'

'The doctor had admitted her to hospital to administer IV antibiotics.'

Lucas frowned. 'For how long?'

'A week.'

He drew in a breath and released it in a slow stream. 'I'm sorry I didn't realise her burn was as serious as that.'

He'd always prided himself on taking care of his staff, from the most senior to the most junior. It frustrated him that Beatrice, his most loyal staff member of all, had hurt herself and he had known nothing.

'Of course this changes everything.'

Ruby's voice contained an element of *I-told-you-so* that jangled at his already overstretched nerves.

'Everything…?'

'I'll have to stay longer than the weekend. You'll need help while Gran's away, and—'

'I will not need help.'

The last thing he wanted was Ruby waiting on him hand and foot. It was bad enough having her here for the weekend. Seven days of trying to avoid her would be unbearable.

'Don't be silly, Lucas, of course you'll need help. I can work remotely for the next week. I can get the castle in some sort of order while Gran has a much-needed rest.'

Lucas saw the sense in her argument, but he also saw the pitfalls if he were to agree—which he was strangely tempted to do. Ruby was not the sort of person he could easily ignore. But wouldn't a week with her be preferable to a stranger filling in for his housekeeper?

'Fine. Stay, then. But I don't want to be disturbed unnecessarily. And once the week is up you'll have to leave.'

'Thanks for being so terribly gracious about it.'

Lucas could hear the sarcasm in her tone and imagined the pert tilt of her chin and the flash of her toffee-brown eyes. 'You're welcome.'

He moved up another step, and he sensed her on the one above him. He could smell not just her perfume but the fragrance of her hair—an apple and vanilla scent that teased his senses all over again. He could hear the soft sound of her indrawn breath and pictured her blinking at him with those wide puppy dog eyes. The desire to touch her shocked him to the core of his being. He had to tighten his hold on the balustrade and keep his other hand pressed against his right side.

'Excuse me. I want to go upstairs to bed.' He spoke through tight lips.

'Lucas?'

Her hand came down on his arm and a wave of heat travelled through his body in a blood-tingling current.

She took her hand away, as if she too felt that electric charge.

'It's way too early to go to bed. You need to have proper nutrition and exercise. And regular exposure to daylight so your circadian rhythms don't go out of whack. I can help you with that.'

'If you think your playing nursemaid is going to change my mind about the wedding, think again.'

He brushed past her but he heard her following him, her footsteps light but determined.

'Forget about the wedding for now. I'm doing this for Gran. I had no idea she wasn't keeping up with things the way she used to. I should've come back before this to check on her. I shouldn't have relied on phone calls. I should have come in person.'

Self-recrimination laced her voice, and it triggered his own gut-clawing guilt.

Lucas stopped walking up the stairs and turned in Ruby's direction. 'It's not your fault. If it's anyone's, it's mine. But with my operation and all, I just—'

'You mustn't blame yourself. Gran is a stubborn old goat who wouldn't listen until I told her the arm was likely to be amputated if the infection got any worse.'

'It won't come to that, surely?'

'Let's hope not.'

'It seems your visit was timely.'

'Yes…'

Lucas knew how much Beatrice missed Ruby, although she never let on. It wasn't the housekeeper's way to wear her heart on her sleeve. But he was feeling a little uncomfortable that she hadn't told him about her injury. Her loyalty was admirable, and her stoicism something he had always admired, but he was her employer and ultimately responsible for her welfare.

He hated it that he was unable to conduct his life the way he wanted. This loss of control was anathema to him. It reminded him of the chaotic rollercoaster of living with his parents as they fell in and out of love with each other repeatedly. One minute they would be passionately in love and all would be well, and then the fights would start. Horrible fights, with cruel insults hurled and doors slammed and voices raised. Then, after his father had moved out—or his mother, depending on who had had the latest affair in order to wound the other—the cycle would begin again.

Sometimes the peace had lasted for so long he'd lower his guard. He'd be lulled into thinking that this time they were going to make it and all would be well. But of course he was always disappointed.

Lucas had learned the hard way not to trust their passion or their promises. A cynical crust had formed around his heart and he longer believed in lasting love. He went into his short flings with his eyes wide open and his guard up.

And that wasn't going to change any time soon.

CHAPTER THREE

RUBY WATCHED AS Lucas climbed the stairs to his suite of rooms, torn between wanting to follow him and needing to keep her distance. At least he'd agreed to let her stay the week, but his stubbornness over her helping him in any way was beyond frustrating. It was also imperative she got him to agree to host Delphine's wedding, but how could she change his mind?

She might not like him much, but she'd have to have a heart as hard and cold as marble not to feel empathy for his situation. He had always struck her as a bit of a loner. He was not like his extroverted parents in any way other than having the same good looks as his father. She didn't even know if he saw his father these days. His mother had died of a brain tumour a few years ago, and his father had remarried within a couple of months and promptly created a new family with a much younger wife in Brazil.

Ruby sighed and went back down to the kitchen to see about dinner. Cooking for her was not just work or even a hobby—it was her happy place. Preparing ingredients, using her creativity to develop new tastes and flavours, brought her immense satisfaction. Her busy life running the wedding business with her friends left little time for a social life, but she didn't let it worry her. She liked the security it gave her to know she was earning her own money and not being dependent on others as her mother had been.

Which was why securing Rothwell Park for Delphine's wedding was of paramount importance to her right now. Convincing Lucas to allow it to go ahead was going to be a big challenge, but never let it be said that she had ever backed down from a challenge.

The bigger the better.

A couple of hours later, Ruby set up the smaller of the two dining rooms for Lucas's meal. She went up the stairs to the master bedroom and rapped her knuckles on the door.

'Lucas? Dinner is ready downstairs.'

She heard him let out a curse word and then the sound of his firm tread as he came to the door. He opened it and stood there glaring down at her—without his sunglasses this time. The outer rims of his irises were a dark smoky grey, the centre an ice-floe-blue with ink-black pupils. His lashes were long and thick, his eyebrows prominent. His hair was tousled, as if he had been raking his hands through it, but if anything it made him look even more attractive. He had taken off his shoes, but he still towered over her.

'I thought I told you I wasn't hungry?'

'And I told you how important it is to eat well. A good diet will help your recovery.'

He gave a rough-edged sigh and his hand fell away from where it was gripping the door. 'I never knew you could be so persistent. I'll be down in a minute. I need to put on my shoes.'

Ruby could have gone ahead and got ready to serve dinner, but she stayed in the open doorway, watching as he tried to locate his shoes. He bumped his foot against the bedside table and let out another colourful curse.

'Damn it to hell.'

'They're over here.'

Ruby went to where the shoes were half pushed under the bed. It wasn't the first time she had entered his room—during her girlhood crush she had slipped in unnoticed several times. Her cheeks warmed as those memories resurfaced. She had been so infatuated with Lucas, so desperately in love with him—or at least with the version of him her teenage mind had conjured. She bent down to pull his shoes out from under the bed, and then straightened and brought them to him. She crouched in in front of him and set them next to the socked toes of his left foot.

You are not going to think about the fact you are on your knees in front of Lucas Rothwell. Gulp. In his bedroom.

Ruby wouldn't have wished blindness on anyone, but right then, with her cheeks hot enough to solve an energy crisis, she was glad he couldn't see her blush.

'Here you go.'

Lucas slipped his feet into the shoes and gave a grimace. 'Thanks…'

Ruby straightened in front of him, conscious of how close they were standing to each other. Never had she been so aware of a man. Of his power and potency. Of his commanding presence and how it affected her. Her body tingled from head to foot. Even the roots of her hair lifted away from the skin of her scalp. Her heart began to beat a little faster—a staccato rhythm that banged against her breastbone and made it hard for her to draw another breath. She knew she should step back, put some distance between them before she was tempted to touch him.

Don't even think about touching him.

But for some strange reason she was unable to step back. Her feet were nailed to the floor by an invisible force she had no way of counteracting.

Time seemed to stand still. The silence stretched. Her heart hammered like the piston in a faulty engine.

Lucas lifted his hand to her face, touching her cheek with the lightest touch, his fingers ever so slowly trailing down to the base of her chin. So close…so *achingly* close to her lower lip that her mouth buzzed and fizzed and tingled in anticipation. She drew in a soft breath and his hand fell away as if her skin had burned him.

'Forgive me.' His tone was so rough he could have been gargling with gravel.

'It's okay…'

Ruby couldn't seem to get her voice above a whisper, or get her heartrate to slow down to anywhere near normal. Her heart was bouncing up and down in her chest cavity as if it was on a pogo stick. His touch had been so light, but it had created a firestorm in her flesh. Stirrings and yearnings and urgings were erupting in places she didn't want to think about. Places she *forbade* herself to think about. The one time she had touched him in the past it had turned into the most humiliating experience of her life.

Lucas stepped away, his forehead cast in a severe frown. 'It's not okay. You have my word it won't happen again.'

I want it to happen again.

Ruby was shocked at where her mind was leading her. Shocked and ashamed and furious with herself. For years she had done everything in her power to avoid touching him. But now the desire—the fervent, aching desire—to touch him beat in her fingertips like a primitive drum. It was an ache in her flesh, an urgent ache to feel his hand gliding down her face. And not just her face but other places on her body. Touching her, exploring her, pleasuring her...

She suppressed a tiny shudder. 'I guess you have to use your other senses to make up for your loss of sight. Touch is one way of knowing how someone looks or what expression they have on their face.'

'I don't have to touch your face to read the pity that's likely there.' His tone was embittered and his expression dark and brooding.

'You think I pity you? If I do, it's not because of your lack of sight. It's because you're refusing to make what you can of your life at present. Thousands—no, millions of people are blind and live happy, fulfilled lives.'

'Please spare me the lecture on how I should live my life.' He spoke the words through white tight lips.

Ruby let out a long sigh. 'I know this must be an awful time for you. Everything has happened so suddenly and, just like after any surgery, it'll take some time to get used to your new circumstances. Everything must seem out of whack for you right now. And

I want to help you get through it. But I can't do that if you aren't prepared to meet me halfway.'

'I don't need your help.'

'When was the last time you shaved?'

A savage frown carved deep on his forehead. 'What?'

Ruby stepped up close to him again and lifted her hand to his stubbly jaw. He flinched as if her touch burned him, but he didn't step away. She placed her hand back on his face, gliding it over the rough regrowth. The raspy sound was loud in the silence. She lowered her hand from his face and tried to ignore the fluttery sensation in her belly. Tried to ignore the tingling in her fingers and the pulse of something dark and silky and secretive between her thighs.

'Unless you intend to grow a beard, you really could do with a shave. I could drive you to a barber, if you like.'

'I'm not going anywhere.'

'I could maybe get one to do a house call.'

'No.' He moved away to search for his sunglasses on the bedside table. He slipped them on and turned to face her with an unreadable expression. 'What? Not going to offer to shave me yourself?'

Ruby could feel another blush crawling over her cheeks. 'I can't imagine you allowing me to come at you with a razor in my hand. Who knows what might happen?'

One side of his mouth lifted at the corner. 'Who, indeed.'

Something about his sardonic tone sent a shiver rolling down her spine and Ruby turned for the door before she was tempted to touch him again. What was wrong with her? Did she have no shame—especially after the blistering set-down he'd given her all those years ago? She had to get a hold of herself. The last thing she needed right now was the complication of developing an attraction to the one man who would never be interested in someone like her.

A few minutes later they were seated in the dining room. Ruby dished up a portion of the casserole she had made onto his plate and filled his glass with wine.

'Bon appetit.'

Lucas leaned down to sniff the steam rising off his plate. 'Mmm, smells good.' His fingers briefly searched for cutlery. He cocked his head, as if sensing she was watching him. 'Is something wrong?'

She flicked her napkin across her lap and picked up her own cutlery. 'It must have been hard to learn how to eat without vision'

'I'm getting used to it.' A frown flitted across his brow and he added, 'I had the help of a very efficient occupational therapist for a couple of weeks.'

'That must have been a great help.'

'She's the mother of three adult children and has zero tolerance for self-pity.' One side of his mouth tilted in an almost-smile, which was a little rueful around the edges. 'I told her she'd missed a great career in the army as a drill sergeant.'

'You won't have been an easy client.'

His smile dropped away and he moved the food around his plate, a brooding frown pulling on his brow. 'No, I wasn't.'

'Why did you come back here to recuperate?' Ruby

asked. 'I mean, you hardly spend any time here these days. I got the impression you didn't enjoy being here.'

He put down his fork and picked up his wine glass. 'I chose it because of the isolation. The press would have a field-day if they found out about my condition. Plus, I know my way around here. I spent my childhood seeking out various hiding places to avoid the battles between my parents.' He took a sip of his wine and put the glass back down, the line of his mouth bitter. 'I don't remember this place as a home. It was more of a war zone.'

'But your parents weren't always unhappy. I remember them being so in love and—'

'I hardly think that was *love*.' Cynicism was ripe in his tone. 'They lived off each other's drama. They got high on it. They weren't happy unless they were making each other unhappy.' He shook his head, as if he still couldn't make sense of his parents' relationship. 'If that's what love is, I want no part of it.'

'Have you ever been in love?'

'No.'

'But you've dated so many women. Hasn't one of them made you feel something?'

'Sure—but lust isn't love.' He picked up his wine glass again. 'I don't stay with anyone long enough to develop feelings for them.'

'But what if they develop feelings for you?'

'I don't intentionally set out to break anyone's heart. I state my terms and those who can handle them accept them.'

'It sounds like plenty of women do accept them.'

Ruby tried but failed to keep the note of disapproval

out of her voice. If what was reported in the press was true, Lucas changed partners faster than a racing driver changed gears.

Lucas took another sip of his wine before answering. 'So, you're not a fan of casual hook-ups?' he asked.

Her cheeks grew warm. 'I have the occasional fling.'

'But you've never fallen in love.'

'Not yet.'

'But you'd like to.'

'Of course,' Ruby said. 'I work in the wedding industry. I would be a hypocrite if I didn't believe in love and want it for myself. I just haven't been lucky enough to find it yet. Nor have either of my business partners, Aerin and Harper—which is kind of ironic, really.'

Lucas made a sound that sounded like a *more-fool-you* snort. He picked up his cutlery again and ate a couple of mouthfuls. But then he paused with his fork halfway to his mouth, as if sensing her watching him. 'Look—I'm sorry about your grandmother. I hope she's going to be okay. If there's anything she needs, or if I can help in any way—'

Ruby reached for her glass of wine. 'Thank you, but I'm sure she'll be fine. Although I still think she needs to be encouraged to retire. She can't work for ever.'

There was a small silence.

Ruby studied his expression, wondering what was going on behind his shuttered features. He was hard to read at the best of times, but now he seemed even more closed off. He wouldn't be human if he wasn't worried about regaining his sight, but she sensed it was more than that. He had a big international business to run, staff to look after, multiple projects running at the same

time. Yet he was unable to travel now—or at least chose
not to until he was confident of a full recovery. No wonder there were lines of worry about his mouth and eyes
that had not been there before.

'That's a conversation I intend to have with her
sooner rather than later,' Lucas said. 'And it's another
reason you can't host your client's wedding here.'

He paused as if expecting her to join the dots.

A stone landed in Ruby's stomach as she finally did.
She put her wine glass down and stared at him. 'You're
not thinking of...*selling* Rockwell Park?'

Even saying the word out loud seemed like sacri-
lege—like shouting a curse in the middle of a church
service. This had been her only stable home, and she
hated the thought of not being able to return to it. It was
her base, the anchor that had kept her safe after bobbing up and down in the turbulent waters of her early
childhood.

If Lucas sold it, she would never walk through the
castle and its grounds again, never wander through the
gardens and the moors beyond. A deep sense of loss
assailed her—a sense that nothing would ever be the
same again. She would not only be losing her sanctuary but a part of herself as well.

'It's too big for one person,' Lucas said, shrugging
one shoulder in a dispassionate way. 'I spend most of
my time abroad these days, so it makes sense to offload
it to someone who'll make better use of it.'

Ruby opened and closed her mouth like a stranded
fish gasping for air. 'But it's your home. The home of
your ancestors. And, wait—what does your father think
of you selling?'

'He signed over the deeds to me upon my mother's death. He has no wish ever to return to England, let alone live here, and nor does his young wife. She finds it too cold.'

Ruby bit her lip, still struggling to get her head around the fact Rothwell Park would not be a part of her life any more. She might not visit more than two or three times a year, but just knowing it was there, that her gran was there, gave her a sense of security.

She hadn't realised how much she'd clung to it until now. Having her beloved sanctuary taken away would be like revisiting the worst of her childhood—the constant moves from bedsit to bedsit as her mother tried to escape yet another unsavoury boyfriend or a drug debt that had got out of hand.

'But what's going to happen to my grandmother? She's lived her for so long.'

'You're the one who's insisting she needs to retire. I'll give her a generous pay-out, of course. And provide her with accommodation for the rest of her life.'

It was a more than generous offer, but Ruby still didn't understand why he was so intent on offloading Rothwell Park. How soon did he plan to sell it? Was selling it just something he was mulling over in his mind while he recuperated, or did he have a timeline in place?

'When do you intend to tell her?'

'Once the sale is finalised.'

Ruby's heart clanged against her breastbone. 'You mean you already have a buyer?'

Lucas's expression flickered with a hint of irritation. 'Why all the drama? It's an offer I'd be a fool to knock back.'

'So, it's all about the money.' It was a statement, not a question—a statement that burned in her throat like a searing hot coal. 'I thought you were nothing like your father, and yet here you are selling your birthright to the highest bidder.'

Lucas leaned back in his chair and curled his top lip in a cynical manner. 'You're welcome to make a counter-offer. The final contract is yet to be signed.'

She glared at him, even though she knew he couldn't see the blistering fire in her eyes. 'You know I haven't got that sort of money.'

And nor would she ever have that sort of money if she couldn't build the business to the heights she and her friends had planned. She swallowed the choking lump in her throat, determined to show no emotion in front of him.

'Ruby.'

His stern schoolmaster tone ignited her anger all over again.

'You're a successful businesswoman. You should know the importance of keeping emotion out of business deals.'

'But don't you feel *anything* for Rothwell Park? Anything at all?'

His features were as hard and cold as one of the marble busts of his ancestors in the gallery. 'As far as I'm concerned, this place is cursed.'

She frowned so hard it hurt her forehead. 'Cursed?'

The cynical twist to his mouth reappeared and he put his fork down with a hard little thud. 'You witnessed it yourself. My parents falling in and out of love. Breaking up and breaking each other. This place reminds me of nothing but angst and ill-feeling. I want nothing more to do with it.'

Ruby gaped at him. 'And you think that's Rothwell Park's fault? It was your parents and their hang-ups that cursed their relationship. It had nothing to do with this lovely old castle and its grounds. It's the people who make a place a home—not the bricks and mortar. Besides, when they were happy, they were truly happy. I have never seen two people more passionately in love with each other.'

Lucas gave a harsh laugh that was nowhere in the vicinity of humour. 'In love? Is that what you'd call it? You saw them through a child's eyes. You were fascinated by them…in awe of them because they were so different from—'

'From my mother?' Ruby lifted her chin, a remnant of pride making her spine as straight as a rod. 'Is that what you were going to say?'

The silence throbbed with a dark energy that seemed to press in from all four corners of the room.

Ruby liked to think her mother *had* loved her once. Not that she had any clear memory of it, but still… The alternative was too awful to think about. Didn't most mothers love and adore their babies? Didn't most mothers bond with their newborn infants and want the very best for them?

Or had her mother always resented her? Hated her for changing her life irreparably before she was ready? Resented the demands a small child had made on her time…resented the responsibility that came with raising a child without a father present. Resorted to drugs and drink to escape from the burdensome task of keeping a child safe.

How could Ruby ever know the truth? Her grandmother refused to speak of her daughter—her only child, who had rebelled against everything she had tried to instil in her. The values, the qualities, the solid work ethic…all ignored, disregarded.

And now, of course, it was too late. Ruby's mother had died of an overdose only days after leaving prison, within a year of Ruby coming to live at Rothwell Park.

Lucas finally let out a serrated sigh. 'You deserved better, Ruby. No one can deny that. But my parents were not shining examples of how to be an adult, and certainly not how to be an adult in a relationship.'

Ruby picked up her wine glass again but couldn't bring herself to drink a drop. It was more something to do with her hands. 'But at least they loved you,' she said. She stared at the wine in her glass and added before she could monitor her tongue, 'I'm not sure my mother ever loved me.'

Most people would have said *Of course she did.* Or offered some other equally useless platitude. But not Lucas Rothwell. Maybe there were some advantages to being a hardened cynic. He spoke the blunt truth instead of wrapping it up in cheap shiny tinsel.

'I'm sorry,' he said in a gentle tone. 'That must be hard to live with…not knowing for sure.'

Ruby gave a wry smile, even though she knew he couldn't see it. She wondered if he would sense it anyway. He seemed to have a sixth sense when it came to her—which, come to think of it, was a scary thought.

Could he sense her growing awareness of him? Could

he sense the way her body responded to his closeness? Could he sense how often her gaze drifted to his mouth and how her mind ran wild with images of those firm lips moving against hers?

She put her wine glass back down on the table and ran her fingertip around the rim, so the soft musical whine of the friction filled the silence.

'I couldn't help envying you growing up here at Rothwell Park,' she said, lowering her hand from the glass. 'It's true I was a little starstruck by your parents—in particular your mother. She was so glamorous and vivacious and charming…the life of every party. No wonder your father kept falling in love with her. I think I did a little too.' Ruby gave a little sigh and added, glancing across at him, 'I miss her. I guess you do too.'

Lucas's mouth twisted in a rueful manner, and a shadow of raw grief passed over his features like the ripple of the wind across a lake. 'Yes…' His hand carefully searched for his wine glass and his fingers moved around the stem, but he didn't lift the glass to his lips. 'It's sometimes hard to believe she's gone.' He tapped his fingers on the base of his glass and added with a frown, 'My father certainly got over losing her quickly. He remarried within weeks of her death.'

'But they weren't together at the time,' Ruby pointed out, even though she too had been a bit surprised at Lionel Rothwell's haste in remarrying.

'No, that's true.'

The silence ticked past.

'Do you think they might've got back together? I mean, if she hadn't got sick?' Ruby asked.

'Don't you think three marriages and three divorces is enough to prove two people are completely unsuitable?'

There was a sharp edge to his tone, an embittered edge that was at odds with what Ruby remembered of his parents' relationship. Or maybe he was right—she had been viewing them through the rose-coloured glasses of a love-starved child.

Maybe she was a glass-half-full type of person, but she'd had to live on hope for most of her life. Hope that things would get better…that life would not be uncertain and scary all the time. Hope had helped her build a business with her two best friends. Hope lived in her heart—hope that one day she would find the love of her life and have a happy family.

And her big hope right now was getting Lucas to change his mind about Delphine's wedding before Rothwell Park was sold.

'Lucas… I know you've already said no a thousand times, but please will you consider holding off on the sale of Rothwell Park until after Delphine's wedding? You're selling in any case. What does it matter if a wedding is conducted here in a few weeks' time? It might be the last time I come here. I know it's not really my home, or anything, but I can't help looking upon it as such. It was so wonderful, coming to live here with Gran after a stint in foster care. Please will you think about it some more? I'll stay here for the next week and get the castle tidied up while Gran's in hospital. You won't even know I'm here.'

Lucas let out a long-winded sigh. 'You don't let up, do you?'

'I've learned you don't achieve your goals in life unless you're prepared to work at it. My credo is: if you've got what it takes, then *do* whatever it takes.'

An enigmatic smile played at the edges of his mouth. She sensed he was mulling something over in his mind. Making calculations that somehow involved her. It gave her a secret thrill to think he might be prepared to cut a deal with her.

'All right, you can hold the wedding here. But I want something in return.'

Ruby's heart did a jerky somersault. 'We're prepared to negotiate on a hiring fee.'

'I'm not talking about money.'

She moistened her parchment-dry lips. 'You're... you're not?'

'I want you to come with me to Greece.'

Ruby stared at him as if he had asked her to go to Mars via Venus. 'But why?'

'Not for the reason you're thinking.'

Her cheeks were so hot she could have fried a couple of eggs on them. 'I wasn't thinking any such thing.'

His smile tilted a little higher on one side. 'I'll organise the cleaning of Rothwell Park while we're away. If I'm not on site it will lessen the chance of a press leak. We'll stay for a week on my private island and—'

Ruby's eyes threatened to pop right out of her head. 'You have a *private island*?'

'I bought it a few months ago—before I was diagnosed with the tumour. It's undergone some extensive renovations since, but I haven't seen the finished result. I have to do a final inspection for the builder.'

'But you can't see anything other than vague shapes and light and dark, right?'

'True, but I can use my other senses. Anyway, you can be my eyes. You can describe everything to me in intricate detail. But it goes without saying that if you betray me to the press the wedding is off, understood?'

'I would never do something like that.'

'I'll organise someone to visit your grandmother at the hospital,' Lucas said. 'She has a couple of friends she plays bridge with occasionally who'll look in on her, so you won't need to worry about her while we're away.'

While we're away...

A frisson passed over Ruby's flesh at how strangely intimate those words sounded. She would be alone with Lucas Rothwell on his private island for a week. A hot tingle rolled down the length of her spine. She would be by his side, talking him through what she saw.

But what if he sensed her heightened awareness of him? What if she was tempted to touch him again? He was a magnet to her iron—a potent, powerful force she was drawn to almost against her will. Almost, because a secret part of her still felt cheated that she had never got to experience the firm, sensual press of his lips on hers.

'But what will I say to Aerin and Harper? They only expected me to be away for the weekend. I'll have to tell them something...' She bit down on her lower lip, not sure she liked the thought of lying to her friends—especially Harper, who had been lied to all her life.

'Tell them you're doing me a favour in order to secure Rothwell Park.'

'They'll think I'm having a fling with you.'

One dark eyebrow lifted. 'Would they disapprove if you were?'

Ruby shrugged. 'Maybe… Especially Harper. I told her a few months back to steer clear of a notorious playboy at a wedding we were doing. But Jack Livingstone was not so easy for her to ignore.'

He jerked upright in his chair like a puppet whose strings had been suddenly tugged. 'Jack Livingstone, the boutique hotelier?' His expression was quickly smoothed over, as if he was conscious of his reaction and wanted to downplay it. 'What happened?' His tone had switched to mild interest, as if he were making polite conversation rather than avidly searching for details.

'He was the best man, and in a moment of weakness she had a one-night stand with him. He wanted to see her again, but she wouldn't return his calls.'

'Why not?'

'He's a playboy and she thinks he only wants to see her again because she's the first woman who's ever said no to him.'

Lucas twisted his mouth as if he understood all too well the way a playboy's mind worked. 'A challenge can be hard to resist.' He picked up his wine glass. 'So, will you come with me?'

A flutter of excitement danced across the floor of her belly. 'How can I say no?'

Later that night Lucas sat in the library, sipping a nightcap on his own, mulling over his decision to take Ruby with him to his island. He wasn't a man to make impulsive decisions, but it made sense to invite her rather than anyone else. Besides, he couldn't bear to be at

Rothwell Park while the place was being cleaned from top to bottom.

It would be too risky being there while strangers came in to clean. Strangers who might purposely or inadvertently let something slip to the press or on social media. Of course, rather than take Ruby to Greece he could have paid someone to accompany him—a member of staff, perhaps. But spending a week on his island with a staff member did not appeal to him half as much as a week with Ruby did.

A week alone with Ruby.

A warning bell sounded in his subconscious, but he blocked it out with logical argument. Ruby wanted something from him and he would give it to her if she upheld her end of the deal. She had too much at stake to betray his trust. He realised with a strange little jolt that he did trust her. She wanted this celebrity wedding to go ahead so she could build her business. He admired her goal-driven focus for it reminded him of his own. Success did not come about by wishing for it. You had to work for it—sometimes doing things you would rather not do.

But he didn't get the sense that Ruby found the prospect of a week in his company on his island all that distasteful. Interesting… Did that mean she hadn't outgrown her crush? She was no longer an awkward teenager. She was a fully grown woman. An intriguing and captivating young woman he found increasingly impossible to ignore.

From the moment Ruby had walked into the library something had changed for him. Something had changed *in* him. Her touch had ignited a spark inside him—lit a fuse that was fizzing quietly but insistently in his veins even now. One might argue that he was being reckless in taking her with him to his island. But something about her made him feel more alive than he had felt in weeks—months, even.

She wasn't the type of woman to kowtow to him. She stood her ground and fought from her corner and argued her case with steely determination. She was passionate and feisty and, God, how he needed someone to make him feel something other than this quiet despair at being at Rothwell Park when he could be on his beautiful island in the sun.

This actor's wedding could be the farewell event before Lucas left Rothwell Park for good. He had no emotional attachment to the place—to him it represented pain and broken promises and shattered hopes.

He would be relieved to drive out through the gate for a final time.

'You're going *where*?' Harper said on another three-way phone call later that night.

'It's only for a week, and it's the only way I can get Lucas to agree to have Delphine's wedding here at Rothwell Park,' Ruby said.

'Why does he want you to go with him?' Aerin asked with a hint of delighted suspicion in her tone. 'What's going on between you two?'

'Nothing.' Ruby was glad it wasn't a video call, because right now her cheeks were glowing hot enough to blowtorch the sugar on the top of a crème brûlée. 'He wants me to see his newly renovated villa. I thought

I might as well go and check it out. I haven't had a holiday in ages, and I happen to be free this week.'

'Playboys aren't worth the trouble,' Harper said. 'Take it from someone who knows about these things.'

'Aren't you being a little hard on Jack?' Ruby said. 'He did want to see you again, but you point-blank refused.'

'Hey, you were the one who warned me about him in the first place.'

'I know—but he asked to see you again, so you must have made an impression on him,' Ruby said.

'I'm not ready for a relationship—not even a fling,' Harper said. 'Work is my focus right now. I shouldn't have allowed him to distract me at the Tenterbury wedding. It was unprofessional of me, and it's all the more reason for me to stay away from him.'

'Well, *I'm* ready for a relationship,' Aerin said with wistful sigh. 'The trouble is finding Mr Right when there are so many Mr Wrongs out there.'

'Don't you mean Mr Perfect?' Ruby said with a teasing note to her voice.

At nearly thirty, Aerin was still a virgin. In fact, she was so terrified of dating the wrong man she hadn't even been kissed.

'Paint me overly cautious, but I don't want a trail of broken relationships behind me before I find my soulmate,' Aerin said. 'I want what my parents and siblings have—true and lasting love with a partner who's perfect for them.'

'Don't we all?' Ruby sighed.

'Which is why I have serious misgivings about you spending a week with a renowned playboy on a private island,' Harper said. 'You had a crush on him before. It wouldn't take much for you to develop one again.'

'Stop worrying about me,' Ruby said. 'I can take care of myself.'

Now all she had to do was prove it.

CHAPTER FOUR

THE FLIGHT TO Athens was uneventful, especially since Lucas had organised a private jet. While they were waiting for their transfer Ruby took the opportunity to buy a swimsuit and a sarong, and other essential items, given she only had her weekend clothes with her. None of which were suitable for a Greek island.

She went back to where Lucas was waiting for her in a private lounge area.

'Did you get everything you need?'

'I think so. How soon do we board the next plane?'

'Not a plane. A helicopter. Stavros, the pilot, is waiting for us now.'

A cold hand of fear gripped at her insides, squeezing, twisting, torturing. She looked out of the window to where a helicopter was stationed. *A helicopter?* Even saying the word in her mind was enough to send her spiralling into panic. Seeing those powerful blades reminded her of a flight when she was a young child, with one of her mother's boyfriends. The boyfriend had seemed to enjoy her terror, and had shredded her tender nerves with his reckless behaviour as pilot.

She hadn't been in a helicopter since. She'd been

lucky in her career so far and had not needed to fly in one, but with the growing popularity of destination weddings she knew it wouldn't be long before she would have to face down her fear.

'Can't we go by boat?' Ruby asked.

'It's quicker by air.'

She shifted her weight from foot to foot, glancing with trepidation at the helicopter waiting on the tarmac in the bright, shimmering sunshine. 'B-but it'd be nice going by boat. The fresh air, the scenery—we might even see dolphins.'

Lucas turned his head in her direction and frowned in concern. 'Are you scared of helicopters?'

His tone was gentle, not the least bit mocking, and it made it so much harder to maintain her emotional distance. Ruby moistened her suddenly dry lips, conscious of how close he was standing to her. His rolled-up shirtsleeve brushed against the bare skin of her arm and an electrifying tingle raced along her flesh and tripped her pulse.

'A little…'

'Have you had a bad experience in one?'

Even though she knew he couldn't see her expression, she sensed he could read her distress signals. Her rapid breathing, her racing pulse, her agitated movements. He could probably even hear her churning stomach.

'When I was seven my mother had a rich boyfriend who had a helicopter pilot's licence. He was also a drug dealer.' She glanced at the helicopter again and shuddered. 'He got a kick out of seeing how frightened I was when he made dangerous moves.' She swallowed and added, 'I haven't been in one since…'

Lucas placed a stabilising hand on her shoulder. 'What a cruel thing to do to a small, sensitive child.' His voice was throbbing with barely suppressed anger on her behalf. 'Didn't your mother tell him to stop?'

'No, she thought it was funny. She liked the daredevil lifestyle he offered and thought I needed to be toughened up.' She twisted her lips and added, 'She blamed me when they broke up a few weeks later. She said he couldn't cope with a kid who still wet the bed at seven years old.'

'Oh, Ruby…'

Lucas gathered her in his arms, resting his chin on the top of her head. His arms were strong and yet infinitely gentle, as if he was reaching back through time to comfort that small, terrified little girl.

Ruby breathed in the scent of him—the citrus top notes of his aftershave with its hints of wood and leather. Her face was pressed against the freshly laundered cotton of his shirt, which was the only barrier between her skin and the toned muscles of his chest. She could feel the steady *tump-tump-tump* of his heart against her cheek and her own heart went into a hit-and-miss rhythm, along with her pulse. She became aware of how close her lower body was to his. Her soft contours moulded against his hard frame, stirring her feminine flesh, igniting needs she fought desperately to control.

Lucas gently put her from him, but kept his hands on the tops of her shoulders. The only sign that he might be as rattled by her closeness as she was by his was a dull flush riding high along his aristocratic cheekbones.

'Hey, you'll be fine with me. I've flown heaps of times and never had an incident. I would fly us myself, except for my current condition.'

'You have a helicopter licence?'

He gave a grim movement of his mouth that loosely passed for a rueful smile and his hands fell away from her shoulders, one of them raking through his hair. 'Yes—not that it's much use to me at present.'

Ruby placed her fingers on the bare hair-roughened skin of his tanned wrist. Another lightning zap of electricity shot up her arm, and she knew he must have felt a similar reaction for he gave a tiny flinch, but didn't move his wrist away from her touch.

'It must be difficult to not know if you will regain your full vision.'

Lucas placed his hand over hers, anchoring it to the strong warmth of his wrist. His expression was difficult to read, given he was wearing his aviator glasses. 'We can take a boat if you can't face flying in the helicopter. But I have engaged a pilot with a lot of experience, and I'll be by your side the whole time.'

Ruby knew he wanted to get to his island as soon as he could, and she was touched that he was prepared to put her concerns ahead of his own. She glanced down at their joined hands and suppressed a tiny shiver. Not of fear but of excitement. His skin was deeply tanned, and the rough, masculine hair sprinkled on his arm and over the back of his hand was a heady reminder of the powerful male hormones charging through his body. The hormones that were signalling to her female ones and sending them a little haywire.

She took a shaky breath and slipped her hand out

of his hold. 'It's okay. I'll be brave. I might get seasick otherwise—and that could be infinitely worse.'

His sudden smile transformed his features, making him appear younger and more approachable. And even more dangerously irresistible.

Lucas held Ruby's small hand in his once they'd taken their seats in the four-person helicopter. He could feel the tremor of her fingers and gave them a reassuring squeeze.

Touching her had become rather a habit—a habit he found increasingly hard to resist. Holding her in his arms had made his blood tingle as it had never tingled before. Her body was slim and utterly feminine, each soft curve stirring his body into rampant lust. Perhaps it was his current sex drought, or perhaps it was because he couldn't see but could only feel. All he knew was that he had to be careful around her. She was not his type and he wasn't hers. A fling between them would be completely inadvisable...even if it was sorely tempting.

Lucas was still brooding with anger over how she had been treated in her early childhood. The cruelty was unpardonable, and all these years later Ruby was clearly still carrying the scars. It was ironic that she'd found coming to live on his family estate so stabilising, for he had never experienced it as anything but a battleground for overblown egos. But, putting his parents' issues aside, Ruby had benefited from living there with her grandmother.

He could understand why she would be upset about him selling Rothwell Park. And she would potentially be even more upset when she found out who was buying it. She had already mentioned the hotel billionaire Jack Livingstone in regard to her friend Harper. Lucas should have told her then and there that Jack was the buyer, but he and Jack had signed an agreement to keep the details confidential until the sale was finalised.

The pilot started the engine and Ruby flinched as the rotor blades began to spin. Lucas lifted her hand and laid it on his thigh, speaking to her through the headset microphone. 'Breathe, Ruby…nice and deep and slow. Exhale on the count of three…let go of all your tension with each breath out.'

She dug her nails into his thigh, as if anchoring herself to him. He couldn't hear above the noise of the engine or through the headset whether her breathing had slowed once the helicopter rose in the air, but gradually her grip on his thigh relaxed.

'Are we up very high? I'm not brave enough to open my eyes yet.'

'And here I was, relying on you to tell me what you see.' He kept his tone light.

Ruby's hand slipped off his thigh and he had to stop himself from reaching for it to bring it back. He sensed her shifting in her seat to look out of the window at her side.

'The water is so blue.'

'What shade of blue?'

'A gorgeous turquoise that makes you want to dive in and swim for hours…'

Her voice took on a dreamy note and he pictured her swimming like a mermaid in the ocean.

'What else do you see?'

'A few white clouds.'

'What type of clouds?'

'Hey, I was never that good at geography. Clouds are just clouds to me.'

Lucas gave a wry smile. 'Are they high or low?'

'High and kind of thready—like stretched out cotton wool.'

'They would be cirrus clouds.'

'Oh, right.' She leaned closer to her window. 'Oh, my goodness. I think I can see dolphins. A whole pod of them. Wow!'

'Describe them to me.'

'There's about ten or so, and they're all swimming in one direction—perhaps feeding on a school of fish. The water on their backs as they breach to take in air shines like millions of diamonds. They're so sleek and nimble, so fluid in the water...'

The breathless wonder in her voice entranced him so much that he could picture what she described in his mind.

'Oh, wow, one has just leapt out of the water and splashed back down. The sun caught his silver back and dorsal fin. I've never seen anything so incredibly beautiful...'

Lucas wished he could see the awe on her face, but he realised that listening to her had its own reward. 'What else can you see?'

'Erm... Oh, there's a boat—well, I guess you'd call it a yacht if you want to get all technical. A luxury yacht. It's white, with a blue and silver trim, and it looks like you could sleep ten people or more on board. And to the west is what looks like a couple of fishing boats.'

'We should be getting close to my island now.'

'Already?'

'I can hear Stavros preparing to descend.'

Ruby put her hand back on his thigh. 'Thank you.'

'For?'

'For making me forget about how terrified I was.'

Lucas could make out the vague shape of her face and lifted his hand to stroke two of his fingers down the slope of her cheek. It was like the finest silk under his fingertips, and he wished he could touch more of her. *All* of her.

'You did extremely well.'

His voice came out sandpaper-rough. He heard the sound of her breath, felt the soft waft of it against his face. She gave an audible swallow and his nostrils flared as her flowery fragrance teased his senses into a drugged stupor. Never had he wanted to kiss a woman more than at this moment. Desire roared in his blood, thundered in his pulse, thickened his male flesh to the point of pain.

He cradled one side of her face, his thumb stroking the rounded curve of her small chin. 'You have incredibly soft skin.'

One of her hands came up to the side of his face, and she moved her fingers across the thick growth of stubble. 'You need a shave.'

Her voice was lightly teasing, but there was a quality to it that spoke to the dark desires swirling in his body. Dark and forbidden desires that threatened to break free of the tight restraints he had around them. He could feel them tugging on the cords of his self-control like a wild animal, fighting, raging, desperately clawing for freedom.

'Are you worried about getting beard rash?' Lucas kept his tone light-hearted, but his intention was deadly serious. He longed to feel the softness of her lips against his. Longed for it like a potent drug.

'I would be…if you kissed me.'

Her voice was as husky as his had been just moments earlier. Lucas ran his thumb across the plump shape of her lower lip, recalling its sweet contour in his mind. 'I'm not sure that would be such a good idea right now…'

'Oh?'

There was a wealth of disappointment in her one-word response.

He gave a rueful twist of his mouth and removed his hand from her face. 'I wouldn't want to shock Stavros.'

'Because seeing you kiss the housekeeper's grand-daughter *would* be shocking, right?'

On the surface her tone was as light-hearted as his, but underneath he could hear a trace of wounded pride.

Lucas took off his headset and hung it over the back of the pilot's seat in front of him. 'That would depend on the type of kiss.'

He could almost sense her frowning at him. 'How would you kiss me? I mean, hypothetically speaking, if we *were* to kiss.'

'That would depend on where we were.' He sent a playful smile her way and added, 'If we were in company, then a light peck on the cheek. But if we were alone…'

He left the rest of the sentence hanging, wishing he could see the expression on her face. He didn't want to question why he was flirting with her. He was enjoying their banter way too much. Enjoying the thought of actually kissing her, moving his mouth against the softness of hers and letting things go from there… His body thickened in anticipation, the turgid heat of his arousal reminding him of the fine line he was walking.

A dangerous line.

A line he had promised he would never walk near, let alone cross.

'But we're going to be alone,' Ruby said. 'For a week. Or do you have staff on the island?'

'Yes and no. There's a maintenance man and his wife who look after the house. Their quarters are on the other side of the island, but they're away at present, visiting their adult children on Santorini. I asked them to organise food and supplies, and for the beds to be made up in the villa, but for the rest of the time we'll be alone until Stavros comes to take us back to Athens.'

Ruby unclipped her seat belt. 'You really are serious about maintaining your privacy, aren't you?'

'You bet I am.'

Maybe he should have organised a chaperon. Maybe he shouldn't have brought Ruby here in the first place. Maybe he needed to get a grip and take their relationship back to what it had been before—distant, formal. But something had shifted in the last twenty-four hours. Something that couldn't be so easily dialled back. There was a new sense of intimacy, a sharing of hurts and wounds from the past that had somehow breached the chasm that had existed between them before.

And being so far away from Rothwell Park added another dimension to their relationship. Being away from his ancestral home always gave him a sense of freedom, a sense of living in the moment rather than in the past. But was living in the moment with Ruby a good idea or a bad idea?

All he knew was that he trusted her to help him sign off on the inspection of the villa for the builder. Her attention to detail was similar to his own—little escaped her. Would she notice the way he was drawn to her, even though everything rational and logical in his mind told him to keep his distance?

He had made it a whole lot harder to keep his distance by bringing her to his island.

They would be totally alone.

CHAPTER FIVE

A FEW MINUTES LATER, Ruby stepped down from the helicopter on legs that were not quite steady—not because of the flight, but because of how close she had come to leaning closer and kissing Lucas.

The temptation to do so had been close to overwhelming. She had forgotten all about the pilot, forgotten all about the dreaded flight—all she had been focussed on was Lucas. In the space of a few hours he had become her entire focus. She was aware of him in a way she hadn't been before. Aware of the magnetic pull of his body to her sensually starved one. Aware of the subtle change in their relationship that was not just about his current blindness but something else—something she couldn't quite describe.

What had she got herself into by coming with him to his private island? Normally she was so straight down the line and sensible. She wasn't the type to do things on a whim, to be impulsive or reckless. But it seemed there was a secret part of her that was all those things— or at least when she was with Lucas Rothwell.

She was starting to understand why Harper had found it so hard to resist Jack Livingstone. What was it about renowned playboys that was so darn irresistible? Not that Ruby had ever considered Lucas a particularly charming man. He had always been so brusque and aloof with her in the past. But his gentle handling of her phobic reaction to the helicopter flight had revealed a tender and compassionate side to his personality that was equally addictive as full-blown charm. Perhaps even more so.

Ruby stood for a moment, taking in her surroundings. The island was larger than she had been expecting, with a forest of cypress pines behind the helicopter landing spot. It was fringed by sandy beaches, one of which had a jetty near a luxury villa.

She lifted her face to the sun to breathe in the salty sea air. 'I feel like I've stepped into a fairy tale.'

'It's a nice place. Serene, peaceful...'

'I love serene and peaceful,' Ruby said, linking her arm through his as they followed Stavros, who was taking their luggage on ahead. 'I used to dream of visiting a place like this when I was a kid. You should've seen some of the places I lived in before I came to live with Gran. It would have made your skin crawl.'

'I hate the thought of you suffering like that.' His voice was laced with anger. 'Some people don't deserve to have children.'

'Careful, there's a couple of steps here on the path,' Ruby said. 'I'm just glad I had Gran and your parents. They were kind to me—especially your mother. I remember once she let me play dress-up with some of her clothes and jewellery. I had the best fun. I pretended I was a movie star. She even gave me a bright red lipstick to use. Gran took it off me, of course. She's not a make-up person.'

Lucas stopped walking to look in the direction of the cypress forest, his brow furrowed in a frown. 'My mother lost a baby before I was born. It was a little girl. They—or I should say Mum—called her Sophia. My father was against naming a miscarried child.'

Ruby's heart contracted. 'I didn't know that. How terribly sad.'

Lucas continued walking along the path with her. 'Yes, I imagine it was. I don't think my father is the type of man to understand how a woman would feel about such things. He refused to talk about it—ever. It was as if it had never happened. My mother was thrilled when she got pregnant with me, but I've always wondered if she was disappointed that she didn't have another little girl to replace the one she lost.'

This time it was Ruby who stopped walking to look up at him. 'But she loved you, Lucas. You're surely not in doubt of that?'

He gave a loose shrug of one broad shoulder, his lips set in a grim line. 'It was a difficult birth, and she had a long bout of postnatal depression afterwards. A nanny was engaged for me, and she ended up staying on until I went to boarding school at six. My mother loved me in her way, but she never stopped grieving for the child she lost. Unfortunately, due to the complications of my birth, there was no possibility of her having any more children.'

'No wonder your parents had such a rocky relationship,' Ruby said. 'There were so many unresolved issues. But I wonder why Gran didn't tell me any of this.'

'Your grandmother is an old-school housekeeper. What goes on up upstairs, stays upstairs.'

Ruby wondered what her gran would think of her spending a week alone with Lucas Rothwell. When she had quickly visited her in hospital, before leaving, she had been a little sketchy on the details, simply saying she was filling in for her as housekeeper.

She resumed walking with Lucas up the path leading to the villa. 'I'm sorry I didn't know more about your mother's pain. I might've been able to comfort her in some way.'

'You did comfort her,' Lucas said with heavy conviction. 'She loved it when you came to live at Rothwell. She would be so proud of you now...to see how you've turned out. A smart and successful businesswoman who sets goals and works hard to achieve them, no matter what obstacles are in her way.'

'*You've* been my biggest obstacle so far.' Ruby gave him a playful shoulder-bump. 'Go on—admit it.'

He made a soft sound of wry amusement. 'But you won me over in the end.'

Ruby wasn't so sure about that...

They said their goodbyes to Stavros and he went back to the helicopter. Within a few minutes Ruby watched it take off and rise into the sky, and finally disappear in the distance. This was it—she was finally alone with Lucas. On a private island, no less.

The newly constructed villa was set on a freshly landscaped area a few hundred metres from the main beach. Ruby shielded her eyes from the blinding sunlight and looked critically at the design. She was no architect, but it was impossible to find fault with it.

The lines were modern and minimalist, a pavilion-style design, and it was built on one level. The front of the villa overlooked a large infinity pool that was only a few steps from the main living area. The use of local stone made the villa blend perfectly into the setting. And, while the garden was still in its infancy, the same stone had been used in the terraced areas, softened by lush greenery here and there.

It was quite easily the most luxurious setting she had ever seen, and the thought that Lucas could not see it and might never do so was particularly poignant.

'It's gorgeous, Lucas. Did you design it yourself?'

'Yes—with a bit of help from a friend who's a building architect.'

'It's a beautiful setting with the forest behind. I can smell the pines from here. And don't get me started about the pool… I don't think I've ever seen a more inviting one.'

'I'm glad you like it.' He reached down to brush his hand against one of the newly planted shrubs near the front entrance. 'These will grow in time. It'll take a year or two to get the garden the way I want it. But gardening is always about patience.'

'I like how you've made the villa blend into the landscape. A lot of modern buildings can look a little out of place, but not this one. I can't wait to see inside.'

Lucas waved a hand in the direction of the entrance. 'Come this way. Stavros has opened up and taken our luggage inside. Let's have a cool drink and then you can have a look around.'

'Sounds like a plan.'

Ruby walked with him inside the front entrance of the villa. The floor inside was of stunning polished marble, in cream and beige tones that reminded her of sand patterns on the shoreline. The view from the full-length windows was spectacular, as beyond the of the pool it faced the stunning blue of the ocean with its fringe of powder-white sand. The interior walls were painted a chalk-white, and to balance it, the light fittings were in a modern minimalist style and matte black. The furniture was also modern and streamlined, but there were classical touches here and there that gave the villa a lovely balance of old and new, adding a depth of character than a brand-new home often lacked.

Ruby let out a breath of awe. 'Oh, my goodness, it's so beautiful…'

A smile curved his mouth and her heart gave a little flick-kick. He was so devastatingly attractive when he smiled. It relaxed his sternly cast features and made him seem more approachable.

'The kitchen is through there.' He pointed to the right of the living area that overlooked the pool. 'I'd offer to help, but—'

'Don't be silly—it's what I'm here for. Why don't you wait on the terrace for me? Do you need help getting out there?'

'No.' A note of pride entered his tone and his features tightened into a brooding frown. 'I think I can manage not to tumble into the pool.'

'I'm sorry…' She bit her lip. 'I didn't mean to—'

'Don't apologise.' He released a short gust of air and twisted his mouth in a rueful line, the harsh lines on his face relaxing slightly. 'I guess I didn't expect to be here for the first time after the build under these circumstances.'

'It must be horrendously frustrating for you.'

'It more ways than the obvious.'

The enigmatic quality to his words made her skin tingle. Was he referring to their almost-kiss on the helicopter?

Ruby found the kitchen and set about organising some refreshments from the supplies his staff had delivered. Within a few minutes she had tall glasses of fresh juice and a fruit and cheese platter on a tray. She carried it out to where Lucas was sitting on one of two sun lounger chairs next to the pool. The roof of the villa jutted out over them, to bring much-needed shade to the sun-drenched terrace.

Ever the well-bred gentleman, he rose when he heard her approach. 'Did you find everything all right?'

'Yes—there's no shortage of food or drink, that's for sure. Here we go.' Ruby set the tray on the table between the two loungers and then handed him a glass of juice.

'Thank you.' He waited until she took her seat before he sat in his. Then he crossed one muscled leg over his bent knee and lifted his glass to his lips.

Ruby found it hard not to stare at him, taking in every one of his features—the way his lips moved against the rim of the glass, the way the strong column of his throat moved up and down as he swallowed, the way his long, tanned fingers held the frosted glass... It made her wonder how it would feel to have those fingers touching her intimately.

Her inner core tightened, moistened, pulsed with a

clawing longing, and she crossed her legs to try and suppress the wayward desires.

'Tell me what you can see right now.'

Lucas's deep voice jolted her out of her study of him.

'Erm… I was actually looking at you.'

One side of his mouth lifted at the corner. 'And what do you see?'

She licked her dry lips and put her glass down on the table between them, the shade and the light sea breeze doing little to cool the heat in her cheeks. 'You seem a little more relaxed now you're here. You've even smiled, which you don't often do.'

A frown carved into his forehead. 'You find that a fault? That I don't find life all that amusing at present?'

'It's understandable that you'd be feeling frustrated and annoyed at losing your eyesight. I can only imagine how hard it must be.'

'Close your eyes and imagine it now. Go on. Sit with me here and experience it like I do.'

'Okay…'

Ruby closed her eyes and listened to the sound of the birds twittering in the nearby shrubbery. The sound of the gentle lapping of the ocean in the distance was soothing, mesmerising, and even the light dance of the breeze amongst the leaves of the shrubbery had a calming effect on her senses.

'It's amazing what you can hear when you can only hear and not see. It's like every sound is magnified.'

'Keep your eyes closed and come over to me. Don't cheat. Find your way by touch.'

Ruby found herself taking up his challenge, wanting to prove to him that she was prepared to put herself in his situation in order to better understand his experience of the world at this point. She had an advantage, though, because she had already seen the table between them, and the general layout of the terrace and the dimensions of the pool.

She walked with slow, cautious steps towards him, sidestepping the table and coming to within touching distance of his legs.

'Now take my glass off me and put it on the table.'

Ruby reached out her hand and finally located the glass in his hand, briefly encountering his fingers as she took it from him. She half turned and placed it on the table behind her, making sure first that the surface was clear and the glass would be not too close to the edge. The amount of concentration it took was a revelation to her, and the dangers of breaking a glass or misjudging where a piece of hard furniture might be placed only added to the stress.

'Gosh, this is a lot harder than I thought.'

'Take my hand.'

His voice had a note of command to it that was strangely compelling. Ruby kept her eyes closed and searched for his hand, finally finding it resting on his thigh.

She curled her fingers around his and lifted his hand. 'Now what?'

Lucas rose in one agile movement, standing so close to her she could feel his knees against hers. 'Are your eyes still closed?'

His tone had a husky edge that sent a shiver racing down her spine.

'Yes…' Her voice was as whisper-soft as the breeze teasing the leaves of the shrubbery.

Her heart beat a staccato rhythm that made her feel light-headed and unsteady on her feet. She could feel herself swaying towards him, the magnetic pull of his male body calling out to everything that was female in hers. It was an irresistible forcefield of longing that made a mockery of her determination to keep her distance.

One of his hands cupped the left side of her face, his fingers splaying across her cheek. Tingling sensations rippled through her body and spot fires of need burned in her female flesh. His other hand tipped up her chin, his thumbpad stroking over the fullness of her lower lip.

'You have a beautiful mouth.'

His tone was still pitched low and deep, with a rough edge that set her pulse racing all over again.

'But you can't see it…or at least not clearly.' Ruby couldn't get her voice above a thready whisper, or her heartrate to settle into a more normal rhythm.

'But I can feel it.'

She snatched in a wobbly breath, her heart skipping all over the place. 'What does it feel like?'

'Soft, sensual, sexy…'

His voice went down even lower, to a deep rumbling burr that made heat flow down her spine like warmed honey.

'I don't think anyone has ever used those three words in relation to me before.'

'I find that hard to believe.'

There was a beat or two of silence. A silence that

had an anticipatory element, like a long-held breath while someone waited for an important announcement.

Lucas brushed his fingertips over her closed eyelids. 'I thought you would've peeked by now.'

'I'm tempted.'

'So am I.'

Something about the cryptic quality of his tone sent another shiver rolling down her spin. Then he cradled her face in both of his hands, his touch light and yet possessive.

'Are you asking me to kiss you?'

'I'm not asking you to do anything you don't want to do.'

Ruby slipped her arms around his waist, abandoning her pride in her quest to feel his mouth on hers, emboldened by the feeling sweeping through her body. The desire licking along her veins was sending heat to all of her erogenous zones. A blistering heat that made her aware of every inch of her flesh—especially where it was in contact with his.

Lucas brought his mouth down to hers in a kiss that was as soft as the landing of a breeze-blown leaf. He lifted it off, but then came back down with greater pressure, his lips moving against hers in a sensual manner that sent every female hormone in her body into a happy dance. He made a sound deep in his throat…a guttural sound that was as primal as an animal growl…and then he deepened the kiss with a commanding thrust of his tongue.

Ruby opened to him with a gasp of delight, her legs almost going from beneath her as desire hit her like a tidal wave. His tongue danced and duelled with hers, teasing her senses into overdrive. His hands were still cradling her face, his lips locked on hers, and their bodies were close enough for her to feel every deliciously hard ridge of his.

His lips moved with greater urgency against hers, his tongue playing cat-and-mouse with hers in darting thrusts that sent heat flowing to her core like molten lava. He shifted position, letting his hands fall away from her face to gather her closer by grasping her by the hips. She gasped at the intimate contact with his bold erection, wanting him with a need that was unlike anything she had experienced in the past.

Lucas suddenly broke the kiss with a muttered curse, releasing his hold on her. He pushed his hair back from his face with a rough hand that didn't appear too steady.

'I didn't bring you here to seduce you.'

There was anger in his voice, but she sensed it was directed at himself, not her.

Ruby licked her lips and tasted the sexy salt of his kiss. 'I know.' She smothered her disappointment behind an airy, light-hearted tone. 'You and me, right? Like *that* could ever work.' She moved away to pick up her fruit juice, adding, 'I'm going to have a little scout around before I make dinner. Is there anything I can get you in the meantime?'

'No.' His lips were set in a grim line and he added after a stiffly released breath, 'Thank you.'

She had only taken half a dozen steps when his voice stopped her in her tracks. 'Ruby?'

Ruby turned to look at him. 'Yes?'

He released a long, jagged breath, his expression as

hard and impenetrable as the stonework beneath his feet. 'It won't happen again.'

It must not happen again, Lucas determined once Ruby's footsteps had faded into the distance.

He was furious with himself for giving in to a moment of weakness—a moment of sensual madness that could only backfire if he allowed it free rein. He could still taste her on his lips…the sweet milk and honey taste that had made his senses spin out of control. He was wary of allowing any dalliance between them. Not because of their history per se, but because he wasn't the knight in shining armour she was looking for.

But it didn't mean he didn't want her.

He did. Damnably so.

But just because he wanted something it didn't mean he could have it. He of all people should know that by now.

Like most people, he had taken his sight for granted, never once dreaming it might be taken from him—even temporarily. His career had been built around his ability to see. The career he loved and had worked so hard to build to this point was hanging by the hope that his sight would be restored. He couldn't envisage continuing as a landscape architect without his vision. Nor could he bear the thought of his condition being media fodder—yet another Rothwell scandal to sell newspapers and gossip magazines. His parents' behaviour throughout his life had put a target on his back. Anything he did, anywhere he went, anyone he associated with drew the press to him like bees to pollen.

This week on his private island was meant to be a

way for him to get away from Rothwell Park while it was being cleaned in preparation for Delphine Rainbird's wedding. To rest, to recuperate, to regroup. Not to indulge in a fling with Ruby Pennington…even if the desire to do so was burning a hole in the armour of his self-control like a blowtorch on butter.

Lucas lifted his face to the sun, smelled the spicy scent of the cypress pines behind the villa redolent in the air. He had only been to the island once before he'd bought it several months ago. He had been too busy juggling various large projects across the globe. How ironic that now he finally had the time to be here he couldn't see a damn thing other than vague shapes. He was a details guy—a perfectionist who prided himself on delivering a high standard on every task he set himself.

He knew many blind people lived happy and fulfilling lives, but he couldn't get his head around being one of them.

He *wanted* his sight back.

He *grieved* for the ability to see.

He *mourned* the loss of little things, like not being able to see the sunset, the sunrise, the smile on someone's face…

Yes, he could manage to dress and feed himself, and he could mostly manage to avoid bumping into furniture, but what he wanted was his old life back. The freedom to come and go, the independence, the autonomy, the agency. He was stuck in a foreign land, on unfamiliar territory, where all he could cling to was a thread of hope that his life would go back to how it had been before.

And he didn't need his sight to recognise that he had

seriously miscalculated how tempting it would be to have Ruby here with him. What had he been thinking, getting her to close her eyes and pretend to be blind? It had only intensified the sensual atmosphere between them. The bewitching atmosphere that had grown from the moment she'd stepped into the library at Rothwell Park and asked him about the wedding.

He could have stuck to his refusal. He could have been stubborn and unbending. But he hadn't wanted to jeopardise her business aspirations. In some ways she reminded him of himself—hardworking, driven, determined. It hadn't sat well with him to thwart her plan. He was selling Rothwell Park anyway. What did it matter if one wedding was held there before he handed over the deeds?

Lucas only hoped his determination to keep his hands off Ruby held out over the next seven days, otherwise he was in deep trouble.

Deeper than he wanted to think about.

CHAPTER SIX

RUBY FOUND THE rooms that had been prepared for her by Lucas's housekeeper. The bedroom was larger than her entire flat back in London, decorated in cream and white, with a luxurious handwoven rug on the floor that threatened to swallow her up to the waist. And the bathroom was stunningly appointed, with the same sand-inspired marble floor and tapware in gold.

The shower area was big enough to have a party in, and there was a deep freestanding bath positioned in front of a window that overlooked a secluded walled garden. A young vine was beginning its climb along the stonework outside, and a bronze fountain with a tinkling flow of water gave the setting a spa-like feel. The large pavilion-style windows of the bedroom had a stunning view of the ocean, to the left of the jetty.

She opened the sliding glass doors leading to the terrace and the briny scent of the ocean filled her nostrils. The lightweight silk curtains, captured by the playful sea breeze, billowed around her and out through the doors like the voluminous skirt of a ballgown.

Ruby caught sight of Lucas, down by the water's edge. He was standing with his back to the villa, his hand thrust deeply into his trouser pockets. Was he still deriding himself for kissing her? The housekeeper's granddaughter who had, yet again, made a fool of herself over him? But he had been the one to start it by insisting she close her eyes and try to see the world from his perspective.

Ruby ran her tongue over her lips and recalled every moment of their heart-stopping kiss. No one had ever kissed her with such intensity, with such exquisite sensuality. He had stirred her body into a swarm of sensations it was still humming with even now.

Lucas turned and faced the villa, and even though Ruby knew he couldn't see her she suspected he sensed her watching him. But how could she *not* watch him? Not be transfixed by him? Captivated by him? He had always held a certain fascination for her—her teenage crush was a cringeworthy reminder of that—and in her callow youth she had elevated him to a godlike status, finding him a powerfully romantic figure: a tortured hero who only needed the love of the right woman to find peace.

Ruby had gauchely, misguidedly, imagined herself as that woman, foolishly thinking she was his perfect soul mate. But he didn't even believe such a thing existed. He was as cynical about relationships as she was hopeful and optimistic. One kiss did not mean anything, and she had better hammer that truth into her brain right now or suffer the humiliating consequences of having her hopes dashed all over again.

Ruby had spent an hour in the dream of a kitchen, preparing dinner. Cinderella had never had it so good. The appliances were top-of-the-range, and the layout was perfect in terms of form and function. She couldn't have designed it better herself.

She hadn't seen Lucas since her glimpse of him by the shore. She *had* noticed a large study at the other end of the villa, near his bedroom suite, though. She hadn't dared to venture into his rooms, even though she'd had the opportunity when he was down by the water. Hadn't she suffered enough embarrassment for one day, with him insisting their kiss would not be repeated?

Ruby set up the dining room that was situated in the middle of the villa, overlooking the pool. The water was lit from the sides of the pool, cast in a stunning blue light. The sun was just about to sink below the horizon, painting the lower part of the sky in tangerine and pink streaks. But above that vivid colour storm clouds were forming in bruised-looking clumps, and in the distance Ruby heard a faint rumble of thunder.

Lucas came in just as she was lighting a candle in the middle of the table. He had showered and changed since she'd last seen him—his hair was still damp and curling around the collar of his light blue shirt. He was wearing dark-coloured chinos and suede loafers without socks, revealing his tanned feet. She could pick up the citrus fragrance of his cologne, the notes as intoxicating as his presence.

'Dinner won't be long. Would you like a drink?'

Who said she couldn't act cool, calm and collected after that blistering kiss?

If he was thinking about their kiss, there was no sign of it on his face.

Lucas placed his hand on the back of a chair at the dining table. 'I'll get it. What would you like? Champagne?'

'That would be lovely.'

Ruby decided against insisting she help him. The kitchen was easy to navigate, and it would be good for him to gain more independence. She stayed in the background, putting the finishing touches to their meal, but acutely aware of his every movement as he took the champagne from the wine fridge and released its cork.

But then he frowned, and turned first in one direction and then another, lines of frustration rippling across his features. 'You might have to help me find the glasses. I'm not sure where Iona has put them.'

Ruby moved over to the cupboard where she had seen the glasses earlier. 'Here we go.' She set them in front of him, standing close enough to him to see a tiny nick in the skin of his lean jaw. 'You cut yourself shaving.'

'Yes.' His mouth was pulled tight, his frown brooding.

'I could have helped you with that.'

He turned his head so he was directly facing her, his expression sardonic. 'And you could've also scrubbed my back in the shower, but I don't think that would have been a good idea, do you?'

The mocking edge to his tone did nothing to slow her pulse. And, while she knew he could only see the outline of her face, surely he could feel the searing heat coming off her cheeks? Her brain exploded with images of him naked in the shower. Images of her touching him intimately with her lips and her tongue, the steam coming off the water nothing to the sensual heat coming off their bodies.

A tiny inner demon in Ruby decided to fight back… to make him admit he was as attracted to her as she was to him. 'Because of our kiss? The kiss you say you won't let happen again even though I know you want it to?'

His hands gripped the edge of the counter, his knuckles showing white. 'You should know better than to get involved with me. I'm not your knight in shining armour.'

'Maybe not—but that's not to say we can't have a little…flirtation.'

He curled his top lip, and his pupils turned as dark and wide as black holes in space. 'A "flirtation"?'

The pitch of his voice lowered to a rough burr that sent a shiver across the floor of her belly.

'Believe me, Ruby, you don't know what you're getting yourself in to. You'd be wise to step back right now.'

'What if I don't want to step back?' Ruby stroked her fingers down the front of his muscular chest with just enough pressure for him to feel the scrape of her nails through the light cotton of his shirt. 'What if I want to get closer? What if I want what you want?'

He sucked in a breath but didn't move away. 'I only have flings. I don't do relationships. Ever.'

Ruby sent her fingers on another exploration, this time along the strongly corded muscles of his right arm. His casual shirt was rolled back at the cuffs, revealing hair-roughened forearms. His breathing rate increased, his nostrils flaring like those of a wild stallion scenting his mate.

'So we could have a fling. While we're here on the island.'

She was a little shocked at her forthrightness. Shocked and yet secretly delighted at her brazenness. Why *shouldn't* she be honest and up-front about what she wanted? She might be an old-fashioned girl at heart, but that didn't mean she couldn't have a little fun before her handsome prince showed up, one day in the hopefully not too distant future.

She tiptoed her fingers over the back of his hand, where it was still gripping the counter, and lowered her voice to a throaty whisper. 'What happens on the island, stays on the island.'

The silence stretched and stretched and stretched, like a thin cord pulled almost to snapping point.

Then Lucas removed his hands from where they were gripping the counter and grasped her by the upper arms. His touch was electric, sending arrows of liquid heat straight to her core. He released a rush of air, as if something tightly bound inside him had suddenly given way.

'Don't say I didn't warn you when the week comes to an end.'

Then his mouth came crashing down on hers in an explosive kiss, his lips setting fire to hers. The kiss deepened with a silken thrust of his tongue through the seam of her lips. She gave a breathless gasp and surrendered to his passion—a passion that more than rivalled her own.

He slid one of his hands along the side of her face, his touch sending shivers skittering across her scalp. He angled his head to reposition his mouth, his lips softening against hers, bewitching her into a trance-like state as hot delight shot through her body from her mouth to her curling toes and back again. An ache built in her feminine flesh…a clawing, desperate, primal need that sent pounding blood to her secretly moistening centre.

Lucas dragged his mouth off hers, his chest rising and falling against her. 'Are you sure about this? Once we do this, we can't undo it.'

His voice was rough and thick with desire, and it made her want him all the more. Ruby linked her arms around his neck, pushing her body even closer to the potent hard heat of his.

'I'm not a silly little starstruck teenager any more, Lucas. I'm a fully grown woman and I want you to make love to me—not because I'm in love with you, but because we're both attracted to each other and it makes sense to make the most of it while we can. No one will ever know.'

Lucas ran his hands down the sides of her body, his hands settling on her hips. 'As long as we're clear on the rules.'

'Do I need to sign something? A contract or a non-disclosure agreement?' Her tone was lightly teasing. 'Loosen up! I'm not going to beg you to marry me. This is just a bit of fun to pass the time.'

Lucas tugged her against him in a ruthlessly possessive fashion that sent another scalding wave of heat through her body.

'Then if it's fun you're after…'

His mouth came back down on hers in a spine-tingling kiss that sent fireworks shooting through her blood. The ache between her thighs grew to a throbbing fever-pitch, and her heart was racing as his lips and tongue wreaked sensual havoc on her senses. He growled something indistinct against her lips, a primitive sound, deep in his throat, that made the blood sing in her veins.

His mouth moved from hers to explore the sensitive skin of her neck. She rolled her head to one side, delighting in the sensual glide of his lips against her skin. He moved his mouth to just below her earlobe, his teasing touch firing up the nerves of her erogenous zones like a naked flame thrown at dry tinder.

'You smell divine…'

His voice was low and deep and thick with desire. His teeth gently closed on her earlobe and a shiver shot down her spine like greased lightning.

'I want you so bad…' His bald statement came out like a groan of desperation.

'I want you too—just in case you hadn't noticed.'

He gave a slow smile against her lips. 'It hadn't escaped my attention.'

He kissed her deeply again, in a long, drugging kiss that ramped up her need to an unbearable level. Never had she felt such intense desire. It pounded in her body like a tribal drum.

Lucas left her mouth to kiss his way down to the top of her shoulder, his hand skilfully sliding the fabric of her shoestring-strapped sundress partway down to reveal the naked upper curve of her breast. He moved his lips across the top of her shoulder, sending shockwaves of heat through her body. She hadn't even realised her shoulder was so sensitive, but under the expert ministrations of his lips and tongue her nerves twirled and twitched and tingled.

His mouth was so close to her breast…so achingly close that her skin tightened in anticipation of his touch.

He brought his hand to the globe of her breast, his touch gentle and yet no less spine-tingling. His thumb rolled back and forth over her tightly budded nipple, and a riot of sensations rippled through her.

'You're perfect…so soft and natural.'

Ruby had never seen herself as model material—in fact, she had suffered from body issues since her teens. She had more than her fair share of acne scars and cellulite, which had always made making love with someone tricky in her attempts to hide her imperfections. She knew she had never truly enjoyed sex the way it was meant to be enjoyed. She always worried that she was being assessed by her partner, compared to other far more beautiful women and found lacking. She often cut such casual encounters short by pretending to orgasm just so she could cover herself up again.

But with Lucas all those insecurities melted away. He couldn't see the tiny pockmark scars on her forehead and left cheek…he couldn't see her dimpled thighs. He could only feel his way around her body. And the way he was feeling his way around her now was thrilling beyond all measure.

'I want to touch you.'

Ruby set to work on the buttons of his shirt, desperate to place her mouth on his salty skin. She uncovered his taut and tanned chest and lowered her mouth to his sternum, licking him like a cat with slow sensual licks that evoked another guttural groan from him and a whole-body shudder.

Lucas picked her up by the waist and sat her on the counter, bunching her dress up and nudging her thighs apart so he could stand between them. He put one of his hands behind her and pushed her hard up against his body. His mouth came back down on hers, harder this time, as if his self-control was hanging by a thread. It delighted her to witness his level of arousal—to know it was *she* who was exciting him.

His mouth moved down to her uncovered breast, his lips and tongue caressing her until she was arching her back in pleasure. He stroked his hands over both her breasts, then cradled them. The gentle warmth of his touch sent a frisson of delight through her entire body. Had anyone ever paid such exquisite attention to her breasts? It was like discovering all the pleasure points of her body for the first time.

'I can tell how beautiful you are just by touching you,' Lucas said in a husky tone.

'I would normally be trying to cover myself up at this point,' Ruby confessed. 'I'm hardly supermodel material.'

He frowned. 'You shouldn't be so hard on yourself. Even most supermodels don't look like supermodels without filters and full make-up.'

Ruby stroked her hand down the length of his lean jaw, then ran her fingertip over his lower lip. 'Did you want to have dinner, or…?'

He smiled a lopsided smile and brought his mouth back down to within a centimetre of hers. 'Dinner can wait. This can't.'

And his lips covered hers in a searing kiss that set her pulses racing all over again.

There was no mistaking his intention as the breathless moments ticked on. He lifted his mouth off hers at last, and worked his way down her body with hot kisses that made her skin tingle and tighten in pleasure. He helped her wriggle out of her knickers, and then he parted her thighs and brought his mouth to the damp centre of her womanhood.

A part of her was shocked at the raw intimacy of his caresses. She had never wanted anyone to pleasure her in such a way before, but with Lucas it seemed as natural as breathing. His lips and tongue parted her swollen flesh and she shivered and shuddered in reaction. She arched her spine, resting her weight on her hands, opening her body to him in a way she wouldn't have thought possible a day ago. The sensations rippled through her in increasing waves, and then she was swept into a whirlpool of explosive feeling that sent tremors through every part of her body. Earth-shattering, mind-blowing tremors, that made her gasp and pant with wild cries of pleasure.

Lucas held her as the last of the shockwaves rolled through her. 'That was just an appetiser...'

The sexy timbre of his voice almost made her come again and Ruby gave another little shiver, her body still trying to rebalance after such a heady rush of sensations. 'I can only imagine what's for the main course, let alone dessert.'

He brushed his bent knuckles down the curve of her cheek, a lazy smile tilting his mouth. 'You sound a little undone.'

Ruby leaned her forehead on his, her breathing still ragged. 'No one has ever done that to me before...you know...like that. I've always shied away from being so...so exposed.'

He eased back to study her, and even though she

knew he could only see the vague outline of her face she sensed he was reading her all the same. Her tone, her breathing, her touch—all would be clues to her emotional state.

'Every part of you is beautiful, Ruby. Beautiful and so responsive. Do you know how much it pleases a man to have his partner receive and welcome his touch with such enthusiasm?'

'I guess I've been hooking up with the wrong men. No one has ever made me feel like that. I thought I was going to pass out with pleasure.'

Lucas smiled and placed his hands on her shoulders, bringing her closer again. 'I found it quite unforgettable too.' His voice had that sexy rough edge again.

Ruby frowned in confusion. 'But you haven't finished... I mean, I had an orgasm but you didn't—'

He placed a gentle finger over her lips. 'I can wait. You've gone to a lot of trouble with dinner. We can finish this later. In bed.'

He could wait...

Somehow his words had her self-doubts popping up their heads again like meerkats. Of *course* he could wait. He wasn't as attracted to her as she was to him. She was a convenient lover—someone he would not have looked at twice if the circumstances had been different. He normally slept with stunning model-types who hadn't a dimple of fat anywhere on their person— filter or no filter.

Ruby slipped down off the counter, hastily putting her clothes back in place, her emotions see-sawing. 'Dinner won't be long. I'm just going to...to freshen up...'

Lucas suddenly caught her by the arm as she went to

go past, his fingers a steel bracelet around the slender bones of her wrist. 'You're upset.' It was a statement, not a question.

Ruby pulled her wrist out of his hold. 'Of course I'm upset. I thought you were as hot for me as I was for you, but clearly I was wrong. I'm sorry you had to suffer the indignity of…of *servicing* me.' She almost gagged on the word, but carried on regardless. 'I can assure you I won't bother you again.'

He let out a long, ragged breath. 'Sweetheart, I want you as much as you want me—even more so. But—'

'Here comes the "but",' Ruby cut in before he could finish. 'Here come the reasons why any encounter between us is inadvisable. I'm the housekeeper's granddaughter…the girl who embarrassed you all those years ago by throwing herself at you. I'm from the wrong side of the tracks. No one in your elevated circles would ever accept me as your partner. I could go on and on.'

'Please don't,' he said in a curt tone.

Ruby blinked away the sudden sting of tears, feeling her throat tighten as if something was stuck halfway down. 'I'm not beautiful. I'm ordinary. And everyone knows you don't do ordinary.'

Lucas took her by the shoulders in a gentle hold. 'Do you know how hard it's been for me to keep my hands off you from the moment you walked into the library yesterday at Rothwell Park? I couldn't see you, but I could sense you in a way I have never done with anyone else.' He gave her shoulders a light squeeze, his expression softening. 'Just because I can control my desire, it doesn't mean it's any less fervent.'

Ruby sent the tip of her tongue over her dry lips, suddenly embarrassed by her outburst. But experiencing such mind-blowing intimacy with him had made her feel incredibly vulnerable—especially since he hadn't taken his own pleasure. How could she *not* think he didn't really want her?

'I'm not used to a man taking his time with me. I haven't had a lot of lovers, and most of the ones I've had have been in a tearing rush to get their rocks off. I've mostly faked an orgasm to get it over with— especially if I could tell my enjoyment wasn't going to be a priority for them.'

Lucas framed her face in his broad hands, his features cast in lines of gravitas. 'Your enjoyment is my top priority. Otherwise there would be no point in continuing our...arrangement.'

His slight hesitation over the word he eventually used to describe their relationship made her wonder if he was regretting inviting her to his island. Everything had changed between them—especially now. *She* had changed. Her body was alive and throbbing with new energy. A sensual energy that sent her blood singing through her veins.

Ruby linked her arms around his neck. 'Do *you* want to continue?'

He lowered his mouth to just above hers. 'You bet I do.'

And then he covered her mouth with his in a kiss that left her in no doubt of it.

Lucas stood beside his bed with Ruby. His hands stroked down the length of her bare arms. Her skin was as soft as the finest quality silk. His nostrils flared to take in more of her flowery scent and he raised one of her hands to his mouth, planting a kiss on each of her fingertips in turn.

He longed to see every nuance of her expression, but he had to be content with reading her with his other senses: hearing the soft gasp of her breath as he brought her closer to his aroused body, feeling the way she moved against him, signalling her growing need, smelling the sweet musk of her arousal. Then there was the thunder of her pulse when he pressed his lips to her neck. Her sounds of encouragement…the breathless sighs and whimpers of female desire that made him want her all the more.

He placed his hands on her hips, holding her against the pounding ache of his male flesh, relishing the feminine contours of her body, delighting in the fiery chemistry that flared between them.

Lucas kissed her slowly, deeply, drinking in the milk-and-honey taste of her as if it was a drug he had never known he wanted until now. He couldn't get enough of her softness, the sweet suppleness of her lips, the shy playfulness of her tongue as it tangled with his.

He kept his mouth on hers as he helped her out of her dress, the fabric falling from her like a sloughed skin. His hands caressed the small but perfect globes of her breasts, and he lowered his head to take each tight nipple into his mouth, subjecting it to warm, moist caresses that made her whimper in pleasure.

'I love it when you do that…' she sighed.

'I love the taste of your skin,' Lucas said, trailing his lips over the upper curve of her breast. She shivered under his touch, and his body hardened even further.

'I want to taste yours.'

Ruby tugged his shirt out of his chinos and then set to work on undoing the buttons. He shrugged it off himself, impatient to have her soft little hands on his naked skin. She smoothed her hands over his pectoral muscles then, stepping on tiptoe, placed her mouth to his neck in a softly nibbling little bite that sent an arrow of lust to his groin.

'You're killing me...' He sucked in much-needed air, his body so hot, so tight, so full of thundering blood that it was part pain, part pleasure.

'That's good to know.' There was a smile in her voice...a sultry smile that made her impossible to resist even if he had wanted to.

But he didn't want to.

He had been fighting his attraction to her because he hadn't wanted any more complications in his life. But this week together on his island would be a perfect solution to scratch the itch, so to speak, and move on. End of story. No follow-ups. No promises. No relationship. No commitment.

'You're still wearing your chinos. I want to see you. *All* of you.'

Ruby wound her arms around his body, leaning into him, her nakedness thrilling him to the core. Her breasts were soft and warm against his chest, her lower body flush against his. She planted a kiss to his lips, a barely touching, teasing kiss that only ramped up his desire for more.

'That's easily fixed.'

Lucas pulled away just long enough to step out of the rest of his clothes, including his loafers. He could sense her eyes moving over every inch of him, and he waited with bated breath for her to touch him. The anticipation was intense. His body was poised, thick with blood, with pounding need, and his heart was hammering like a piston, his breathing increasingly ragged. Had he ever been this turned on before? Had anyone got him so worked up? Was it because of who she was? Someone he had known for a long time? Someone he had seen grow from child to woman?

Someone he could no longer ignore.

He couldn't see her clearly, but he could feel every sweet curve of her body. He could feel the silky texture of her skin and how it sent searing heat through his own. How could he have thought he'd be able to resist her touch? How could he have thought he had a hope of keeping his physical distance when his body craved her like a drug?

But he could still keep his emotional distance—just as he always did in his flings. He assured himself that this fling with Ruby would be no different, even though a tiny corner of his mind beeped a tiny warning sound…

He ignored it.

Ruby placed her hand on the middle of his chest, then slowly, achingly, torturously slowly, sent it down lower, lower, lower…until it was just above his groin.

'You're so…big…' There was a note of awe in her voice.

'I'll take things slowly if you're nervous.'

'I'm not nervous,' she said, wrapping her hand around his tight length. 'I'm excited.'

Lucas shuddered at her electrifying touch. Her soft

hand moved up and down, her finger rolling over the head of his erection where pre-ejaculatory fluid oozed.

'Condom.' His voice came out hoarse, as if his tonsils had been filed with a blacksmith's rasp. 'I need a condom.'

'Where are they?'

'In my wallet.'

Where the hell had he put his wallet? His mind was suddenly blank. He was so aroused there wasn't enough blood going to his brain to get it to function.

'I've found it.' Ruby moved to the bedside table and he heard her take a condom from his wallet, and then the soft thud as she dropped the wallet back on the table. 'Here we go.'

She came back to him and pressed the tiny packet into his hand.

'Why don't you put it on me?'

'Okay…'

He could imagine her biting down on her lower lip in concentration. He listened as she opened the packet, and then shivered in delight as she rolled the condom over him.

Lucas pulled her close and clamped his lips down on hers, gliding his tongue through her lips to tango with hers in a sexy duel that sent his senses into overdrive. His cupped her neat bottom with his hands, guiding her womanhood against his erection, wanting her so fiercely it was like a fever in his blood.

He finally lifted his mouth off hers, his breathing heavy. He took her hand and pulled her down to the bed. Once she was lying there he came down beside her, balancing his weight on one elbow, his other hand caressing her left breast.

'This is the first time I've made love with someone since my surgery.' Lucas wasn't sure why he was revealing such information to her, but it had come out in a moment of unguardedness.

That tiny *beep-beep-beep* in the dark corner of his mind sounded again. *Get physically close, not emotionally close.* But it was hard to keep his emotional distance with Ruby. She got under his guard like smoke under a locked door.

'Are you nervous?' The twin chord of concern and surprise in her soft voice made something in his chest contract.

'Not really. I've been making love long enough to be able to do it with my eyes closed. But it's different somehow.'

'Different in what way?'

Lucas moved his hand from her breast to the slim flank of her thigh, his expression rueful. 'It's a new experience to rely only on touch and hearing and taste and smell. I can only imagine how you look.'

'I'm kind of glad you can't see me. You might be disappointed. In fact, I'm sure you would be.'

Lucas frowned and cupped her chin in his hand. 'Stop being so negative about yourself. You are an accomplished and beautiful young woman. I've always thought so.'

'I have cellulite.'

'So? Don't most women?'

'And I have acne scars.'

'I've never noticed them.'

It was true. He hadn't. But he *had* noticed and was increasingly noticing more her emotional scars.

'Only because you've done your best to ignore me since the night of that wretched party.'

'Sweetheart, listen to me.' Lucas used his no-nonsense tone. 'If I ignored you or avoided you it was only so you could get over your embarrassment. I didn't want to make you feel any more uncomfortable than I already had by dressing you down the way I did. Besides, I hated being at Rockwell Park—especially when my parents were there together in one of their honeymoon phases. I was always looking for excuses not to be there.'

Ruby let out a serrated sigh. 'So it's not my fault you're selling it?'

He frowned. 'How could you think it's your fault?'

He heard the movement of her shoulder against the sheet as if she had shrugged. 'I just wondered...'

He stroked his hand down her cheek. 'Stop wondering. It's strictly a business decision. I want to offload it so I can concentrate on other things. It's a white elephant to me. I'll be glad to drive out through those gates for the last time.' He leaned down to kiss her lightly on the lips. 'And speaking of concentrating on other things...' He circled the erect bud of her left nipple with his finger. 'I'm going to make love to you like you've never been made love to before.'

She gave a little shudder and nestled closer. 'That sounds exciting.'

'It will be.'

Lucas brought his mouth back down to hers, losing himself in the sweet taste of her. Her lips were soft and yet insistent, opening to him with whimper of delight that made goosebumps prickle over his skin. He positioned himself at her entrance, stroking her first with his fingers. She gasped and moved against him, urging him on with breathless sounds that jeopardised his plan to take things slowly. Her moist, fragrant heat was irresistible, and he drove forward with a deep, guttural groan of pleasure.

Her body wrapped around him, enclosing him in the tight cave of her womanhood. Shivers coursed over his flesh and his heart raced, his senses reeled and his mind whirled as he thrust and thrust and thrust in the most primal and pleasurable of dances. Ruby picked up his rhythm, moving her body with his as if they had made love together in a past life. He could hear her every breath, every gasp and whimper and cry of pleasure. He could feel the way she responded to him, and it heightened his enjoyment in a way he had not been expecting.

Lucas read the signals of Ruby's body and stroked her intimately to help her go over the edge. He held her shuddering body in his arms as her orgasm rippled through her. Her pleasure triggered his own release, and he thrust himself into oblivion with a hoarse cry. The aftershocks went on and on, until he finally collapsed, spent, satiated, stunned.

He'd been having sex for years, and yet this time it had felt...different. So different it was as if he had slipped into a parallel universe where all the rules had changed. Sex was not just about physical pleasure, but was a complex, layered experience in which body and mind were inextricably involved.

Ruby's hands moved in sensual strokes over the still-twitching muscles of his back and shoulders. 'It must've been good for you. You've got goosebumps.'

Lucas propped himself up on one elbow and used his other hand to finger-comb her silky hair. The apple scent of her shampoo teased his nostrils.. 'It *was* good. Better than good.' He smiled and leaned down to kiss her soft lips.

She sighed and wound her arms around his neck, her legs still sexily entwined with his. He realised with a jolt that he didn't want to be the first to move away. He was *always* the first to move away. Always. So why wasn't he moving? Why was he holding her as if he never wanted to let her go? He would have to let her go once this week was up. That was the deal.

'It was good for me too. The best ever, in fact.'

She nestled against him and he held her close, listening to the soft and rhythmic sound of her breathing.

Lucas wasn't old-fashioned enough to be concerned about how many lovers she'd had before him. Although it was concerning that she hadn't always enjoyed sex the way it was meant to be enjoyed.

But then, wasn't that true for him too?

CHAPTER SEVEN

DINNER HAD BEEN served a little later than Ruby had planned, but she was hardly going to complain. She sat with Lucas in the dining room an hour or so later, her body still tingling from his lovemaking.

Every time she thought of him possessing her, a tiny frisson of pleasure coursed through her most intimate feminine muscles. She glanced at his hand, where it was holding his wine glass, and recalled with another delicate shiver how it had felt to have those clever fingers caress her.

Lucas brought his glass up to his lips and took a sip of wine. He lowered it back to the table, his expression somewhat preoccupied. Was he already regretting the new dynamic of their relationship?

Ruby picked up her own glass. 'You look like you're worrying about something.'

He blinked, as if he had completely forgotten she was sitting opposite him. 'Sorry.' He gave an on-off smile. 'That was a lovely meal...thank you for going to so much trouble.'

'It was my pleasure.' She took a tiny sip of wine and

then returned her glass to the table. '*Are* you worrying about something?'

He shrugged one broad shoulder. 'The usual things—work, staff issues, the sale of Rothwell Park.'

'Delphine Rainbird's wedding?'

Lucas let out a gust of a sigh. 'Not particularly. We've made a deal and I'll honour it. But don't expect me to make an appearance while it's going on. I've been to enough weddings to last me a lifetime.'

He picked up his glass again and drained the contents, setting it back down on the table with a thud that sounded as definitive as a punctuation mark.

'I love everything about weddings,' Ruby said, refusing to be put off by his brooding frown. 'Being present when two people make a permanent commitment to each other is wonderful to witness. So emotional and romantic. Of course I'm usually too busy with the catering to see as much as Harper and Aerin do, but if I haven't been able to snatch a few moments here and there I love to watch the video later.'

'Close to half of all marriages end in divorce. Those are risky odds, if you ask me.'

'I know, but most people start out with the right intentions. Few couples stand at the altar thinking they're going to get a divorce. Love doesn't always die. It gets damaged. And then pride makes people give up, instead of nurturing their relationship back to health.'

His mouth curled in a cynical manner. 'You really are a die-hard romantic.'

'I want what most people want. I want what my mother never found—nor even my gran, for that matter. I want a love that lasts, a love that heals rather than hurts, a love that builds up rather than knocks down. A love that is respectful and kind and enduring.'

'Good luck.'

Ruby pushed back her chair and began to clear the table. 'One day you're going to meet someone who challenges everything you believe to be true about relationships. It's like tempting fate to say you don't believe in love.'

He gave a half-laugh tinged with scorn. 'Isn't it tempting fate to say you do? You'll only get your heart broken.'

'And is that what scares you the most? That your carefully guarded heart might get dented?'

There was a silence. A long awkward silence. Like a pause in the wrong place in a piece of music.

Lucas slowly rose from the table, his expression now unreadable. 'I hope you're not making the mistake of confusing great sexual chemistry for something else.'

Ruby began stacking their used plates with a noisy clatter. 'I might not have had the level of experience that you've had, but I'm not that much of a fool.'

Or was she? It would be all too easy to 'catch feelings', as the modern term went. They were having a fling, a temporary 'arrangement', but how could she protect herself from falling in love with him? He was her total opposite—an aloof cynic who had built an impenetrable fortress around his heart. She was a foolish, open-hearted, optimistic moth, and he was the bright light she could not help being attracted to, even though it might spell disaster.

'Ruby…' Lucas let out a rough-edged sigh. 'I don't want you to get hurt. You've been hurt too much already.'

'I can take care of myself.' Ruby put the plates on a tray and then turned back to him, adding, 'I've been doing it for most of my life.'

He placed his hand on her wrist. 'I know you have.'

His tone was suddenly gentle, soothing. His hand moved up to cradle one side of her face. His body was so close to hers a wave of fresh need whipped through her like a roaring backdraught of flame. His thumb moved back and forth across her cheek in a tender caress that made something in her chest spring open.

'You're brave and strong and resilient,' he said. 'So many people would have fallen at the first hurdle, but you've fought hard and fought fair to get what you want in life. I admire you for it.'

Ruby inched closer to the warmth of his body and his arms came around her and held her close. She rested her head on his chest, listening to the thud of his heart. His hand stroked the back of her head in slow, rhythmic strokes that sent shivers across her scalp and down her spine.

'The only thing that kept me going during my childhood was hope. I clung to it so desperately… I needed it like a lifeline. Each day I would wake up and pray that today would be different—that my mother would turn a corner and be the kind of mother I wanted and needed. I didn't get that wish granted, but my gran did her best to make up for it.' She glanced up at him. 'I guess hope is my default setting while cynicism is yours.'

Lucas pressed a kiss to the middle of forehead, his expression wistful. 'I wasn't always so cynical. I remember being highly optimistic as a child. But I got worn down by my parents' rocky relationship, by the broken promises they made to me and to each other. It was easier in the end not to hope at all. To wait instead for the bubble to burst—as it always did.' He let out a jagged sigh and added, 'I'm trying to be optimistic about my sight returning, but it's tough going.'

Ruby could only imagine how difficult his childhood must have been, and how those emotional wounds still impacted him today. 'Oh, Lucas...' She gently stroked his lean jaw. 'I was so envious of you, growing up at Rothwell Park. You seemed to have it all. A castle to live in, expansive grounds, money and status and two parents who loved you.'

'They didn't know how to love a child unconditionally,' Lucas said. 'They were too self-absorbed—in particular my father. My temperament was too serious for them. I think they'd imagined I would be as outgoing and gregarious as they were. They found it impossible to relate to me and I to them.'

It was a shock for Ruby to see things from his perspective. But it touched her that he felt comfortable enough to share such information with her. He had never done so before. Did that mean he was lowering his emotional guard?

'I understand now that I was only seeing the good bits,' she said. 'Not the bad bits about your life back then. Anything would have been better than what I had grown up with, and that made it harder for me to see the problems you faced for so long. And now you have to deal with the loss of your eyesight and the worry that it might not fully come back. I wish there was something I could do to help you get through this difficult time.'

He smiled a lopsided smile. 'You *are* helping. More than you probably realise.'

Ruby made a business of straightening the collar of his casual shirt. 'You don't regret bringing me here?'

He gathered her closer and rested his chin on the top of her head. 'No. Do you regret coming?'

She leaned back to look up at him. 'You're joking, surely? What's not to love about this place? It's private, it's gorgeous, and luxurious beyond anything I've experienced before.'

There was a slight pause, and then he asked, 'Any regrets about us?'

'How can I regret having the best sex of my life?'

He cupped her left cheek in his broad hand, his expression inscrutable. 'A week is all I'm offering.'

'I know.'

Why did he have to keep reminding her? Why torture her with the clock ticking on their 'arrangement'? She knew the terms. She'd accepted the terms. Wanting more was out of the question. She knew him well enough to know he wouldn't budge on this, even though a tiny flicker of hope still burned in her chest.

His thumb moved across her cheek in an idle caress. 'Our relationship will never be the same again after this. It's not like we can go back to what we were before.' His hand fell away from her face and he stepped back. 'I need you to understand that.'

'Do you have this conversation with all your lovers?'

A ripple of tension passed over his features. 'I don't normally have a pre-existing relationship with my lovers.'

'So you only hook up with strangers? Is that what you're saying?'

'It's less complicated that way. No one gets hurt.'

Ruby resumed the task of clearing away the dinner things. 'I have nothing against casual sex, but don't you get a little tired of the…the impersonality of it?' She placed a wine glass on the tray and glanced at him. 'I mean, you never really connect with them other than physically. Doesn't that get a little boring after a while?'

He shrugged in a dismissive manner. 'Probably no more boring than having sex with the same person for years on end.'

Ruby frowned. 'But how can you say such a thing is boring when you've never been with someone long enough to get to know anything about them beyond their name? And sometimes maybe not even that?'

The line of his mouth was cynical. 'Go on believing in the fairy tale, Cinderella. Don't let me burst your bubble. I hope you find what you want. I hope what you want actually exists.'

'It does exist for some people,' Ruby insisted. 'You mentioned the divorce rate before, but what about the percentage of couples who *do* stay together and have fulfilling and rich lives, being there for each other? I'm not talking about volatile couples, like your parents, but couples who are stable…who love each other through all of life's ups and downs. The couples whose bond is even deeper when they have children and then grandchildren. The sort of couple who love each other more each year, rather than less. Who find joy in each other…who respect each other and lovingly build their relationship as they age.'

'That's the ideal—but who's to say it's reality? Don't most people talk up their lives? Wax lyrical on social media about their so-called soul mate? What goes on behind closed doors is another story.'

Ruby let out a breath of frustration. 'I don't think I've ever met a more cynical person than you. It's like you can't allow yourself to believe in love because you know deep down it has the power to hurt you. But the thing you fear the most is often the one thing you need to embrace, in order to reach your potential.'

Lucas gave a crooked smile that didn't reach his eyes. 'You'll have your work cut out trying to convert me, Ruby. Don't waste your time and energy on a lost cause.'

He walked out without another word and Ruby's shoulders slumped on a sigh. Was she being a fool to think he had the potential to change? He had so many good qualities. He was hard-working and stable and generous, and he cared about his staff. But he stubbornly refused to believe in lasting love. His chaotic childhood would not have helped—watching his parents fall in and out of love repeatedly would have made anyone question whether love could be trusted to last. But her childhood had been even more chaotic, and way more love-deprived, and yet she was still ever hopeful of finding a soul mate.

It's not going to be Lucas Rothwell... a little voice inside her head informed her, in an unwelcome but timely dose of reality.

Their week together on his private island was not even a fling. It was an 'arrangement', so they could both achieve their goals. But how could she stop herself from wanting more? His lovemaking had shown her what had been missing in her previous relationships. He had opened up a world of sensuality to her—a dizzying world of physical delight that she knew on a cellular level she would be hard pressed to find with anyone else.

How could she want anyone else when it was Lucas who made her flesh tingle from head to toe?

How could she want any other man's lips to kiss hers when his set her on fire?

Lucas walked out to stand by the pool, listening to the rumble of thunder in the distance. A storm had been brewing for the last couple of hours, but it was still too far away for him to pick up the glare of any lightning flashes. The brooding weather seemed to match his mood, with the electrical energy in the air signalling atmospheric change a reminder of what was going on between him and Ruby.

Change that could not be reversed.

He had set a seven-day limit on their arrangement, but was a week going to be enough? The first day was almost over and he was already anticipating the next and the next and… Then what? What about when he got to day seven? Would this ache in his flesh have died down by then? Or would his body be as on fire as it was now?

He was already tempted to extend their arrangement, but he didn't want her to get the wrong impression about his motives. It had never been his intention to complicate their relationship. Hurting her was the last thing he wanted to do. She had been hurt too much already by people who should have loved and protected her. How Ruby hadn't ended up as cynical and jaded as him was a miracle, but she stubbornly refused to give up hope.

Hope that one day someone would sweep her off her feet and ride off into the sunset with her.

Lucas rubbed a hand over his face and tried not to think of who that person might be. He only hoped it would be someone who took the time to understand her, to be patient and gentle with her. Someone who would admire and respect her as he did for overcoming such a rough start in life.

The sky lit up in front of him with a flash of lightning, closely followed by a booming crash of thunder. The storm was getting closer by the second.

But the savage storm in his body, and in his mind, was even closer.

Ruby turned on the dishwasher in the kitchen and just then the horizon lit up with silver swords of lightning stabbing at the sea followed by the sound of a booming crash of thunder.

She went and stood next to the open door leading to the terrace. 'Lucas? Don't you think you should come in? That storm is getting pretty close.'

He turned and came over to where she was standing, his expression difficult to read. 'Time for bed?'

She sent the tip of her tongue over her lips, feeling a wave of heat flow through her lower body. 'Did you want me to sleep in my room or...?' She left the question hanging in the air, along with her hopes.

Lucas took one of her hands and lifted it to his mouth, his lips brushing her fingers in a light caress that sent a shiver rolling down her spine.

'Or...?' There was a teasing note in his tone.

'Or...sleep in yours.'

He tugged her a little closer, bringing her up against the deliciously hard frame of his body. 'What do you think?'

His eyes gleamed with erotic intent and her body was swamped with another tidal wave of longing. 'I think it makes sense to make the most of the time we have here.'

His gave a lazy smile. 'My thoughts exactly.'

He placed his hands on her hips, holding her against the primal throb of his body. His mouth came down and covered hers in a kiss that triggered a firestorm in her flesh. His tongue entered her mouth with the same earthy drive as his body had done, making her gasp with delight. Her tongue met his in a sexy tangle that made her blood simmer and her heart pound. Desire throbbed and pulsed between her legs with each flicker of his tongue against hers.

Another zig-zag of lightning cracked overhead, and an almost instantaneous boom of thunder. But the wild weather only seemed to heighten the electricity fizzing between their bodies.

Lucas groaned against her mouth, deepening the kiss even further, one of his hands going to the base of her spine and pressing her harder against his body. Ruby kissed him back with the same intensity, winding her arms around his neck, letting her fingers play with the curls of his hair that brushed against his collar.

He broke the kiss to bring his mouth to the neckline of her dress, his lips blazing a fiery trail across her skin. 'Ever made love in a storm before?' he asked.

'No. Have you?'

'Not that I can remember.' He nibbled on her earlobe, sending another shiver skittering down her spine. 'But first we need protection.'

Ruby glanced warily at the sky outside. 'But surely we can't get struck by lightning under the shelter of the terrace roof?'

'I meant a condom.' He nibbled her other earlobe and added, 'But making love with you *is* a little like being struck by lightning.'

'Right back at you, buddy.' Ruby gave a half-laugh. 'I don't think my body will ever be the same again.'

Lucas frowned and stroked her cheek with his index finger in a gentle touch. 'Have I rushed you? Made you sore?'

His voice was full of concern, and that made it so much harder to control her feelings. Feelings she had promised would not exist between them during their 'arrangement'.

'No, of course not. I just meant making love with you is so different…so wonderfully different from what I've experienced before.'

What were her chances of finding such perfect chemistry with someone else? She might be an optimist, but even she could see there might be a problem finding a partner who met her needs as wonderfully as Lucas. Who else would she love as she loved him? Had she *ever* stopped loving him? Her teenage crush had simply grown into a more mature love. A love that didn't disguise his faults but accepted them as part of who he was.

But he didn't love her. He refused to love anyone. His heart was a cordoned off with razor wire.

His frown loosened, but didn't entirely disappear. He seemed to be mulling over something in that quiet, reflective manner of his. 'Promise me you won't settle for second best in your future relationships,' he said.

'Your pleasure is equally important and should never be sacrificed simply to feed a man's ego.'

'I know, but sometimes it's been hard to be totally comfortable with my partners,' Ruby said. 'I guess that can improve over time, but no one I've met so far has been worth the effort.'

His hands moved up to give her shoulders a gentle squeeze. 'Let's hope you do meet someone who's worth the effort. I hate to think of you being unhappy, Ruby.' He sighed and added, 'What's worse is the thought of me being the one to make you unhappy.'

'I understand this isn't for ever. You really don't have to keep reminding me.'

He gave an enigmatic smile. 'Perhaps it's not you I'm reminding.'

His tone had a husky edge, and he leaned down to press a lingering kiss to her mouth. Ruby's lips clung to his, her senses on high alert, her heart beating hard and heavy as his mouth moved with mastery against hers. He gave a deep sigh of pleasure and drew her closer to his body, igniting her desire like a match to kindling.

Was he rethinking the timeline on their arrangement? A week was such a short period of time. Dared she ask him to extend it? Or should she leave things as they were, hoping he would come to see the sense of enjoying the chemistry they had for a little longer?

CHAPTER EIGHT

FOUR DAYS LATER, Ruby sat by the pool watching Lucas swim lengths. By counting his strokes he was able to judge when to do a flip-turn at each end.

She would never tire of watching his lean, athletic body slicing through the water with breathtaking efficiency. His skin had developed an even deeper olive-toned tan, but due to her fairer complexion and limited swimming ability she stayed in the shade, and only jumped into the shallow end of the pool to cool off.

The week was rushing past, and he hadn't mentioned anything more about the timeline on their relationship.

Once she had meticulously gone through the builder's checklist with Lucas they had slipped into a holiday mode routine that was intensely relaxing, and a refreshing and much-needed change for her, given how hard she had been working over the last few months.

Lucas, too, looked more relaxed and at ease than he had at Rothwell Park, although there were times when she caught him staring into space with a frown on his face. She knew he was worried about his eyesight and how it would impact on his career if it didn't return.

But whenever she encouraged him to talk about it he quickly changed the subject.

He was in contact with his staff via phone each day, but he kept it to a minimum and spent the rest of the time with her. They went on long walks around the island and Ruby would make a picnic to carry in a backpack, so they could lunch in the little bay on the other side of the island. She couldn't remember a time when she had felt so at ease with someone. Lucas even asked questions about her work, showing an interest in all the things she planned to do to build her business with her friends.

Lucas stopped swimming and came over to lean his forearms on the edge of the pool, close to where she was sitting. He scraped his wet hair off his face, his eyes narrowed against the bright sunlight.

'Jump in with me and cool off.'

Ruby gave a playful laugh. 'If I jump in with you I will definitely *not* be cooling off.'

His smile was broad, his teeth shining white against his tan. 'Come here.'

His tone had an arrogant note of command about it, but instead of annoying her, it excited her. A frisson of delight coursed through her and her pulse picked up its pace.

'You can't make me.'

'Can't I…?'

His silky tone sent a shockwave of lust through her core. Then he launched himself out of the pool in one supremely athletic movement, droplets of water landing on her from his glistening body.

'Hey!' She tried to shift out of the way by rolling onto one hip. 'You're making me wet.'

Lucas placed his hands on each arm of her sun lounger, effectively caging her in. 'That's the plan.' His mouth was just above hers, and his voice was deep and rough around the edges. 'I love it when you're wet for me.'

Ruby shivered, and couldn't take her eyes off his mouth. The smiling contours of his sculpted lips sent hot pulses of need through her. Those lips had been on the most intimate parts of her body, sending her to paradise and beyond so many times she had lost count.

She linked her arms around his neck, bumping her lips against his once, twice, three times. 'I want you.'

He smiled against her lips. 'I want you more.'

She reached down and stroked the thickened ridge of his erection, smiling a sultry smile. 'Mmm, what's got you all excited?'

'You.'

Lucas adjusted the sun lounger so it reclined a little further, then pushed her legs apart and kneeled between them. He stroked the seam of her body through her bikini bottoms, the light caress sending shivers cascading down her spine and tightening every nerve in her pelvis in anticipation. Then he nudged the fabric aside and placed his mouth on her most intimate flesh. He tasted her, teased her, tantalised her. Until she was sobbing with pleasure, her whole body shaking, as the rippling, rolling, crashing waves smashed through her.

Ruby finally managed to sit upright, her senses still reeling, her body experiencing delicious little after-shocks. 'I can't let you get away with rendering me senseless without some sort of payback...' She sprang off the sun lounger and commanded him, 'Lie down.'

Lucas lay in the space she had just vacated. 'Should I be nervous?'

'Very.'

He gave a whole-body shudder and sucked in a breath. 'I can hardly wait.'

Ruby worked her way down his body from his mouth to his bellybutton and back again, in teasing kisses and caresses that made his breathing rate escalate. Then, on her next journey down his body, she went a little lower, stopping just above the jut of his erection.

'You're torturing me...' he groaned, and gripped the edges of the sun lounger as if to anchor himself.

'That's the plan...' She echoed his own words and then, kneeling down beside him, licked along his skin from the shallow cave of his bellybutton to the hem of his swimming trunks. Then slowly, ever so slowly, she peeled his trunks down, her gaze drinking in the potent length of him. 'Mmm...now, where will I start?' she mused, trailing a lazy finger from the head to the base of his erection and then back again.

He gave another shudder and muttered a curse-word, his body twitching in anticipation. Ruby placed her mouth on him, licking and stroking him with the tip of her tongue, delighting in the guttural groans he was making, delighting in the thrill of pleasuring him in a way she had not done with anyone before. It had always seemed too raw and intimate, and yet with Lucas she relished the texture of his skin and the taste of his essence.

She worked on him until he was close to the edge,

his groans increasing with each silky movement of her mouth against his rigid flesh. And then he finally let go, his body racked with a series of violent shudders. She watched the flickering emotions on his face—the agony, the ecstasy, the exhilaration, and then finally the relaxation.

Lucas opened his eyes and turned his head towards her. One of his hands came up and touched her lightly on the face, her nose, her lips her chin. 'That was... amazing. *You* are amazing.'

Ruby shrugged. 'Not bad for a beginner, I suppose.'

He frowned. 'You mean you haven't ever—?'

'No. You're the first partner I've wanted to do that to. It never felt right for me before.'

He finger-combed her hair back from her face, his expression thoughtful. 'It's not an experience I'm going to forget in a hurry.' He let out a shuddery breath and added, 'But then, there's a lot about this week I'm not going to forget.'

Ruby sat on the edge of the sun lounger next to him and tiptoed her fingers down his forearm. 'It's going so quickly...'

'Yes...'

A silence fell.

'Ruby?'

'Yes?'

He stroked his hand up and down the length of her arm from shoulder to wrist. 'Thank you for being with me this week. It's been what I needed—some time out to think about my situation going forward.' He gave a rueful smile and added, 'If it hadn't been for you coming that day to Rothwell Park and asking about Delphine's wedding, I would probably still be sitting brooding on my own in the library.'

'Why did you ask me to come with you?'

He moved his head in a side-to-side motion, as if trying to think of an appropriate answer. 'The builder's checklist had to be done... But truly I didn't intend for anything like this to happen between us.' He ran a lazy finger over the slope of her left breast. 'Or at least that's what I told myself. But I found it hard not to kiss you, to want you... And when you seemed to want me just as much—well, I figured it was the perfect opportunity to indulge in a fling.'

'Is that what we're calling it now? A "fling"? I thought it was an "arrangement".' Ruby kept her tone light and teasing.

His mouth twisted again. 'I'm not sure what to call it any more.' He brushed his finger over her lower lip, his expression cast in contemplative lines. 'You're not like any other lover I've had in the past.'

'Yes, well, that's because I've never gone near a catwalk in my life and nor am I ever likely to.'

Lucas took one of her hands and gave it a gentle squeeze. 'I wish you wouldn't be so negative about yourself. I've met stunning women who have bored me within seconds. You're both beautiful *and* interesting.' His other hand came up to cup her cheek. 'And so sexy I can barely keep my hands off you.'

But how beautiful would he think her if he got his sight back?

She was not in the same class of attractiveness as his usual partners by any stretch of the imagination. And her insecurities were hard-wired into her personality—

drummed into her by the cruel comments of her mother and many of her unsavoury boyfriends. And if Lucas thought her so irresistible, why had he placed such a strict time limit on their relationship?

A soft little sigh escaped from Ruby's lips. 'You're great for my ego. I don't think I've ever had so many nice things said to me in my entire life.'

Lucas continued to hold her hand. 'I guess your gran isn't one to splash compliments about. But she loves you and is enormously proud of you.'

'I know...but there's a part of me that feels unlovable. I mean, if my own mother couldn't love me, who else could?'

'It's understandable you feel like that, given what you've been through.' His thumb stroked the back of her hand in a soothing fashion. 'But you can't let your mother's inadequacies as a parent dictate your life going forward. She might not have been capable of loving you, or anyone, but there are plenty of other people who are.'

But he wasn't one of them, was he? He liked her, and he enjoyed her company, but he didn't love her the way she wanted to be loved. Was it because of the way he'd seen love growing up? The way it had been expressed via his parents?

The sound of a mobile phone ringing sounded in the ensuing silence.

'That's my phone,' Ruby said, reaching for her sarong. 'I'd better answer it. It might be Gran calling.'

She got to her phone on the table inside the villa just in time to see it was Aerin on the line.

'Hi, Aerin.'

'I have good news and bad news—which do you want first?'

'Let's go with the bad news.'

'Delphine wants to bring the wedding forward.'

Ruby frowned. 'Forward by how much?'

'She wants to get married next weekend.'

'Next weekend?' Ruby's response came out as a squeak. 'Are you serious?'

'Apparently there's been a sudden change in the shooting schedule for the movie she's filming, so the wedding has to be brought forward. It's the only time she has available now. It's going to be a nightmare to pull it off, but I think we can do it. Harper is okay with the change. And we don't have any other bookings next weekend, so there's no reason why we can't rise to the challenge.'

Ruby had every confidence that Aerin would be able to pull it off, and Harper was always one to be prepared for a sudden change in plan. But would Lucas be okay with the change? She would have to fly back tomorrow to organise her catering team. Catering for a wedding was not as easy as putting a picnic together. There was so much planning and preparation to do before the event. And she would have to make sure the cleaning team had left Rothwell Park in tiptop shape...

'So what's the good news?'

'Delphine insists on paying us a bonus for the date-change.' Aerin named a figure that made Ruby's eyebrows lift. 'I told her I'd check with you first, before I confirmed it.'

'We'd be crazy not to accept,' Ruby said. 'Tell her it's a yes.'

She ended the call and glanced at Lucas, still lying on his back on the sun lounger out on the terrace, his hands propped behind his head, his eyes closed against the bright sunlight.

She walked back out to him and he opened his eyes and reached for one of her hands. 'How's your gran?'

'It wasn't my gran.' She sat down beside him. 'Lucas, there's been a change of plan. Delphine wants to get married this coming weekend instead of next month. I'll have to fly back tomorrow to get ready. I know we agreed on a week here together, but I have so much to do...'

Lucas sat upright and laced his fingers through her hair in a light caress that sent shivers across her scalp. If he was disappointed that their week was being cut short he didn't show it on his face.

'I'll call Stavros to pick us up first thing tomorrow. Will you be able to do everything you need to do in such a short time?'

'I think so. I've done a couple of big weddings at short notice before. And it will be easier doing it at Rothwell Park because I know the kitchen so well. But it's still a huge challenge.'

He gave a crooked smile and stroked a lazy finger down the slope of her nose. 'I'm sure you're more than up to it.'

Ruby bit her lip. 'Lucas...you know how we agreed that what happens on the island, stays on the island...? I'm sorry for cutting our time together short by three days, but—'

He captured her hand and entwined his fingers with hers. 'We don't have to cut it short.'

She blinked and swallowed. Could this mean he was keen to continue their relationship? Hope flared in her chest and she felt a bubble of excitement in her blood. 'What do you mean?'

'We can continue our arrangement.'

Her heart skipped a beat. 'Until when?'

His expression gave nothing away. 'Let's leave it open-ended for now. The sale of Rothwell Park will be finalised in the next few weeks, so I'll be moving out. And you'll have to head back to London in any case.'

Her hope lost some ground, sinking back down to reality with a painful thud.

'You'll have to head back to London in any case.'
She'd be going alone.

Lucas was only offering her an extension on their arrangement. An extension was good, but the timeline was still in place—a definitive timeline that left her wanting more. Aching for more.

She looked down at her hand, encased in his large one, and something in her chest tightened like a vice. 'And where will you go?'

'That depends.'

She glanced up at him. 'On whether you regain your sight?'

'Yes...' His tone was weighted, and a flicker of worry passed over his features.

Ruby stroked a hand down his jaw. 'You mustn't give up hope. It might not return as soon as you want, but hopefully it *will* return.'

His smile was not quite a smile. 'I'll just have to wait and see.' His mouth twisted further, and he added with unmistakable irony, 'Or not.'

Ruby was relieved to find, once they got back to Rothwell Park, that the cleaning and gardening teams had done a brilliant job. The castle sparkled from top to bottom, and there wasn't a weed or blade of glass out of place in the expansive gardens. Even the weather had brightened. There were no gloomy clouds on the horizon, no threat of rain, and while the air was still cool, the sun was out in a clear blue sky.

Her gran had left hospital and was staying with a friend in the Lake District, seemingly enjoying her new, quieter pace of life. Ruby's team were arriving the following day, as well as Aerin and Harper, which left only tonight for her to be truly alone with Lucas before all the frenetic activity began.

She was still blissfully relieved about him extending their arrangement. She had been so sure he would stick to his plan of *What happens on the island, stays on the island.* Could it mean he was developing feelings for her? More lasting feelings? It was hard not to cling to hope, for he made love to her with such exquisite attention to her needs.

Their physical chemistry was unquestionably divine, but his companionship was also something she found increasingly enjoyable. Their chats over dinner or on their long walks had opened her up to his world of landscape design, and the worries he had about resuming his career if his sight didn't return. His willingness to share such moments of vulnerability with her made her feel closer to him than she had felt to anyone else—even, to some degree, her two best friends.

Ruby was finding it impossible to imagine going back to her single life now that she had experienced being in a fulfilling relationship, even if it had only been for a few days. It was a world apart from any relationship she'd had before, so how could she not hope it would continue, perhaps for ever?

Lucas had taken himself off to the library to make some phone calls to his staff a couple of hours ago, so Ruby set a tea tray and took it in to him. The door was ajar, so she nudged it further open and carried the tray over to the windows, where he was standing with his back to the room. He turned and faced her, a smile relaxing his features.

'Tea for two?'

'Yes, because tomorrow this place will be crawling with people.' Ruby set the tray down and picked up the teapot. 'Thank you for being so good about the sudden change. And about allowing us to use Rothwell Park. It's a dream come true for us to host such a big celebrity event.'

His smile became twisted. 'As long as you don't expect me to make an appearance. Weddings bring me out in hives.' He stood next to one of the chairs and she handed him a cup of tea. 'Thanks.' He took the cup and waited for her to take a seat before he too sat.

Ruby picked up a teaspoon and stirred her own cup of tea. She put the spoon down again and took a sip, watching him over the rim of her cup. A frown was carved on his forehead and one of his fingers was tapping the side of his cup in a restless manner.

She put her cup on the table between them. 'Is everything okay?'

He blinked and reset his features into a less brooding expression, but she could still see shadows moving behind his gaze. 'Just work stuff. A project that needs my attention. But what can I do?' He let out a sigh of frustration. 'Clearly nothing at the moment.'

'Oh, Lucas, it must be so frustrating for you. I wish there was something I could do to help.'

'You've already helped more than I can say.' He let out a long sigh and leaned forward to place his own cup on the table. He sat back and continued in a wry tone, 'Patience was never one of my strong points.'

Ruby stood and went over to stand by his chair, stroking his ink-black hair, her body pressed close to his side. One of his arms came around her waist and a thrill went through her at his touch.

He pulled her down to his lap, one of his hands cradling the side of her face. 'You're very good at distracting me.'

'Am I?'

He pressed a soft kiss to her lips. 'You know you are.'

'I find you pretty distracting too.'

'All the more reason for me to stay out of the way while you do your wedding preparations.'

Ruby stroked the hair back from his forehead. 'I'd like you to meet Aerin and to say hi to Harper again.'

His brows snapped together. 'Why?'

'Because we're using your family home as a wedding venue and they'd like to thank you for your generosity.'

He dislodged her from his lap and stood and went to stand at the windows again, his back turned towards her. 'You can thank me for them.'

'But it would be so nice for them to—'

He swung back to face her, his expression set in intransigent lines. 'What have you told them about us?'

'Nothing.'

He gave a rough-sounding laugh. 'How did you explain our days on the island?'

Ruby licked her suddenly dry lips. 'I didn't tell them about your eyesight, and I didn't tell them we were having a fling. In fact, they both warned me against doing any such thing.'

'Maybe you should've heeded their warning.'

'Maybe I should have.'

She stood and began clearing away the tea things, feeling her heart contract at the way he was pushing her away. But how could she regret some of the most magical days of her life? Days filled with sensual pleasure and delight. Days she would remember for ever.

Lucas let out a stiff curse-word and came over to her. He placed his hands on the tops of her shoulders and turned her to face him. 'I'm sorry for being in such a foul mood.' He gave her shoulders a gentle squeeze and added, 'Thank you for keeping my condition a secret from your friends. I can't bear people's pity.'

Ruby wound her arms around his waist and laid her head on his chest. 'I understand. I'd probably be the same.'

He held her close for endless seconds, then he eased back to lift her face with a finger beneath her chin. He searched her features, as if willing his eyes to see her more clearly. But maybe it was better that he couldn't, for she was finding it hard to hide the feelings she had for him. The feelings that had grown against her will, against her better judgement, against the advice of her best friends, against all reason. Feelings that could not be so easily dismissed as a silly little teenage crush. Feelings that were deep and strong and yet painful, because she was gambling on the slim chance that he might one day return them.

His lashes lowered to half-mast over his eyes and his mouth came down on hers in a kiss that melted her bones and curled her toes and sent her pulse racing off the charts. His tongue glided into her mouth to mate with hers in an erotic dance that sent blazing heat to her core. His arms moved around her, bringing her closer to the hard frame of his body. He groaned against her mouth—a guttural groan that spoke of urgent primal need spiralling out of control. The same primal need that was barrelling through her body in tidal waves of searing, blistering heat.

'I can't stop wanting you,' he said, in a tone that seemed to hint at deep frustration with himself.

'I want you too,' Ruby said. 'So much it hurts.'

He held her face between his hands, angling her head so he could deepen their kiss. The kiss went on and on, sending her senses into a tailspin. His lips were soft and cajoling, and then hard and insistent, ramping up her need for him to fever-pitch. He lowered his mouth to the sensitive skin of her neck, the teasing movement of his lips sending shivers down her back. He set to work on her clothes and she worked on his, her hands less efficient than she would have liked. But finally they were both naked and Lucas had sourced a condom.

'You came prepared,' Ruby said with a sultry smile.

'I've learned to be prepared around you. You turn me on in a heartbeat.'

Lucas lowered his mouth to the curve of her right breast, his tongue circling her nipple in a spine-tingling caress. He took the nipple gently between his teeth, then sucked on her, drawing her nipple further into the warm cave of his mouth. Hot arrows of pleasure shot through her body and molten heat pooled in her core. He moved to her other breast, subjecting it to the same deliciously erotic caress, and she felt her legs weakening as the pleasurable sensations rippled through her in waves.

Lucas guided her down to the floor and then came down beside her in a tangle of limbs. He stroked her hair back from her face, his eyes glazed with lust. 'Are you sure you don't want to take this upstairs, to a comfortable bed?'

'No time for that.' She pulled his head down so his mouth came back to hers.

His kiss was long and deep, his breathing as hectic as hers. Then he thrust into the seam of her body with a harsh groan. 'You feel so damn *good*…'

Ruby caught his fast rhythm, her body gripping him, wanting him, needing him. His thrusts became deeper, harder, faster, but she was with him all the way. Her senses were on fire as the pressure built in her most intimate flesh. She was wet and swollen, tight with need. He placed a hand beneath one of her buttocks to lift her pelvis to receive him deeper, and the friction intensified, electrifying. Tiny flickers of pleasure became a ferocious fireball of flames and flashing fireworks as her orgasm swept through her. She gasped out loud as the sensations exploded in her flesh, her body thrashing beneath his as the waves pulsed through her. Lights flashed behind her closed eyes and scorching heat flowed to every inch of her body.

Lucas followed with his own explosive release, his harsh cries echoing in the cavernous silence of the library. He collapsed on top of her, his head against the side of her neck, his warm breath a caress on her skin. 'Am I too heavy for you?'

'No.'

'Good, because I don't think I can move right now.'

Ruby stroked her hands over the taut muscles of his back and broad shoulders, a smile curving her mouth. 'Nice to know I have that effect on you, since you do the same to me.'

There was a peaceful silence.

Lucas finally propped himself up on one elbow, his free hand lazily stroking the curve of her cheek, his expression suddenly serious. 'I wish I could see you more clearly.'

There was a note of wistfulness in his tone that plucked at her heartstrings.

'I can tell when you're smiling, but that's about all.'

Ruby brushed his lower lip with her index finger. 'I have more freckles since we got back from Greece.'

'Where?'

'On my nose.'

He bent down and kissed the bridge of her nose. 'I've always found your freckles kind of cute.'

He placed another kiss at the corner of her mouth, setting every nerve on high alert.

'In fact, there's not a part of you I don't find irresistibly attractive.'

And his mouth came down to cover hers again.

During the early hours of the morning, Lucas woke from a deep and restful sleep to find Ruby nestled against him, fast asleep. He ran an idle hand up and down the silky skin of her arm, breathing in the honeysuckle scent of her body, feeling her fragrant hair tickling his nostrils where her head was tucked below his chin. He never failed to marvel at the texture of her skin, the sweet taste of her lips, the sensual warmth of her body. He couldn't get over the way she responded to him with such enthusiasm and delight. His desire for her hadn't abated at all—it had become more fervent.

He began to drift back to sleep, but then a worry began to nibble at the wainscoting of his mind...

He had done something he had never done before. He had extended a fling with a lover. Not only extended it, but left it open-ended. Before now, even if he hadn't actually told a lover their end date, he had always had one sketched in his mind. But with Ruby it was as if his playboy rulebook had been torn up. He had ignored his own rules, put them to one side, in order to indulge in a fling that wasn't like any other fling he'd had before.

Was it because she wasn't a stranger he had met in a bar? She wasn't a casual lover—someone who wanted a good time not a long time? Ruby was after the damn fairy tale, and yet he was drawn to her by an irresistible force he couldn't explain, let alone control. Was it because he already had a relationship with her? One that went back years? Was that what was making it so freaking hard to define a timeline? Or was it the mind-blowing sex between them that kept getting better and better?

He couldn't remember having a partner who was so in tune with him physically. He was no stranger to good sex—great sex, even. But with Ruby it was on a whole new level. Was it because he couldn't see her but only feel her? Because he could only taste and smell and touch her? Had his other senses intensified the experience, making him wonder if making love with anyone else was going to be as good, regardless of whether he got his sight back?

Ruby murmured something and nestled closer. He felt something in his chest flare open, and a sensation of warmth seeped into all the cold corners of his guarded heart.

Careful, buddy, don't let things get too serious. Don't get too close. A fling is a fling, no matter how long or short it is. Stay in control.

Lucas dismissed the warning of his conscience. Of course he was still in control. He wasn't going to let things get out of hand just because he had extended the timeframe on his relationship with Ruby. He might be enjoying the explosive chemistry between them, but that didn't mean he was losing control of his emotions.

He *never* lost control of his emotions.

Falling in love was something that happened to other people, not him. He had a line drawn in his mind and nothing and no one was going to make him step over it. Ruby might be refreshing and endearing and super-sexy, but he wasn't going to suddenly morph into a knight in shining armour.

Not now. Not ever.

Not possible.

CHAPTER NINE

RUBY WELCOMED HER best friends and business partners to Rothwell Park the following day, along with her catering team. Once her team were busy setting up in the kitchen she met with Aerin and Harper in the less formal of the three sitting rooms, for a quick catch-up over drinks and nibbles.

'These look scrumptious,' Harper said, reaching for one of the savoury tartlets Ruby had prepared earlier. 'There goes my diet. I'm so hungry I could eat a horse and chase the rider—and maybe the saddle and bridle wouldn't be safe from me either.'

'You don't need to diet,' Aerin said with a tinkling bell laugh. 'I think you look amazing right now. Your skin is glowing and your hair is so shiny. Have you had a treatment?'

'Yes, I was thinking so too,' Ruby said. 'I don't think I've seen you look better.'

Harper took another tartlet off the plate and waggled her eyebrows at Ruby. 'I could say the same about you. Four days on a private Greek island with Lucas Rothwell seems to have agreed with you. So, when do we meet him?' She popped the tartlet in her mouth and chewed with obvious enjoyment.

'He's not feeling very sociable at the moment,' Ruby said, hoping her hot cheeks weren't giving her away. 'Weddings kind of freak him out, given how his parents married and divorced each other three times.'

How else could she explain why he wouldn't meet them? She hadn't told them he was blind, after his request for privacy.

But Harper had obviously picked up on something, for she leaned forward with a narrowed look. 'What's going on? There's something you're not telling us.'

'Nothing's going on,' Ruby said, averting her gaze.

'So how was it? The island?' Aerin asked, her eyes wide with interest.

'Amazing.' Ruby took a parmesan sablé off the platter and put it on her plate. 'The villa is gorgeous, and it has a wonderful infinity pool set in front of it, so most of the rooms on that side of the villa look out over it. The gardens aren't fully grown, but they'll be a showpiece once they're established. There are several lovely beaches, and there's a long private jetty and a pine forest that covers almost two-thirds of the island. I'll show you photos later. But first we'd better run through the wedding programme.'

The less she talked about Lucas and the island, the better. Revealing too much of her relationship with him would mean revealing her feelings about him. Her friends had already warned her about losing her heart to a man who couldn't commit.

Harper stopped raiding the platter to fix her gaze on Ruby. 'So, did you sleep with him?'

Ruby was aware of the heat storming in her cheeks. 'I don't want to talk about it. Look, we have Delphine's wedding in a day's time and—'

'You did!' Harper said, slapping her own knee. 'I knew you wouldn't be able to resist him. Don't say I didn't warn you.'

Aerin had a look of concern on her face. 'Are you *still*...sleeping with him?'

Ruby blew out a breath. 'We were only going to have a fling while we were on the island, but then we had to come back early for Delphine's wedding, and now...'

'So, that's a yes,' Harper said. 'Well, I guess it's your life and your heart and all that. But I can't see it ending well—especially if he doesn't want to be seen in public with you while you're together.'

Aerin chewed at one side of her mouth, her gaze steady on Ruby. 'You're in love with him, aren't you? I mean, *really* in love.'

Ruby let out another long sigh. 'I tried so hard not to fall for him, but I guess I've always had feelings.' She picked up her drink and stared at the contents for a moment before adding, 'Not that he returns those feelings. We're just having a fling, that's all. That's all he ever has—flings.'

'I know the type,' Harper said with an eyeroll, but then continued in a more compassionate and reflective tone. 'It really sucks to fall for someone who's unattainable. But sometimes I wonder if that's what happens to former care home kids like us. The people we loved as kids didn't love us the way we were supposed to be loved, so we tend to fall for men who are the same. Totally unattainable men who are not able to love us the way we want to be loved.'

Ruby frowned in confusion. 'Are you saying you're in love with Jack Livingstone?'

Harper rapid-blinked, like an animal sure it was about to become roadkill, and then she screwed up her face in distaste. 'No, of course not.'

'I think you're both being a little hard on Lucas and Jack,' Aerin said. 'Not all playboys stay unattached for the rest of their lives. Look at my dad, for instance. He was a notorious playboy until the day he met my mum. Then he couldn't get a ring on her finger quick enough, and they're still as in love as the day they met.' She gave a dreamy sigh and added, 'Wouldn't it be wonderful if all three of us could find a partner like that?'

'Personally, I'm happy on my own,' Harper said. 'Call me hypocritical for working as a wedding photographer, but I don't want the complications of fitting my life around some guy who expects his pipe and slippers brought to him each night.'

'I think most men are a little more woke than that these days,' Aerin said with a light laugh. 'But seriously, Ruby...' Her expression sobered. 'Only you can decide what to do. But it seems to me a positive thing Lucas wants to continue the fling.'

'I know... But, like Harper said, I've had a lifetime of getting my hopes up only to have them dashed,' Ruby said. 'Lucas has always been a closed-off sort of person, but he's opened up about a bit of stuff over the last few days—about his childhood and his parents and their crazy relationship. And, to be honest, I too have shared things I've only ever shared with you two before. I kind of feel Lucas and I have got to know each other on a different level. A more intimate level.'

'Yes, well…if you're getting naked with him, it doesn't get more intimate than that,' Harper put in.

'I think it's more than that,' Ruby said. 'I feel more comfortable around him than ever before. And I think he does around me.'

'Do you feel comfortable enough to tell him how you feel about him?' Aerin asked.

'I don't know…' Ruby chewed at her lower lip, wondering how Lucas would take it if she told him how she felt. Would he reject her as brutally as he had all those years ago? He had told her the rules—and yet he had changed the rules…a little. Only a little, but that fed her hopes. Or was she being foolish to hope his locked-away heart could ever be opened?

Opened to *her*?

Lucas was in his study when Ruby came in, just before dinner. She closed the door behind her with a soft little click. She approached his desk and, although he could only see the blurry outline of her body, he could see she was wearing a baby blue dress. He would enjoy taking her out of it later. He caught a whiff of her peony and tuberose perfume and his senses reeled.

'Have your friends settled in?' he asked.

'Yes. I put Aerin in the blue room and Harper in the yellow room.' She paused for a beat and added, 'I told them you weren't feeling very sociable at the moment and don't like weddings. I couldn't think of any other excuse for why you weren't keen to meet them.'

A twinge of guilt jabbed him for being so hardnosed

about keeping out of everyone's sight. 'I'm sorry, but it's best if I stay in the background.'

He heard the floorboards creak as she shifted her weight from foot to foot. He sensed she had something to confess. He could read the little tell-tale signs so well—the hitched in-breath, the rustle of her clothes, the wringing of her hands.

'Lucas…? I'm sorry, but I did tell the girls about us… about our fling. But they won't tell anyone else. I trust them to keep it out of the media.'

Lucas let out a stiff curse-word and rolled his chair back from the desk. 'Was it necessary to tell them? They're only here for a couple of days. Surely you could have kept it a—'

'I don't know how close you are to *your* friends, but, no, I couldn't keep it from them,' Ruby said in a tight little voice. 'In any case, they guessed—or at least Aerin did.'

'Guessed?'

He was so attuned to her he heard her lips part softly before she spoke. 'I didn't realise having amazing sex for the first time in my life would leave signs upon my person, but apparently it has.' Her tone was decidedly wry.

Lucas moved to where she was standing. He slowly stroked his hands down the length of her arms and then captured her wrists. 'I'm sorry for being touchy about my privacy. I just want to keep my private life out of the press—but not because I don't want to be seen with you.'

'I understand…'

Lucas put his finger beneath her chin and lifted her

gaze to his blurry one, wishing with all his heart he could see her expression in finer detail. 'Do you?'

Her tongue slipped out and swept across her lips. 'I'm not sure it's going to do my image much good being seen with you, either.'

He frowned. 'What do you mean?'

'I'm in the wedding business. What does it say about me that I'm having a fling with a playboy who's made it perfectly clear he will never settle down?'

Lucas tightened his hold on her wrists as the blood thickened in his veins. Being this close to her always sent his blood racing south. He was addicted to her and he could do nothing to stop it. It was a fever in his system—a raging fever that took over his rational brain, pushing aside all his reasons for keeping his distance.

He didn't *do* long flings, and yet he was already thinking of ways to keep her with him. Not for ever, but for longer than he would normally consider. He was starting to find it hard to imagine making love with anyone else. That had never happened to him before. In the past, the lure of the next lover had always pulled him forward.

But not this time—which was deeply concerning. He had to get a grip and keep control of this escalating need for her before it got out of hand. A fling was a fling, no matter if it lasted a week, a month or a couple of months.

He was *not* falling in love.

'I hardly think people are going to judge you for having a bit of fun,' he said.

Ruby moved a little closer, and he felt her lower body igniting his with flickering flames of lust.

'Is that all I am to you? A little bit of fun?' Her tone was light and playful, but he sensed a chord of disquiet underneath.

Lucas released her wrists and framed her face in his hands. 'You are way much more than that.'

And then his mouth came down on hers like a magnet drawn to metal. Her lips tasted of strawberries, and he wondered if he would ever eat that fruit again without thinking of her. His tongue met hers in an erotic dance that made a tingle move down his spine and the backs of his legs.

No, he was not falling in love. But he was falling deeper in lust.

And, if he was any judge, so was she.

The day of Delphine Rainbird's wedding arrived and Ruby was up before dawn, working with her team in the kitchen. The florist had been the day before and the castle looked stunning, with whimsical floral arrangements everywhere. The ballroom where the reception was being held looked like a fairyland, with gleaming candelabra on the tables and scattered rose petals in an array of colours. The silverware was polished and the starched white tablecloths were set with silver-embossed crockery.

Ruby wished Lucas could see everything, but even if he had his sight she knew he would avoid coming anywhere near the wedding. It would be too triggering for him, given the three weddings of his parents, all held at Rothwell Park, and all subsequently ending in acrimony and bitterness.

Harper came in with her camera bag and a sophisticated digital camera slung around her neck. 'Looks fabulous, Ruby. I'm heading upstairs to take some shots of Delphine and her bridesmaids getting ready. It's great that the weather's looking good.'

Ruby glanced out of the windows and smiled. 'Yes, but Delphine's so happy she wouldn't mind if it was sleeting or snowing outside.'

'Miguel seems pretty chuffed too,' Harper said, fiddling with the settings on her camera.

'Yes…' Ruby bent down to pick up a stray rose petal from the floor and held it to her nose, sniffing the clove and peppery smell of an old English rose.

'Are you okay?'

Ruby put the petal on the table nearest her and turned to look at her friend. 'I'm fine. Tired, though. I barely slept last night.'

Harper raised her eyebrows. 'Let me guess—not because you're nervous about the wedding, but because you were in Lucas Rothwell's bed, having amazing sex till the wee hours?'

Ruby's cheeks were so warm they threatened to wilt the rose petals. 'I know you don't approve, but I can't seem to help myself.'

Harper let out a heartfelt sigh. 'I do know what that feels like. That night I slept with Jack…' Her brow furrowed into a frown of self-disapproval. 'It was like I had zero self-control. I still can't believe I had a one-night stand with him—with anyone, for that matter. And at a wedding, for God's sake. A wedding where I was supposed to be working—not cavorting with the best man.' She blew out a breath and side-eyed Ruby. 'I left one of my favourite earrings in his hotel room.'

'Have you got it back?'

'No.'

'Why not?'

Harper's expression tightened. 'Because he insists on giving it back to me in person, and I don't want to see him again.'

'Do you want me to get it for you?'

Harper aimed her camera at the bridal table and took a couple of shots. 'I've already suggested that, but he was pig-headed about it and said I could only get it back if I agreed to see him. So—goodbye, favourite earring.'

Ruby had known Harper long enough to know how stubborn she could be when she made up her mind about something. 'You're not only being hard on Jack, you're being hard on yourself,' she told her. 'You're only human, and he *is* pretty darn hot.'

Harper made a scoffing noise and took another round of photos. 'I've taught myself to resist hot men.'

'Good luck with that,' Ruby said in a wry tone. 'That's not quite working for me at the moment.'

Lucas could hear the wedding in full swing downstairs but he stayed in his study, trying not to remember the wild celebrations of his parents as they'd repeated their mistakes time and time again. If that was love, then he wanted nothing to do with it.

There was a tap at the door and he stiffened in his chair. He had told Ruby no one was to be allowed in this part of the castle. Was a member of the press snooping about in his private quarters? It reminded him of being chased by the media as a child, cornered like a terrified animal, cameras pointed at him like guns.

Would he be tomorrow's biggest headline? Would his health issue be splashed over every media outlet? Why had he agreed to this damn wedding being hosted here? He should have known it would come to this. That some sneaky journalist would hunt him down and—

'Lucas? It's me,' Ruby said. 'I've brought you something to eat and drink.'

He breathed out a sigh of relief and rose from his chair to go and unlock the door. But his emotions were still in disarray. Emotions he didn't want to acknowledge. Vulnerability being at the top of the list.

Ruby was carrying a loaded tray of delicious-smelling food and he suddenly realised he was starving. Not just for food but for her company. It had been hours since she'd left his bed that morning. Long, boring hours of him aching for her. Wanting her. Needing her and being angry with himself for it. Furious that he was finding it so hard to resist her. Annoyed with himself for being more in lust with her than ever.

He moved out of her way so she could put the tray on his desk. 'You shouldn't have bothered. Aren't you supposed to be working?' His tone was brusque and unwelcoming, but he couldn't get his heartrate back to normal.

Ruby put the tray down and turned to look at him. 'My team have got everything under control.'

Unlike him. He was so out of control emotionally he could barely think straight.

'Are you okay?'

Lucas scraped an impatient hand through his hair. 'Of course I'm okay. There's a freaking celebrity wedding downstairs that sounds exactly like my parents' ones. Why *wouldn't* I be okay? I just hope they've drawn up an ironclad prenuptial agreement, because we both know how this is going to end.'

'They have,' Ruby said matter-of-factly. 'Have you heard of Drake Cawthorn, the celebrity divorce lawyer? He's an expert in prenups. He's a friend of Aerin's older brother. He drew up a prenup for Delphine, given her assets are worth so much more than Miguel's. In fact, it was Miguel who insisted on it, so that proves how much he loves her.'

'Does it?'

'Maybe I shouldn't have bothered bringing supper up to you.'

He heard her pick up the tray again. 'I'm sorry, Ruby.' He let out a long sigh. 'When you knocked on the door just now I was convinced a journalist had hunted me down. There were so many times in the past when the press followed me, looking for an exclusive on my parents' relationship. I hated the attention, the intrusion, the exposure. The thought of that happening again under my current circumstances—well, you can probably imagine how it feels to be cornered and unable to escape.'

Ruby put the tray back down on the table. 'I made sure no one could get to this part of the castle. I locked all the doors on my way up. Besides, I thought you might be hungry by now.'

'I am,' he said, taking her by the upper arms and drawing her closer. 'I shouldn't have kept you awake so long last night. You must be tired.'

She wound her arms around his neck. 'I can handle it.'

Lucas pressed a lingering kiss to her mouth, feeling his pulse racing at the softness of her lips, the silken touch of her tongue against his. The alluring curves of her body pressed closer and closer until he was fit to burst. He finally dragged his mouth away and placed his hands on her hips. 'So, what have you brought me to eat? It smells delicious.'

'Lots of things.' She slipped out of his hold and began serving the food onto two plates. 'I thought we could have a champagne supper up here.'

He heard the sound of bubbles being poured into glasses, and then Ruby pressed a champagne flute into his hand. The glass was cold against his fingers, and the soft hiss of rising bubbles was loud in the silence.

'What are we celebrating?' He tried but failed to keep the cynicism out of his tone. 'Another wedding at Rothwell Park that has a higher than average chance of failing?'

Ruby let out a weary-sounding sigh. 'Look, I know this wedding is triggering for you. But if you could see how much Delphine and Miguel love each other you'd know how well-suited they are.'

Lucas took a long draught of champagne before putting the glass down on the desk. 'Yes, well, that's the point, isn't it? I *can't* freaking see.' He raked a hand through his hair. 'I can't see a damn thing—and I want to so badly.'

The fear that he might never see again gripped him by the guts with a cruel hand. He knew plenty of people lived with blindness—lived good and productive lives—but he needed his sight to work at the job he loved. He could not do it without his sight.

'Oh, Lucas...' Ruby put her own glass down and wrapped her arms around his waist, her cheek pressed to his chest. 'I wish I could wave a magic wand and make everything right for you.'

Lucas absently stroked the back of her head, his emotions sawing at his insides like savage teeth. 'I don't believe in magic. I don't believe in miracles.' His voice came out through gritted teeth.

I don't believe in love.

And yet...and yet...something was picking at the lock on his heart, trying to prise it open when all he wanted was to keep it shut.

He had been honest with Ruby over his struggle to accept permanent disability. Even more honest than he had been with his specialist. The solid, impenetrable armour he hid behind was falling off, shield by shield, plate by plate, bolt by bolt, and if he didn't do something, and do it quickly, he would be completely exposed and vulnerable.

'But I *do* believe in magic and miracles, and maybe that's enough,' Ruby said.

'It's not enough,' Lucas said, and put her from him.

He needed distance. He needed to control this relentless drive to bring her closer and let her in.

He *had* to control it.

He picked up his champagne glass and drained it, putting it down again with a thud. 'You should go back downstairs, Ruby. I'm not in the partying mood.'

The sound of music and high-spirited revelry downstairs wasn't helping his state of mind. Three times he had heard such sounds at a wedding in his home and what had come of it? Nothing but bitterness and smashed hopes, leaving echoes of sadness in every nook and cranny of the castle.

Ruby came up behind him and placed her hand on the small of his back. A bolt of electricity shot through him. 'Can we just have our supper? The wedding will be over soon.'

Lucas turned and stared down at the pale oval of her face. She was no doubt tired and hungry, and yet she had taken the time to bring him a sample of the wedding feast. Surely the least he could do was enjoy it with her.

He brushed his bent knuckles down her left cheek, his expression rueful. 'I seem to have trouble saying no to you.'

Ruby placed her hands on his chest. 'I seem to have the same problem.' Her voice was whisper-soft, her face uptilted to his. 'What are we going to do about it?'

He could feel the soft waft of her breath on his lips and desire hit him like a punch. 'This might be a good place to start,' he said, and pressed his mouth to hers.

CHAPTER TEN

SOMETIME LATER, RUBY poured the last of the champagne into their glasses and handed Lucas his. They had finally got around to having the supper she'd brought up—but not before making exquisite love on the floor of his office. And even though they were both back in their clothes her body was still humming with aftershocks, and any tiredness she'd felt before was completely gone.

Lucas took a sip from his glass and then put it to one side. 'Would you like to dance?'

Ruby looked at him in surprise. 'What? Now?'

He held out his hands to her and she placed hers in them. 'We can hear the music from up here.' He drew her into the circle of his arms and they moved in time with the romantic ballad. 'You'll have to forgive me if I crush your toes.'

'I don't think there's much chance of that.'

There was more chance of him crushing her heart. But she didn't want to think about that now.

She breathed in the familiar smell of him, the citrus and leather scent that never failed to intoxicate her senses. 'This is nice…' She swayed in his arms, tipsy on champagne and his company.

'Mmm…' His breath stirred the hair on top of her head and a shiver coursed down her spine. 'I might have to rethink my bias against weddings. This one has been better than any I've been to before.'

Ruby glanced up at him. 'How many have you been to? Apart from your parents', I mean.'

'A few, but they bored me to tears.'

'Are the couples still together?'

'Only one.'

'Oh…'

There was a beat or two of silence, broken only by the music drifting upstairs.

Lucas stopped dancing and looked down at her. 'When will you be leaving for London?'

Something in Ruby's stomach tilted sideways. Of course. She would be leaving this bubble of happiness sooner rather than later. Lucas was selling Rothwell Park. They couldn't stay here together for ever. She was not in some fairy tale romance with him. She was in a fling and it had a timeline.

'I—I'm not sure. We have another wedding in Gloucester in a couple of weeks, but…' She didn't know how to finish the sentence without betraying her feelings for him. Without betraying her fragile hopes that he'd return them.

Lucas held her slightly aloft, his expression inscrutable. 'I've been thinking about what happens next.' His hands gave hers a light squeeze. 'Between us.'

Ruby swallowed, and her heart skipped a beat or

two. 'I have to go back to London, and you're selling Rothwell Park, so…'

He drew in a long breath and let go of her hands as the same time as he released a stream of air. 'Yes, well, about the sale…'

'You've changed your mind?'

His brows snapped together and his jaw locked tight. 'No. The sale is going ahead.'

'Oh…' Her chest deflated on a sigh.

'Why are you so fixated on this place? I told you before it's a white elephant to me. A burden I want to offload as soon as I can.'

'And I've told *you* before it's the only home I ever knew as a child,' Ruby said. 'It was the first place I truly felt safe. I hate the thought of never being able to come back here.'

He moved to stand behind his desk, as if he wanted to put a barrier between them. 'I'm sure you'll be able to come back here. Jack Livingstone is planning on turning it into a boutique hotel. You might even get mate's rates if your friend Harper asks nicely. Don't they have some sort of history?'

Ruby stared at him blankly. 'Jack Livingstone? *He's* the buyer?'

'Yes. He has a chain of boutique hotels.'

'I know who he is.' She swallowed again and asked, 'Am I allowed to tell Harper, or is this news confidential?'

He gave a loose shrug of indifference. 'Do what you like. It makes no difference now. I signed the contract electronically this morning. It actually worked in my favour when Delphine brought her wedding forward. It meant I could wrap things up a little faster.'

Ruby couldn't seem to get her head wrapped around the fact that Lucas no longer owned his family estate. And nor could she understand how cool and detached he was being about it. Surely he felt *something* about leaving his childhood home behind?

'So, when do you plan to move out?'

'I'm also going to London soon.'

'How soon?'

His expression was still difficult to read, although there was a line of tension around his mouth. 'Don't worry. We can still see each other in London.' He pulled at the cuff of his shirtsleeve, as if it was annoying him, and added, 'That is, if you're still happy to continue our arrangement?'

Something about his tone sent a chord of disquiet through her. He sounded as cool and detached as he had when discussing the sale of his ancestral home. How long did he intend their 'arrangement' to last? And why had she allowed *him* to dictate the terms? She had given up her own agency to indulge in a fling with him that she had known from the start could never go anywhere.

At least he had been honest about it from the get-go. Brutally honest. She was the one who had conjured up a fairy tale fantasy of them staying together for ever. Just like she had as a foolish teenage girl. She had imagined a future with Lucas Rothwell in which he was madly in love with her.

Ruby sent the tip of her tongue over her carpet-dry lips. 'I'm not sure what you're offering me. "Arrangement" sounds…temporary.'

'It sounds temporary because it *is* temporary,' he said in a crisp tone. 'What else did you think I would be offering?'

Ruby pressed her lips together, her chest so tight she could barely draw in a breath. 'I've wondered after these last few days together if things have changed between us. If you have changed.'

He made a rough sound at the back of his throat. 'Why would I want to change?'

'I meant in your feelings about me.'

There was a silence so thick a pin dropping would have sounded like a metal pole crashing to the floor.

Lucas let out a curt swear-word. 'You know, I'm getting a weird sense of déjà-vu. The champagne has gone to your head if you think anything has changed in that regard. You knew the rules when we started this. You can't say I didn't tell you what to expect.'

How cruel of him to remind her of her embarrassing teenage crush. Didn't he realise how much she regretted making such a fool of herself back then? And she would be making an even bigger fool of herself if she revealed her feelings now. Better to end things with her pride intact.

'If you don't mind, I think we should end our arrangement now. Tonight.'

'Tonight?'

Was that a hint of shock in his tone or was she imagining it?

'Why tonight?'

'We've both achieved our goals. Delphine's wedding has gone off without a hitch and you've sold Rothwell

Park. We can part ways now, without hard feelings. Or, worse, catching feelings neither of us want.'

His forehead was screwed up in a perplexed frown. 'Catching feelings?'

'Falling in love.'

Lucas placed his hands on the back of his chair, his knuckles showing white beneath his tan. But his expression was as blank as the wall behind him. 'Okay. We end it now.' His voice revealed even less than his inscrutable features.

'Thank you for allowing us to hold the wedding here. It was very generous of you not to charge a fee and—'

He held up a hand like a stop sign. 'Can we just leave it at that?' He closed his eyes and pinched the bridge of his nose. His hand fell away from his face and he let out a rough-sounding breath and glanced in her direction. 'I hate goodbyes.'

'Yes, well… I'm not too fond of them either.' She looked at the remains of their supper on his desk. 'I'd better clear this away before I—'

'Leave it.'

'But—'

'I said, leave it.' His tone brooked no resistance.

Ruby stepped away from the desk, her heart as heavy as an anvil. 'I hope you get your sight back, Lucas.'

'Thank you.'

She hesitated by the door, wishing and hoping he would call her back and say he had made a terrible mistake. That he did love her. That he didn't want her to leave.

A sob rose in her throat at the thought of never seeing him again, but she quickly disguised it as a cough. 'Excuse me. It's been a long day. And I think all those flowers downstairs are triggering my asthma.'

'Ruby?'

She turned to look at him, glad he couldn't see the tears tracking down her cheeks. 'Yes?' She was proud of how indifferent she sounded—as if her heart *wasn't* breaking into a thousand and one pieces.

His throat rose and fell over a tight swallow. 'Thank you for helping me get through a rough time. I'm not sure what I would have done without you...especially with your gran out of action.'

'That's okay. I had a good time.'

One side of his mouth curved upwards, but it was a stretch to call it anywhere near a smile. 'Take care of yourself, won't you?'

'You too.'

There was another beat or two of silence so thick it was almost palpable. And then Ruby turned and walked out without looking back. The door shut behind her with a soft thud that sounded eerily like the closing of a book. End of story.

But this one—*her one*—didn't have a happy ending.

Lucas let out a breath and let go his iron grip of the chair and flexed his aching knuckles. He should be happy, right? The fling he shouldn't have had in the first place was over. And all done with cool politeness rather than rancour and ill feelings. Why then did he feel so...so angry? So disappointed?

A heavy weight of disappointment he could not explain was sitting in his chest. He had always intended to end his fling with Ruby. He ended all his flings with lovers. He never gave anyone the opportunity to leave him. He left first. That was one thing he had learned from his parents—the person who left had the most control, and thereby suffered the least hurt. And the one thing he avoided in life was getting hurt. Loving someone gave them the power to hurt you. Why would he allow anyone that sort of power over him? He didn't. He wouldn't. He hadn't.

And yet...

Ruby closing that door had sent a shockwave through his chest, snatching the very air from his lungs. He had intended to continue their fling a little longer. How much longer he couldn't say. It was unusual for him, but he had never had a clear idea of the timeframe on his fling with Ruby. It had been as blurry and vague as his vision...the end point had always been in the foggy distance.

But it was here. Tonight. Now. A line had been drawn through their relationship as clear as if he had drawn it himself. Ruby would leave Rothwell Park tomorrow and he would never see her again. But then he hadn't seen her for the duration of their fling. Not clearly—not in detail, not in the way he'd longed to see her.

Was that why he was so angry? Was that why he was bitter, because she had ended it so abruptly? He clenched his hands into fists, furious with himself for wanting her. For needing her. For aching for her spine-tingling touch...

He was a man who didn't need anyone. He was a man who didn't get close.

He was still that man. He hadn't changed.

He was a man who didn't love.

Ruby ran into her friends on the way back to her room.
The last thing she wanted was a post-mortem on her
relationship with Lucas, but Harper and Aerin were
too observant to miss her reddened eyes. They followed her into her room and closed the door behind
them.

'What's happened?' Aerin asked, grasping Ruby
by the hand. 'Have you been crying?'

Ruby brushed at her eyes with the back of her hand.
'I've ended things with Lucas…' She bit down on her
lower lip to stop it from trembling.

'Oh, Ruby…' Harper sighed. 'Maybe it's for the
best, hon. Us Cinderella-types don't belong in a rich
man's world.'

Aerin handed Ruby a tissue. 'I'm so sorry. I wish
there was something I could do to make you feel better.'

Ruby blew her nose. 'I'll be fine. I knew the risks
when I got involved with him. He told me from the
outset our fling was only temporary. But how can you
put a timeframe on your feelings? How do you switch
them off like that?' She snapped her fingers for effect. 'I
think I've always loved him.' She choked back another
sob and wiped at her eyes. 'I'm leaving in the morning.
First thing. I don't want to see Lucas again.'

'Are you sure you should rush off like that?' Aerin
asked with a concerned frown. 'What if he changes his
mind? He might see things differently in the morning.'

Ruby's shoulders slumped on a sigh. 'He won't see
things differently. He's made up his mind to live his

life without needing anyone. And now I've ended the fling, because to continue it knowing he's never going to change would end up hurting me more in the end.'

'Oh, I'm so sorry things have turned out like this,' Aerin said. 'But I guess you know him better than anyone else.'

'I only know what he allows me to know,' Ruby said. 'He won't let me in. I thought he was starting to—telling me stuff about his parents and so on—but when push came to shove, no. He locked me out. He refuses to love anyone. Why did I think he might love me?'

Harper eyed her for a long moment. 'Did you tell him you loved him?'

Ruby shook her head. 'No, and that's one thing I'm immensely grateful for. I couldn't bear it if I'd gushed over him like I did when I was sixteen. Urgh! Can you imagine how embarrassing that would have been?'

Harper's expression communicated her staunch approval. 'You gotta maintain your pride, sister.'

'There's something else I need to tell you...' Ruby began to shred the tissue with her fingers.

Harper looked at her in horror. 'You're not...*pregnant*?'

Her friend had a mortal fear of getting pregnant, as her own mother had done, by a man who didn't stand by her and refused to acknowledge or even meet his child because he was already married with a family. Harper had ended up in care from the age of eight, after her mother died by suicide. Although her father had promised to visit a few times after her mother's death, he hadn't followed through. And, unlike Ruby, Harper had never been chosen to live with a relative or reside with a permanent foster family.

'Of course not,' Ruby said. 'It's about the new owner of Rothwell Park.'

Harper's eyes rounded even further. 'Lucas is selling?'

'It's a done deal,' Ruby said. 'And you'll never guess who's bought it.'

The colour drained from Harper's face and she gave a convulsive gulp. 'Jack Livingstone?'

'Yep. He's going to turn it into one of his boutique hotels.'

'Well, I can safely say *I* won't ever be staying here again,' Harper said with emphatic determination.

'Nor will I,' Ruby said, with a sigh of sadness that was bone-deep.

Lucas heard Ruby's car leave before dawn the next day. He had lain awake most of the night at war with himself. One part of him had wanted to go to her, to tell her to stay, the other had wanted to push her away. It had been like revisiting the pain of his childhood, reliving the walking out of one or other of his parents and having to deal with the devastation of the other.

Watching the rollercoaster of emotions in the person left behind had left an indelible mark on him. He would not be like his mother, clawing at his father, begging him to stay, to give her one more chance. And he would not be like his father, who'd told his wife he loved her and then gone off and had affairs with younger women when his wife's up-and-down moods wore him down.

Lucas knew he was doing the right thing for himself, let alone Ruby, by letting her go. He didn't have the emotional hardware to maintain a long-term relationship. He wasn't cut out to be the fairy tale knight who rode off into the sunset with his princess. It wasn't fair to promise things he had no ability to give. It was better to let her go so she could find someone who *could* give her those things: love, commitment, a family.

But...

He would miss Ruby. Deeply. He would miss her in so many ways—the sound of her pottering about the castle kitchen, the fresh flowery scent of her fragrance, the tinkling of her laugh, the warm press of her body against his. Oh, how he would miss the sweet curves of her body. The taste and feel of her, the intensity of her kiss and her touch.

A crippling ache seized his body with a pain so violent it took his breath away. Making love with her had been the most erotic, pleasurable and exciting experience—one he would never forget. Every moment was etched on his mind, on his body, on his senses.

Lucas was glad he was moving out of Rothwell Park. Staying here now would be too hard without Ruby. She brought life to the place, she lit up the dark corners, and she added colour to every room. Not a colour he could see, but one he could sense. She brought a lightening of the sombre atmosphere…a freshness that was like a summer breeze, blowing out the stale air of sadness that had clung to Rothwell Park for so long.

He was almost glad he couldn't see Ruby drive away. He had watched his parents take turns leaving and each time it had been emotional torture, knowing he would have to pick up the pieces left behind.

But this time there was only himself to deal with, only his own emotions to handle. He still didn't get why he was so angry. So bitterly disappointed that Ruby had ended their arrangement before he was ready.

Why hadn't he been ready?

CHAPTER ELEVEN

One month later...

RUBY WAS GLAD when a rush of wedding bookings came in soon after she got back to London. Although the meticulous planning and organising of menus that involved didn't entirely take her mind off Lucas, at least it distracted her.

But being around loved-up couples who were excitedly planning their upcoming weddings was a form of torture. Why couldn't she be like them? Blissfully happy with the love of her life? If anything, she loved Lucas more than ever. How could that be? Was something wrong with her? She was supposed to be moving on with her life. A month had passed and yet she was still heartsore and lonely—*more* heartsore and *more* lonely than she had ever been. It was like being handed a grand prize and then realising it didn't belong to you after all.

Lucas didn't belong to her. He didn't belong to anyone. He was an island, not unlike his own Greek one. *Urgh.* Why did she remind herself of those wonderful days on his gorgeous island? It was like rubbing salt into a wide, seeping wound. Would it ever heal? Or would she always feel this aching sense of loss for what might have been if only things had been different?

But how could things be different if Lucas couldn't allow himself to love her? To love anyone? Or was it because she was unlovable? The old self-doubts plagued her—what if it was *her* that was the problem? Harper was right—they were all Cinderella-types who didn't belong in a rich man's world. Lucas's world had always been out of reach for Ruby. She had lived in it in a vicarious sense, on the fringe, but she had never truly belonged?

Love was supposed to conquer all, to bridge all gaps and chasms, but what hope did she have that Lucas could ever love her?

None. Zilch. *Nada.*

It reminded her of her childhood, of her gnawing relentless emotional hunger to be loved by her mother. But her mother, like Lucas, has been incapable of it. Some people locked away their hearts or were damaged so much that they shut down their emotions.

She would never know why her mother had never loved her, but she had to assure herself it wasn't because of her—it was her mother's issue.

And she had to accept that Lucas not loving her was not because *she* was unlovable. Her gran loved her, her friends loved her—even her clients loved her.

Harper came into Ruby's office with her camera bag slung over her shoulder. 'How are you doing?'

Ruby painted a smile on her face. 'I'm fine. Distracting myself with work. You know the drill.'

'Yeah…' Harper leaned down to put her bag on the floor and winced. 'I certainly do.'

'Are you okay?'

Harper straightened and rubbed a hand at the base of her spine. 'I've got a nagging backache. I think lugging all that gear around is wrecking my spine.'

'I have some paracetamol in my handbag.'

Harper sat gingerly in one of the client's chairs in Ruby's office. 'I've already taken some and it did nothing.'

'Maybe you should see a doctor? Or a physiotherapist?'

Harper shifted in her chair, obviously trying but failing to get comfortable. 'Nah, I'll be okay in a day or two. I probably need to lose a bit of weight and get a bit fitter—especially before I head to Paris in six weeks for the book shoot.'

Harper wasn't one to crow about her achievements, but she had been selected to contribute to a coffee table book featuring the work of up-and-coming photographers.

She focussed her gaze on Ruby. 'Speaking of weight, you look like you've lost a lot, and you've got dark circles under your eyes.'

Ruby sighed. 'Yes, well… I don't seem to have much appetite for anything just now. And I find it so hard to sleep.'

'You miss him, huh?'

'Like you wouldn't believe.'

'Has he contacted you?'

'No.'

Harper shifted her head from side to side. 'You have

to move on, hon. You can't let the end of one little fling get you down.'

'I know, but I keep hoping I got it wrong about him… that he does love me after all.' Ruby gave a self-deprecating grimace and added, 'Remind me how many years I did that with my mother?'

Harper rolled her eyes. 'You and me both.'

Lucas woke from yet another fitful sleep and opened his eyes. Something was different… The once vague outlines of his bedroom furniture had sharpened—not by much, but they were less blurry and amorphous.

He sat upright and rubbed at his eyes, squinting against the bright sunlight beaming through the windows of his London apartment. He threw off the bedcovers and padded over to the window. Even from his penthouse height, he could see more than he'd been able to see the day before. The stunning view should have lightened his spirits, but if anything it did the opposite.

What was a stunning view if you had no one to share it with?

He turned back to the bed and felt his chest tighten at the stark emptiness of his crumpled white sheets. He pictured Ruby in his bed and an ache gripped him deep in his gut. Maybe he shouldn't have come to London. Maybe he should have gone back to his island. But going back there without Ruby would be too…difficult. And the thought of taking anyone else was unthinkable.

Would he have to sell the island? How else could he move on? He couldn't allow himself to be haunted by memories of his time with Ruby. And it had been such a short time. When it came down to it, their fling had been one of his shortest.

Why, then, was he struggling to let her go?

Because he hadn't wanted to let her go.

The realisation was like a zig-zagging bolt of lightning shooting through his brain. Of course he hadn't wanted to let her go. She had been a part of his life for years, and when the end of their fling had come he had fought against it. Fought violently. Not wanting to accept he would never see her again.

He had closed his heart to love, closed his mind to emotion, never wanting to end up like his parents. And yet he was unable to move forward because he missed Ruby so much. He ached for her in every bone of his body. He searched for her in his dreams and he woke alone and lonely in his bed, his body yearning for her. He had mistaken his feelings for simple lust, but that was a lie. A blatant lie he had told himself to protect himself from vulnerability.

The physical intimacy he'd shared with Ruby had been wonderful, but it was their emotional connection that had taken it to the next level. That was why he hadn't wanted their fling to end. He loved her with his body and his mind and his heart.

But did she love him? She hadn't said so. Was he a fool to think she would be interested in resuming their fling?

Lucas scraped a hand through his hair and sighed. He had half an hour before he was meeting his father for a quick coffee. Lionel—Lucas couldn't remember the last time he had called his father 'Dad'—was flying in for a business meeting. He could think of a dozen things he'd rather be doing this morning, but he hadn't seen his father in over a year. At least he would be able to *see* him—perhaps not as clearly as he would have liked, but still it was an improvement, and he was thankful for it.

The coffee shop was in Mayfair, and Lucas saw his father sitting at one of the tables in the window as he approached. His father was looking down at his phone, no doubt scrolling through endless emails and messages, his life so busy he could only slot in ten minutes for his son.

Lucas realised with a jolt that he was like his father in more ways than he cared to admit. Before he'd lost his sight, hadn't he been the busy man, with no time for anything but the most fleeting of relationships?

His father looked up from his phone when Lucas came to the table. 'Lucas. Nice to see you. Sit down. I've just got to send this email to my lawyer in Brazil.'

Lucas sat opposite and the waitress came over and took his order for coffee. His father continued to tap away at his phone, a frown on his forehead.

'Your lawyer?' Lucas asked when he could stand it no longer. 'Is everything all right?'

His father put his phone down on the table, his expression sheepish. 'Rosa is leaving me.'

'Should I ask why?'

'I probably deserve it.' Lionel Rothwell sighed. 'I had a tiny little fling with someone I met at a party. Rosa found out.'

'I'm starting to lose count of how many times you've been married and divorced.'

It was hard for Lucas to erase the cutting judgement in his tone. But how many times did his father have to go through this before something changed? Before *he* changed?

'I guess I'm not the settling down type...' Lionel toyed with his teaspoon. 'A little like you, I guess. Once a playboy, always a playboy, right?'

'People can change,' Lucas said. 'You can change if you're motivated enough. Do you love Rosa?'

'Of course.'

'Have you told her?'

'Heaps of times.'

'Have you shown it? Words are cheap. Actions are more important.'

But who was he to be giving his father advice on love? He hardly qualified as a relationships expert. He was a failure at relationships. He had failed at the one relationship he valued the most—his relationship with Ruby. Why hadn't he realised until this morning that his anger over her ending their fling was because he loved her?

He loved her. He loved her. He loved her.

The words were like beams of golden bright light shining into a room after a lifetime of shadows. They were like seeing sharp detail after months of seeing nothing but blurred edges. The scales had finally fallen from his eyes and he could see what had been staring him in the face all this time—he loved Ruby.

And didn't her actions tell him she felt the same about him, even though she hadn't said the actual words? He had been so locked down emotionally, so blind emotionally, he hadn't even recognised his own feelings—let alone hers.

Ruby had told him once that the thing people tried

so hard to avoid was often the very thing they most needed to grow as a person. He had been avoiding love all his life. Avoiding it, blocking it, sabotaging it just like his father.

But no longer.

He was not going to run away from the fear of loving someone fully. He was not going to shy away from a wholehearted commitment. Ruby deserved her fairy tale, and he would knock himself into shape as Prince Charming if it was the last thing he did.

Lionel picked up his coffee cup, his expression mocking. 'Listen to you. What's made you such an expert on love, eh? Or should I say who?'

'Did you ever truly love Mum?'

Lionel reared back as if insulted by the question. 'Of course.' He frowned and added, 'I married her three times, didn't I?'

'And divorced her three times.'

'Yes, well... That's all in the past.'

'But it's not,' Lucas said. 'You're reliving it now by divorcing Rosa. What about getting some counselling? Or having a go at making your relationship work instead of calling time on it or having an affair with someone else who catches your eye?'

Lionel shrugged and picked up his phone again. 'When a relationship is over, it's over.'

'I don't believe that,' Lucas said. 'I used to, but not now. You keep sabotaging your relationships because you're frightened of loving someone totally. You always have a get-out plan.'

'What's got into you?'

Lucas pushed back his chair and stood. 'I'm sorry.

I can't stay. I have to see someone. Urgently. I hope you work things out with Rosa. For her sake as well as yours and the children's. Please send them my regards.'

Lionel looked at him with a frown. 'But I've come all this way to catch up with you.'

His tone sounded like a petulant child's, and it made Lucas realise again how immature his father was. His father had never truly grown up, taken responsibility or faced reality. Lucas could not bear to turn out like him. That would indeed be his biggest failure if he did. His father walked away when things got difficult. He didn't stay and work through problems, and he didn't for a moment even consider himself a part of the problem—which was a problem in itself.

Lucas gave a bark of a laugh. 'A ten-minute slot in your busy day? That's not a catch-up—that's an insult. It doesn't surprise me that Rosa's fed up if you slot her in like you do everyone else. If you love someone, you make time for them.'

Lionel had the grace to look a little ashamed. 'I'm not good at relationships...you of all people should know that.'

'I do know it—but I also know you can change if you want to badly enough.' Lucas moved around to his father's side of the table and laid his hand on his shoulder. 'Don't waste yet another opportunity for growth.'

Lionel briefly laid his hand over Lucas's. 'It was good to see you, son.'

'It was great to see you too, Dad,' Lucas said, and he meant it in more ways than one.

Ruby was in her home office, designing a menu for a wedding for an older couple who had once been childhood sweethearts but ended up marrying other people. Now in their fifties, and both widowed, they had reconnected and fallen in love all over again.

Such happy stories were part of the joy of Ruby's career, but the downside was that it made her ache for her own happy ending. Surely she wouldn't have to wait until her fifties to hear those special words from the love of her life?

She had heard nothing from Lucas—which, prior to their fling, would not have been unusual. Months, even years could go by with zero contact. But in that short time during their fling they had shared so much together—more than she had shared with anyone else. Their intimacy had made her hope he had fallen for her as hard as she had for him.

She'd tried to douse her hopes and move on with her life, distracting herself with work and spending time with her friends, but no amount of activity and socialising could ever fill the void of loneliness of having loved and lost the only person she wanted.

Ruby had just clicked 'save' on her laptop when her doorbell rang. She wasn't expecting anyone. Harper and Aerin had been over the previous night for a movie and homemade pizza. Harper had still been complaining about her niggling backache, but she wouldn't see anyone about it. Ruby knew better than to nag, but it did worry her that Harper wasn't her usually hale and hearty and healthy self.

She pushed back her chair and peeped through the security hole in her front door. Lucas was standing there, with a bunch of red roses in one hand, and her heart came to a juddering halt. She unlocked the door and opened it, her stomach a hive of activity. Excitement, nerves, confusion, hope—all were churning around in there.

'Lucas?'

'May I come in?'

'Sure.' She closed the door once he was inside. 'I didn't expect to see you.'

Lucas handed her the roses. 'These are for you.'

His voice was so husky it sounded as if he had swallowed some of the roses' thorns.

She bent her head to smell the blood-red blooms. Trust a landscape architect to give you the real thing, not those hothouse ones without any scent.

She looked up at him again. 'You're not wearing your sunglasses.'

He smiled, and her heart gave a soft little flutter.

'That's because I can see a little better.'

'Really? I'm so thrilled for you.'

Ruby put the roses to one side, too nervous to find a vase. Did she even have a vase? She'd broken her only one a few months ago and hadn't got around to replacing it. Why was he here? Just to tell her he had his sight back? Or dared she hope he had come for some other reason?

'Ruby.' He held out his hands to her. 'Come here.'

She slipped her hands into his broad ones and it was like coming home. His fingers wrapped around hers and firmly squeezed, as if he never wanted to let her go. She had never seen his expression so tender. Had he changed his mind? Did he want to resume their fling? But how could she settle for a fling when she wanted the for ever fairy tale?

'Can you forgive me for taking this long to realise what I should have seen a month ago?' He swallowed, and then continued in the same hoarse tone. 'I love you, my darling. I think I fell in love with you the first time we kissed. I'm so ashamed it's taken me this long to understand how I feel. To even recognise how I feel.'

'Oh, Lucas…' Ruby flung herself at him so violently he almost lost his footing. His arms wrapped around her and held her tight, and it was just as well, for right then her heart was threatening to beat its way out of her chest in excitement and joy. 'I'd given up hope that you could ever feel anything for me. I can't believe you love me.'

Lucas tipped up her face so he could lock his gaze with hers. 'Does that mean you love me too? I took a gamble, hoping you do. You didn't say anything back at Rothwell Park the night of the wedding.'

'Of course I love you.' Ruby beamed up at him, so happy to be able to say it out loud at last. 'I wanted to tell you then, but my pride got in the way.'

He cradled her face in his hands, his touch so gentle it melted her heart. 'I think it was better that you didn't. I needed to suffer a bit. More than a bit, to be honest. I'm not used to feeling so wrecked after a break-up. I'm usually the one who ends a relationship. So I put it down to a bad case of pique. I only realised today that it's because I love you and want to spend the rest of my life with you.'

Ruby looked at him with wide eyes. 'Are you proposing?'

He gave a sheepish grin. 'I guess I am… But not doing such a great job of it.' He got down on one knee, holding her hands in his and looking up at her with an abundance of love. 'Will you do me the honour of becoming my wife, my life partner, my soulmate, my everything?'

Ruby hauled him to his feet and threw her arms around him again. 'Yes! How could I not want to marry you? You are the only man I could ever love. I think I've been in love with you since I was sixteen. I can't tell you how miserable I've been. There is no worse industry to work in than the weddings one when you're nursing a broken heart.'

'Oh, my poor, sweet darling.' Lucas hugged her again, resting his chin on the top of her head. 'I was miserable too. I couldn't sleep. I couldn't think straight. I was lonely, and aching for you the whole time, but I kept telling myself it was because you had ended our relationship, not me. I can't believe I've wasted the last month thinking I didn't feel anything serious about you.'

She looked up at him again. 'You said you only realised today?'

'I met my father this morning,' Lucas said with a grimace. 'It was like looking at myself in the future. He never made time for my mother, and nor does he for his present wife—who is about to become his ex-wife if he doesn't take on board what I told him.'

'What did you tell him?'

'I told him that words are empty, that actions speak louder. That he can change if he wants to badly enough.' He smiled crookedly and continued, 'And then I realised what I was saying to him applied to me…that I was at risk of turning into him in the future. A too-busy man who goes from one broken relationship to the next. You see, constant busyness was my way of distracting myself from wanting the things I told myself I didn't want. Love, commitment, a family. It wasn't until I lost my sight that I had to stop and take stock. And I hated every second of it. That's why I was such a brooding bear that day you came to the library at Rothwell Park and asked me about Delphine's wedding. I could no longer hide behind my overpacked diary and my big moneymaking projects all over the globe. I was stripped down to my most basic, and it scared the freaking hell out of me.'

Ruby stroked his lean jaw and smiled up at him. 'I kind of like you stripped down to your most basic.'

He grinned wolfishly at her. 'We'll get to that in a minute. But first let me tell you how wonderful it is to see you. You're still a little blurry, but I can see the sparkle in your beautiful eyes. I can even see the new freckles on your cute nose.'

He lowered his mouth to hers in a kiss that spoke of deep, abiding love. A love that she could trust, that she could depend on, that she could rely on no matter what.

Lucas lifted his mouth from hers and smiled down at her with his eyes shining. 'I really should have called in on your gran to ask her permission for your hand in marriage. What do you think she's going to say about us getting married?'

'She'll probably have a heart attack,' Ruby said. 'I didn't even tell her about our fling. I wanted to, but I couldn't bear the lecture I'm sure she would have given me.'

'She'll be happy for us,' Lucas said. 'She'll be happy you've found the love of your life and happy I have too.'

'Is that how you really see me? As the love of your life?'

'I didn't think it was possible to be this happy. I

was always terrified of getting too close to anyone in case they left. I think it's something I learned from my parents. Watching the repeated train wrecks of their relationship made me shy of getting into an intimate relationship where I had little or no control.' He stroked her bottom lip with his thumb. 'But you, my beautiful girl, changed everything. You brought light to my darkness. You unpicked the lock on my heart. You gave me the motivation to change and I can't thank you enough for that. Remember when you said that often the thing people try to avoid is the very thing they need to face to grow as a person? I realised I needed to stop shying away from loving someone. And that someone, I am thrilled to say, is you.'

Ruby gazed up at him with love and adoration. 'I love you with all my heart. I can't wait to be your wife. I still can't quite believe this is happening. It's like a miracle.'

'I said once to you that I didn't believe in magic or miracles, but you are both to me. You've shown me what it's like to feel whole. To embrace emotion instead of hiding from it or pretending it's something else.'

'I was so frightened I would spend the rest of my life without you,' Ruby said. 'I was trying hard to move on, but I couldn't. It was impossible to think of a future without you in it.'

'We'll have a great future because we've both learned from the past. Not everyone does. Let's promise each other we'll work through stuff together, never give up on each other.'

'I promise with all my heart.'

Lucas brought his mouth back down close to hers. 'I love you and I will always be there for you.'

And he sealed his promise with a kiss that left her in no doubt of his heartfelt commitment.

* * * *

COMING SOON!

We really hope you enjoyed reading this book. If you're looking for more romance, be sure to head to the shops when new books are available on

Thursday 12th May

MILLS & BOON®

Coming next month

THE SECRET SHE KEPT IN BOLLYWOOD
Tara Pammi

It was nothing but sheer madness.

Her brothers were behind a closed door not a few hundred feet away. Her daughter...one she couldn't claim, one she couldn't hold and touch and love openly, not in this lifetime, was also behind that same door. The very thought threatened to bring Anya to her knees again.

And she was dragging a stranger—a man who'd shown her only kindness—along with her into all this crazy. This reckless woman wasn't her.

But if she didn't do this, if she didn't take what he offered, if she didn't grasp this thing between them and hold on to it, it felt like she'd stay on her knees, raging at a fate she couldn't change, forever... And Anya refused to be that woman anymore.

It was as if she was walking through one of those fantastical daydreams she still had sometimes when her anxiety became too much. The one where she just spun herself into an alternate world because in actual reality she was nothing but a coward.

Now, those realities were merging, and the possibility that she could be more than her grief and guilt and loss was the only thing that kept her standing upright. It took her a minute to find an empty suite, to turn the knob and then lock it behind them.

Silence and almost total darkness cloaked them. A sliver of light from the bathroom showed that it was another expansive suite, and they were standing in the entryway. Anya pressed herself against the door with the man facing her. The commanding bridge of his nose that seemed to slash through his face with perfect symmetry, the square jaw and the broad shoulders…the faint outline of his strong, masculine features guided her. But those eyes…wide and penetrating, full of an aching pain and naked desire that could span the width of an ocean…she couldn't see those properly anymore. Without meeting those eyes, she could pretend this was a simple case of lust.

Simon, she said in her mind, tasting his name there first…so tall and broad that even standing at five-ten, she felt so utterly encompassed by him.

Simon with the kind eyes and the tight mouth and a fleck of gray at his temples. And a banked desire he'd been determined to not let drive him.

But despite that obvious struggle, he was here with her. Ready to give her whatever she wanted from him.

What did she want? How far was she going to take this temporary madness?

Continue reading
THE SECRET SHE KEPT IN BOLLYWOOD
Tara Pammi

Available next month
www.millsandboon.co.uk

MILLS & BOON

THE HEART OF ROMANCE

A ROMANCE FOR EVERY READER

MODERN

Prepare to be swept off your feet by sophisticated, sexy and seductive heroes, in some of the world's most glamourous and romantic locations, where power and passion collide.

HISTORICAL

Escape with historical heroes from time gone by. Whether your passion is for wicked Regency Rakes, muscled Vikings or rugged Highlanders, awe the romance of the past.

MEDICAL

Set your pulse racing with dedicated, delectable doctors in the high-pressure world of medicine, where emotions run high and passion, comfort love are the best medicine.

True Love

Celebrate true love with tender stories of heartfelt romance, from the rush of falling in love to the joy a new baby can bring, and a focus on t emotional heart of a relationship.

Desire

Indulge in secrets and scandal, intense drama and plenty of sizzling hot action with powerful and passionate heroes who have it all: wealth, status good looks…everything but the right woman.

HEROES

Experience all the excitement of a gripping thriller, with an intense romance at its heart. Resourceful, true-to-life women and strong, fearless face danger and desire - a killer combination!

To see which titles are coming soon, please visit

millsandboon.co.uk/nextmonth

LET'S TALK

Romance

For exclusive extracts, competitions
and special offers, find us online:

JOIN US ON SOCIAL MEDIA!

Stay up to date with our latest releases, author news and gossip, special offers and discounts, and all the behind-the-scenes action from Mills & Boon...

 millsandboon

 millsandboonuk

 millsandboon

it might just be true love...

MILLS & BOON
Desire

Indulge in secrets and scandal, intense drama and plenty of sizzling hot action with powerful and passionate heroes who have it all: wealth, status, good looks...everything but the right woman.

MILLS & BOON

HEROES

At Your Service

Experience all the excitement of a
gripping thriller, with an intense romance
at its heart. Resourceful, true-to-life
women and strong, fearless men face
danger and desire - a killer combination!